LOVE'S PURE LIGHT

A Christmas Novella Collection

SUSANNE DIETZE, SHANNON MCNEAR,
DEBORAH RANEY, JANINE ROSCHE

BARBOUR BOOKS
An Imprint of Barbour Publishing, Inc.

WHILE SHEPHERDS
WATCH ARE KEEPING

by Susanne Dietze

DEDICATION

For pastors, whose hearts are for Jesus and His people,
and whose tasks are many: teacher, preacher, counselor,
pray-er, evangelist, plumber, dishwasher, groundskeeper,
builder, fixer, human resource manager, techie, author,
accountant, and friend. Especially Karl, my favorite pastor.

ACKNOWLEDGMENTS

With many thanks to my editors Rebecca Germany and Ellen
Tarver; my agent Tamela Hancock Murray; the delightful, sweetheart authors in this collection; and you, the readers who allow us
into your homes this Christmas. Thanks also go out to my supportive family; my crit partner Debra E. Marvin; and most of all, the
Lord Jesus, whose birth we celebrate in this joyful season.

*There were in the same country shepherds abiding in the field,
keeping watch over their flock by night. And, lo, the angel of
the Lord came upon them, and the glory of the Lord shone round
about them: and they were sore afraid. And the angel said unto
them, Fear not: for, behold, I bring you good tidings of great joy,
which shall be to all people. For unto you is born this day in
the city of David a Saviour, which is Christ the Lord.*

LUKE 2:8–11 KJV

CHAPTER 1

Massachusetts
Sunday, December 3, 1899

The moment the final notes of the closing hymn fell silent, wind whistled in through the loosened lead casing of one of the church's stained glass windows, snaking down the Reverend Seth Shepherd's neck. He shivered, but not just from cold. He was anxious over the realization that yet one more thing around the gray stone church required repair.

But for now, he had a worship service to conclude. Seth gazed out at his congregation, the families clustered together for warmth, the widows in the first two rows, friends scattered here and there, and the lone visitor sitting halfway back on the left side. Each had come to church bearing burdens of some sort, and each needed the Lord's touch today. "May the Lord bless you and keep you," Seth began, offering the benediction.

The wind gusted, followed by a disheartening series of scratching, sliding sounds coming from above. Seth gulped. Not the roof again.

"Oh dear," frizzy-haired Ora Cole said from the organ bench.

After agreeing with Ora's sentiment, Seth refocused his concentration and completed the benediction from the book of Numbers. "Amen."

"Amen," the parish echoed.

"What was that noise?" Paulie Mack, one of the younger Sunday school students, popped to his knees. The lad's heavily pregnant mother, Sylvie, tugged him back to sitting, finger to her lips.

"It's a good question, Paulie." Seth hurried down the aisle and out of the sanctuary to investigate. Normally he'd recess and chat with parishioners by the red church door, but no one would mind forsaking postservice greetings today, not if the problem was related to repairs. Why didn't they teach skills like that in seminary, alongside Greek and theology?

He could have used them last February, when the worst blizzard in local memory swept over the area. He'd thought the church unaffected by the weather until he and Ora walked in one morning to a leak in the sanctuary ceiling. Dripping water had warped two pews, mildewed a tapestry crafted by the Ladies' Guild, destroyed a dozen Bibles and hymnals on the rack by the narthex, and seeped into the storage closet, ruining their assortment of Christmas decorations, including a porcelain nativity set that had turned pink when the red ribbons above it bled dye onto it.

There hadn't been much money in the church coffers back in February to replace the pews, Bibles, and hymnals, but things were even tighter financially now. Seth had no doubt that his congregants were as anxious about the scraping noises as he was, because the noise meant something else was wrong.

The door latch was like ice in Seth's hand as he turned it to open the door into the cold morning, revealing the snowy churchyard—with several roof tiles scattered over it.

February's repairs hadn't held for long, had they? But what should he have expected? The matter had been seen to by volunteers, led by an inexperienced fool: Seth himself. At twenty-seven, he was ill-equipped, unable to give this, his first parish, what it most needed. Someone capable.

Perhaps once he finally received the call to the New York City post he'd been groomed for, he would feel as if he knew how to do his job. The next pastor of this little stone church would surely be far better qualified to lead the congregation.

Or maybe his parents were right and he would be a disappointment there too.

Meanwhile, his parishioners clustered around him on the chilly church steps, murmuring, eyeing the tiles and looking up at the roof.

"We can't afford to fix it again." Albert Tillson, the pear-shaped grocer and church treasurer, rubbed the back of his neck.

"Is the roof gonna leak again?" Paulie asked.

"Hopefully not." Was it a lie or wishful thinking on Seth's part?

Lord, this church is in Your capable hands, but You know we lack the money to pay for supplies and capable labor. How will this work?

Maybe he shouldn't have phrased his prayer that way. Maybe he should have ended his prayer asserting trust in God's providence, not countering it.

His shoulders sank. He couldn't even pray right.

"I'll get out the ladder and assess the damage. My hope is this will be a quick patch-up."

"I'll help." Organist Ora Cole, who'd passed her sixtieth birthday some time ago, patted Seth's elbow. "I used to climb trees. My father called me Squirrel Girl."

Broken tiles, Seth could handle. But if Ora fell? Seth took her hand from his elbow and squeezed it. "You're a gem, Ora. Maybe you can hold the ladder steady."

Her craggy lips pouted. "I'd rather go up there. A little ice doesn't scare me."

"Me neither. I want to go on the roof." Paulie tugged his mother's cloak, even as she shook her head.

"May I be of assistance?" An unfamiliar feminine voice with a hint of a southern drawl drew Seth's gaze around. It was the visitor, a tall, pretty woman in her twenties wearing a fancy bonnet and a purple coat the same hue as today's advent candle.

Well-dressed as she was, there was no way she was a roofing expert. "Thank you, ma'am, but it's just a few tiles."

Please, God, may it only be a few tiles.

"Take this for the building fund then." She opened the drawstring of her purple velvet bag and pulled out a bill.

He didn't look at the denomination, because whatever it was would most definitely help. In fact, it was an answer to the feeble, grumbling prayer he'd offered a minute ago. *Thanks, Lord, for providing.*

And thanks too, to the dark-eyed visitor. "I'm grateful for your generosity, ma'am. We're glad to have you worshipping with us today. Are you visiting Millerton?"

"For Christmas, yes. Staying with my uncle." A golden-brown lock of hair came loose in the wind, and she shoved it behind her ear. "He's not much for church, I'm afraid. I'm Miss Jessalyn Grant."

He wasn't familiar with any Grants in the area. "Seth Shepherd." They shook hands, and then she took a step away to allow for another parishioner to speak to him, but he wasn't quite finished with her.

"Hope to see you again next week, perhaps?"

"I plan on it." Her full-lipped smile defrosted his toes a touch.

Something tugged his robe. He looked down with a smile. "Yes, Paulie?"

The fair-haired lad with a gap where a front tooth should be rocked on his heels. "Father's not here today on account of being too angry."

"Paulie," his mother scolded, but her sad eyes met Seth's. "I'm sorry, Pastor, but it's all too much for Hiram right now."

"What is?" He had to watch his words, since Sylvie might not want everyone to hear the details, although the whole congregation already knew how anxious Sylvie and Hiram Mack were about the pregnancy. Well, not the pregnancy, exactly. The fear of it ending too early, as her last four pregnancies had. She still had two months before this baby was due. If it was born now, could it survive? Seth's heart sank even lower at the thought of the Macks going through yet another loss.

Sylvie's eyes narrowed. "You didn't hear the news, Pastor? The mill. It's closing."

He must not have heard right. The mill was the town's main industry. It employed most of his parishioners. "That can't be correct."

But other congregants were nodding and a few even swiped tears from their eyes. How did Seth not know this? Anger at the situation and guilt over his ignorance warred in his chest. "When did this happen?"

"We received letters yesterday. All of us." Sylvie's lip trembled. "As of New Year's Day, the Chester Mill will be closed."

"And with it, your jobs." Seth could hardly take it all in.

"Wool's all I know," a man said. "I'll have to leave Millerton for another mill town."

"I don't have anywhere else to go," Ora added. "My late husband worked in that mill, and I intend to be buried right beside him here in this churchyard."

"If our customers leave, we'll have to open shop somewhere else," Albert Tillson lamented.

Others added their fears and distresses, and Seth rested a hand on Sylvie's shoulder. "I'm sorry, Sylvie. And utterly astonished. Why would Francis Chester close the mill?"

"Why indeed." The voice wasn't Sylvie's. It came from the visitor, Miss Grant. Her eyes were narrowed, her jaw set. She may be a stranger here, but she certainly didn't like hearing the news about the mill closing.

What a compassionate soul.

"I'm not sure." Seth moved his hand from Sylvie to Paulie's head. "I'll talk to Francis Chester this afternoon. Ask him to reconsider, or at the least, get some answers."

"You've tried before, but he won't talk to you, much less see you," Ora insisted. "Like Scrooge in that Dickens story. Hates ever'body and ever'thing."

Others muttered agreement. Seth couldn't blame them for their grumbling, borne of their distress. Fear was heavy on his parishioners' minds. What could Seth say that wouldn't sound hollow? What platitude would give them comfort when the future looked disturbingly uncertain?

None from his lips. But he could remind them of God's promises and seek the best help he could. "Why don't we pray? God will provide a way, I'm sure of it. He always does."

The folks gathered around him for prayer, and at the final amen, Seth felt as if the burden had lightened a fraction, since they'd offered the matter up to the Lord. But there was still work to do.

"I'm going to get out of these robes and climb up on the roof, but afterwards I'll be here for a few hours if anyone needs to talk."

"I'll fetch some roofing nails from the shop," Albert said.

In a swish of purple, Miss Jessalyn Grant marched down the swept path to the street, which reminded him that he still had her donation in hand. "Albert?" He handed the bill to the grocer. "This goes into the repair fund."

Albert took the bill and whistled. "Mighty generous."

God had provided for the roof repair, and He could easily provide jobs for Seth's parishioners.

The hardest part of trusting God was being patient.

Jessalyn entered the wood-paneled foyer of her uncle's three-story corner house, stripping off her gloves. Despite the fact that the weather was far chillier than she was accustomed to in her native South Carolina, her core was burning—with anger.

The mill was closing?

"Uncle Francis?" She raised her voice without a lick of concern for sounding unladylike to the staff, as Father would have noted. Uncle Francis employed a housekeeper, Mrs. Appleby, who cooked his suppers, but she took Sundays off.

"There you are. I was beginning to wonder if you'd return in time for luncheon." Her uncle's words preceded him from the parlor, but then he appeared in the threshold, a graying, slender fellow around her height with sharp green eyes and thick sideburns that shaped his lean cheeks like parentheses. "Long sermon, eh?"

"It was well delivered and thoughtful, in my opinion." She followed him back into the cozy parlor, decorated in rich brown and gold.

His glance was sharp. "I detect an edge of ice in your tone. What's got you in a dither? The pews? Uncomfortable blocks, as I recall, and set too close together for a man to sit without his knees hitting his chin."

At least he remembered something of the interior of the church after so many years.

"If I am in a dither," Jessalyn said, moving to stand before the warmth of the crackling hearth, "it is because I heard you are closing the mill."

"From the pulpit? That pastor's as bad a gossip as everyone else."

"Not from him. The parishioners were discussing it." The pastor hadn't struck her as a gossipy sort, but she'd only just met him. Still, there was something about his kind, light eyes and the way he smiled at not only her but the children in the congregation, that made her believe he was good-hearted and—

Jessalyn waved away the ridiculous direction of her thoughts. There were far more serious matters at hand. "Uncle, tell me it is not true."

His face hardened a fraction. "If I sell the mill, that's my business."

"Selling is one thing. Closing it and selling the equipment and land is another thing altogether. You employ over half the people in Millerton. Your workers will lose their livelihoods, and Christmas is but a few weeks away."

"I know all of that, and I regret it, but it cannot be helped."

"Tell me you have a buyer who will keep the mill open and employ everyone."

"You are the most unabashed girl of my acquaintance, have I told you that of late?"

"Not yet this visit, but I've only been here a day and a half.

Besides, I'm long past girlhood, Uncle, and I've been called worse than unabashed." Too free with her brain, according to her father. "So is there a buyer?"

"No, there is not. I did try, but I cannot wait for one any longer."

"But why sell? I cannot believe you are weary of the work. Nor do you look ill, but. . .are you, Uncle? Is that it?" Fear skittered through her belly.

"Pah. I've long told you, a bowl of gruel each morn, a portion of fruit each eve, and a daily constitutional in brisk air makes a man fit. And no, I am not weary of work. The textile mill is no longer profitable enough, is all."

Profits. This was entirely about money.

Jessalyn dropped into one of the fireside chairs. "I can look at the books, you know. Mama used to call me her darling nipcheese because I can find pennies in the tightest of budgets."

"She was a smart one, unlike your father." He sat beside her.

"That is an entirely different discussion." For many reasons. Her father found her ability to keep accounts to be an unattractive trait in a husband-seeking female. That wasn't why she left home to spend Christmas with Uncle Francis though. "We are talking about the mill. Perhaps I can find areas of loss that can be remedied."

"Thank you, but it can't be helped. My mill isn't the only one failing to flourish either. They're closing all over New England. That's why I can't find a buyer."

Her gaze fell to her feet. "I hadn't realized. And I am sorry. But can nothing be done? What of the employees?"

"I regret this, I do, but this is business, poppet."

He wasn't completely coldhearted about his workers' plight. She could see it in his eyes. "Then let's try to save it, Uncle. It's Christmastime after all. A season of miracles."

That's when she lost him. His gaze hardened and shifted to the bisque nativity set she'd placed on the mantelpiece this morning. "I noticed what you did there, putting the nativity where *she* used to place it. I won't remove it, out of respect for you and the dearest woman ever to walk the earth, but there's no such thing as miracles, Jessy. Only fools believe in them."

She wasn't offended. "You're calling me and Aunt Joan fools, then?"

"I want my lunch." He stood. "Join me in five minutes at the table if you care to, but there will be no more discussion of miracles. Or the mill. I'll not suffer dyspepsia on account of unpleasant topics, thank you very much."

Jessalyn sat alone in the parlor for a minute, staring at the white bisque nativity set. It was small, six inches tall, all one piece with the holy family under an A-frame shelter. Joseph's head bent down so he could view the Christ child, as did Mary's.

Aunt Joan set it here on the mantel every Christmas. She'd loved it as a reminder of the season, a reminder of Jesus' birth. But then she'd died and Uncle rejected Jesus because, in his grief-induced opinion, Jesus hadn't protected his wife. His choice to separate from God and the church ached Jessalyn's heart, as did his subsequent decision to pursue the things of the world, such as wealth—but unlike other people, namely, her father, he was at least honest about it. Uncle Francis was no liar, so when he assured Jessalyn of his care for her and opened his home to her this year for Christmas, she knew he meant it.

She'd accepted the invitation gladly to escape her situation at home. But she'd also come with the hope and prayer that she'd somehow be able to help her uncle find his way back to the Lord. This choice of his to close the mill and put half the town out of work did not bode well for his spiritual health.

Oh Lord, what are we to do with Uncle Francis?

She'd prayed that prayer for years. Now she added a new one. *You can provide for those working at the mill. Maybe help Uncle Francis see reason? Lord, what is best here?*

Her prayer was interrupted by the loud and persistent rumbling of her stomach. Bother. Spiritual needs disrupted by earthly ones.

She would have lunch with her beloved Uncle Francis, and she would not mention anything to upset him. But afterward?

There had to be something she could do to lighten the burden on those about to lose their jobs. But what?

CHAPTER 2

The red church door squeaked open at Jessalyn's push. The air within the stone building was not much warmer than the air outside. The stove must have been banked after services. She snuggled her hand back inside her warm winter muff.

What was the etiquette for visiting church on a quiet Sunday afternoon? Did one maintain silence in case someone prayed in the pews? Or should she call out for Pastor Shepherd? He said he'd be here this afternoon, but she didn't wish to disturb him. She tiptoed into the sanctuary.

Good thing she had not called out. Someone was indeed sitting in the pews, his dark head of curly hair bowed in prayer, his wrists resting on the pew in front of him. Pastor Shepherd, his shoulders curved, not in resignation, but in a posture of obedient surrender, as if the yoke of his burden wasn't unbearable since his Master had placed it there. How long had he sat like this, praying?

She should leave him be.

A tendon in her ankle snapped. Pastor Shepherd's head jerked upright and swiveled around. "Miss Grant?"

"Forgive my interruption."

"Nothing to forgive. The conversation will pick up where it left off later." He was up and in the aisle before she could blink, tall and lean in his dark suit.

"You're off the roof. I hope the matter was easily resolved."

"Alas, it was a temporary patch. I know working on the Sabbath isn't ideal, but something had to be done now in the event that wind will blow in snow. Tomorrow I'll purchase some supplies to do a more thorough job. Your generous donation to the building fund will be spent on those supplies. I hope you don't mind."

"That's what it was for."

He leaned against a pew and regarded her. "What brings you back to church? Did you forget something in your seat? I didn't see anything when I tidied up, but I might have missed it."

"Actually, I wished to speak with you." She took a deep breath. "Earlier, I failed to mention that my uncle is Francis Chester, owner of the textile mill." It was impossible not to sigh at the tightening of the skin around his eyes. "You've had dealings with him, I presume."

"Actually, no, I do not know him, only *of* him." And obviously the reputation he knew Uncle Francis by was not a good one. "I've called on him thrice since my arrival in Millerton last year in order to remedy that, but he has not been, er. . .receiving visitors."

Jessalyn smiled. "It's because you are a clergyman. He is angry with the Lord."

"Ah. I've experienced that particular situation a time or two."

"I am fond of Uncle Francis. He opened his home to me for

Christmas this year, and for that I am ever grateful to him. But he changed after his wife's death, accumulating money over treasures that last, as it were. That is one reason why I have come back, sir, to ask you to pray for my uncle. My primary concern is for his spiritual well-being, of course, but I'm concerned about his decision to close the mill too."

"It is my honor and a privilege to pray. Perhaps, with you in town, I might also be able to finally have that talk with him."

"I doubt he'd listen, whether the topic is the mill or God, but if the Lord presents an opportunity, yes, I would be grateful if you would speak to him." Her finger traced the carving on the pew's edge, garnering her courage. "That isn't the only reason I've sought you out, however. From what I gathered this morning, the church is not flush with funds, and your parishioners will be holding tight to their coins, I expect, since they will soon be without work. If the church needs more repairs, like that window there, they will not be able to provide it."

He glanced over his shoulder at the whistling window casing. "That is true. And if my parishioners must leave town to find new work, there could be few of them left here in the new year to care about the repairs."

Oh Uncle Francis. Have you any idea what you've done in the name of profit?

At least Jessalyn had found something she could do. "Then I'd like to offer something in the way of coin, but also, myself."

"You're proficient with lead window casings?" he teased.

His smile warmed her chilled toes. "Alas, no. Nor can I purchase the mill and save everyone's jobs. But I could help with the church's financials. I am an excellent bookkeeper, if I may say so, quick at sums and handy discovering places where cash hemorrhages. I could offer

18

references, but they are not local, and it would take too long to procure them, but I assure you I have experience. I kept my mother's accounts before she died and helped other women back home with their investments and budgets. If you're willing to show me the church's books and budget, I might be able to locate areas where money could be put to better use."

She steeled herself for his rejection.

"Splendid." He rubbed his hands together. "I do my best with the books, and so does Albert Tillson, but a fresh pair of eyes would be most welcome, especially if you're able to spot areas of improvement."

It took her a full two seconds to respond. "Really?"

One of his dark brows rose. "Did you expect an argument?"

"Frankly, yes."

"Why?"

I'm a woman, for one thing. "I'm a stranger to you."

"There is nothing sensitive in the account book. Records of tithes are kept elsewhere."

As was proper. But it still didn't change the fact that few people had ever willingly handed over their accounts to her, beyond Mother and the widows back home. She'd have been glad to assist others, but Father had been mortified when she'd suggested volunteering her skills to the church back home.

"Men don't wish to be usurped by a woman. It's unnerving, at the least. Who will marry a female who might be smarter than he?"

Clearly Pastor Shepherd was not like the men of Father's acquaintance.

"When could you start?"

"I'm available now."

"Now?"

What else had she to do but wrap a few Christmas presents for her uncle and set the table for the supper she'd left simmering on the stove? "I should admit an ulterior motive though."

Such things were loathsome to her, but perhaps he'd understand this one.

Pastor Shepherd's dark brow rose again. "I admit to great curiosity."

"I am all discretion when it comes to these sorts of manners, but if I find a way to improve the church finances, would you consider granting me permission to tell Uncle Francis? Nothing specific, just that I helped. Then he might allow me to look at the mill's accounts. And possibly find a way to save it."

"A worthy ulterior motive if I ever heard one. Let's fetch those books for you, then." Pastor Shepherd gestured for her to precede him through a door tucked off to the side of the front of the church. The office, no doubt.

She lifted her head high as she strode over the stone floor, and she couldn't hold back a smile. It felt good to be needed for something by someone again.

Besides, it was good to have tasks at hand. The busier she was this holiday season, the less time she'd have to feel lonely.

Escorting Miss Grant to the church office, some of the tension in Seth's shoulders eased. It had seemed like that tightness of his muscles had become a permanent part of him since the storm last February, a constant physical reminder of his weaknesses. Miss Grant may not be able to accomplish anything—with the books or with her stubborn uncle—but at least she was going to try. He felt less alone with her here.

He led her into his office and pulled a thick leather book from his second desk drawer. "The ledger includes an expanded budget as well as itemized bills. You'll quickly note how hard last year's storm hit us, and this isn't a wealthy parish."

"Thankfully, the Lord doesn't measure us according to our worldly goods."

"A welcome reminder." Especially in light of the letter he'd received from his father yesterday. Seth's parents thought this church too small to be of value. They'd be far more comfortable with his calling when he joined the large staff of the grand church back in New York City.

So would Ethel, his sweetheart. Or whatever she was. When he left for Massachusetts, she said she wouldn't consider his suit until he returned to New York. She had no interest in living anywhere else.

Except church work wasn't the sort of thing where one chose where one was sent. Ethel would understand someday.

Meanwhile Jessalyn Grant tugged off a glove to thumb through the ledger. "Where is the budget? I can't—ah, there it is. Ah, I see," she murmured as her eyes scanned the document. She didn't flinch or gasp, he'd give her that.

"It's too cold in here, so you may take it back to your uncle's house if you wish. You'll certainly be more comfortable there. I only ask that you keep it safe and private. I don't want it examined without my knowledge, or that of the elders."

"Of course, and I won't take long. You'll need it tomorrow to record today's ingathering, I'm sure."

He'd already locked the bag of coins in the safe before climbing up on the roof. "I hope you find something for us. Not just for the church's sake, but so you can persuade your uncle to allow you to do the same with the mill's books. Clearly it's losing money, for him to close it. Maybe you can find something to help."

Her eyes took on a fatigued, heavy look. "The mill isn't losing money. It's just not turning a profit. And that is all Uncle Francis sees."

"A dismal way to view the world."

"If one does not believe in God and lives only for himself, one has little motivation to pay much mind to the needs of others."

"His responsibility is to himself alone." Which resonated with all he'd heard of Francis Chester.

"He wasn't always that way. And as I said, he is quite dear to me." She pulled her glove back on. "There is almost a month before he closes the mill. I will strive each day of it to woo him back to compassion. Ebenezer Scrooge became a new man in *A Christmas Carol* after all."

"Alas, that's fiction."

"Truth is often stranger, however."

It was dreadfully cold in the office and their business was completed, but for some reason, Seth wanted to prolong the conversation. "Are you an admirer of Dickens, then?"

She hugged the ledger to her chest. "Half of his works, perhaps. The other half?"

"Pastor!" A small voice shouted from the sanctuary.

"Excuse me." Seth passed Miss Grant and rushed from the office. "Paulie?"

The boy's cheeks and nose were red, his eyes shiny, his little chest heaving from a hard run. Seth crouched before him so they were eye to eye. "What's wrong?"

Paulie swiped his running nose on his red mitten. "Mama needs somebody."

The baby? Seth's throat tightened. "I'll fetch the doctor."

"No, it's not that. It's Papa. Mama said he reeks like a still and she can't lift him up to bed on account of her stomach being so big." He puffed out his cheeks.

So with the news of the mill's closure, Hiram had resorted to drink. And Sylvie needed someone, anyone, able-bodied enough to put him to bed.

Seth rose and met Jessalyn's concerned gaze. "I beg your pardon, Miss Grant, but I must go."

"Of course." She shoved her hand into her pocket and then extended it to the boy. "I always find my mouth is a little dry after exercise. Care for a lemon drop?"

"Sure, thanks." He scooped the yellow sweet from her hand.

Seth gripped the boy's tiny shoulder. "Wait one moment while I fetch my coat and hat."

"Yessir."

Seth gathered his outerwear and then joined Miss Grant and Paulie in the narthex. Over the boy's head, he met her gaze. "Thank you, Miss Grant." Seth led them outside into the brisk afternoon and paused to lock the door behind him. The old mechanism finally slid into place after three attempts. One more item for the list of things requiring repair.

"Good day, gentlemen." Miss Grant marched out of the church-yard, still clutching the ledger to her chest.

"Good day." He pocketed the key and looked down at Paulie. "Let's help your father, shall we?"

He couldn't fix everything wrong with the church or in the lives of his people, but this he could do. Lifting an inebriated man to his bed and comforting the fellow's frightened wife wouldn't impress his father, but Seth couldn't help hoping his heavenly Father would approve.

At least Someone loved him without condition.

And God had sent Jessalyn Grant to look at the ledger. For the first time in a long time, Seth felt something he'd often preached about but lost along the way.

A sense of hope.

CHAPTER 3

You won't be lonesome today whilst I'm at the mill?" Uncle Francis donned his heavy coat in the foyer Monday morning after they'd finished breakfast. "I hate leaving you by yourself all day, Jessy, my girl."

"Nonsense." Jessalyn slipped his fine woolen scarf from its peg on the coat tree and wrapped it around his slender neck. "I have plenty to keep me occupied today."

"Good. I wouldn't want you mooning over your father marrying that Bernice person."

The unpleasant reminder of what transpired back in South Carolina set a pang through Jessalyn's chest, but she forced a smile so he wouldn't notice her pain. "I have errands, including a stop at the church."

His brows arched. "The pastor put you to work?"

"Not like you think. I volunteered." She couldn't tell him about it though. She'd told Pastor Shepherd she wouldn't. Not yet.

"You are a kind girl, Jessy." He kissed her cheek. "Do try to have a little fun though. The housekeeper will be by, but she has a key, so you may come and go as you like."

After he left, she gathered the ledger and quit the house. Her boots made crunching noises on the snow-dusted walk. At least there hadn't been heavy accumulation to penetrate Pastor Shepherd's patchwork on the church roof.

She could hear the thwacks of a hammer before she passed through the low gate. Sure enough, when she turned into the churchyard, there was Pastor Shepherd on the roof, bundled in a coat and hat, striking nails into the tiles. The church organist, Ora something-or-other, held the ladder from her spot on the ground, even though the reverend wasn't currently on it.

"Good morning," Jessalyn greeted the organist, who was dressed in men's trousers and a flannel jacket, an ensemble that looked far more comfortable than Jessalyn's wool skirt and gathered-sleeve coat. Then again, wearing a corset tended to make everything uncomfortable.

"Miss Grant, is it?" Ora peered up at her. "Come to visit the pastor? He's a bit busy."

"So I see." She stepped back, the better to watch him swing the hammer. She was no judge, but he seemed more than proficient. In fact, he seemed downright—

Do not say, "attractive."

He caught her looking and grinned. "Hello, down there."

"Hello. I've come at an inconvenient time, I see."

"Actually, that was the last nail." He scooted closer to the edge of the roof. "I was able to purchase all the supplies I needed, thanks to you."

"Ridiculous." Her mother had taught her that the better steward one was of one's resources, the more there would be for God to use to further His kingdom.

Pity Uncle Francis didn't see it that way. Or her father either. But this was not the time to think about Father. Or Bernice.

She held up the ledger. "I've returned this to you."

"I'm eager to hear what you learned."

Ora threw up her hands. "Are you going to keep yelling at one another, or will you be coming down, Pastor? It's a mite cold out here."

"Sorry, Ora." His smile looked abashed. Charmingly so.

Stop it, Jessalyn. You act as if you've never seen a nice-looking man before.

Ora gripped the ladder. "Ready for you."

The ladder wobbled while he made his descent. Jessalyn would add a new ladder to the list of things the church needed to replace or repair, along with that loose window casing and the sticky lock. And the threadbare rug and filling the poor box—

"Miss Grant?"

Pastor Shepherd stared at her, his brows meeting in a quizzical V.

"Sorry. Woolgathering."

"That's what we do around here. Woolgathering." Ora elbowed Jessalyn in the corset. "Because of the woolen mill. It's a joke. Funny, isn't it?"

"Clever." Jessalyn's laugh was too late, but Ora didn't seem to mind.

The pastor gestured toward the church door. "Why don't we go inside, and you can show me what you've discovered. It's warmer than yesterday, I promise."

Good. Jessalyn's toes stung. "I'm not accustomed to weather like this."

"Where you from?" Ora preceded her into the church.

"South Carolina." Ah, it was much warmer here in the narthex.

Ora turned, blocking Jessalyn's entrance into the sanctuary. "Do you knit?"

"Ma'am?"

"Knit. Since you're staying awhile, perhaps you'd like to join our Friday group, making baby blankets and sweaters and such for those in need. We meet at my house."

"I'd love to." Anything to hold the loneliness at bay. "What a wonderful idea."

"It was Pastor's notion, clothing and warming the poorest in the community, regardless of whether or not they're church members. Same with the monthly luncheons here, where everyone walks away with a loaf of fresh bread."

Pastor Shepherd shrugged. "Ora insists I visit the circle Friday to see what it's like, so I'll see you there. For a minute, anyway."

Ora shifted so they could enter the sanctuary. "I've got things to do in here. See you Friday, if not before, Miss Grant."

"Jessalyn, please."

"And I'm Ora." She meandered toward the organ bench.

"Maybe she doesn't know who my uncle is, to have issued me the invitation," Jessalyn said when she and Pastor Shepherd were ensconced in his office, far cozier today than yesterday, with the little corner stove warming the space.

Leaving the door open, he shed his coat and bid her to sit. Morning sun streamed through the east window onto the desk, giving the pastor's curls a bronze sheen as he sat across from her behind his desk. "Or maybe she is reaching out in friendship regardless of your relations."

Reaching out in friendship without a motive. Now that was a refreshing thought.

"How is Mr. Mack? If I may be so bold as to ask. It's none of my business."

Pastor Shepherd scratched his head, mussing his curls. "He's well enough. Probably has a dreadful headache today. I'm not condoning his decision to drink in his distress over losing his work, but I can sympathize with his fears. The people here rely on that mill."

"They also clearly rely on you."

"Me?" He seemed surprised.

How could he be so shocked? "Paulie could have run to anyone, but he came to you. You're a safe haven. They trust you."

"Aren't people trustworthy in general?"

"Surely you know better than that." She tried to make it sound like a lighthearted jest, but she was dead serious. She'd been deceived by those closest to her.

Pwa-wa-wa!

Jessalyn jumped in her chair. Mercy, she hadn't expected Bach's *Toccata and Fugue in D Minor* to blare through the organ pipes like that.

"She'll quiet in a minute," the pastor shouted, grinning.

Now that she wasn't frightened by the shock of it, Jessalyn might as well enjoy the concert. She settled back in her chair and listened, staring unfocused at a landscape painting of a snowy scene with a lit church in the distance.

As Pastor Shepherd had predicted, Ora moved on to something softer after about two minutes. "Silent Night," slow and hushed, different than Jessalyn had ever heard it played, but beautiful. How moving it would be to hear the song performed thus on a dark Christmas Eve.

"I think we'll be able to hear ourselves now." The pastor took the ledger Jessalyn had set on his desk. "Sorry I didn't warn you, but I didn't know she'd do that. Sometimes she likes to play loudly to start. She says it gets her fingers going."

"Isn't it customary to begin with scales? That's what I do." Jessalyn tried not to laugh.

"You play the organ?" He looked up from the book.

"Oh no, organs are terrifying. So many pedals and knobs. But I'm passable on piano. I'm much better at math."

"So I can see." His lean fingers traced the notations she'd inserted as bookmarks. "You found a few math errors. Good."

"Those are minor mishaps."

"That's good to know. What's this?" He held up one of her notes.

"A suggestion. Your budget for missionary funding is at zero, but there is money left over in this budget, in a fund called Outreach. I assume that means the monies are used locally. I wondered why— not that it is my business—but if the church elders choose not to spend it in that area before December 31, the funds could be transferred to church repairs and the budget adjusted next year to reflect this year's spending."

His light eyes scanned the document. "There's money remaining in Outreach because Ora and a few of the other widows donated food for the monthly luncheon so we didn't need to buy any. I doubt we can adjust next year's budget, but it's good there are funds available now."

"Another area that could possibly be manipulated is this column here, Facilities Management. That's an exorbitant price for fuel."

He looked at her as if he didn't expect her to know the price of coal. But not in a bad way, like he didn't believe her. Just that he was surprised. "We're sparing in our use of fuel around here, I assure you."

"I am not accusing you of poor stewardship." Indeed, while it was warmer in here than it had been yesterday, it was still too cold, in her opinion. "I suggest investing in more modern stoves, which are far more efficient than what you have in place." That stove in the corner could have warmed her grandparents' toes.

"You're right. I'll make a note of it. If we have a church to budget for in the New Year." He stopped himself, shaking his head. "Sorry. That's a lack of faith talking."

"I think it's normal to wonder how everything will turn out when one's troubles are heavy." At least it was for her. She still had no answers when it came to her own struggles, but she was glad to be away from her father and his wife for the month. Perhaps the time and distance would help her perspective. "Here, let me show you where I found a place to easily tighten the budget."

For the next fifteen minutes, she pointed out the areas where coins could be saved, and one place where Mr. Tillson's subtraction error revealed an unexpected surplus.

Pastor Shepherd's shoulders relaxed. "That's amazing. Not enough to pay for the window repair, but a start. Thank you."

"Then I'll pay for it. I prefer not to freeze at the Christmas Eve service," she teased.

His lips turned down. "That sort of repair could be quite expensive. I could never ask you to—"

"You're not asking. I'm offering. I've long believed all my possessions are the Lord's, not mine, and I should use them when He directs. This is one such circumstance. Your people bear enough burdens, thanks to my uncle, and they shouldn't have to worry about scraping coins together to fix the window. Not when I can do this small thing. Will you send me the bill?"

"Yes, thank you, Miss Grant." But he wasn't as excited as she thought he'd be. Unsmiling, he seemed downright despondent.

A shiver coursed through her, and not from the cold.

Miss Grant's shudder drew Seth's attention out of himself and back to her, a woman who had whirled into his office with a gift in her hands, like manna from heaven. She must be cold, here in this lukewarm office, to have shivered like that. He should let her be on her way, back to the comfort of her uncle's manse. "Thank you for your help, Miss Grant. I won't keep you any longer."

She didn't budge from her seat though. "Pardon my saying so, but you do not look pleased about something. The window repair? I am good for the bill, I promise you."

"That isn't it. I've bungled this. Forgive me." He mussed his hair. There was no easy explanation beyond the truth. But could he share it with her, not only not a parishioner but a virtual stranger? Confessions usually went the other way around where he was concerned, with folks telling him their struggles and sins.

He didn't know Jessalyn Grant, but the urge to confide in her was strong and at the same time quieting, like he'd been working out in the cold for too long and at last had come inside to a blazing fire to thaw out. So he met her intelligent gaze and smiled.

"I am grateful for your assistance, Miss Grant, and even more than that, I appreciate your response. You saw a need and addressed it out of your ability—a response of stewardship. But my first impulse to your offer was far less noble. It was nothing short of greed."

Her jaw tensed. "What do you mean?"

"One of my personal weaknesses. Rather than thank God for the blessings He provided through you, my thoughts leapt to wanting more. An end to our troubles, financially at least. You saw the ledgers. You know the church is not wealthy, and times will only get harder on my parishioners with the mill closing. A large donation could change all of that."

It wasn't an unrealistic yearning either. His comfortably well-off family could cover the cost of the church repairs without noticing a pinch. If they were at his home church in New York, the leaks, loose tiles, sticky locks, drafty windows, and ancient stoves would have been addressed the moment they showed the first sign of wear, funded by a well-padded endowment.

Jessalyn's face went blank. "You want more from me?"

"Not you. God." He wasn't proud of himself. "For a moment there, I wanted God's hand, not His face. I forgot that God asks us to trust Him to provide how and when He wills. And in my experience, His provision is more often through faith, endurance, and sometimes sacrifice. Not by raining manna, or in our case, dollar bills. So when you saw that I was not pleased, rest assured, it had naught to do with you or your generosity. It had entirely to do with dismay at my lack of faith."

Her wide eyes glanced at the ceiling, as if considering. "I think it is human nature to wish such a thing. Trusting God can be difficult when one cannot see where one is going." She shifted, readying to rise. "Abraham waited how many years for God's promise to come to fruition?"

God hadn't promised Seth anything when it came to this church, but His other promises—including that He'd never leave or forsake him—kept him going on the most difficult days.

"Thank you, Miss Grant. For your help with the repairs, for examining the ledgers, and for listening. Pastors sometimes fumble along like everyone else. Or at least I do."

"I do not think you are fumbling, Pastor Shepherd. On the contrary, you have guided me today, although you didn't know it. By speaking so plainly. I'm comforted to know I am not the only person who sometimes wishes God would draw me a signpost."

"With an arrow pointing the way," he added, unable to hold back a grin. "And a mile marker."

"So one knows when a time of rest is coming." She stood.

He followed suit, walking behind her toward the church. "Instead, we walk by faith with His Word as a lamp to our feet. And thank God for that lamp."

Ora's playing was louder here by the door. A familiar tune, "Greensleeves," which was used for a popular Christmas song, "What Child Is This?"

"I like this one," Miss Grant said. " 'Whom angels greet with anthems sweet, while shepherds watch are keeping,'" she sang along with the notes, then smiled. "It reminds me of singing carols around the spinet at my aunt Estelle's. Her house is always festive, decorated with greenery, and, best of all, the nativity set her father carved from maple and painted with great skill. Mary, Joseph, and a shepherd adoring baby Jesus."

"It sounds like a beautiful and precious heirloom."

"It is. Aunt Estelle arranges it on a table with a red tablecloth by the parlor window. When I was small, I used to kneel by it. I always thought it would be fun to be carried about like the sheep, over the shepherd's shoulders. Once I begged my father, and he tossed me over his shoulders and took me up to bed like that."

The spark that had been in her eye when describing the nativity diminished at the mention of her father. Seth was about to ask what was wrong, but Ora concluded the song and Miss Grant pushed through the door to the sanctuary.

"Brava, ma'am." Miss Grant applauded the organist, her claps muffled by her gloves.

Seth joined in the applause. "Truly lovely."

"Lovely won't do, Pastor. Not this year, with the mill closing. The parishioners deserve a *perfect* Christmas Eve service."

Perfect wasn't realistic. But special? Memorable? A service that would encourage and bless his people in later times of darkness? Seth would do his best.

He'd be failing, though, if he didn't do one more thing before accepting all was lost as far as the mill was concerned. "Miss Grant, may I walk out with you?"

"Going somewhere?" Ora cocked her fuzzy white head.

"The mill. The best Christmas I can give my flock includes speaking to the mill owner on their behalf, don't you think?"

Now it was Ora's turn to applaud.

CHAPTER 4

O f course I'm going with you." Jessalyn had to hurry along the walkway to keep up with Pastor Shepherd's long strides, an unusual
occurrence for her, considering her height equaled many men's.

"I don't wish to put you in the center of this muddle, Miss
Grant."

"I am already in the center of it. Francis is my uncle."

"I wouldn't wish for him to be upset at you for being with me."

"I will never apologize for my faith or my friends who share it."

He didn't argue with her after that. They traversed the opposite
way from Uncle Francis's cozy, large home, turning onto a street
she hadn't visited. Then another and another. The houses here were
smaller, closer together. This close to the Merrimack River, the wind
felt a mite colder too.

One more turn, and there it was, a behemoth brick structure
surrounded by smaller outbuildings. Jessalyn had never visited the

mill on her earlier visits. Father hadn't thought it appropriate for ladies. "It's huge."

"That it is." Pastor Shepherd opened the office door, admitting her to a blue-wallpapered waiting area appointed with straight-back chairs, glowing lamps, and gilt-framed landscapes of the Merrimack River. Across the room, a double set of doors was marked with a discreet No ENTRY sign. The mill's true work must lay beyond those doors.

A woman with a graying topknot and a creased brow rose from behind a desk. "Welcome to Chester Mills. May I help you?"

"I'm Mr. Chester's niece." Jessalyn smiled. "Will you tell him Pastor Shepherd and I are here to see him?"

"He is in a meeting, I'm sorry to say."

"We will wait." She spun back to the pastor. "I shouldn't have spoken for you, I'm sorry."

"No, I'd like to wait as well."

The woman gave a curt nod before she disappeared through a door behind her. Jessalyn glanced at the pastor. "She seems efficient, so we'd better hurry."

"With what?"

"Peeking inside the mill."

"And why would we do that?" Pastor Shepherd's smile was crooked.

She hurried to the double set of doors and looked up at him. "I've heard the most terrible things about textile mills, and I hope to ensure my uncle does not run such an establishment."

"I admit I'm curious, although I've not heard a bad word about the conditions here."

Jessalyn pushed open the heavy door, revealing a hallway. Dull thumps and whirring sounds were her guide through a short maze of office halls, and then, through one last door, they came to a warehouse illuminated by lamps and large windows. Tidy, swept rows separated machines whose purposes she couldn't begin to fathom. It smelled of warm metal and the subtle but particular odor of wool that made Jessalyn's nose twitch. The employees at their tasks or walking past were dressed warmly, and all were adults. No harsh child labor here, thanks be to God.

"Lost, my dear?" Uncle Francis said loudly from behind her so he could be heard above the noise of the machinery.

Jessalyn spun, her skin tingling with embarrassment at having been caught. "I was curious."

Pastor Shepherd's smile fell. "Forgive me. I'd always wondered how some of these machines worked."

"That is not why we're here, and you know it. Uncle, this is my doing."

"I am not surprised by the fact." Uncle Francis gestured toward the door they'd come through. Jessalyn preceded the men out until they reached the relative quiet of the reception area, where the woman behind the desk leveled Jessalyn with a look of disapproval.

"Sorry, ma'am." Pastor Shepherd tipped his hat at her.

"If either of you wanted a tour, you only needed to ask." Uncle Francis folded his hands before him. "But visitors may not stroll in there. It could prove dangerous to them and to my employees. However, I doubt you came here to investigate the safety of the mill. What's this about, Jessy? Why are you here with him?" He pointed at Pastor Shepherd without looking at him.

The pastor didn't seem offended. "Perhaps we could have a moment in private?"

"All you clergy want is money for a God who doesn't do anything."

"I don't want money," Pastor Shepherd said. "All I desire is to discuss the mill's closure and its ramifications for your employees."

Uncle Francis ignored him. "You and I already discussed this, Jessalyn."

"It bears discussing again. Please hear us out."

"You clearly care about your workers. The mill is clean, safe, and warm. So I wonder, in light of that care, could you not explore another avenue, rather than closure?" Pastor Shepherd's tone was even, considerate.

Jessalyn's was probably far more pleading. "You are not losing money."

"Nor am I making any," her uncle retorted. "This is about profit. Business."

"I understand you've tried to sell it. What if you give it more time?" Pastor Shepherd held up a hand, as if offering a physical option.

Uncle Francis laughed. "Keep your job at the church, Reverend, and leave the business matters to those with a tad bit of knowledge."

Pastor Shepherd's face hardened into a mask, as if he'd been hurt by the comment somehow.

That wouldn't do. Jessalyn squared her shoulders. "Pastor Shepherd allowed me to look at the church's account books, Uncle. I found a few things to help. I know I've asked you already if I may view the mill's books, but now that I saved the church a few pennies, perhaps you'll allow me to do the same here."

"It will take more than a few pennies to keep the mill profitable."

"It won't hurt to let me try, will it?"

He waved his hand. "Please don't concern yourself, Jessy. I have capable people who do that."

She waited a moment before responding. "You're saying I'm not capable?"

He flushed. "That's not what I meant."

But the damage was done. He'd poked the old wound Father had made. Since she could hold a pencil, she'd been keeping accounts, and Father had insisted she wasn't proficient. No matter how many times she proved him wrong, he shamed her for behaving in an unfeminine manner. Before Mother died, he'd scolded her for encouraging Jessalyn. *"She's already old enough as it is, without a husband. We'll never marry her off at this rate."*

Uncle Francis may not feel the same, but he'd dismissed her, and it hurt.

Uncle Francis reached for her. "Jessy—"

"I know, Uncle." One look at his anguished face told her he regretted his words, but she didn't wish to be touched right now. She wanted to hide.

Pastor Shepherd was on her heels as she rushed outside. "Miss Grant? I'm sorry."

"As am I."

He rushed to her side and kept her quick pace away from the mill. "You seem upset with your uncle."

"I am."

"I suppose you'll be returning to South Carolina, then?"

His disappointed features surprised her, as did his question. "Oh no. This. . .incident is not enough to send me home. I came to get away from my father. My aunt Estelle or aunt Lila would have taken me in, but they are practically his neighbors."

"I'm sorry there's a difficulty there." He didn't pry, but his eyes held questions.

She didn't mind telling him the truth. By unspoken agreement, their pace slowed. "My mother died a few days before Christmas last year."

"I'm sorry. How difficult."

"It was, but I made a new friend at the library shortly thereafter. Bernice. She'd known the loss of a parent—her father—and her financial situation was tenuous, since the family was supported by her two brothers who'd rather spend coin on whiskey than shoes for their siblings. Despite that, she was generous with me in every way, writing me encouraging notes, baking me treats to cheer me, listening to me when I was sad. I grew to trust her implicitly."

"I take it from the lack of cheer in your tone that is no longer the case."

She sighed. "One day I returned from an errand to find her at the house with my father. She'd been many times, of course, and I assumed she was there awaiting me, but to my shock, they announced their betrothal."

"You'd no indication it was coming?"

"Not one. Except for two or three times, Bernice was never at the house when Father was home, and those few occasions they spoke only pleasantries. I realized that she had come to the house on the pretext of seeing me other times, knowing I was not home, in order to see my father."

"Are you certain of that?"

"All I'm certain of is that once the betrothal was announced, she wanted naught to do with me. No more friendship, only the cool, haughty treatment of a stepmother—and one who is younger than I am." She met his concerned gaze. "Bernice probably learned about my mother's death and wanted a way to meet my father, or once she met him, she enacted a plan to worm her way into his life. Either way, her friendship with me was a ploy. Now she is free of financial hardship, and neither of them wants much to do with me."

He was silent for a moment, regarding her. "You must feel betrayed."

"My father and my friend were supposed to be trustworthy, but ultimately they weren't. That is one thing I appreciate about Uncle Francis. He may make decisions I dislike, but he doesn't lie. He takes me as I am. Or at least I thought he did."

"Because he won't allow you to look at the accounts?"

She nodded. "I know he didn't mean it to come out as it did though. He doesn't want to hurt me."

He kicked a clump of snow. "I know something about difficult families, but I must say, you are good to him, Miss Grant."

"Do call me Jessalyn, please. My surname reminds me of my new stepmother too much right now. Besides, I'm not one of your flock, nor am I staying here past Christmas. I do not think it entirely improper, in private at least, for us to speak as friends."

That assumed they would speak in private again. As friends. Jessalyn's face warmed.

"A pretty name." He smiled. "I suppose you must call me Seth, then. After all, we are allies, trying to sway your uncle to see reason. And return to the Lord too." They'd reached the intersection where she needed to continue on straight to reach Uncle Francis's house, and he should turn right to return to church, but he didn't turn his body that direction. "May I escort you to your front door, Jessalyn?"

It was tempting to say yes, even though the desire to continue chatting out in the cold was not at all like her. Perhaps her eagerness was a manifestation of her loneliness, now that she'd lost her father and Bernice. Things between her and Uncle Francis weren't that good either. She wanted a friend. And there was something about Seth's eyes and his kindness that drew her in a way she hadn't felt in some time.

But theirs was a temporary friendship, so she must do what she always did when loneliness loomed: keep busy. "Thank you, no, Seth. I've taken you from your work long enough."

"Not true. I went on behalf of my parishioners."

So he had.

She realized she hadn't moved yet. Neither had he, but he was probably waiting for her to go on her way first. "Until Sunday, then?"

"Friday. The knitting circle."

"Oh, that's right."

In the meantime, they'd both pray. And ponder. Perhaps there was nothing to be done about the mill closing, but Jessalyn could still do something to make Christmas a little brighter for the families in town. "I'll see you there."

Once Seth returned to the church, he executed a few tasks before setting out again to make inquiries into someone with experience repairing stained glass casings. If the matter of the drafty window could be seen to this week, his parishioners would certainly be grateful. Especially if the temperature dropped any lower.

Throughout the rest of the day and the days that followed, he prayed about the mill, Francis Chester, and Jessalyn Grant. Should he have agreed to call her by her first name and suggest she do the same with him? It pushed a boundary between clergy and parishioner, perhaps. But then again, she was not of his flock. After Christmas she would return to South Carolina, and he would likely never see her again.

What a dismal thought. She was an intelligent, honorable lady

whose openness blessed him in a way he hadn't expected. Her difficult family situation grieved him, but her experience reminded him
he wasn't alone in having a parent who found his child disappointing. Although for completely different reasons. Pastoring wasn't as
impressive a profession to Father as business. Profit over people—
Father would understand Francis Chester's motto. Seth's father
would have been overjoyed if Seth had been born with a head for
accounts, like Jessalyn.

Ethel, his blue-eyed sweetheart in New York, would agree too.
He hadn't received a letter from her since September. Had she grown
tired of waiting for him to prove himself a good enough pastor to
earn the New York post? Had he disappointed her too?

In the meantime, the Lord had given him work here, although
he wouldn't be working, exactly, at the knitting circle. Visiting, more
like.

He knocked on the organist's door Friday afternoon with a jug
of October's apple cider in hand.

Ora welcomed him with a grin. "Come in and be useful."

Useful? "Is there something I can do, other than knit?" He
entered the warm foyer and shrugged out of his coat.

"Not a thing. My Obadiah knit, you know. Good skill for a bachelor man like you to have. You can help us with our aim to give at
least one knit good to each family affected by the mill's closure by
Christmas."

He had to duck his head to enter the cozy parlor packed with
women from his parish, from Sylvie Mack and other married women
to a few widows and Jessalyn Grant, who gave him so warm a smile
he couldn't help but forget his discomfort at being the lone male
present.

Ora gestured at the vacant spot on the worn brocade sofa by

Jessalyn. "Come on in, Pastor. That's my spot. Sit in the middle, and I'll teach you."

Between her and Jessalyn? That sofa wasn't big enough for the three of them, but he took the seat, as instructed, while Ora set the jug of cider on a table beside a teapot and some baked goods.

"Never had a man in our knitting circle before." Alice Tillson, who kept the shop with her husband, Albert, grinned at him.

"To be frank, I hadn't planned to do more than chat with you ladies and—oh, thank you, Ora." She had plunked two large knitting needles into his lap, followed by a ball of duckling-yellow wool.

Then she squished between him and the sofa's arm. "You've got no choice. You're learning today."

Jessalyn lifted a white rectangle for his perusal. "It's not that hard, honest."

"Most of us have knit since we were tykes," Alice agreed.

"And we're fast, which is good, because there's a lot to do." Ora looped the yellow yarn around one of Seth's needles, far too quickly for him to tell what she was doing, much less repeat it himself. "After last winter's bad storm, we're preparing just in case God sends another. Like squirrels gathering nuts. Did I ever tell you my father called me Squirrel Girl?"

More than a few times. "Because you climbed trees."

Ora's cousin Marianne Redbud hooted. "Did she ever. I used to get a crick in my neck calling her down to come play."

Stories of the women's childhood antics had them all laughing within minutes. Despite the number of people crammed into Ora's parlor, Seth found himself settling into the sofa, fully aware of Jessalyn's shoulder pressed against his. Nevertheless, he tried to focus on Ora's instructions, yet produced stitches that looked uneven and lumpy. He managed to make a few long rows of yellow before the others stood to go home. "It'd make a good scarf for a pencil, maybe."

Jessalyn laughed as she tucked her yarn and needles into a purple brocade bag. "If you practice at home, think of how much will be accomplished by our next meeting."

Earlier today he would have balked at coming back. But now? He wasn't sure he wanted to leave. In fact, he wanted to spend more time with Jessalyn. "What are you working on?"

"A baby blanket. Sylvie says there are several little ones coming into the community this spring."

"Six, by my count." Sylvie rested her hand over her protruding stomach.

Much as he enjoyed sitting with Jessalyn, Seth was drawn to take advantage of the opportunity to speak to Sylvie. He'd visited the Macks earlier this week to chat with Hiram, but a word with Sylvie would be good too. Dropping his project on the coffee table, Seth approached her, glad for the cover of others' conversations so they wouldn't be easily overheard. "How's Hiram?"

"Glad you came by to talk and pray with him. He promised me no more drinking, no matter what happens with the baby or the mill. This is a hard time for us, but I'm glad he won't turn to drink anymore."

"Me too. I told him I'd visit him next week to talk again."

"We appreciate that, Pastor." She looked down. "I'm trying to focus on God rather than my circumstances, but it's so hard. I don't want to lose another baby."

He squeezed her shoulder. "I'm praying."

"And we're grateful for it."

Marianne interrupted then, and he was caught in a few conversations before he could retrieve his yellow pencil scarf. Er, project.

"Thanks, Ora, ladies."

"Want your jug?" Ora lifted it.

"Finish the cider, and I'll fetch the jug later." He turned back, finding Jessalyn tugging on her gloves. "How was your week?"

"Uncle Francis is still being stubborn about the mill as well as about letting me look at the books." Her jaw set. "I haven't given up hope, however."

"That's the spirit."

She turned toward him, her back against the others in the parlor. "Sylvie Mack looks pale. Is there something I can do for her?"

He shook his head. "She's lost several babies since Paulie."

"How sad." Jessalyn's hand went to her chest. "Anxiety about her husband losing work can't be helping things. I'll add her to my prayers."

"Pastor?" Alice Tillson called behind him. "Before you go, I wondered if you have a moment to talk about the candles for the Christmas Eve service. The order came into the store, but they sent the wrong ones. Care to look at them to see if they'll work?"

"You are needed here, aren't you? How wonderful to be needed." Jessalyn sighed. "I'll see you Sunday, Seth."

He liked that she called him by his first name. "Until Sunday, Jessalyn."

He discussed the candles with Alice, not a situation where he was particularly *needed*, as Jessalyn said. But he became aware of how much he was a part of this community.

Once he left Ora's, the cold nipped his nose and the wind hinted at something colder blowing in. It would be good to be in his little parlor tonight.

Except that when he turned the corner, his plans took a turn. A tall man carrying a small valise banged on the church door. Seth couldn't see his face, but he recognized the man's form and tilt of his head. "Father?"

The man turned, and sure enough, it was Father, his round cheeks pink from the cold wind. "There you are. No one's here to let me in, eh? No sexton or secretary?"

"You know we don't have those, Father. Just me and the organist." Seth enveloped his father in a hug. "Good to see you, but what brings you to Millerton?"

"I thought it would be faster if I brought these in person." Father pulled back and dug into his breast coat pocket, withdrawing a few letters. "It's time."

"Time?" What had Seth forgotten?

"There's to be a vacancy at the church at home in the new year, and it's yours if you want it."

CHAPTER 5

Mine if I want it.

    Which, of course, he did.

But as Seth reread the letters Father had brought with him, his stomach felt hollow.

Perhaps it was because of Ethel's letter.

"I have already accepted an invitation for New Year's Eve but will be prepared to receive your call midday the first of January."

She'd written a little more, of course, but not much. There was no sense of excitement, no endearments. It was more a summons than an invitation.

The letter from the head pastor at the New York church was courteous but similarly brief. It mentioned a competitive salary but nothing about how he would function as part of a team in ministry. Perhaps those details would be discussed in person.

"You seem sullen." Father came out of Seth's bedroom early

Sunday morning. Seth had offered his bed and slept under a pile of blankets on the short parlor sofa. Father glanced around the snug but sparsely furnished parlor. "I'd have thought you'd be celebrating the fact that you'll be out of this place soon. Perhaps within the year you'll have a wife to provide a more comfortable home."

Ethel? Seth had wanted that for a long time, hadn't he? But did he still?

What was wrong with him? Perhaps he was just tired. Sleeping cramped on the sofa could do that to a fellow. He scrubbed his face with his hands. "I'll brew us some coffee."

"You'll cheer once you've had a cup or two."

Seth hoped so, because it was never good to go to Sunday worship feeling like a disgruntled bear. Especially now that Father had his arm around him in an awkward sideways hug that ended with a thump of his fist on Seth's bicep. "Your mother and I are pleased. Well done."

He hadn't done anything, but he understood what his father meant. Seth ducked into the kitchen to begin the coffee, his emotions a muddle. He had yearned for their approval for as long as he could remember, but he couldn't help but wish his father could be proud of him for who he was, even if he was here in Millerton.

When the clock struck half past nine on Sunday morning, Jessalyn put away the letter she'd received yesterday and had reread twice. It was a Christmas note from her school friend Mabel Perkins, but one line in particular made Jessalyn pause. Should she tell Uncle Francis about it?

It would be a risk. She hadn't discussed anything her uncle deemed unpleasant since the incident at the mill, but Mabel's letter made her want to try again. Should she? Perhaps the best thing to do was wait for the Lord to tell her when to ask.

She donned her coat and gloves in Uncle Francis's foyer, and then went to find him in his favorite chair in the parlor, cup of coffee in hand, woolen lap rug over his knees. She smiled, knowing how he'd respond to her invitation, but she wanted to ask anyway. "I'm leaving for church, Uncle. Care to join me?"

"You know the answer to that." He caught her gaze. "You still love me even though you're upset about the mill?"

"I will always love you, Uncle."

"I'm not sure I deserve that."

"Love isn't something you earn, I don't think." If it was, would God love her?

"You still willing to look at the mill books?"

"Are you sure?"

"I'd like you to verify the bookkeeper's math tomorrow. Will you?"

"Of course. Thank you." Was this the Lord's answer in regard to timing? In for a penny, in for a pound. "I received a letter yesterday from my friend Mabel. We went to finishing school together, but she married a lawyer in Lowell. She mentioned he'd been occupied of late with the sale of a textile mill, and the proceedings went well." Mr. Stone, probably the partner at the firm where Mabel's husband worked, had been exceedingly pleased, according to Mabel. "It indicates someone is buying mills. May I ask for details?"

"I assure you, poppet, everyone who's expressed interest in buying my mill has been a vulture who only wants to pay half of what it's worth. They won't care about the employees, and I'll not lose money like that, no sir."

It was worth a try. "Thank you for letting me look at the accounts, Uncle Francis."

His mouth curved the slightest bit upward. "You looked like your mother just now, all big-eyed and sweet."

For all his bluster and orneriness, it was clear as polished crystal that Uncle Francis was in pain—over Mother's loss, over the loss of his wife, and probably over the loss of his relationship with God as well. When Aunt Joan died, he could have turned to God but chose instead to walk away. He'd gotten lost, but she would never stop praying for him.

She wiped a budding tear from her eye. "I miss Mother. It's nice to know you do as well."

His gaze returned to the fire crackling in the hearth. "I'm sure your father does too. That's why he married that Bernice so fast. It made him less lonely."

"Probably. I don't think he misses *me* though. Otherwise he wouldn't have been so quick to agree when I said I wanted to come here for the holidays. In any case, I'm glad he's not lonely. Mother wouldn't have wanted that."

"She wouldn't have wanted that for you either. Which reminds me, is something going on with you and that pastor fellow? Beyond trying to talk me out of closing the mill, that is."

"Seth? And me? Of course not."

"Oh, 'Seth' now, is it?" He grinned.

"Don't tease." To avoid his gaze, she adjusted the angle of Aunt Joan's bisque nativity on the mantelpiece. It must have been moved when it was dusted. "We're friendly, that's all, and we're working on the knitting project together. Nothing remotely. . .*you know.*"

"If you say so, but you're a catch."

"I'm twenty-eight, Uncle. Father says once a woman passes twenty-four she is no longer viewed as—"

"I don't give a buttered crumpet what your father says, and that age stuff is ludicrous. You're a pretty gal with a good brain and even better heart. Now shoo, go on to church before I say something more about your father I may or may not regret."

"Goodbye, then."

"Say hello to *Seth*," he teased.

"Oh, I will," she teased back as she left the parlor. "I'll tell him you expressly wished for me to bid him a good day."

His laughter chased her out of the house.

At church Sylvie beckoned Jessalyn to sit with them. It was her first time to meet Hiram, a friendly man, but abashed, maybe because most of the congregation knew he'd turned to drink last week. But today he was in God's house. Jessalyn was genuinely glad for that.

She recognized everyone from last week except for a dark-haired gentleman of middle years who sat in the front pew. She paid him no more notice, however, and concentrated on the service, especially Seth's sermon about John the Baptist and repentance.

She needed to repent of a few things, especially her attitude where her father and Bernice were concerned. For the past few months, she'd been unable to grapple with the way Father treated her once he announced his intention to wed Bernice. Nor could Jessalyn heal from the pain inflicted by Bernice's abandoning her that same day. Now that she had some distance and had talked over the matter with Seth and Uncle Francis, however, she could see that Bernice must have been miserable at home to have gone to such lengths to find a husband. And Father was clearly lost and lonely without Mother.

It didn't justify their cold treatment of Jessalyn, but acknowledging their pain did soften something inside her. Her relationship with them would never be the same, but it didn't mean she should spend her life resenting them.

At the end of the service, Jessalyn brought up the rear of the line of parishioners greeting Seth at the door. His smile warmed her, and she thanked him for the sermon. "I have work to do in that area."

"Don't we all?" His smile warmed her from her core.

A glance right and left assured her she couldn't be overheard. "Good news. I've been granted access to the mill's account books."

His features lightened. "That's wonderful. Have you discovered anything useful?"

"Not until tomorrow—"

Jessalyn realized she was no longer the last one in the line. The man from the front pew had come up behind her.

Seth extended an arm in a posture of including the man in their conversation. "Jessalyn Grant, meet my father, Gideon Shepherd."

His father was here? Jessalyn extended her hand to him. "Wonderful to meet you, sir."

"And you." His stiff posture communicated otherwise though.

Jessalyn felt her eyes narrow. Hadn't Seth mentioned something about having family difficulties? Perhaps this had not been an easy visit.

Before she could think of something else to say, Ora marched up to Mr. Shepherd. "So you're Pastor's father. I'm Ora Cole, the organist. Your boy is a fine preacher and middling knitter."

"Knitter?" Mr. Shepherd's expression remained unchanged, except for a twitch of his eyebrow.

"He's participating in a Christmas project," Jessalyn explained.

"We're determined to create at least one warm knitted good for each family affected by the mill's closure by Christmas," Seth said.

His father didn't blink, much less smile.

"Speaking of, a few men were inspired by your attendance, Pastor, and will be joining us this week. Circle's at my house again, Friday, you two." With a nod, Ora left them.

Mr. Shepherd turned to his son. "Pity I won't be here to see it. I doubt any of the clergy at home would be caught knitting stockings."

A wave of displeasure roiled through Jessalyn at Mr. Shepherd's implied censure of his son, and the desire to defend him crested up to her throat. "I, for one, am delighted there will be more men offering their skills to help the less fortunate, thanks to your son's attendance. His investment in the community is inspiring, to say the least."

"I see," Mr. Shepherd said, as if he'd seen something different entirely. Like Jessalyn's heart on her sleeve.

She'd best go before she said the wrong thing. "I should rejoin my uncle now, if you'll pardon me. Good day."

Seth's appreciative smile elicited one of her own.

She returned home to a lunch of biscuits and a tomato-fish bisque. They spent the afternoon at leisure, enjoying the Sabbath.

Monday morning, however, Jessalyn was ready to look at the mill's accounts.

As her uncle had said, there weren't any glaring errors, and the mill was breaking even. In her estimation, part of the problem was the abundance of textile mills in the region, creating competition. But more troubling was the structure of management. Shareholders took a larger percentage of profit than Jessalyn thought appropriate, and what excess remained went to manager bonuses. There was little left, with such competition, to increase employee salaries, make improvements, or even go toward Uncle Francis himself. When she mentioned the subject to her uncle, he shook his head.

"I can't restructure without throwing good money away."

"You'd ultimately make up for the losses."

"At my age, though, that's not a risk I'm willing to take."

Not even at Christmas.

In exasperation, Jessalyn retired to her room. Looking out her window over the frosty landscape, she considered visiting the church, but she wasn't sure when Seth's father was leaving and she didn't wish to interrupt their visit, especially not with bad news.

Instead, she wrote letters to her aunts and, after prayer, one to her father—in the spirit of a possible reconciliation.

I love you as much today as I ever have. My heart is heavy at the state of affairs between us—all three of us. May we make amends? Nothing would please me more.

Your loving daughter

Hopefully he'd receive her note early enough to reply before Christmas. A kind word from him would be a gift indeed.

She was about to put away her pen when she paused. Uncle Francis hadn't granted his permission for her to ask Mabel about her husband's work with the sale of a textile mill—but he hadn't said no either. What could it hurt? Perhaps Mabel's husband could provide information about prospective buyers. And if there was indeed someone interested in paying fair price for the mill, it would be a far better Christmas gift to her uncle than the silk necktie or silver-knobbed serge umbrella she'd purchased for him.

As she carried the letters out to the post, her hopes were high, much like they'd been when she was a child writing letters to Santa Claus. But now her hopes were not placed in the man in the sleigh, but the Lord, who heard her prayers and answered them, one way or another. Sometimes in ways she did not want, but He'd been faithful all the same. She could never argue with that.

She wasn't sure when Seth's father was leaving town, so she refrained from calling on the church to inform him of what she'd found in the mill's accounts. The news would wait until Friday when they met at Ora's for knitting circle. When the day came, she gathered her knitting bag and walked to Ora's cozy house.

Alas, she couldn't tell Seth much of anything beyond hello when she arrived. He was surrounded by three white-haired widows—two flanking him on the sofa, one in front of him, bent over his work—who offered their opinions on what he was doing wrong. Then the woman on his left, Marianne Redbud, snatched his project and fixed whatever error he'd made.

Seth looked at Jessalyn and shrugged, grinning.

She hid her laughter by ducking her head.

Seth wasn't the only man, as Ora had said. Three senior-aged husbands came along today, as did Paulie, since school was out for the day. He plopped at his mother's feet and worked on an uneven but soft-looking blue rectangle attached to knitting needles. "See? My blanket is for the baby."

"Good work, Paulie." Seth nodded at the project. "You could teach me a few things."

"I think I could." Paulie scrutinized Seth's yellow—whatever it was.

Everyone laughed, but Sylvie's smile didn't look natural. Was she thinking about losing the baby, or perhaps wondering what Hiram would do for work once the mill closed? As Jessalyn knitted, she prayed for the Macks. And then she set aside her white blanket and started a new project.

It didn't take long. When she finished, she topped her fist with the Christmas-green baby cap she'd made, like a puppet wearing a hat. "What do you think, Paulie?"

The little boy smiled at the way she'd positioned it on her hand. "Looks good, I guess. I like the little tassel."

"It's for your baby brother or sister, and I'll make you one that matches if you like the color."

He squinted. "I like it fine, but mine would need to be bigger."

"Big enough for you, I promise."

"How will you know how big to make it?" His hands patted his head.

She pulled out her measuring tape. "This way."

He scooted over on his knees, and she wrapped the tape around his blond head.

"What do you say to Miss Grant, Paulie?" Sylvie nudged him.

"Thank you, ma'am."

"You're welcome."

"And I get a tassel?"

"Absolutely."

He grinned, and he wasn't the only one. Seth's smile was—well, there was no word for it but captivating.

Oh goodness. She really must stop being a ninny and start on Paulie's cap. Two stitches in, however, she looked up.

Seth held up his project and rolled his eyes.

She shrugged as if it wasn't that bad.

He gave her a pointed look when Mrs. Redbud took over his project again, as if to say, *See?*

She held her needles just so and lifted her hands so he could watch her, since he wasn't holding his quite right.

He squinted at her hands.

It was hard not to laugh.

"Edna, it's nigh on suppertime," one of the older men said as he stood.

Jessalyn hadn't noticed how much the daylight had dimmed outside. Uncle Francis would be home soon if he wasn't already. She tucked her yarn and needles into her brocade bag and stood. As the others murmured and prepared to leave, Jessalyn noted the booties, caps, adult-sized sweaters, scarves, shawls, and other items the group had completed piled atop the coffee table. They appeared to be close to meeting their goal of providing every family in need with something warm this Christmas. "What a blessing this will be to the community, Ora. Thank you for allowing me to be a part of it."

"Glad for your contribution." Ora patted her arm. "You're almost done with that blanket."

Jessalyn would have liked a moment with Seth, but he was occupied with the older men by the cookie table, discussing the price of coal. Ah well. It wasn't as if she had any real news about the mill's accounts, so it could wait. She bid goodbye to the group as one.

Ora tugged Seth's sleeve. "Walk that lady home, Pastor. It's getting dark."

"Of course." Seth nodded to the men and walked toward her. Jessalyn didn't miss the knowing expressions on the other women's faces, but they were mistaken. There was nothing budding between her and Seth except for the mutual prayers for Uncle Francis and their attempts to prevent the mill closure.

In the foyer, they donned their coats and hats. "I still can't knit," he muttered under his breath.

"You're not here to knit. Not really. You're here to encourage. And now other men are coming."

"I've learned when one is facing hardship, it often helps to focus on helping someone else." His hand was on the doorknob. "Ready?"

She nodded and preceded him outside. The temperature had dropped, but the sky was cloudless. She tugged her cloak tighter around her shoulders.

"I've been anxious to speak to you, but it was a busy week with my father's visit, the window and door lock repairs, and a few administrative matters," he said. "But I've prayed about your opportunity to look at the mill's accounts. Did you learn anything?" The look on Seth's face was so hopeful, she hated to disappoint him.

"I found areas to improve. The shareholders insist on too high of dividends, and then there is the problem of competition in the area. I suggested a restructure of the organization as well, but my uncle is not interested."

"Why ever not? Oh, hello, Mrs. Wilton."

The woman passing them on the street peered at them with curious eyes. How silly. There was nothing burgeoning between them besides their concerns for the town and her uncle. It had been so long since she dared hope any man could care for her—

"So?" Seth drew back her attention. "Did your uncle explain?"

"He doesn't want to entertain the financial risk. But I had one last idea."

"I'm intrigued."

She explained about Mabel's letter, mentioning her husband's work in the sale of a textile mill. "She said something about Mr. Stone being pleased with his work—I assume Mr. Stone is a partner at the firm, but in any case, Mabel's husband did a good enough job that he received a plump Christmas goose for his efforts."

"Then he must have done well," he said, smiling over the goose, no doubt. "And now you wish to find out if that buyer is interested in purchasing Chester Mill?"

"Yes, or if Mabel's husband knows of other prospective buyers. But I'm not telling my uncle. If it fails, no harm was done. If it succeeds, it would make a wonderful Christmas gift to us all, wouldn't it?"

"It would indeed." His unhurried smile sent a jolt through her. *Stop this foolishness, Jessalyn. Talk about something—anything. Now.* "How was your visit with your father?" she blurted.

His steps slowed, as if he didn't wish to end their time together. Jessalyn's heart skipped a beat. Two beats. Then smacked against her rib cage hard and fast.

"I need a friend, Jessalyn. May I confide in you?"

"Of course." Her breath swirled in the air between them.

He shoved his hands into his pockets. "I'm leaving Millerton. After Christmas."

There. Seth had told someone—told Jessalyn—which made the whole thing feel more real.

But maybe he hadn't done such a good job of it, because Jessalyn's face clouded with confusion. "Since you can't travel at Christmas, I imagine it will be enjoyable to spend New Year's with them."

He glanced around to ensure they couldn't be overheard, but now that they had turned from the main road onto the residential street where her uncle lived, there was no one about. "No, Jessalyn. I was offered a position at my home parish in New York City."

Her intelligent eyes narrowed. "You're moving. Why? You don't like it here?"

"On the contrary, I'm fond of it. It's not home, of course, but that doesn't mean it hasn't become a home to me." He'd never realized it until this moment, when he spoke it aloud. He loved Millerton.

"What about the church here? Your flock?"

"Someone new will come, unless there's no one left in town to need a church."

"There will always be someone left. Ora. Widows and people who have nowhere else to go." She looked down. "I'm sorry. I am not in a position to judge, but I cannot help but be. . .surprised."

She didn't sound surprised. She sounded disappointed, which pierced his gut like a knife. "It's been the plan for a long time."

He didn't say whose plan, and she didn't ask, but her face changed into a bland mask. "You have someone waiting for you, then? A sweetheart."

He was so startled by her guess that when she started walking, it took him a moment to catch up to her. "There is someone, yes, but it's more than that. Remember what you said about your father disapproving of your bookkeeping skills? Well, my parents don't approve of my skills much either."

"How so?" She looked at him then, but her eyes were guarded.

If he was confiding, he might as well tell her everything. "My two brothers have business sense, like my father, but my lack of it disappointed my family. In fact, everything I've ever done seems to disappoint them, including pursuing my calling to be a pastor."

"How could they disapprove of that? I would think you'd be their favorite preacher."

"Sunday was the first time a member of my family has heard me preach, actually. They've never visited me before." He couldn't look at her. "They prefer their church, and if I join the staff, as they wish me to do, perhaps they'll recognize I have some value." He cringed, outwardly as well as internally. "I know how bad that sounds. I can hear it myself."

"Your value is in being God's child. I am sorry your parents and your sweetheart do not understand that."

"Ethel isn't my sweetheart. I realize she never really was and never will be. She sent a letter with my father, and in reading it, I saw we aren't even friends. How can I marry someone who's not my friend?"

They'd reached the walkway to her uncle's grand house, and she stopped. "So this change is not about Ethel or your desire for a new assignment."

"No."

"It is about your parents' blessing. Are you sure you'll have it if you take that position?"

No, he wasn't. Father had seemed pleased by the offer from the New York church, true, but there was no guarantee Seth would capture his father's lasting favor. But he'd never been this close to receiving it before. "I have to try. For my parents' approval."

"And this change meets God's approval?"

Perhaps her question hit him so hard in the solar plexus because it wasn't offered with malice or bite, but honesty, more of a request that he take the situation to God in prayer. Hadn't Seth done that? His entire life, since he'd come to know God and entrust his life to Him, hadn't he asked Him for His guidance?

"God hasn't answered that particular request yet, but if He's anything like my father, then I'm sure He's disappointed in my work here too. I've failed."

"That isn't true."

"Isn't it? The church isn't thriving, much less growing in numbers or discipleship. The facility is a mess and needs things I'm not equipped to provide. The new pastor's sure to be more adept than I am at hammering and fixing windows."

"They don't need a handyman. They need you. The person who feeds the poor each month and inspires menfolk to knit for their neighbors and prays for them and puts their husbands to bed. To be their pastor."

"No one's ever needed me, Jessalyn. I disappoint everyone. Trust me when I say the parishioners will welcome a new pastor. A better one."

"It's ten days to Christmas, and you'll be gone along with the mill."

"The timing isn't ideal, I agree. But if most of the parish leaves to find work elsewhere, I wouldn't have a job here anyway."

Jessalyn lifted her hands, knitting bag and all, and shook her head vehemently. "Stop—"

"But it's inevitable. The mill will close, followed by the church, due to lack of ability to sustain itself, and I'd be sent elsewhere anyway. No matter what happens, I'm leaving Millerton."

"You're leaving?" a familiar voice said behind him.

Now, too late, he understood Jessalyn's frantic signals. Ora stood behind him on the walk, mouth agape, the tasseled green baby cap in her plum mittens. She thrust it at Jessalyn. "You forgot this, Miss Grant, and I thought you might need it as a guide to make Paulie's hat."

Then she spun away, hurrying as if she couldn't get away fast enough. Her back was to them, but Seth could tell by the way her plum mittens brushed at her face that she dashed away tears.

This was not how he'd planned on anyone finding out. And he certainly hadn't expected anyone to be upset about the prospect of his leaving.

He couldn't let Ora go like this. "Sorry, Jessalyn. I need to run after Ora and explain. May I call on you later? I owe you a finished conversation about this."

"You don't owe me a thing, Seth. But you do owe it to your flock." With that, she mounted the steps to the porch and let herself into her uncle's house, leaving him out in the cold.

CHAPTER 6

The following Sunday morning, one week before Christmas Eve, Jessalyn took her seat in church by the Mack family, feeling not the least bit prepared for worship. Seth was leaving Millerton, abandoning the people who needed him most?

And she was abandoning any hope of a continued friendship with him.

All the time she'd been warning herself not to get carried away, she'd allowed herself to be encouraged by his smiles and their easy rapport and the way the other women in the church looked at them as if they saw a blooming romance.

Jessalyn had been a fool. First with Bernice, now with Seth.

Ultimately, Seth's decision was none of her business. She was nothing to him but a temporary confidant. She would be sure to keep a good distance between them from now on, and she'd concentrate on other things. That was her motto, wasn't it? Busyness held loneliness at bay.

Since the service hadn't started yet, she tugged a Christmas-green hat from her handbag and offered it to Paulie. "I finished last night."

"Thanks, Miss Grant." He tugged off his gray cap and pulled on the green one. "Fits just right."

Sylvie and Hiram chuckled. Hiram even playfully swatted the tassel atop Paulie's head. Ora started to play the organ, and Jessalyn opened her hymnal and concentrated on the service.

Seth entered the church, singing the hymn. Bags pouched under his eyes, and his face was lined with fatigue. But he conducted himself well, and his sermon on preparing one's heart for Jesus, not just for Christmas but for His coming again, was well researched and thoughtful.

And cut short when Sylvie stood up, her face stricken.

"Sylvie?" Hiram took her arm.

Seth rushed down the aisle toward her. "Are you in pain?"

"I was." Sylvie flushed red as St. Nicholas's suit. "Sorry to cause such a commotion during the sermon, Pastor. It hurt something awful, and I thought—but it's passed now."

"You thought the baby died again?" Paulie asked.

Jessalyn stood and rubbed small circles on Sylvie's back. "Why don't we take you home and call for the doctor."

Seth met Jessalyn's gaze. "I'll come by after the service."

"Thank you, Pastor." Hiram gathered his wife while Jessalyn took Paulie's hand.

After the slow walk to their modest but snug home, she helped Sylvie change into a nightdress, but by then, the only discomfort Sylvie seemed to be suffering was the pain of embarrassment. "I can't believe I interrupted church like that."

"No one minds." Jessalyn tucked a heavy blanket over Sylvie's feet. "I'm sure they're all praying for you."

Sylvie sniffled. "I don't know how we'll manage, Jessalyn. I'm trying to be cheerful for Hiram about the mill closing, but I'm gonna lose this baby—"

"You don't know that." Jessalyn took Sylvie's hands. "Your job right now is to rest and let God work on everything else."

Sylvie nodded, swiping her damp cheeks with her palm. Jessalyn would have said more, but the doctor arrived, so she went downstairs to join Hiram in the parlor.

But there was already someone with him. Seth's low voice met her ear as she reached the bottom stair, hidden from their view by the wall, and she stood still, wishing she didn't have to pass through the parlor to find Paulie. She didn't much want to talk to Seth right now.

"This is a hard time, Hiram, but drinking won't solve a thing," Seth was saying. "You've got to be the husband and father God wants you to be, here for your family when they need you."

"You're right," came Hiram's strangled voice. "I was a coward before."

Jessalyn shouldn't be listening to this, but before she could move, Seth kept on.

"Any man'd be scared. It's human to be afraid. The shepherds were frightened on Christmas, remember? The angel had to tell them to fear not, so they must've been petrified."

"Guess I never thought of it that way." Hiram cleared his throat. "I've been doing what you said, Pastor. Praying and reading the Psalms. It's helped a lot."

This seemed a good time to make her presence known. She took the last step loudly and entered the parlor, avoiding Seth's gaze. "Where's Paulie?"

"Playing outside with the Nichols boy."

There went her excuse to be "needed" elsewhere. When Hiram offered, Jessalyn had no choice but to take a seat in one of the horsehair stuffed chairs.

Seth reached out to lay a hand on Hiram's shoulder. "May we pray?"

Jessalyn might be angry at Seth for abandoning his church, but she joined in. His prayer resonated within her, and together the three of them lifted Sylvie to the Lord. And then Hiram's need for a new job, as well as their friends and neighbors in the same plight.

When they finished, Jessalyn had no answers, but she did have peace and confidence in God's strength. She had no idea how He would work these things out, but she had to trust.

Even with Seth, who watched her with sad eyes.

The doctor came downstairs, stroking his thick brown mustache. They all stood up, and then the doctor gripped Hiram's shoulder and smiled. "Nothing wrong. Baby's healthy enough to do a jig, is all."

Hiram let out a breath. "So it's not coming yet?"

"No, sir. Sylvie needs rest though. The strain of the mill closing isn't helping her situation. And with her history, we need to ensure she is calm going into delivery."

"Yes, sir." Hiram swiped away relieved tears. Jessalyn did too.

After promising to return with supper, Jessalyn made her exit, glad Seth wouldn't be leaving with her. He wasn't there when she came back at half past four with a crock of stew, but Ora was, donned in a vibrant orange apron.

"I'm staying over as long as I'm needed. No knitting circle this week," she told Jessalyn before she left. "The projects are all pretty much finished."

"I have a little more to go on my blanket, but I'll deliver it to you in a day or two."

Ora leaned in to whisper. "I knitted a scarf for Pastor for Christmas, but I'm not sure I'm giving it to him now. He explained why he's leaving, but I don't like it."

Jessalyn could only hug the organist. "It will be well, I'm sure of it. I don't know how, but it will."

"But you're leaving too, and I don't like that either."

Really? "I'm a virtual stranger, Ora."

"Are you? Worshiping with us, praying with us for your uncle to change his mind about the mill, doing what you can to help us. You're one of us, don't you think?"

Jessalyn pondered the question through the next few days. Christmas was in less than a week, and soon she'd have to think about returning to South Carolina. Her aunts would be glad to see her, but would her father? Would Bernice? There'd been no response letter.

Thursday, four days before Christmas, she did receive mail, however. A foot-long wooden box arrived from Aunt Estelle. Uncle Francis had just come home and carried it into the parlor for her, setting it on the elegant mahogany coffee table—an act of recklessness, inviting the box to scratch the table like that. "What's this? A Christmas present?"

Jessalyn sat on the velvet sofa before the table. "She sent gifts with me on the train."

"Then where are they? I want my present." Uncle Francis rubbed his hands together with feigned glee.

"Your presents will go under the tree when we get one."

His brows rose. "Ah yes. A tree."

"Do not say you forgot about a Christmas tree."

"All right then, I shall not say it." He pressed his lips together.

"You're incorrigible." Jessalyn slid the box to the sofa, where any splinters would do less damage than they would on the fine table. "I thought you were waiting until closer to Christmas Eve."

"I haven't had a tree in years, but I suppose we should have a proper tree. Right there." He pointed to the bay window. "You and I will make merry, won't we?"

She'd hoped so. "Have you decorations, or should I make them?"

"Make, purchase, whatever you desire. The storekeeper, fellow by the name of Tillson, will add what you need to my account."

"I shall go to the store tomorrow, then. But how shall we procure a tree?"

"There's a market for that sort of thing beginning tomorrow. I shall leave work early, and we'll pick one out, eh? Oh, but we can't. You have that knitting square."

"It's a circle, and it's been canceled."

His twitching lips told her he knew very well it was a circle and not a square. "Then I shall meet you here at three o'clock. Now, will you open that box, or am I to be kept in suspense until the twenty-fifth?"

It felt a little more like Christmas now, with her uncle whistling a carol as he fetched a tool to remove the lid from the box. She joined in singing as he used a hammer claw to tug the nails free, and then with a flourish, he indicated she should open the box.

On top was a folded sheaf of paper. Jessalyn read the contents aloud.

Darling Jessalyn,

Greetings and best wishes for a festive holiday. Your aunt Lila and I miss you, but just because you are not here for

Christmas doesn't mean we can't send Christmas to you. The nativity set is yours now. You mustn't argue with me when next we meet, for I've intended to give it to you since you were a little girl. You know its story, how your grandfather carved all the pieces and painted them to help his family remember the story of our Lord's birth. Please set them somewhere for you and Francis to enjoy.

You are in our hearts and prayers.

With affection,
Aunt Estelle

Jessalyn and Uncle Francis dug through the fresh-smelling sawdust in the box to retrieve the smaller box within that housed the nativity. Together they arranged the figures: first, Joseph in his brown robe, his expression protective; next, Mary, sweet-featured and clad in blue; then the baby Jesus, lying in his bed of straw. Last, Jessalyn set out the green-robed shepherd, sheep snuggled over his shoulders, his gaze fixed on the Christ child.

Seth's words about the shepherds being afraid struck her anew. This six-inch figure certainly didn't look as if he'd received a fright, but the real shepherds certainly must have, to have encountered the heavenly host like that.

Yet even in their fear, God brought them good news and peace. He still did to His weary, frightened people, didn't He?

People like her, and Sylvie and Hiram and Ora. She had no idea what would happen after Christmas, when the mill closed and she had to make plans to return to South Carolina. But until then she had four days to enjoy the experience of being part of something again, and she determined to enjoy every minute.

∞

Friday afternoon, Seth left the Macks' as Ora arrived, a vermillion scarf swathed about her ears, chin, and neck. She'd been as prickly as a pincushion with him since she'd overheard him tell Jessalyn about the New York position, even though he'd sat her down to explain things. She hadn't much cared for the explanation though.

But every day was a chance to make peace with her, so he smiled and held the door open for her. "Hello, Ora. Sylvie will be glad to see you."

Ora's bundled chin jerked up. "Hello, Pastor."

"May I help you with that?" He reached for the package she carried.

"No need. It's only yarn." She slipped past him inside the house.

He retreated back into the small foyer. "I hear the knitting circle will continue through the winter."

"With menfolk too. Thanks to you, I s'pose," she said sourly. "But what do you care? You'll be gone."

"I'm always going to care, Ora." He'd be hungry for news of them all, in fact. It struck him suddenly that he'd miss the birth of Sylvie's baby. Pain panged in his gut.

Ora sniffed. "Well, I'm not leaving. They'll have to pry my fingers off that organ."

Whoever *they* were. "You're a treasure, Ora. Truly. And a friend."

"You do seem miserable at the prospect of going back to New York." She seemed mollified by the idea.

How could he be miserable? He was going home to the bosom of his family, where he'd be recognized by them at last. Why didn't he feel happier? Was it the guilt of leaving them?

"Where is everybody?" Ora set the yarn down on the floor.

"Hiram's at the mill. Paulie's out playing, and Sylvie's upstairs. The doctor was just here and said Sylvie's in good health. She wants to cook Christmas dinner, in fact."

"She will do no such thing. Jessalyn and I are making sure this family is well cared for."

Jessalyn. He'd missed her company this past week. He'd been disappointed to learn there was no need for the knitting circle to meet today, because he'd have liked the opportunity to see her again. He'd planned to call on her—at an hour when her uncle was there to chaperone, of course—but calls on sick parishioners and counseling folks about to be let go by the mill had kept him occupied each evening.

Lord, grant me the opportunity to make peace. This is the season, isn't it?

"You and Jessalyn have done a wonderful job, Ora. Thank you. There's just one problem at the house that I can see. It's not ready for Christmas. The tree market is here today, isn't it? I'm going to go buy the Macks a tree."

"That's the best idea you've had in a while." She shooed him out the door. "Go on. Ask if they have any scraps we can use to decorate the church on Christmas Eve, will you?"

Scraps? Maybe he could buy something larger to twine into garland. "I'll ask."

"It's all we'll have this year. That blizzard last February ruined the nativity and the ribbons we've always used."

"God's house will look beautiful, nevertheless."

The air was crisp and dry as he strode to the wide alley between the bakery and the stationer's that served each December as a temporary market for pine trees. A few dozen trees were propped against the brick walls while several others leaned against a display rack. The aromas of pine and woodsmoke, paired with the chatter and laughter of the crowd bustling around, took him back to his childhood. The tree meant Christmas was here, and he and his brothers used to whoop with delight at its arrival.

Seth enquired about scraps, was informed by a man with few teeth to wait a moment, and in the meanwhile, he set about his search for the perfect Christmas tree. He pulled out a few trees and twirled them to view all angles before deciding on one about four feet high. It would look perfect on the side table by the Macks' window—

"Buying a tree?"

Jessalyn? He spun, tree still in hand. She looked so—*homey* wasn't the right word. But she was like the feeling of home. Comfort and calm.

He'd missed her.

And he should probably say something before she thought him daft. "It's for the Mack family. It's a surprise."

"A thoughtful one." Then she looked up and waved. "Uncle Francis has found a tree. I should go."

"Wait." He wanted to touch her, but he couldn't. Not the way things were between them. "I don't wish to part with you like this. I wish for us to be friends."

"Pastor?" The man with half his teeth nudged his arm. "My boy and I will deliver some greens to your church tomorrow. Won't be much, I'm afraid."

"Whatever the amount, it will be most welcome. Our decorations were destroyed in the blizzard last year. Nativity, ribbons, everything."

"I'll make 'em as big as I can, then," the man said before walking off.

Jessalyn chewed her lip. "I agreed to help Ora and a few ladies decorate the church tomorrow, but I had no idea there would be so little to work with. I've just bought yards of ribbon for Uncle Francis's house, but he won't notice if I neglect his bannister and tie bows for the church candlesticks instead."

"May we talk more tomorrow, then? Please?"

"I—suppose."

Francis Chester ambled forward. "Jessy? Good afternoon, Pastor. Fine tree for the rectory."

They shook hands. "It's actually for the Mack family, and I'd best be on my way to deliver it. Have a good evening. See you tomorrow, Jessalyn."

She didn't look happy about it, but he couldn't blame her, he supposed. He excelled at disappointing people.

After paying for the tree and carrying it over his shoulder to the Macks', he entered the house without knocking. "Merry Christmas," he called.

Hiram, Paulie, Ora, and a robe-wrapped Sylvie stood in the parlor, still as statues.

"What's wrong?" The baby?

Ora sighed. "Paulie wasn't outside like you thought he was. He overheard us talk about you leaving."

Seth lowered the tree to the tied rag rug. "I didn't plan to announce it until after Christmas."

"What's three days?" Hiram turned away.

"Don't you like us?" Paulie scowled, a far cry from the expression Seth had hoped to see on the boy's face once he carried the tree through the door.

"I like you a lot. God calls people to go sometimes."

"And if he's got a call, we can't argue with God," Sylvie added, her voice forcefully bright. "Now wipe off that long face and look what Pastor's brought, Paulie. A tree."

"Right kind of you." Hiram took it, his tone bright but his expression grim. "Smells like Christmas."

No one could meet Seth's gaze. He finally gave up and returned to the rectory, but he didn't feel the sense of peace he usually enjoyed there. Tonight the walls were too close. He put his coat back on, lit a kerosene lamp, and unlocked the church. He set the lamp on the front pew and sat beside it, shutting his eyes.

He'd disappointed everyone here by pleasing his parents. Who was he disappointing most?

Or perhaps more importantly, who should he be most concerned about disappointing?

He tried to pray, but Paulie's face kept darting across his mind. Then Paulie's parents', Ora's, the Tillsons', and each of his parishioners', one after another. He'd failed them time and time again, struggling to repair this drafty, leaky building. Trying to persuade Mr. Chester to keep the mill open. Not helping the poorest of their community in any permanent way, despite his prayers and best attempts to clothe and feed them.

Three days to Christmas, and he'd thought leaving them would be the best gift he could offer them.

He rested his elbows on his knees, lowered his head into his hands, and prayed.

Chapter 7

Jessalyn would never be invited to join a church choir, but desperate times called for desperate measures. She cleared her throat. "Why don't we sing?"

The other women decorating the sanctuary this cold Saturday afternoon—Ora, Mrs. Bridges, Mrs. Tillson, and two others who hadn't been at the knitting circle but were deft with forming bows—looked at her with questioning eyes.

"Sing what?" Ora asked.

"Christmas carols." Considering they were decorating the sanctuary, decking the stone halls with a garland of pine and red ribbon, there was an absence of Christmas cheer here. In fact, things felt downright gloomy.

"We're not feeling festive, I guess," Mrs. Tillson said. "Not with the mill closing, and of course you've heard the pastor's leaving. Paulie told our boy Lou, and the Macks confirmed it. Now everyone with ears in Millerton knows." She sighed and returned to tying garland with twine. "Seems like he and your uncle both are looking out for their own interests. The way of the world, I guess."

After the way Bernice wiggled her way into Jessalyn's life in order to sidle up beside Father, and Father's treatment of Jessalyn afterward, Jessalyn had come to believe the same thing about people. Then she'd met Seth and thought he of all people was different. Compassionate. Giving. A man of service. But she'd been fooled again.

As if summoned by her thoughts, Seth entered the sanctuary from the office, carrying the rickety ladder he'd used to climb atop the roof to fix tiles. He greeted everyone, but his smile didn't reach his eyes or round his cheeks. Lines etched his cheeks and framed his mouth in an unhappy expression, and dark circles beneath his eyes testified to sleepless nights.

He didn't seem like a man who was doing what he wanted. Recalling his explanation to her, she considered his reasons for leaving. In Seth's view, he was honoring his family's wishes. She could certainly understand wanting one's parents—in her case, her father—to notice and appreciate the person God had made one to be.

And oh how it hurt.

Her heart shifted inside her rib cage.

Seth passed by her with the ladder. "You've done a wonderful job, ladies." He set the ladder up against the back wall by the exit to the narthex.

Ora bustled toward him, carrying the largest of the wreaths, a pine and pine cone creation entwined with red ribbon. She held the ladder while he climbed it. "I miss our old decorations."

"It's different, to be sure, but just as lovely." He reached down for the wreath. Then, stretching his long arms, he hung the pine circlet where everyone would see it when they went home. The red ribbons trailed down to the doorway, and Jessalyn wondered if Paulie or any of the other boys would jump to flick at the ends after church tomorrow evening.

"Jessalyn and Alice brought ribbon, which helped." Mrs. Bridges peered around, her eyes narrowed like a mole's in the daylight. "But for the life of me, I don't see where you put the nativity scene, Ora."

Ora brushed pine needles from her hands. "I put it in the refuse heap ten months ago. It turned pink, remember? Those red ribbons got wet in the big leak and bled all over everything."

Mrs. Bridges frowned. "Why didn't you wash it?"

"Dye doesn't wash out, and diluted bleach didn't work either," Ora challenged. "So I tried painting it, and that turned out even worse. What does it matter? We don't need a nativity scene to remind us of the true meaning of Christmas, do we, Pastor?"

Down from the ladder, he smiled, a far more genuine expression of affection than the one he'd greeted them with earlier. "No, we don't, Ora."

"I have a set we can use," Jessalyn volunteered. "It's small, but I'm happy for the church to use it on Christmas Eve. My grandfather carved and painted the figures."

"Is that the one you told me about?" Seth hoisted the ladder again. "It's an heirloom."

"One that I'd be happy to share. I'll fetch it when we're done here."

"We're done, I'd say." Ora pointed to the completed garland. "All we need to do is add bows and hang it, and we don't even need the ladder. Go on."

Ladder in hand, Seth stepped closer to Jessalyn. "May I come with you? I can bring the nativity back with me. Save you a trip back out in the cold."

Yesterday he'd asked if they could speak today. She had reluctantly agreed. This seemed as good a time as any to talk, so she nodded.

The lines around his mouth eased. "Give me a moment to put this away and fetch my coat."

Jessalyn's fingers were sticky with sap dollops, which made donning her gloves a little slower than usual, but she was ready when Seth returned. She waved goodbye to the women busy with the garland. "See you tomorrow, ladies." Since Christmas Eve fell on a Sunday this year, they would have a short worship service at the usual time in the morning and then meet again in the late afternoon for the Christmas Eve service.

Alice Tillson fisted her hands on her hips. "Pastor, while you're at the Chester house, will you try once more with Jessalyn's uncle? Ask him to reconsider closing the mill, seeing as it's two days to Christmas?"

"That is my intent, yes." He tugged his hat lower down his brow.

"You give him something to think about," Ora encouraged.

"I shall try." He cleared his throat. "Ladies, I may be taking a position in New York, but I want you to know it is not because I don't care for you all."

"We know." Ora looked at the others, then back at him. "We wouldn't be so angry with you for going if we didn't care for you either."

Tears stung Jessalyn's eyes as Seth exchanged embraces with each of the women. She wasn't the only one with damp eyes, but Seth's were clear and soft when they left the church. Ora's words had given him a sense of peace, to be sure.

Jessalyn looked up at him. "You needed to hear that, didn't you?"

"I did." Seth smiled. "This has been far more difficult than I ever imagined it would be."

They turned onto the street, keeping a comfortable pace. "I think I better understand now, Seth. My father disapproves of me too. But I've not tried to fit into his mold."

"If I'd submitted to my father's will, I wouldn't have gone into the ministry." Seth snapped an evergreen twig from a small pine planted close to the walkway, filling the cool air with the rich smell of the tree. "This is the best way I know of to please them though."

"I hope you and your ministry both flourish in New York. Truly."

"That means a great deal to me, Jessalyn. Thank you."

His gaze was so sincere, her heart lurched in her chest. Was Seth as lonely and aching as she was?

At least he had a clear path in front of him. "Your parents must be delighted about your return."

"I assume so." His gaze was on the cloudless, pale blue sky.

"They haven't written? Your mother? Or. . .Ethel?"

He had said he wasn't interested in pursuing marriage with Ethel, who was surely a beautiful and dainty creature, but now that he was going home, he might change his mind.

"Not a word from anyone, but I'm not surprised. I wrote Ethel to wish her well and inform her I would not be available New Year's Day, so I'm sure she read between the lines that I won't be calling. She won't be disappointed. As for my family, my brothers always send toffee and dried fruit, and my Father brought me his and Mother's gift, the lone present awaiting me Christmas morning. I haven't peeked beneath the brown wrapping, but it's shaped suspiciously like a book."

At his quirked brow, she couldn't help but smile. "But there is still a surprise there. You don't know which book it is."

"True. Knowing my mother, it could be poetry. Or a treatise on economics, if my father selected the gift."

"Or a cookery book," she teased.

"Perhaps a farmer's almanac," he countered.

"Or Mother Goose."

He laughed. "Now that would make for entertaining evenings by the fire."

It was amazing how easily they fell into this sort of rapport, where they teased and laughed. Even when she was hurting and they would soon be parting. Permanently. She still liked being around him.

They turned onto Uncle Francis's street. "Did you send your family books too?"

He shook his head. "Woolen goods produced by members of the knitting circle. I paid them to create shawls and scarves a few months ago."

His thoughtful presents for his family supported his parishioners financially as well as showcased their skills. "They sound like gifts from the heart in more ways than one."

His smile shot heat to her cold toes.

Jessalyn scolded herself for her reaction. She may have softened toward him, true. She better understood his choice to leave now, and from the start, they'd been friends, paired in their desire to pray for her uncle and urge him to reconsider closing the mill. There was also an element to their particular friendship that was rare even among old friends. A camaraderie.

And he'd said he was no longer interested in courting Ethel.

But she mustn't allow herself to have feelings for him. Or, rather, deeper feelings than she already had.

Friends only she reminded herself as they mounted the steps to Uncle Francis's porch. "Come in and speak to my uncle. Would you care for eggnog? I made it last night." Her uncle's housekeeper was away for the holidays, and Jessalyn had enjoyed taking over the kitchen.

"It sounds delicious, if it's not too much trouble."

"Not at all." She admitted them to the foyer, where she tugged off her gloves. "Uncle, I've brought a guest."

Uncle Francis emerged from the parlor, his smile twisting to a grimace when he beheld Seth. "Don't ask me to church."

"Good day to you as well, sir." Seth doffed his hat.

"I've invited Pastor Shepherd in for eggnog, Uncle." Jessalyn kissed his warm cheek. "Care for a cup?"

"I can't resist your concoction. Just the right amount of nutmeg."

While the men went into the parlor, Jessalyn shed her outer-wear, washed the sap from her hands, and fixed a tray of cookies and a pitcher of eggnog from the icebox, along with three crystal cups. She carried the tray into the parlor, which was redolent with the scents of pine, woodsmoke, and the bayberry candles she had purchased at the Tillsons' store. Seth and Uncle Francis stood before the tabletop tree by the front window, admiring the decorations she and Uncle Francis had added to it yesterday: red and white ribbons, tiny cornucopias filled with wrapped candies, paper stars and snowflakes, and candles clamped in brass clips, ready to be lit on Christmas Eve.

Catching sight of her, Seth rushed toward her, arms extended to relieve her of the tray. "Lovely tree."

Their fingers brushed as he took the tray, their touch sending a jolt up her arms. Afraid to meet his gaze, she looked instead to her uncle. "We had a wonderful time decorating, didn't we, Uncle?"

He nodded. "Looks like Christmas now."

"Shall I place it here?" Seth paused beside the coffee table.

Jessalyn nodded and sat before it, pouring two cups for the gentlemen. Taking the cup from her—without touching her fingers this time—Seth sipped. "Delicious."

Jessalyn handed her uncle his cup. "We shall have to make do with but one nativity scene for a few days. I'm loaning Aunt Estelle's to the church, since theirs was destroyed last winter."

"As long as your aunt Joan's stays here." Uncle Francis took it from the mantel and cradled it in his hand.

"Of course."

Seth set down his cup and moved toward the wooden nativity figures displayed on the side table. He took the shepherd in hand, turning it just so in the lamplight to catch the nuances of the figure's features. "They're exquisite. Your grandfather carved and painted these?"

Uncle Francis grunted. "My father, before I was born."

"He was a skilled artisan, sir." Seth smiled.

"He was," agreed Jessalyn. "Oh, I shall fetch the box to transport them back to church." She'd only put it in the hall closet, so it took but a moment to retrieve the rough wood box it had been shipped in. Back in the parlor, she withdrew flannel rags from the box for wrapping each figure. She started with Joseph, who was the largest and heaviest.

Seth glanced at Jessalyn, his gaze heavy with meaning that she understood without words. He would now initiate a conversation with her uncle about the mill, as he'd promised to the women at church. She hoped her small nod communicated her support, and she began to pray.

Seth turned toward her uncle. "What brought you to Massachusetts, Mr. Chester?"

"Opportunity. I missed my family, of course, but if I hadn't come here, I wouldn't have met my dear Joan." Uncle Francis stared down at the bisque nativity in his hands, his cheeks mottling, as if he held back emotion.

Poor Uncle Francis. When a knock sounded on the door, he was quick to set down Aunt Joan's nativity on the velvet chair cushion and excuse himself for the front door.

Seth frowned. "He mourns her still."

"I expect he always will. She was a treasure of a woman." Jessalyn packed up the wooden figure of Mary, whose serene face was ever in an expression of quiet contemplation over her firstborn Son. "I pray Uncle Francis hears us today."

"God has it in hand, I am sure. I've prayed for your relationship with your father as well. Have you received correspondence from him?"

"Not yet." Jessalyn wrapped the baby Jesus figurine in soft flannel and laid it in the box beside the Mary figurine.

"No present either?"

"Not so much as a book on economics," she said with a smile. "But to be truthful, there is only one thing I want from my father. His desire to be reconciled with me."

"I hope that is the gift he ultimately sends, but if not, I pray God grants you the grace to handle whatever the future holds in regard to your father. Come what may."

It was a pastoral, kind thing to say, full of hope for reconciliation and blessing, but more than that, his prayer for grace touched her heart. Jessalyn looked down, her gaze catching on the figure in his hands. "You and that shepherd have something in common, you know."

"The name?" he teased.

"That you tend flocks in service to the Good Shepherd. And you are quite clearly, in my eyes, called to it."

He handed her the shepherd, his long fingers lingering over hers to ensure the figure did not slip from either of their grasps. "I am not sure I am doing the right thing. Leaving."

With reluctance, Jessalyn withdrew her hand and tucked the shepherd in a flannel rag. "I do not know God's will, but I heard what you told Hiram the other day. I didn't mean to eavesdrop, but I was caught on the stairs. You were urging him to be the husband and father God wants him to be. It was sound advice, and I realized. . ." She met his gaze, almost losing herself in their dark depths. "I realized you're trying to be the son God wants you to be."

His gaze fixed on the box. "But Jessalyn, am I the pastor God wants me to be? The man?"

And at the moment, standing this close to him, all she knew was how easily it would be to tell him everything in her heart. Her uncertainties. Her fears. Her feelings. Even for him.

He stared at her, unblinking, and for the first time in her life, Jessalyn forgot how to breathe.

Seth couldn't remember his own name. Jessalyn's eyes were soft and large in the lamplight. So pretty. In his twenty-seven years, he'd never beheld such a face, sweet in features but also honest, open, radiant with care for others. Never had a friend, male or female, challenged or encouraged him in his relationship with God or his work the way she had. He'd never met a woman who could make him feel this confused yet at the same time this peaceful—

"Jessy?" Francis Chester's voice carried an excited tone. "You've a letter."

Seth spun away and found his abandoned cup of eggnog. He

took a swig, hoping the cool drink would quell his suddenly hot skin.

Jessalyn rushed past to her uncle. "Ah, wonderful. I'm expecting news."

"What sort of news?" Francis handed her the letter.

"I shan't say, for it could be a Christmas present for you."

Ah, yes. Jessalyn had told Seth about her letter to her friend Mabel regarding potential buyers for the mill.

"Minx. Alas, I think unlikely, since the letter is from your father. But I trust it is good news." His voice tinged with hope.

Seth's stomach filled with equal parts optimism and dread, and he offered a silent prayer. "Perhaps I should take the box and leave you to your afternoon." He could return later to talk to Francis about the mill.

"No, please stay. I am certain it is naught but Christmas greetings." She moved to a small desk in the corner and retrieved a silver paper knife from the top drawer. Seth continued to pray as she scanned the contents, her features hardening by the second.

Whatever the news was, it wasn't what she'd hoped.

Her uncle peered over her shoulder, his upper lip curling. " 'Rejection,' he says? If anyone is guilty of rejecting kin, it's him, discarding you. He succumbed to that Bernice's schemes, and the pair of them made your life so miserable you didn't feel welcome in your own home. How is that rejection on your part?"

"It's well, Uncle."

"It is not at all *well*. Pastor, can you believe what my brother-in-law has done to his only child?"

"I cannot," Seth said. He didn't need to know what the letter said. Jessalyn's hands shook.

The paper rattled in her fingers as she offered the letter to Seth. "Read it."

Seth carried the letter closer to the glass lamp and read the unfamiliar script.

You ask if we may make amends with one another, yet you are the one who behaved ill, questioning your stepmother's sincerity. Your rejection of her is beyond the pale. As a female of advanced age, it is past time you explored your independence. Your things will be packed and waiting for you in the carriage house upon your return.

"Jessalyn," he whispered. "I'm sorry."

Francis pulled Jessalyn into the half circle of his comforting arm. "Jessy did none of those things he says she did."

"I did question the suddenness of it all and short betrothal," she admitted. "And Bernice's sincerity in her friendship with me. Those are both true. I assure you though, I did my best to approach Father with calm and love, rather than fear or anger."

"Of course, poppet. Anyone who knows you can be sure of that. And the haste with which they wed was indecent. How could you not question them?" Francis's gaze caught on something out the parlor window. "Someone's come calling?"

Sure enough, a mud-speckled but well-sprung carriage pulled into the circular drive. They all moved closer to the window for a better look.

"Are you expecting guests?" Seth glanced at Francis and Jessalyn, who shook her head. Neither she nor her uncle seemed to recognize the caller, a tall man with a sharp chin, looking to be in his early forties, too young to be her father.

With a harrumph, Francis stepped away from the window. "This is not a good time, whoever he is. I'll send him away."

"It's all right, Uncle Francis." Jessalyn swiped her eyes.

Her uncle paused in the threshold to the foyer. "He's no friend of mine, and if this is business, he can wait until the twenty-sixth."

"I'm sorry." Jessalyn turned back to Seth. "You came for a nativity scene and important conversation with my uncle, but you've also heard a fair bit of our family's unpleasant affairs."

"And they break my heart. Jessalyn, I'm sorry for your pain."

"On the contrary, I am sorry for him."

Out in the foyer, Francis was not using the most welcoming tone of voice with the mysterious caller, insisting the man call at the mill the day after Christmas. The man replied that he was from Lowell, and Jessalyn gasped, her eyes shining, not with tears, but excitement.

"Oh! Uncle Francis mustn't send him away. What if it's Mr. Stone?" She dashed out to the foyer.

Stone—the name seemed familiar enough. Clearly he should remember, but he couldn't snag the memory. He didn't have to wait long, however, for Jessalyn's voice carried into the parlor, insisting the visitor come inside.

"I called at the mill first," the man explained. As he entered the parlor, he removed his hat to reveal wavy dark hair sprinkled with silver. He carried a leather bag—an expensive one too, like Seth's father would use to bring work papers home. Francis followed after him, eyes narrowed in suspicion.

"What have you to do with this man, Jessy?"

She took her uncle's arm in a calming gesture. "First, I must confirm, are you Mr. Stone?"

"I am." The man's gaze took in Seth and the Christmas tree. "Forgive me for interrupting, but I could not wait to meet with you."

"I assure you, your visit is most appreciated. I am Jessalyn Grant. We share a mutual acquaintance in Mabel Perkins. You know her husband, Dorian, I believe?"

"Quite well." Mr. Stone grinned. "Sharp fellow, that one."

Mabel. Oh! That Mr. Stone. A partner at the law firm that handled the sale of a textile mill. Well, this was good news, indeed.

"Allow me to introduce my uncle, Francis Chester, and our pastor, Seth Shepherd. Would you care for eggnog, Mr. Stone?"

"That sounds wonderfully festive, Miss Grant."

The gentlemen waited for her to fetch a fresh cup and sit down on the sofa before lowering to their designated chairs, Francis to his favorite chair, where he'd wedged the bisque nativity by his knee, and Mr. Stone in the seat closest to her uncle. Seth didn't sit, however. "Perhaps I should take my leave," he offered for the second time.

Francis leaned forward, ignoring Seth and his offer. "I am eager to hear about your business with me, Mr. Stone."

With steady hands, Jessalyn poured eggnog for their guest. "Mabel Perkins, my school friend? Her husband is a lawyer. And Mr. Stone is a partner in his firm."

Francis's jaw set. "You took it upon yourself to contact him, Jessy?"

Mr. Stone grinned. "No, but I am glad she wrote to Mrs. Perkins, if you are indeed selling Chester Mill."

Seth couldn't interject into this business discussion without intruding, nor could he very well leave now, so he moved behind Jessalyn. Only when he was there, hands on the sofa above her shoulders, did he realize he probably looked as if he protected her. She didn't need it, but he wanted to be there for her all the same.

And he couldn't help but notice the way her shoulders relaxed a touch at his nearness.

Francis wasn't the least bit relaxed, however. "Did you come here because you know of someone interested in buying my mill, Mr. Stone?"

"That is precisely why." Mr. Stone finished his eggnog. "And that man is me. I am not a lawyer, Miss Grant. I was the firm's client."

Well, that changed things.

"Why do you want my mill?" Francis glowered. "You've not even seen inside it. Or looked at the accounts to see how it is faring. Did you tell him what you saw in the books, Jessy?" He glared at Jessalyn.

"No, Uncle. I showed no one."

Mr. Stone crossed his ankles. "I need not see the books to suspect the mill is not making a grand profit."

Francis's chin lifted. "So you seek a bargain, like everyone else. Or do you want the machinery? Or the land?"

Mr. Stone tipped his head, as if he was enjoying this. "What if I seek all of it? Land, building, and machinery? The mill in its entirety. Nothing has to change at all."

"Nothing?" Seth couldn't help but speak out. "Not even the workers?"

"I cannot run a textile mill without employees, so no, I would not dismiss them." Mr. Stone set down his eggnog. "I see this has caught you by surprise, Mr. Chester, but when Dorian Perkins mentioned your plans to sell, I didn't dare wait should another buyer express interest."

"You wish to continue operating the mill when it is not turning a large profit." Francis sounded skeptical, which Seth could well understand.

"I'm a businessman, Mr. Chester, same as you, but I'm also distraught by the closure of textile mills here in our beloved state. What I have done is I have bought underperforming mills and brought them together under one company to reduce competition."

"You noted the problem with competition, Jessalyn." She was sharp indeed, and Seth couldn't help but grin down at her.

She looked back and smiled at him, then flushed as if she sat too close to the fire.

Mr. Stone's chair creaked as he leaned forward. "I own six mills now, and yours, should you sell it to me, would be the seventh in my company. I have references as well as a solid offer for your consideration." Mr. Stone reached down to a pull a file from his leather bag. "Here."

Francis's face was inscrutable, but his knuckles were white as he gripped the pages. "I need time to review the documents before I respond."

"Certainly. My contact information is on the first page, but if you make a decision quickly, I am staying at the inn on Main Street overnight. Hopefully the weather cooperates and I am able to be home tomorrow in time for Christmas Eve services and supper with my family."

When he stood, Jessalyn, Seth, and Francis walked him to the door. He entered his carriage, and Jessalyn sighed, hands to her chest. "Perhaps we should have invited him to supper, Uncle Francis."

"Supper?" Francis spat. "You've presumed enough for one day, I'd say."

Seth grimaced. "Jessalyn has tried to help you, sir."

"Help? I told her I was not interested in her contacting her friend."

"You didn't say no." But she flushed. "Not exactly."

"But I didn't say yes, and you pressed forward, interfering with my business." He stomped to his chair and sat down in a huff.

"I am sorry." She stood beside the chair. "I was trying to find a way to save jobs, and I hoped Mabel's husband would have some advice. Maybe there would be inspiration for us, but she never wrote back. I didn't know Mr. Stone would come."

"The world has gone mad, with strangers swooping in to steal my mill and my niece going behind my back." Francis poked at Jessalyn's letter with his finger. "And my own brother-in-law spurning his daughter? What of peace and goodwill, Pastor, eh? What sort of man turns someone out at Christmas?"

All was silent for a quarter minute except for the sparking and snapping of the fire in the hearth, while Seth held back words about Francis closing the mill, removing the livelihoods of half the town. Jessalyn was thinking the same. Seth could tell by the way her lips pressed together.

Then Francis realized it too. "Me, I suppose."

This, perhaps, was the moment God answered Seth and Jessalyn's prayers to talk frankly with Francis. "Sir, you are no monster. You are a man, fallible and fallen, like the rest of us."

"I don't want to hear this twaddle." Francis stood up.

Seth had forgotten the bisque nativity was at his side. So had Francis, it seemed, for as he stood, he knocked the nativity from the chair. Seth lunged, as did Francis, but neither was fast enough.

The nativity shattered on the parquet wood floor.

"What have I done?" Francis's voice was a whisper as he stared at the pieces at his feet. "Oh Jessy, my darling girl, what have I done?"

CHAPTER 8

Jessalyn fell to her knees, brushing fragments of Aunt Joan's bisque nativity into her hands. "It was an accident, Uncle."

"Indeed. And can be repaired." Seth was on his knees too, gathering shards.

It would take time and a fine paste, but Joseph's head could be glued back into place on his shoulders, and so could Mary's right hand. Jesus in the manger would be an easy fix. The shelter of their stable, however, took the brunt of the fall, and she would never be able to set it to rights in a way that wouldn't show.

"No, Jessy, stop."

She looked up at the catch in his voice.

"It's too late. I didn't see."

His brow furrowed, Seth rose to stand beside Uncle. "But now you do see, don't you, sir? You see and you will never be the same, but you may be healed. Scarred but healed."

Jessalyn looked at him in confusion. Didn't Seth understand Uncle Francis grieved over Aunt Joan's precious nativity, a piece of her he cherished? But as her uncle slumped back into his chair, head in his hands, he groaned. "She would despair of me, Pastor, if she could see me."

She? Aunt Joan?

Jessalyn gulped. Seth had heard what she hadn't in her uncle's words. This was not about the nativity at all, but about her uncle's choices. The nativity shattered, and Uncle Francis's heart seemed to have shattered with it.

Seth gently set the pieces of bisque he'd collected on the coffee table. "I never had the honor of meeting your late wife, but I doubt she would ever despair of you, sir. She loved you, that much is evident."

"And I love you still. Now and always." Jessalyn rested a hand on Uncle Francis's shaking shoulder.

"God abandoned me when Joanie died, I thought, anyway, so I decided I had to look out for myself. But that's what your father has done, Jessy. I don't blame him for remarrying, but he shouldn't have cast you away in his grief. Nor should I have cast away everyone in my grief, either."

"You didn't cast me away. You opened your home to me."

"That doesn't make up for me not caring about anyone else though."

Jessalyn prayed for the right words, even as she spoke. "It is never too late to make new choices, Uncle. Christmas is a time of promises fulfilled, one of them being God sending His Son so we might be redeemed. Aunt Joan took hold of that promise."

Seth rested a hand on Uncle Francis's other shoulder. "You are loved by the Lord, sir."

"I am not worthy of it."

"None of us are." Seth shrugged.

"Surely you are, Pastor. And Jessy."

Seth's gaze lost focus. "I have hurt numerous people. Questioned God. Put others before Him, especially myself. Pastors are not immune from sin, Mr. Chester. We are as broken as anyone else."

"I'm not sure I can be fixed." Uncle Francis took Jessalyn's hand. His fingers were cold, bony.

She rubbed warmth into them. "Fixing takes time. But renewed? That can happen in an instant."

He nodded and let out a breath, and Jessalyn's eyes welled with tears. The Lord had answered her and Seth's prayers for an opportunity to speak truth to her uncle.

"Sir?" Seth met her uncle's gaze. "May I pray with you? And talk?"

"I think that would be. . .helpful." Uncle Francis glanced at Jessalyn. "Will you stay?"

"As long as you like."

They bowed their heads, and Seth led them in prayer.

Jessalyn tidied the parlor after Seth took the wood-carved nativity to church. He'd stayed another hour after they prayed, answering her uncle's questions and speaking boldly about God's offer of salvation.

She was exhausted but also happy, humming Christmas carols. Never before had their lyrics seemed so precious to her, proclaiming the ancient promises of God fulfilled in the gift of Jesus—promises claimed by Uncle Francis minutes ago, here in this room. The air still felt charged and sweet from it all.

He'd retired to his room once Seth left, weary and needing time alone, which she could understand. But the next morning, Christmas Eve, he said he was still overwhelmed and declined her offer to attend the morning service.

She didn't press. Nor did she ask if he'd looked through the documents offered by Mr. Stone yesterday. Something held her back from asking about it, so she kissed his cheek before she left for church. "I may be late. Our circle members will be delivering the knitted items to folks. By the way, I glued Aunt Joan's nativity last night. It isn't perfect though."

"Neither am I." He smiled sadly as she took her leave.

She sat with the Mack family but found it difficult to concentrate on her prayers when Paulie, who wore the green cap she'd made for him, fidgeted beside her. After the service, when he no longer had to sit still, he wriggled between Jessalyn and his parents.

"Tomorrow's Christmas," Paulie said, which, of course, explained everything.

"Today will be fun too," she told him. "Visiting neighbors to pass out gifts made by the knitting circle. And later we have church, my favorite service of the entire year. It's dark and cold, but there is something so peaceful about it."

"I guess it's my favorite too then."

Jessalyn waited in the pews with the Macks and members of the knitting circle for Seth to finish greeting other parishioners so they could distribute the woolen items they'd fashioned. Jessalyn couldn't help but notice Aunt Estelle's nativity was nowhere to be found in the sanctuary, however. When Seth approached the group, rubbing his hands together, she was compelled to ask where it was.

"It's not time yet." Seth grinned. "I'll put it out before the service this evening. Thank you for the loan, once again."

"My pleasure."

"I'd hoped your uncle would join you today."

"So did I, but he wasn't quite ready."

Ora fisted her hand on her narrow hip. "Pastor, shall we go?"

"By all means."

No sooner were they out in the churchyard though, when a well-dressed couple alighted from a carriage parked on the street. The way the man was turned to speak to the driver, Jessalyn couldn't see his face, but the woman, whose hooded cloak revealed a hint of her dark curly hair, looked up and frowned.

Seth's steps faltered. "Mother?"

His parents had come for Christmas? They'd never visited him, much less heard him preach, and Jessalyn rejoiced at the turn of events.

"Seth," his father called, beckoning him away from the group.

"No!" someone cried out. Sylvie. Jessalyn spun to find her friend doubled over, face purple with strain.

"The baby." Hiram gripped Sylvie by the arms, holding her up off the snowy ground. "Someone get the doctor."

"I'll go." Albert Tillson kicked up snow as he ran.

Hiram's anguished gaze was on Seth. "It's too early, Pastor. Help."

"Seth?" Mr. Shepherd repeated.

Jessalyn could only pray, watching Seth rooted on the walkway between his parents and Sylvie. What would he do?

Her heart broke when he jogged to his parents' side, leaving Hiram and Sylvie huddled over on the walkway.

Seth didn't need to think twice. He kissed his mother and slipped his father the key to the rectory. "Make yourselves at home. There's ham in the icebox for lunch. I'll be there when I can."

His father blinked. "But—"

"This is urgent, I'm sorry." Seth regretted leaving his parents like this, but he couldn't abandon the Macks. He rushed back and came alongside Sylvie. "Can you walk?"

"I don't know," she said through gritted teeth.

Hiram grimaced. "I can't carry you, sweetheart, not with my back out."

"But I can." Seth bent, placing one arm beneath Sylvie's knees, the other at her back. In one swoop, he had her in hand. "Ora, take charge of the deliveries. Jessalyn, will you watch Paulie?"

"Of course." She held the boy's shoulders and bent to his ear. "Everything will be all right."

Seth prayed as he followed Hiram to the Macks' cottage. Once inside, he had to take the staircase sideways so Sylvie wouldn't bump her head on the wall, a trick to be sure, but they managed, and he laid her atop her bed, Hiram at his heels.

"It hurts," she said, her face etched in pain. "The baby's coming. I can't stop it."

She would know far better than Seth, so he didn't argue. "Then shall we pray until the doctor arrives?"

She nodded, and, tears in his eyes, Hiram took her hand.

"Lord, You formed this child. You know it's early days for him yet, so we ask Your help trusting Your will. Strengthen Sylvie, we pray, and deliver her of a healthy child when it is Your perfect time."

He continued praying, for peace, for faith, for their home and marriage and Paulie, with thanksgiving for all of God's gifts, until the doctor arrived and shooed him out.

He waited in the parlor until Hiram came downstairs a short time later, his face grim. "The baby's coming for sure."

Seth enveloped him in a brotherly embrace. "Courage, Hiram."

"How will I help her if this baby dies too? How will we go on when I have no work at the end of the week?"

"The Lord is working. I don't know how, but He is." Seth couldn't help wondering if Francis Chester would sell the mill to Mr. Stone. He didn't know if the offer was sound, but after yesterday, Francis's heart had been softened. He didn't dare say a word of it and get Hiram's hopes up though. "You're not alone."

In the meantime, he could pray and scrounge for something for Hiram to eat. His parishioner—his friend—would need his strength.

When Jessalyn and the circle members returned to the church after distributing the knitted items, they learned from Albert Tillson that the doctor was still with Sylvie, and the baby was coming, ready or not.

Jessalyn patted Paulie's head. "Then you, young man, are coming home with me."

"Won't my mama wonder where I am?"

"I'll tell her," Ora said. "Just bring him to church with you tonight, and we'll make plans from there, if necessary."

"Sounds good." Jessalyn reached for Paulie's hand. "My first question for you is very important, so answer carefully."

Paulie's face screwed up. "What?"

"We require something hot to drink when we arrive, to warm our hands and tummies. What should we have? Eggnog or hot chocolate?"

"Chocolate." Paulie was quick to answer.

"Excellent choice."

Uncle Francis was not at home when they arrived, but he'd left a note, saying he was attending to last-minute business. Perhaps at the mill, for the shops were closed, this being Sunday. What else could he be doing?

For the rest of the afternoon, she kept busy. She set Paulie at the dining room table so she could cook tonight's supper in the adjacent kitchen while he snacked, colored, and created ornaments for their tree. All the while, she prayed, her heart calm until she glanced at the clock just past three thirty. Where was Uncle Francis? And what news of Sylvie? Why had Seth's parents come to Millerton? Were they angry Seth had gone with Sylvie? Was Seth still with her or with his parents?

"Miss Grant, I said, do you like it?" Paulie shoved a picture he'd drawn up to her nose.

She could barely focus on it, but there was enough green in a triangle for her to determine he'd colored a Christmas tree. "It's wonderful."

"It's for Mama."

"She will adore it."

The front door opened, and her heart lurched in her chest. "Uncle Francis?"

"Who else would it be? Ah, I see we have a visitor." Uncle Francis dusted snow from his shoulders as he peered into the dining room. "Hello, young man."

"I'm Paulie Mack."

"His father works at the mill," Jessalyn said, her eyes large to communicate she'd explain Paulie's presence later. "Where have you been?"

"The mill, where else?"

"Shouldn't you take off your coat?"

"Not if we're to make it to church on time. Haven't you looked at the clock?"

"You're coming?" Praise the Lord!

"Of course I am. Grab your mittens and hats, and I'll bank the fire. We need to leave now. I want a good seat."

"They're all good seats," Paulie said.

"Not in my experience." Uncle Francis poked the disintegrating log in the hearth into embers. "Come on now, you two."

He didn't have to ask her twice. "Put on your hat, Paulie."

On the walk, Paulie danced ahead of them, turning his face to the sky, mouth wide open as if to catch snowflakes. In a low voice, Jessalyn explained Sylvie's situation to her uncle. "It could turn out to be a sad Christmas."

"Aren't you the one who told me Christmas is a time of miracles? Look at me. I'm *going to church*."

"True." She glanced ahead. "Careful, Paulie. The walkway is slick."

He turned, his tongue out, and a white speck on it melted. Jessalyn laughed. "You caught one."

"Tastes like water."

Jessalyn could only agree as she took his hand and they entered the churchyard. "Oh my. Will you look at that."

Candlelight glowed from the garland-draped windows of the stone church, giving it a warm, festive appearance. Organ music carried through the cracked-open door, a sweet carol. "It's beautiful."

"It is," Uncle Francis said. Taking her arm, he led them inside, and they took their seats a few pews from the front. The church was already half full, but within minutes it was near capacity. Uncle Francis gestured toward a small table near the altar, where Aunt Estelle's nativity had been set up. They shared a smile over Paulie's head.

Seth's parents entered and sat in the very front. Were they affronted by Seth's choice to tend to Sylvie? He'd done the right thing, and she planned to tell Seth so. Later, of course. After the service, which, according to the toll of the bell, was about to begin.

Seth entered the sanctuary from the office, gesturing at Ora to wait before playing the opening hymn—not his usual way of starting the service. But at his grin, a thrill went through Jessalyn.

"Tonight our church family celebrates two births. One of our Lord and Savior Jesus Christ, of course, but also the birth of Ruth-anne Mack, born to Sylvie and Hiram twenty minutes ago. I am delighted to report that while Ruthanne is small, she and Sylvie both are in excellent health."

"Huzzah!" Paulie whooped, jumping onto the pew. "I'm a brother!"

"Huzzah indeed," Seth answered.

Jessalyn tugged Paulie down while the congregation clapped.

Seth smiled at Jessalyn, and then turned to indicate to Ora that she could begin the opening hymn.

The service was wonderful, full of joy and hope and expectation. The news of little Ruthanne's birth, paired with their celebration of God's gift of Jesus, created a heartfelt praise from the congregation that made Jessalyn's heart swell within her chest.

She was still smiling when the closing hymn, "Joy to the World," finished and their voices and Ora's notes echoed through the stones. Seth offered a benediction, and though he didn't recess down the aisle like he usually did, everyone started to replace their hymnals into the pew racks and gather their belongings.

"Wait," Uncle Francis called.

"Mr. Chester?" Seth stepped toward him. "Have you something to say?"

"I have an announcement." Uncle Francis joined Seth at the front of the church while everyone who'd stood resumed their seats.

Jessalyn's heart, already swollen with joy, nearly exploded. Was he going to say what she hoped he would say? She met Seth's knowing gaze.

"I'm Francis Chester, as most of you know, owner of Chester Mill."

"We know who you are," a man said with a grudging tone.

"I don't blame you for your animosity. Trust me when I say my decision to close the mill was business. Nothing personal. Until yesterday, when I realized my decision was personal for everyone who worked for me. For that, I apologize and ask your forgiveness. I already asked God for forgiveness, and Pastor here assures me I have received it from above, but that doesn't mean I don't need to seek yours too." He looked down, clearing his throat. "I have other news. Yesterday I received an offer to purchase the mill, but I have to tell you, it wasn't a great one."

Mr. Stone hadn't offered a fair price? Jessalyn's heart sank to her stomach.

Seth too looked disappointed. "That's a shame."

"Well, one thing I know is business. And the prospective buyer, Abner Stone of the Massachusetts Woolen Company, was still in town this morning, so I made him a counteroffer, which he accepted."

"What are you saying?" Seth asked, clearly speaking for the murmuring crowd.

"I'm going into partnership with Mr. Stone. He will be the new owner of the mill and keep on all employees, but I'll still have a hand in Chester Mill for five years to ensure things go properly and my workers are treated well."

One of the men stood up. "Our jobs are saved?"

"Yes, and I'll send out a letter when the mill reopens on the twenty-sixth saying so. Merry Christmas."

The congregation erupted into applause again. And a few tears. Paulie tugged Jessalyn's sleeve. "Does this mean Papa has work still?"

"It does."

"That'll make him happy, I think."

"I think so too."

Uncle Francis returned to their pew. "You have a home with me here, if you want it, Jessy."

Jessalyn blinked back tears. She had a life in South Carolina, beyond her father and childhood home, but the prospect of staying seemed right. "Thank you, Uncle."

"I too have an announcement." Seth drew everyone's attention back to the front of the church. "First, I'd like to introduce my parents, Gideon and Grace Shepherd. I am pleased they're here to celebrate Christmas with me—with us—this year. Not because it's my last Christmas, as you all have heard. But because I'm glad they can experience my home. You see, I'm not taking the position in New York City. I don't believe God is calling me anywhere but right here, so if you all will still have me, I'm staying."

"About time you came to your senses," Ora said from the organ bench.

"Son?" Mrs. Shepherd gaped.

Seth spoke to her with a look of tenderness, but Jessalyn couldn't make out his words once the congregation started chattering. Seth recessed to the back of the church to greet everyone, but Jessalyn couldn't leave just yet. She wasn't sure who was in charge of Paulie, for one thing, and for another, her uncle was suddenly surrounded by folks thumping him on the back and thanking him.

Jessalyn made her way through those folks and past others until she reached the Shepherds, who stood staring at one another in the front of the church, looking as regal and foreign as the wise men must've looked in Bethlehem. "Excuse me. My name is Jessalyn Grant."

"I remember you," Mr. Shepherd said.

"Good evening." Mrs. Shepherd looked as if she held back tears.

"You must be proud of your son," Jessalyn said.

"I'm not sure I understand what you mean." Mrs. Shepherd sniffed. "He could have chosen a more secure position with better wages and prestige."

"He's made a choice to do what God has called him to do, where He has called him to do it. No amount of wages or prestige can compete with that."

"What's this?" Seth approached their little group.

"Why aren't you greeting parishioners?" Jessalyn asked.

"Because they're all still in here chatting. No one's at the door." He laughed then sobered when he saw his mother's face. "Mother, I'm sorry to disappoint you."

"No, you're doing the right thing, I suppose. Miss Grant put it in a different perspective for us."

Seth met Jessalyn's gaze. "Is that so? I'd like to hear more about this. And have a few words with you, if I may?"

He had more to say to her? About what? "Why don't you all come to the house for a light supper?"

"Mother? Father?"

They nodded, and Jessalyn clapped her hands. "I'll see to Paulie and then warm a few things on the stove. Come when you're ready."

"Paulie's with the Tillsons. They'll take him home."

Sure enough, her young friend was playing with the Tillson boy, Lou, and Alice waved at Jessalyn. "Very well, then."

She gathered her uncle, and they hurried home to light fires in the parlor and dining room. She tidied Paulie's crumbs and paper scraps from the table while soup warmed on the stove. She heard the knock as she finished setting the table.

This was like the Christmases she was accustomed to, with friends arriving and smiles on faces. Seth carried a familiar wood box, and when Uncle Francis invited the Shepherds into the dining room for a cup of eggnog, Seth held back.

"I'll help Jessalyn set up her nativity in the parlor, if that's all right."

"Fine by me," Uncle Francis said, winking at Jessalyn.

"Gracious, what a day." Jessalyn led Seth into the parlor, where small tongues of flame licked at the fresh logs just set afire by her uncle. "Tell me about the baby."

"Beautiful. Tiny but healthy, according to the doctor. Lungs working well, judging by the way she was screaming." He tugged his ear as if it was still affected.

She laughed. "That's wonderful."

"It really is." He set down the box and opened it, pulling a rag-wrapped figure from the top. When he revealed the shepherd, Seth looked at Jessalyn as if he hadn't seen her in ages. "You were right, you know."

"About what?" It was hard to think when he was looking at her like that.

"I'm a shepherd. My job is to tend the sheep given to me, and move when there's a nudge—from the Lord, or an angel, in the case of the literal shepherds tending their flocks in Bethlehem that night two thousand years ago. But I don't have a nudge of the Lord to go. I realized it for certain when Sylvie had her pains. I'm supposed to be here."

"Your parents are sad, I think." Could he endure their continued disappointment?

"I wasn't expecting them, you see. They came thinking Mother would get to see what this place was like before I moved home, which, of course, won't be happening now. But I'm glad they're here all the same. Even though I'm disappointing them."

"I'm sorry. I thought perhaps. . ."

"I can live with their disappointment. But I can't leave this church. I thought I had so little to give the people, but you showed me that what they wanted all along was the very thing God wanted me to give to them—my heart."

"That is true. I'm glad you're staying."

"What about you?" He enveloped her hand in his warm ones. "I think your uncle needs you."

"He's offered me a home here. I've been accepted for who I am by the people here, and I haven't felt part of something in a long while."

His lips twitched. "The knitting circle would be glad if you stayed."

"Would they?" She smiled. "If I stay though, I won't give up on my father. Or Bernice."

"I'll pray and hope alongside you, if you stay." He licked his lips. "Will you stay? Please?"

"You want me to?"

"Very much." His gaze burned into hers. "I love you, Jessalyn. I have never known a love like this. You remind me of what's important and challenge me, and when you smile at me, I feel like my heart's going to explode out of my chest. You are truly the most beautiful thing I've ever seen. Will you allow me to court you?"

She'd never known anything like this either. Like her heart shone almost as bright as the star of Bethlehem. "I would be both honored and delighted, Seth."

He glanced at the Christmas tree. "I regret I don't have a present for you."

"No cookery book?"

He laughed. "No. But I offer you my heart."

"And you may have mine."

"Jessy?" Uncle Francis called from the foyer. "Some of us would like to eat supper and light the tree."

"Coming," she called. "Hurry, Seth, let's set up the nativity."

They did, laughing like children, fingers fumbling from excitement. And once it was finished, Seth gripped her hand. "Wait."

He pulled her toward him for a kiss, short and soft.

Now that he'd kissed her, that brief exchange wouldn't do at all. Jessalyn cupped his head of delicious dark curls and pulled him closer for another kiss. And then another. There wasn't mistletoe hanging above them, but they didn't need it.

"The soup's probably cold," she said after a while.

"I'd take your kisses over supper any day," he said. But he pulled back with a reluctant grin.

Holding hands, they made their way to the dining room.

EPILOGUE

December 23, 1900

With tender care, Jessalyn Shepherd placed the wood-carved figures of Mary, Joseph, and baby Jesus in the perfect spot—under the bottom branches of the small but fragrant Christmas tree she and her husband had set atop the table in front of the rectory's parlor window. After supper they'd decorate the tree, and all would be ready for Christmas. "Seth, help me with the last one."

With a loving smile, Seth took the shepherd figure from her hand. "It would be my honor." He adjusted the shepherd so the figure's face appeared to stare down at the Christ child in adoration.

"Perfect." Jessalyn stepped into Seth's side so she could lean her head on his shoulder.

His arm went around her waist, his hand settling near her rounded midsection. "Next year, there will be a little one here to enjoy these Christmas delights with us."

The baby would arrive in late spring, and he or she would be too small next Christmas to do more than watch the flickering candles, pretty ornaments, and heirloom nativity scene in wonder. But in a few years? "The baby might love the nativity as much as I did when I was little."

"And we will tell the story of how it came to be in your possession, from your grandparents to your aunt Estelle, to you." Seth kissed her temple.

"But for tonight, we'll enjoy decorating the tree with Uncle Francis. My, is that the time? He'll be here any moment." The carriage clock on the mantel showed two minutes to the hour, and Uncle Francis was nothing if not punctual. "I'd best stir the stew."

As her wooden spoon scraped against the pot's bottom, she could hear the loud rap on the front door. Ah, there he was.

"Jessy?" Uncle Francis called.

"Coming." She replaced the lid atop the pot and moved back to the parlor. "I thought we'd decorate the tree as soon as we've finished supper—"

Uncle Francis and Seth weren't alone in the snug parlor. Father and Bernice stood in the center of the room, unexpected, uninvited, but most welcome. Jessalyn's hands went to her mouth in surprise.

"Hello, Jessalyn." Father removed his snow-dusted hat. His hair was a little grayer, his cheeks a little fuller, and there was pain in his eyes. "I hope you don't mind our coming unannounced."

She met Seth's smiling gaze. "No, we are glad to see you. Both of you." Oh, she'd been hurt by him and Bernice last Christmas, and she was hurt whenever she thought of how Father had cut her out of his life, but she'd spent the past year praying for reconciliation with the pair of them and writing monthly letters.

The pain hadn't ended with that decision. Her father and step-mother hadn't acknowledged her wedding to Seth, nor the news of her pregnancy, but she kept on writing and praying. And now they were here. She had no idea what the Lord would do with their strained relationship, but He'd worked a miracle bringing them here.

Bernice fiddled with the curls at the back of her auburn coiffure, testifying to her unease with the situation. Like Father, she'd put on weight, banishing the lean, hungry look she'd borne before her marriage. "You have a lovely house."

"Thank you." Seth came alongside his bride. "Jessalyn has made it a true home."

"She's done wonders here in Millerton too," Uncle Francis added. "Thanks to her efforts, the woolen mill is thriving now that it's associated with Stone's Textiles."

Jessalyn resisted the urge to roll her eyes. "That's entirely because of you and the Lord, Uncle."

"You're the one who brought me to their attention. In any case, it'll be a Merry Christmas for the employees this year, with a bonus too."

Her father and Bernice offered awkward smiles.

This wouldn't be easy, would it? But they'd taken a step. Jessalyn held out her hands in a gesture of welcome. "Will you join us for supper? Afterwards we will decorate the tree. Please stay."

"You are kinder than I am, Daughter. Yes, we would love to sup with you."

While Seth helped Bernice from her coat, Father shed his own. His gaze caught on the nativity. "Estelle gave it to you?"

"Last year."

"Your mother would be pleased. About that, and the baby too." Father glanced at her rounded tummy.

"She'd be pleased we're together this year too." Jessalyn offered a silent prayer. "Come, take seats at the dining table. I'll bring in the stew."

Seth followed her into the kitchen. "Let me help." He took the china tureen from her hands and carried it to the counter by the stove, where he ladled the stew into it. "This is a shock. Are you well?"

She nodded. "Are you?"

He set down the ladle and took her face in his hands. "It's the answer to prayer, my love." He peppered a kiss between her eyes, and then another on the bridge of her nose. "It's our first Christmas as a family, and I cannot think of a better way to celebrate."

Jessalyn leaned up on her tiptoes to kiss his lips. "Our first of many."

"Many, many," he agreed, kissing her again. "You know what I said last year," he whispered after a minute, his breath warm on her cheek. "I'd take your kisses over supper any day. But I suppose we shouldn't keep them waiting."

"I suppose not." Sighing, she pulled back. "They've come a long way."

"So have we, sweetheart. So have we."

It was true. Between these Christmases, they'd found their identities in Christ, not in who their parents wanted them to be. They'd found one another and married. Soon they'd have a precious baby in their arms, a son or daughter to love and raise.

As wonderful as this Christmas was already, next year's was sure to be even better.

Susanne Dietze began writing love stories in high school, casting her friends in the starring roles. Today, she's an award-winning, RWA RITA®-nominated author who's seen her work on the ECPA, Amazon, and *Publisher's Weekly* Bestseller Lists for Inspirational Fiction. Married to a pastor and the mom of two, Susanne lives in California and enjoys fancy-schmancy tea parties, genealogy, the beach, and curling up on the couch with a costume drama. To learn more, visit her website, www.susannedietze.com, and sign up for her newsletter: http://eepurl.com/bRldfv

THE WISE GUY AND THE STAR

by Shannon McNear

DEDICATION

To Aunt "Me," my mother's baby sister and younger of my aunts Beulah, who would certainly have been "that aunt" to my children had she the opportunity. And to my great-grandfather Wilsie Benjamin Wells, for his service in the Great War.

ACKNOWLEDGMENTS

Thanks to the staff of the Osceola & St. Croix Valley Railway Fall Colors Express in Wisconsin, who let me run loose like the child I felt I was and patiently answered all my questions; and to Peter Jackson for his excellent documentary work *They Shall Not Grow Old*, which brought to life those faces and voices like nothing else. The 1921 edition of *The Official Guide to the Railways* was my source for route schedules and information. Any inaccuracies are mine. Thanks also to my husband for woodworking details. I'm grateful to the entire staff of Barbour Publishing, who make this process an absolute joy. To Tamela, my agent, who is so very supportive and encouraging. To Lee, Jen, and Michelle for reading and critiques. To my family, of course, who seems my greatest frustration but is really my greatest motivation. And, of course, to our Savior, the entire reason for celebrating Christmas. May we never lose the wonder of this season!

When Jesus was born in Bethlehem of Judaea in the days of Herod the king, behold, there came wise men from the east to Jerusalem, saying, Where is he that is born King of the Jews? for we have seen his star in the east, and are come to worship him. . . . When they had heard the king, they departed; and, lo, the star, which they saw in the east, went before them, till it came and stood over where the young child was. When they saw the star, they rejoiced with exceeding great joy. And when they were come into the house, they saw the young child with Mary his mother, and fell down, and worshipped him: and when they had opened their treasures, they presented unto him gifts; gold, and frankincense and myrrh.

MATTHEW 2:1–2, 9–11 KJV

CHAPTER 1

Charleston, South Carolina
December 1919

S tella Shepherd stepped inside the huge building of Union Station, stared about her at the hustling crowd, then lifted her eyes to the arching beams high over their heads. Why had she ever thought she'd be comfortable traveling so close to Christmas? Away from home. Away from family.

Well, family who extended some modicum of warmth at least.

"Stella girl, you best get a move on, now!"

At the voice of Old Joe, her aunt's manservant, behind her, Stella swallowed hard, took a better grip on her satchel and suitcase, and fastened her gaze on the retreating form of her aunt, sailing through the crowd ahead of her like the battleship she was oft compared to. But still she couldn't move.

This trip was an adventure, Mama said. And surely, if she and Papa had thought it a bad idea, they'd not have allowed her to go with Aunt Lila.

Or, as the case may be, let Aunt Lila talk them into allowing her to go.

"Stella!" came old Joe's booming admonishment.

Aunt Lila glanced over her shoulder, her arched brows rising even higher.

No more hesitation now. Stella scurried after her, weaving between the other travelers.

The rumble of the steam engine echoed through the busy station and vibrated in the stone floor, growing stronger as she neared the train stretching the length of the station platform in front of her.

Aunt Lila reached the platform and paused but a moment, again, to make sure Stella was following, then after a few words to the conductor, stepped aboard. Stella's chest squeezed. No need for anxiousness here, as she could see clearly which car Aunt Lila had entered. The older woman merely wanted to find the best seats, was all.

Others were crowding forward, however, as she made her own approach. They all formed a loose line at the train steps, people exchanging brief smiles despite the air of urgency. A whistled tune floated from a few places ahead of her, the opening notes of a well-known Christmas carol, and then a man's deep, resonant voice broke out with, "God rest ye merry, gentlemen!"

A second voice, masculine but nearly a tenor, joined him, "Let nothing you dismay."

A few others murmured along. "Remember Christ, our Savior, was born on Christmas day," and Stella's own throat unclenched as her vocal chords warmed in response to the song.

But she could bring herself to nothing more than a hum as the line moved forward.

The song faded at the end of the first chorus, and the line had reduced to half. As the fedora-clad, mustachioed man who'd started the singing approached the train steps, Stella shuffled forward. A thump from behind coincided with the heel of her shoe catching on a crack in the pavement, sending her stumbling into the man in front of her. "Oh! I'm so sorry!" she said.

He turned, alarm flashing in his eyes as she recovered herself.

"Please excuse me, miss," said a crackling voice behind her.

Stella discovered her assailant to be a bent, bearded figure with rheumy eyes. "I am fine, but are you all right, sir?"

He bobbed a nod, his face creasing in apology. "Yes, thank you for asking."

She turned back in line to catch the younger man in front of her regarding her gravely from under the brim of his soft cap. Dark hair fell over eyes that could be either blue or gray. He met her gaze and nodded as well.

She'd also drawn the attention of the two singers ahead of her. The man with the mustache paused with his foot on the lower step, apparently waiting to see that she was all right, then with a quick grin, turned and mounted the steps. His companion shot her a smile and a wink before launching back into a hearty, "O-oh tidings of comfort and joy," and bounding up the steps.

The younger man rolled his eyes, shook his head, then with a wry half smile followed the other two.

The tightness returned to her throat, joined by a warming of her cheeks. Doubtless they were now bright red.

Holding her satchel in front of her, she climbed the steps into the train car. The smell of coal smoke mingled with that of bodies a bit too close together, but not overwhelmingly. And there was Aunt Lila, a little more than halfway back on the right, bending to stow her handbag then straightening to look for her. The crease between her brows smoothed when their eyes met. Stella offered a smile, but

Aunt Lila only shook her head.

Oh, but she was weary of feeling like a recalcitrant child, lumped in with the rest of her siblings. Although, to be fair, Aunt Lila never said a word. It was more in a look, the tilt of her head. Why she'd chosen Stella to be her companion on this journey was anybody's guess.

Not that she was ungrateful. Heavens, no. "*The opportunity of a lifetime,*" Mama's voice echoed again.

And maybe—just maybe—something on this journey would satisfy the restlessness that had bedeviled her so, this last year and more.

The line into the train car moved slowly, filing between the seats covered in teal leather with shining brass fittings. Two of the men ahead of her took the space across the aisle from Aunt Lila, while the third, right in front of Stella, took the one behind.

Why did it give her a small measure of relief that they'd be nearby?

Aunt Lila moved aside to let Stella in next to the window, flashing a quick smile. "You'll want the better view, and I don't blame you. There's just something about watching the world go by from the window of the train."

"Thank you, Aunt." After stowing her suitcase in the overhead rack, Stella slipped into her seat and tucked her satchel sideways on the floor, at her feet.

At last she could catch her breath.

"All aboard!"

The conductor's final call carried above the low hum of chatter from the other passengers. Tucked safely in his seat, Nat Wise glanced across the other passengers in the car, an assortment of hats and bare heads, men and women, with the occasional child. No one else entered the car, so he set his hat on the seat beside him and reached into his pocket for his penknife and the chunk of balsa wood nestled beside it.

Just the act of drawing the two items out, the weight of the knife in one hand and the cool not-yet-smoothness of the wood in the other, was soothing. He peeked across the aisle at Gold and Frank. Both were quiet, watchful in that way they all shared since coming back from the war. They had their eccentricities too—it just happened that Nat's came out in his fondness for carving.

The still-folded knife tucked in one palm, he turned the wood over in his hands, assessing the grain and texture as much by touch as sight before unfolding the knife and beginning to carve. The pale, already nicked, block of wood was just shorter than the length of his hand. "See the form inside," his grandfather had said, and he was doing his best.

Out of habit, he turned his hat upside down on his thigh, and drawing his handkerchief from his pocket, lined the inside of the hat with the cloth before unfolding the knife and applying the blade to the wood. Just the sharp edges of the block at first.

The rumble of the train engine grew, and a slight shudder in Nat's seat and the floor beneath his feet signaled that they were in motion. Outside the window, the buildings of downtown Charleston began to slide by.

The murmur of his brothers' voices caught his ear, and he glanced over. Gold and Frank were introducing themselves to the women in the seats across the aisle, one older with an understated air of wealth and importance, and the other the pretty girl who had pitched forward into Nat when bumped from behind, while in line to board.

"I'm Lila Montgomery, and this is my niece, Stella Shepherd."

The older woman's voice carried a cultured southern accent.

"I'm Goldwin Wise, and these are my brothers Frank and Nat."

The girl's gaze barely skimmed them before her face turned toward the window, but the older woman's regard lingered. "Lately returned from the Great War, by the looks of you."

"Yes, ma'am," Frank answered. "All three of us served in France."

She gave them a warm, if brief, smile. "What a blessing to see you returned safely. Your mother must be very happy."

Gold cleared his throat. "Our mother is very happy, I expect. She's been in heaven these past six months and more."

"Oh, I'm so sorry." The woman's hand went to her ample bosom, and she angled another glance back at Nat. He met it with the briefest smile of his own—an acknowledgment from one who had tasted of a similar grief to another. "Are you traveling to or from home, then?"

"From, ma'am," Gold said easily. "We're on our way to St. Louis to look for work, and if we can't find any there, then to Kansas City."

Nat shook his head a little. His oldest brother would tell their whole life story before it was over with.

"Well, that's enterprising of you," Mrs. Montgomery said.

He smothered a chuckle. Enterprising? More like desperate. He'd heard the British boys had it even worse, having spent four years and more at the front lines, coming home to no jobs and friends or family who behaved as though there never had been a war. It had been just over a year for Nat and his brothers, and that was bad enough.

The train gave a jerk, and Nat's breath caught. Flexing his fingers around the block of wood, he forced himself to draw in a quiet lungful of air and hold it for a few seconds before letting it out, slowly and smoothly. Then his fingers returned to their task.

"Our family often jokes," came Gold's voice again, "that we're the three Wise guys. Only boys in a sea of girls."

The older woman's tinkling laugh greeted his statement, genteel but not forced, and pleasant to the ears. Her spoken response, however, was lost to the hum of the train and other passengers. Nat peeked, and the girl beside her was now turned, listening as well.

She was a pert, lovely thing, with hair done up in a simple knot, the color of pale honey in the light from the window, and her eyes—yes, they were a sea green. He shouldn't stare, but he kept sneaking glances and leaning a little so he could catch a better view over the seat backs.

Sweetness and innocence. Nothing he hadn't seen in his own cousins—and sisters too, he supposed, once upon a time—but something about this girl just caught his attention.

He snorted softly and applied himself more thoroughly to the wood. Of course it wouldn't have anything to do with the way she'd pitched into him in line. Or how her wide eyes had met his own, their shade reminding him of stormy ocean waves in the early morning light.

Which in turn brought back a memory of leaning on crutches at the side rail of a steamship headed back to the good old US of A. With the side of his fist, still clutching his penknife, Nat rubbed absently at the lingering ache in his thigh.

Would everything forever be a reminder? Even the blue-green of a pretty girl's eyes?

CHAPTER 2

A unt Lila could draw conversation from a lamppost, Stella was
sure.

Only half listening, she watched out the window for the first few
minutes, fascinated by the way the buildings slid by. Charleston was
already awake and bustling, its streets populated by early-morning
passersby as well as a mix of horse-drawn conveyances and box-like
Model-T motorcars and trucks.

The man in the seat across the aisle from Aunt Lila answered
her question about family in a tone that Stella registered as forced
glibness over sorrow. Stella swallowed hard but didn't look over until
his "three wise guys" comment. At that she couldn't resist a glance
and was immediately caught by the life in both his and his brother's
faces. As if they held all the secrets of the world behind their eyes
but chose life and adventure despite the hardship.

From what Papa had told them of the war and the awfulness on the front, that was a weighty choice indeed.

She peeked over the back of the seats at the third brother, who sat with head bowed, carving something she couldn't quite see over a handkerchief spread across his hat, balanced between his knees. Well, that was remarkable—a man careful enough not to let his mess spill over on the floor, or at least trying to contain it. Papa was a good and dear man, but Mama often fussed at his carelessness with common things, like leaving his socks wadded up and lying just short of the laundry hamper, or dropping toast crumbs everywhere except on his saucer.

As if he could feel her eyes on him, he looked up and met her gaze with a slight smile, then ducked his head again to his task.

Warmth washed over her, head to toe. There was something about his look—a sweetness within the sorrow, perhaps—that tugged immediately at her. His older brothers were daring and eye-catching, for sure—she thought again of them breaking out in song as they were boarding the train—but the quietness here begged her curiosity.

As did the question of where they were from. She tried to place their accent but couldn't, quite, although it sounded distinctly northern, similar to Papa's and yet different. Surely they'd mentioned where they were from while talking with Aunt Lila, so it would be impolite to ask.

She gave a silent sigh and peered out the window again. And here she sat, with Aunt Lila and his brothers between them. If they were headed for St. Louis or beyond, however, might there be an opportunity somewhere to chat with him?

Aunt Lila and the most talkative Mr. Wise had moved on to discussing the vagaries of business and how the war had both helped and hindered. Mr. Wise expressed his surprise at Aunt Lila being so knowledgeable. "Oh, I was experienced in the business world before you were properly breeched," she said with a smile. "My husband simply humored me at first by indulging my interest but soon found I had a sense for the fine details he hadn't patience for." Her smile took on a sad tinge. "Then when he became ill, it was a natural thing for me to take the reins. The business he started continued nearly without a hitch after his passing. I miss him, but I see it as his way of providing for me, and I have always been grateful."

"Well." Mr. Wise sat back, rubbing his chin with one thumb. "That is remarkable indeed, and I wish you many years more of success in it."

Aunt Lila thanked him with a nod.

Their conversation lagged after that, and Aunt Lila pulled a much-folded copy of the *Wall Street Journal* out of her satchel. Stella supposed she should do the same with a book, but for now she preferred to gaze out the window at how city changed to pine woods and farm fields, fallow now for winter. A few house gardens held patches of green with collards and onions, regardless of whether the dwelling was a small shack or large and stately.

Individual homes became less numerous, and forests alternating with fields more so. The train crossed a muddy creek then steamed on. Stella blinked, a wave of sleepiness overtaking her as the sameness of the countryside dulled her interest, even when they stopped every several miles to let people board and depart.

It had been an early morning indeed. Stella bent her arm, and leaning on the window, fell asleep, lulled by the deep chug of the train and the rocking of the car.

Mrs. Montgomery didn't fit Nat's idea of a businesswoman. With her sensible though fashionable clothing, graying hair upswept to a neat chignon, a dimple flashing in her cheek when she'd turn and smile at Gold and Frank, she looked like she ought to be someone's grandmother. She could definitely match Gold in talkativeness, which reminded Nat of their own granny.

The girl—Miss Shepherd, was it?—was napping, her head moving slightly with the motion of the train. Nat let the corner of his mouth lift. He didn't blame her.

About midmorning she stirred. Not that he was watching for her to wake up. She swiped both hands over her face, looked around, and with a quiet word to her aunt, slid past the older woman and made her way up the aisle, lightly catching the seat backs as she went, presumably for balance. The skirts of her simple long coat and sensible wool skirt swayed. Did she have trouble navigating the motion of the railcar while wearing those fashionable heeled shoes? He couldn't imagine it would be easy.

The blade of his penknife slipped, providing a forcible reminder that he ought to stop staring and pay attention to his carving. Though no one would have witnessed his puppyish attention to the girl, Nat's neck and face flamed. He really was just too pathetic.

When she returned to her seat a few minutes later, he was careful to keep his gaze and head properly down.

Stella thought she'd never been more ready for lunch.

She followed Aunt Lila through the sliding door at the rear of their car out into the small, open area where the back of their car nearly abutted the front of the next with only a few inches to step over. She glanced at the rolling countryside and tangles of winter-bare South Carolina forest slipping past. Then gripping the rails provided for such a purpose, she extended her foot across the heart-stopping space and hopped over.

It wasn't as frightening as she expected, not that Aunt Lila would ever give any indication of such, only a little tricky with her heeled pumps. Ahead of her, Aunt Lila swept through the sliding door of the next car, barely glancing back to make sure Stella followed.

Down the aisle of another coach car filled with passengers, some of whom watched in curiosity and some who kept gazes averted. Men and women alike in sober suits and coats, a few children intermingled. Stella hated having to keep her hands out to brush the sides of the seats to steady herself. It seemed so forward—but worse would be to fall into some stranger's lap or elbow him in the ear. And she'd already had the mortifying experience of being tossed against a stranger before even setting foot on the train.

They passed through without incident, and stepping from one railcar to the other was less tricky. This time, however, the sliding door opened to a narrow passageway angling to the right, where steamy warmth and men's voices echoed, boisterous and cheerful. Stella turned the corner into a long, narrow hallway, steadying herself by the handrail running underneath the windows lining the right wall. Doorways to the left revealed themselves to be kitchens, pouring forth delicious smells borne on waves of heat and populated by energetic cook staff, ebony faces gleaming above white shirts, trousers, and aprons.

Aunt Lila threw a dimpled smile over her shoulder. "The train galley. Isn't it a sight?"

Then she disappeared around the corner. Stella hurried down the passage after her and narrowly missed a tall, immaculately dressed waiter emerging from one of the doors on the left. "Upsy-daisy!" he exclaimed.

"Oh! I am so sorry!" she said breathlessly, and he chuckled, dipping his dark head.

"Making it a habit of running people down, are you?" came a jaunty comment just behind her.

Stella twitched around, hand on the rail at the corner, to see one of the Misters Wise from the seat across from her and Aunt Lila.

His smile deepened. "First it was my brother, and now that poor, helpless waiter?"

Surely he was merely teasing, but even so, she could feel her color rise like a hot wave across her face.

"Ah, Gold, give the girl a break already," came another voice, and this time it was the very brother she'd stumbled into, leaning aside a little to catch Stella's eye and offer a grin. "Always the wise guy."

She smiled back, flashed a glance at Mr. Goldwin Wise, and whisked herself along in Aunt Lila's wake.

The dining room quite took her breath away with its charm. Tables along either wall stood draped in white, one side seating two and the other, four, beneath windows flanked by checked curtains. Aunt Lila chose an empty table for two and turned toward her with another dimpled smile.

As she and Aunt Lila took their seats, Stella tried not to notice, much less be surprised, that the Wise brothers chose the table across the aisle.

Who was making a habit of certain behavior now?

She unfolded her napkin. Another immaculately groomed waiter set two glasses of ice water on the table, his wide grin white against dark cheeks. "Good noon, ladies! Might I start you off with a cup of coffee or tea?"

"Tea, please," Aunt Lila said.

Stella gave him a smile of her own. "I'd like coffee."

"Very good. Cream and sugar with that?"

"Yes, please."

The waiter turned, and a similar conversation took place across the aisle. "Coffee, coffee, and coffee," the waiter said. "Very good, sirs! I'll have that out to you in a jiffy."

As he moved on, one of the older Wise brothers leaned an elbow on their small table, further dwarfing it. "Coffee, tea, and a meal," he said, addressing the other two men. "Imagine—and to riffraff like us."

"They'll let anyone on the train, seems like," the mustachioed brother quipped.

"Hey, speak for yourself," the youngest brother said—or at least she presumed he was youngest, with the way the other two hassled him.

"Ah, you're as much of a wise guy as either of us," the first answered.

"Only 'cause you're such a bad influence."

"I dunno, Frank. I remember him instigating as many shenanigans as we did, don't you?"

"More," was the response, not missing a beat.

Stella exchanged a smile with Aunt Lila. The brothers' humor was nothing if not infectious.

CHAPTER 3

Nat stared at the steaming chicken swimming in sauce and flecked with seasonings. Predictably, his brothers were already eating, just short of bolting down their food.

"What's wrong with you?" Frank said.

Nat shook his head. "This is the fanciest meal I've ever seen."

A fork angled toward his plate. "If you don't want it. . . ," Gold drawled.

Nat wasn't so slow that he couldn't smack his oldest brother's knuckles with the flat of his butter knife. "Mine. I just want to enjoy looking at it for a minute."

Gold smirked. "Well, don't wait too long. It'll get cold."

Nat picked up his roll, and splitting it, generously applied butter. "Still better than cold rations outta a can."

Frank lifted his coffee cup as if in toast. "Or the daily dose of dysentery?"

Gold chewed a bite of collards. "Hey now, I kinda miss army life."

"Yeah, I miss it like the mosquitoes in winter." Nat dug his fork into the chicken and found it so tender he didn't even need a knife. Better to cover his feeling of being overwhelmed by comfort and plenty with joking around. His brothers would never let him hear the end of it if he appeared to be sentimental.

The meat was melt-in-your-mouth good. Nat couldn't help the way his eyes closed for a moment as the full flavor hit his tongue and filled his mouth.

Miss army life, indeed. Not a chance.

It did in fact have the effect of making him glad to be alive, rather like the sweet smile of that girl sitting with her aunt on the other side of the dining car. Nat resisted the urge to glance over at her. His chest was still aching a bit from the impact of that brilliant grin she threw him and Gold before scampering out of the galley area earlier.

He was not on this trip to find a girl. Not even to engage in a bit of harmless flirting, if there was such a thing.

Frank leaned over the table and murmured, "Looks like Miss Shepherd isn't the privileged bit we might expect."

Nat did glance over at that. The girl savored her meal with obvious enjoyment, eyes closed, lips curved, with her aunt giving her an indulgent smile. Some quiet comment by Mrs. Montgomery brought Miss Shepherd's eyes open again, sparkling, and then she laughed. An honest body-shaking laugh, not the polite titter of so many ladies of society.

He had to drag his gaze away.

"She's quite the looker," Frank said and winked at Nat.

He felt the heat climbing from under his collar and across his face. "Keep your mind on the job," he grumbled and shoveled in another bite.

Frank chuckled. "Hey now. Gold's the one who's officially employed here, not us. But what's the harm in just enjoying a pretty face?"

Nat scowled. "Girl like that wouldn't look twice at any of us, and you know it."

Gold, who'd been laughing along, suddenly got all wistful. "Too true. At least not until we find gainful employment, and not just as a railway bull."

"Maybe not either of you," Frank said, "but I'm the good-looking one of the bunch." He angled a smirk at Nat. "And as scrawny as you are. . ."

"Hey, I'm still Mama's favorite," Nat snapped back.

"Of course you are," Gold said. "You were the baby. . .and the one who fulfilled her wish to have sons named after the three gifts of the wise men."

Oh, here it came. Nat's ears began to burn already.

"Yeah, Merrrrrvin," Frank drawled, drawing out the syllable that provided the sound-alike for the aforementioned biblical gift.

"And don't you forget it," Nat muttered, then made the mistake of glancing over at the women across the aisle.

Mrs. Montgomery's gaze was averted, but her lips twitched as she raised her teacup to her lips. Miss Shepherd, however, watched openly, eyes wide. Nat promptly ducked his head and buried his nose in his coffee cup.

If he wasn't so doggoned mortified, he might've lingered to bask in the way those sea green eyes gathered all the light around them and then shone it back as starlight.

But he'd no right to be lingering, least of all on a girl as sweet and fresh as she was.

Stella's book lay open on her lap, almost forgotten, as she watched the western South Carolina hills roll by. Luncheon had been oh so delicious but left her a little drowsy and unwilling to focus on the printed page.

Aunt Lila leaned toward her. "We're almost to Augusta. Usually that's where we change trains, but this particular train goes through to Atlanta."

"So many stops."

"Many people riding, especially this time of year. Freight also sometimes takes priority over passengers, which is why you see us stopping on sidings so often."

Stella was about to follow with a question when one of the elder Wise brothers hovered in the aisle. *Gold,* she remembered, distinguished by his lack of a mustache. Would that make him the eldest, according to what she heard of the inspiration of their names?

He cleared his throat. "Pardon me, ladies, but would you wish to join us in the lounge car for a game of rummy or cribbage?"

To Stella's surprise, Aunt Lila said, "Young man, that would be delightful."

And so they trundled off to the lounge car, where Stella and Aunt Lila wedged into a bench seat behind a small table. Mr. Wise procured a deck of cards from a nearby cabinet and set to counting them. The dark-eyed, mustached brother—Frank—claimed the chair facing Aunt Lila, while the younger brother, Nat, settled onto the padded bench, less than an arm's length from Stella. He promptly drew out the handkerchief she'd seen earlier, spread it across his lap, and set to whittling again.

The seated brother gave him a hard look. "Still working on that, are you?"

The youngest Mr. Wise didn't even look up. "I am."

Stella tried to make out what was taking shape beneath his pen-knife, but somehow his fingers and the blade managed to shield its details from her eyes. He glanced up, however, as if acknowledging her curiosity, and offered a shy smile.

The brother counting cards sat down, triumphant. "Amazing—they're all here."

"Of course they are." Aunt Lila beamed as if she were the man's own grandmother. Stella had to stifle a laugh. "A fine establishment such as Southern Railway would do nothing less than make sure their decks of cards are complete."

Mr. Gold Wise grinned, revealing deep slashes in his cheeks as he shuffled the cards. Very charming. "You have much faith in the railways, ma'am."

"They have never done me wrong, in all my days of travel," Aunt Lila answered, her smile unwavering.

"Well then." Mr. Wise tapped the card edges on the tabletop to even the deck and began dealing them out. "I am frankly surprised you fine, upstanding ladies are willing to play cards with the lot of us."

Aunt Lila pretended indignation, giving him a sidelong glance as she gathered her cards. "Should we suspect you of nefarious doings?"

"Of course not," his brother said, and Stella caught the rueful smile and shaking of the head by the youngest.

Why did the thought occur to her that these men were not all they seemed?

Yet there was no denying, either, the odd sense of comfort and safety they evoked—a sense that until now she'd only felt with her own Papa.

Cards dealt, Stella assessed her hand. An ace of hearts, a two of hearts, but also a two of clubs. Assorted other cards that might be worthwhile. The mustached Mr. Wise picked up the six of clubs that lay faceup, then discarded a three of hearts. Stella schooled her face and suppressed a sound of dismay as Aunt Lila drew the top card from the deck, looked at it, then discarded it on top of the three. A jack of spades. She considered her cards again, lingering on the king of spades. Well, that could work. She picked up the jack and discarded a seven of diamonds.

"Miss Shepherd, what about your family?" the eldest Mr. Wise said, scooping up her discarded seven.

Stella riffled the corners of her cards. "Papa is a minister, and Mama is a housewife. I am the oldest of five, which of course keeps Mama very busy, especially when I'm not home."

Both elder brothers gazed at her with something akin to surprise, and despite his absorption in his carving, the younger's glance also lingered.

"What?" Stella stammered, appealing to Aunt Lila. "Did I say something amiss?"

"Oh no," Mr. Gold Wise answered, as the mustachioed brother drew a card and promptly discarded it. "It's only—I'm astonished that a good Christian girl would be allowed to indulge in such frivolous worldly pursuits as a game of cards."

Aunt Lila's dimple flashed, but not without a bit of an edge. "Not at all," she said quickly. "A friendly game of rummy between traveling acquaintances is certainly permissible, as long as we are not engaging in sinful pursuits alongside. We are not gambling, are we? Or indulging in drunkenness? No? Well then. Nothing to be ashamed of here."

With that, she picked up the top discard with emphasis, inserted it into her hand, and plunked down a two of diamonds in its place.

Oh. That would make things more difficult. Stella debated for a second or so, then with deliberate nonchalance, drew the two and set a queen of clubs on the discard pile.

"Hmm, making this tough now, are you?" The corner of Mr. Wise's mouth lifted as he stared at the queen. Finally, he drew a long breath and let it out, reached for the queen, and after sliding it among the others, drew out three cards and laid them in a row.

All queens. Including the queen of spades. Suppressing another sigh, Stella glanced longingly at her king and jack of that suit.

"Good job," she said, forcing a tone of cheerfulness.

Mr. Wise flashed a brief grin. "Oh Miss Shepherd, your sports-manship quite takes all the fun out of it."

She fastened him a mock glare. "Should I endeavor, then, to muster a more competitive spirit?"

Both men let loose with a gale of laughter, Aunt Lila joining them. To her other side, the youngest Mr. Wise closed both hands around his carving as his form shook with silent hilarity as well.

She let her lips curve in a cool smile and, with a lift of her brows, nodded toward the middle brother. "Your turn, sir."

CHAPTER 4

S he was unbelievably—and nearly unbearably—adorable, the way she matched wits with his brothers and held her own.

And he should not, under any circumstances, even be noticing this fact. Much less dwelling on it.

He considered the three queens Gold had laid down. Miss Shepherd's delicate thumb brushed across the corners of the cards in her hand, lingering on the king and jack missing one of those queens.

The turn came around to her, and she reached for a card off the deck. Another king. Without hesitation, she tucked it in next to the other and discarded the jack.

Good girl. His brothers could win at rummy any old time.

Incredibly, on her next turn, she picked up a third king and laid them all down. Gold nodded approvingly, then Frank laid down a midrange five-card run in diamonds. Mrs. Montgomery played cards on both Gold's set and Miss Shepherd's. And then Miss Shepherd collected a three of hearts and laid that down with a two and an ace, and smiled at the group in general.

Gold laid down another run. Frank presented three jacks. Mrs. Montgomery played a jack on those.

Miss Shepherd reached for the deck and hesitated, her hand lingering. Just then a uniformed man approached Gold, and bending, whispered something in his ear. Gold gave a quick nod and, with an apologetic smile, rose from his chair. "Ladies, I regret that I must go attend a matter. Nat, would you play my hand for me?"

"You gotta be kidding me," he grumbled, but folded his knife in one hand and tucked away the carving-in-progress with the other.

After carefully gathering his hanky with its burden of shavings and twisting it closed into a little bundle, he shoved it deep into a pocket then took Gold's place at the table and picked up the cards.

Not much to work with—three left, all unconnected. "Hmm," he grunted, barely above a breath, and felt Miss Shepherd's eyes on him. "It's still your turn, I believe," he said.

She smiled, genuine and open, and lifted a card off the deck, then tucked it into her hand and discarded.

Oh, so darling.

Frank kicked his foot, and without thinking Nat grabbed the next card off the deck. Ah, there—an eight, to match another in his hand. He discarded one of the other two, equally without thought.

Frank eyed him sternly before swiping the card Nat had just tossed down. He paused for but a moment before throwing down another run, this time in clubs. "One card," Frank announced.

Mrs. Montgomery tsked and Miss Shepherd exclaimed softly. Both still held three cards.

"Well, drat." Mrs. Montgomery tapped her fingers against her cards, drew one from the deck, rubbed her chin, then chose another to discard and made an impatient wave to Miss Shepherd.

She chewed her lip for a moment, then drew from the deck. A crease appeared between her brows, and with a little shake of her head, she threw the card down on the discard pile. Her gaze met Nat's in the briefest of smiles.

The card she'd just put down was an eight. Nat blew out a silent breath, then picked it up, laid the trio on the table, and discarded the last one.

"Oh, you sorry piece of. . ." Frank fumed, as Mrs. Montgomery gave a wordless exclamation.

"Yes, very sorry," Nat said, looking back up into Miss Shepherd's shining eyes.

She laughed. "Oh no! Not at all. Very well done!" Her giggle was light and free, and something around Nat's heart unclenched.

"Well then." He gathered up the cards and handed them off to Frank for another shuffle and deal—they'd always been scrupulous about each other's turns—then folded his hands on the tabletop and scoured his brain for a polite question to ask.

Mrs. Montgomery saved him the trouble. "I hope all is well with your brother."

"Oh yes," Nat said. "Just a bit of. . .business. . .that he picked up before the trip." He angled a glance at Frank.

"Something we're hoping might turn into regular employment if St. Louis doesn't pan out," Frank added.

"Aha," Mrs. Montgomery said, her expression carefully cordial.

Nat gave her a smile. "Nothing illegal or immoral, I assure you."

"Quite the contrary," Frank said. Then counting the cards laid before him, he nodded and set the deck in the center of the table and turned over the top card.

"Now you have my curiosity piqued," the older woman said mildly.

Frank chuckled. "I'm sure I do."

Mrs. Montgomery's eyebrows rose, and one of Miss Shepherd's arched by itself. He couldn't help but smile again.

"You play first this time, ma'am," Frank said to Mrs. Montgomery. She dipped her head, took the card that was face up, and laid down a run of four, in hearts. They all oohed over that.

"Obviously I didn't shuffle well enough," Frank said, chuckling.

Mrs. Montgomery dimpled. "Obviously."

They played that hand and were into another before Gold returned. Nat offered him the cards, but he shook his head a little and remained standing, swaying with the motion of the train.

Frank drew and discarded. Mrs. Montgomery drew and laid down four aces. Miss Shepherd took her discard and laid down three kings. "There you go with the kings again," Nat said, and was gratified to see the color rise in her cheeks despite her sweet smile.

Somehow he also couldn't help the grin tugging at his own mouth in response. Another thump landed on the side of his shoe.

While he drew a card, doing his best to appear nonchalant, Mrs. Montgomery consulted her watch. "We should return to our seats after this next hand or so. We'll arrive in Atlanta soon."

"Will you be picking up the next train right away, ma'am?" Gold asked.

Her glance toward him was sharp and searching, but her smile remained bland. "Oh, I have a stop to make in Atlanta before we continue on, although we aren't sure how long that will take."

Gold nodded. "I see. Godspeed on your journey then, whenever that is."

They finished the hand, with Miss Shepherd winning, and Nat

and his brothers offered their congratulations while she and her aunt slid from their seats. She shook Nat's hand without hesitation, her eyes glinting a deep green in the lounge car's overhead lamps. "If we do not see you again, may God bless the rest of your travels."

"Thank you, Miss Shepherd." Her grip was warm against his, and stronger than expected. "And yours as well."

Releasing him and maneuvering so her aunt could get by, she flashed a dimple very like her aunt's. "I'll be praying you and your brothers find employment very quickly."

"Thank you," he said, and meant it.

"And thank you for a diversion for an hour or two," Mrs. Montgomery chimed in.

They shook hands all around before the ladies made their way back to the coach car. Nat and his brothers watched them go, and then Gold snapped his fingers to bring their attention back.

"So, I take it that was related to our business with Walker?" Frank asked.

Gold nodded. "I'll be meeting with him in Atlanta after we've boarded the *Cincinnati Special*. He'll let us know specifics later, but there is definitely the suspicion of someone boarding sometime after Chattanooga but before St. Louis, for the purpose of causing trouble."

"Well, that narrows it down," Frank muttered.

Gold made a sound of agreement, then added, "He says he's most appreciative that all three of us are willing to be on the alert, and is willing to make it worth our time if there really is trouble." An eye roll and shake of the head attended his words.

"As if we needed money to coax us to do the right thing," Nat said.

"Exactly so." Gold chewed the inside of his cheek for a moment.

"But if they want to pay us, we won't turn it down either."

Stella settled back into her seat beside Aunt Lila and glanced out the window at the beautiful Georgia hills. Did she dare ask? She held her breath a moment, then turned to her aunt. "I can tell you're thinking about something."

Aunt Lila's dimple deepened. "You always were too curious for your own good."

Stella giggled. "Curious or simply observant?"

Her aunt's blue gaze slid toward her then away. "Depends upon the day, dear girl."

They both sighed, almost as one, then laughed. Emboldened, Stella pressed, "Do you think they're up to no good?"

Aunt Lila let out another sigh. "I don't know, child. I would like to think not."

Stella nodded. "Me too. I—I rather like them."

Her aunt sent her another searching look, this one tempered by a dimple. "Liking is just fine, under the circumstances."

An ache lodged somewhere near her heart. "Circumstances being that we shan't see them again?"

"Precisely." Aunt Lila gave a crisp nod.

Stella settled more firmly into her seat and watched the southern edge of Atlanta slide into view.

Soon enough the train slowed and came to a stop at the station. Stella grasped her suitcase in one hand, satchel slung over her shoulder, and exited the train along with Aunt Lila. It was just after four in the afternoon, but it felt like they'd been traveling a week.

Aunt Lila glanced back and must have seen something of Stella's weariness. "Only a bit longer, child, and you'll have a chance to rest and refresh yourself—and a night's sleep to boot."

Stella summoned a smile and kept trudging on after her through the crowd.

They reached the desk of the railway concierge, and Aunt Lila set down her suitcase. Stella held on to hers, glancing around, barely listening as her aunt inquired after messages. The clerk searched then handed her a folded paper, and Aunt Lila straightened, unfolding it.

A sound of dismay escaped her.

That did seize Stella's attention. "What is it?"

"Oh, my business contact has telegrammed to extend his regrets that he's unable to host us for the evening, or meet with us. His entire family has influenza. Perhaps on my return trip, he says."

A chill swept Stella at that, and a wave of weariness. "Oh, that's very much too bad for them."

The threat of influenza the past couple of years was enough to send anyone scurrying. Too many had died from the epidemic, which hit just as the war was coming to a peak—and still died, though with less frequency. Mama's soup pot simmered continually, and somehow their own family had escaped anything more than a relatively mild outbreak.

"It is, at that." Aunt Lila glanced across the busy station. "Well. Plans must change, then. Let us see if we can hurry and get tickets for the next stage of the trip."

They dashed to the ticket counter, where an impassioned discussion between Aunt Lila and the clerk revealed that there were no sleeper compartments available for the evening's journey, but plenty of room remained on the coach with reclining steel chairs. "I suppose it can't be helped," Aunt Lila said, and fished in her handbag for the correct amount of bills.

The clerk handed over the tickets, and the women scurried for the train, even as the conductor stepped out onto the platform and called, "All aboard!"

He beamed at them as they neared. "Good afternoon, ladies! It's a cozy one, but still a few seats left."

Stella's heart pounded in her chest as they climbed the steps. It was a near thing, but—at least they'd made it.

Inside the coach doors, Aunt Lila hesitated. Stella leaned around her to look—the only empty seats were those beside someone else. Except—

The trio of now-familiar faces were upturned toward them, with welcoming grins tinged by surprise. The youngest, in his seat just behind the other two, glanced across the rest of the car, seemed to take immediate stock of the situation, and rose to speak to a gentleman across the aisle who likewise had an empty spot between himself and the window. The older man glanced up, looking none too happy, but nodded and moved aside.

"Well, ladies!" the eldest Mr. Wise said as they neared. "I'm sorry for whatever misfortune befell you, but it's good to see you again."

Still standing in the aisle, the youngest Mr. Wise took Aunt Lila's case and hefted it to the rack above, then reached for Stella's. Their eyes met as she clumsily passed him the suitcase, his hand brushing hers. Drat the blush rising to her cheeks, but he only smiled and tossed the case to the rack, sliding others aside to make room. "There," he said, and waved her into the seat he'd just left.

"Thank you." She still couldn't decide what shade his eyes truly were.

"Yes, thank you so much, young man," Aunt Lila added, and once Stella slid into the window seat, settled beside her.

With a deep breath, Stella leaned back and closed her eyes. Aunt Lila's chuckle brought them open again. "Well, child, I could wish my associate had informed me earlier, and then we'd be riding in comfort in a drawing room sleeper."

"I don't mind the crowd," Stella said. Then when her aunt angled her a look, she added, "Well, not so very much."

Aunt Lila laughed again. "I suppose being the oldest of a minister's family, you are quite used to making the best of a hard situation—and to making things easier on everyone else. Aren't you?"

Stella blinked. She didn't want to admit it, but it was so.

Her aunt's smile sharpened. "As I thought." She gave a little sigh. "I love Jessy dearly, but she asks too much of you."

"I think. . ." Was it true? "Mama does a marvelous job at everything. I hope I'm half the blessing she is."

Her aunt reached a gloved hand over and patted Stella's knee. "You certainly are a credit to her and Seth."

Stella's throat thickened. "I. . .try. Mama and Papa mean the world to me. Surely you know that."

Aunt Lila was the one to blink this time. "I know. And it's a good part of what makes you who you are, dear girl."

She gave Stella a last squeeze, then bent to pull a book from her satchel.

CHAPTER 5

Nat thought he was likely to die before dinner came for their car—seven o'clock or after. His seating companion had resisted attempts at conversation, which probably accounted for very little, since Nat was so much less garrulous than either of his older brothers. But he was content enough to keep it that way, and after offering his most polite thanks to the man for giving up his solitude and allowing Nat to sit with him, he fell to carving again, still being careful to catch the shavings. He ignored the scowls from his seating companion as folks traveled up and down the aisle on their way to and from the dining car and his stomach growled with increasing intensity.

At last the steward came through and announced their turn. Nat quickly bundled up his things and tucked them away, then shuffled out of his seat and led the way. His former seat was currently unoccupied, except for satchels and wraps, as was his brothers'. How long had they been gone? He'd have noticed if the stewards had taken them for the previous shift, but hopefully the ladies hadn't waited so long for their meal. He passed through the kitchen car, the older gentleman hard on his heels. Nat smiled to himself. The man must be just as hungry as he was.

Entering the dining car, Nat hesitated and scanned the tables. Two half-filled four-person tables were all that remained, and the farthest—

Without thinking, and without shame, he angled straight for the far open table. He would not turn down an opportunity to dine with Mrs. Montgomery and the lovely Miss Shepherd.

As he neared, both looked up from their perusal of the small paper menu and broke out with welcoming smiles. Nat could not help his answering grin. "Ladies, might I—" He glanced back and found his seating companion right behind him, even now. Well, that was a little surprising. "Might *we* join you?"

"Of course!" Mrs. Montgomery's dimples were out in full force. Miss Shepherd's smile was no less dim, despite her very pretty blush.

Averting his eyes so he wouldn't appear too eager, Nat tucked himself into the chair closest to the window, facing Miss Shepherd. The older man harrumphed slightly and took the chair across from Mrs. Montgomery. Introductions were promptly made, during which Nat learned his companion's name was Mr. Jensen of Birmingham, Alabama. The waiter interrupted further conversation, took their drink orders, explained the menu choices, then whisked away again.

Mrs. Montgomery fixed her attention on Mr. Jensen. "So what brings you this way, sir?"

To Nat's amazement, the older man straightened and shed his curmudgeonly air. "Grandchildren. In Louisville. Haven't seen 'em in, oh, three, four years."

"Well. I've no grandchildren myself, but I consider my great-niece here—and her younger sisters and brothers—as good as my own in that regard."

Mr. Jensen turned his gaze upon Miss Shepherd. "And you're from Charleston, you say? What is it your father does, young lady?"

Nat successfully kept himself from shaking his head in amazement at the older man's sudden willingness to converse.

She beamed as if he'd paid her a compliment. "My father's a minister, sir."

"Well." Mr. Jensen sat back. "I suppose those are needful."

She laughed. "They are indeed, sir."

Mr. Jensen looked as if he wanted to say more—likely something derogatory—but he thinned his mouth and refocused on Mrs. Montgomery. "And what of yourself, ma'am?"

"I am in business, carrying on my late husband's trade."

"Shipping or manufacturing?"

"A little of both. My niece and I are bound for St. Louis and then Kansas City, where I'll likely stay through Christmas and the New Year."

The waiter delivered their coffee and tea then accepted their thanks with a nod. Nat glanced over his shoulder to see if Frank and Gold were anywhere in sight, but they were not. At the moment, he didn't even care.

Mrs. Montgomery dunked her tea bag up and down in her cup and half smiled. "We'd planned to stay overnight in Atlanta with a business associate, but he was unable to meet us. So we continued on the train, although I vow by morning I may rue not having a sleeping berth."

Miss Shepherd merely shrugged one shoulder and smiled, sipping her coffee.

"It is something of an adventure, I own," Mrs. Montgomery went on.

"The train's decent enough," Mr. Jensen said, "if a little crowded." He glanced at Nat and left no doubt as to exactly why he'd said so.

While Nat struggled not to choke on his sip of coffee, Miss Shepherd leaned forward a little. "Isn't it though? Thank you so much for letting Mr. Wise sit by you so my aunt and I could remain together."

"Well." The older man harrumphed again, scowling for but an instant before bending what Nat was sure was the rustiest smile ever on the young woman. "I am glad I could be of service."

If Mr. Jensen had been his brother, Nat would have kicked him under the table.

"And of course, thank you"—and now she bent the full weight of that glorious smile on Nat—"for thinking of it to start with."

For a moment, all he could do was smile back like an idiot. "It was no trouble at all," he said finally.

And he was very glad neither of his brothers was there to witness the moment, or he'd never hear the end of it.

The youngest Mr. Wise was, in absence of his brothers, a most pleasant dinner companion.

Stella had cringed a little when she and Aunt Lila had been seated on one side of a four-person table, with no idea who they'd be sharing the meal with. So it was with much relief, although not a little surprise, to look up and see Mr. Wise, seating companion in tow, headed in their direction with so much determination on his face.

A look she wasn't even sure in retrospect she'd read correctly.

As amusing as it was to play cards with the brothers Wise, she'd been too focused on her cards and the game play—not to mention too bashful—to take the time for lengthy study of any of them. Sitting across a table at dinner and engaging in focused conversation was a different matter entirely. There was something a little fearsome about the two older brothers that the youngest lacked, while he possessed a quiet winsomeness his older brothers didn't quite achieve. It provided an interesting contrast. His wit proved just as quick, however, if less brash, and his face open and, if Stella were completely honest with herself, rather nice. Possibly even handsome.

Now, where had that thought come from?

She buried her nose in her teacup and gratefully welcomed the distraction of the first course of their dinners being served. A lovely cream soup with crackers, which she spooned with great concentration while Aunt Lila chatted away with Mr. Jensen as if they were long-lost friends. She glanced over at Mr. Wise and found him laughing silently at Aunt Lila's snappy retort to something Mr. Jensen had just said, and a giggle nearly escaped her as well.

It didn't help at all when Mr. Wise caught her eye and gave her the barest wink.

This time she went nearly facedown in her bowl.

After a moment, she dared glance up again and found him distracted, so she let her regard linger. Lamplight accented the strong lines of his jaw, cheekbones, and forehead and glinted off a wavy mop of brown hair that managed to look dashing and a little rakish despite its untidiness. His eyes were at the moment relaxed, but she still couldn't decide if their color was blue or gray, even just across the table. His mouth seemed the most expressive, however, somber in one moment, then flattened with some unknown emotion, then quirking up at the corner.

Suddenly he turned and found her watching him. His eyes widened a fraction then crinkled, lips curving ever so slightly, but he didn't look away.

And, heaven help her, neither did she, though she could feel the color rising in her cheeks again. Why must she be one of those who blushed so easily?

In this light, his eyes looked gray, nearly silver.

"Mr. Wise, where are your brothers this evening?" Aunt Lila asked.

Relief and annoyance warred over the interruption of the moment.

"I'm not really sure, Mrs. Montgomery," he answered smoothly.

She smiled. "No matter, I suppose. It has been a delight to get to know you without the benefit—or is that the distraction?—of their company."

Aunt Lila had so neatly spoken Stella's thoughts that she found herself guiltily tucking her chin again. But the youngest Mr. Wise's smile went awry with what appeared genuine pleasure, and he dipped his head in a way she found altogether charming. "You flatter me, Mrs. Montgomery. The honor is all mine."

Dinner was finished, people had for the most part settled back into their seats, and the stewards were beginning their tuck-in routine, handing out blankets and inquiring after the passengers' comfort. Though the lights were pretty well dimmed at this point, Nat kept his whittling out as long as he had even a shred of illumination to work by.

"So what is it you're working on there, young man?"

The slow, quiet voice of his seating companion startled him, after the hours of curmudgeonly silence before dinner. He opened his hand to reveal the form, still rough. "Well, what is that?" Mr. Jensen asked, plucking it from his palm and turning it about.

Nat chuckled. "It's supposed to be a wise man—you know, as in a nativity piece—but I'm not finished yet. Obviously."

"Ah, I think I see it now." The older man angled it this way and that.

"I have another that's closer to done." Nat pulled it from his pocket and offered it up for the man's inspection.

"Ah." Mr. Jensen rubbed a thumb over the various curves and creases. "You have an eye for this."

"It isn't much."

"Not yet, but I can tell that it will be." Mr. Jensen fixed him with a look of great interest. "Have you carved many of these?"

"These are the first," Nat admitted reluctantly.

The older man laid the pair in Nat's hands again. "Are you making an entire nativity?"

"Just the three wise men. At least so far." Nat rolled them gently side to side, one in each hand. "If my mama were still this side of heaven, they'd be for her, of course. Now I'm not rightly sure who they're for." He smiled ruefully. "I started them on a whim, my brothers and I being named after the three gifts of the wise men and all."

"Oh?" Mr. Jensen's brows shot up, so Nat had to explain. The older man grinned. "Yes. . .yes, I could see that being fitting." He glanced over the backs of their seats at Nat's two brothers. "Very fitting indeed."

Nat could only stare at the older gentleman and wonder what thought was behind that comment. But Mr. Jensen just smiled again and pulled his blanket up under his chin.

He should put his knife and carving away and try to sleep as well. He'd had precious little of it in the past weeks. The steady hum of the rails accompanied by the deeper chug of the engine and the sway of the coach suggested that falling asleep, and perhaps staying there, might indeed be less of a chore than it had been.

And so he tucked everything into his pockets, unfolded the blanket the steward had provided, and leaning back his chair, settled in.

Waking flowed into dreams, where Daddy and Mama presided over some unknown holiday celebration and his sisters and cousins ran about, laughing and shrieking, with his brothers adding to the commotion. Then the scene changed. The hum of conversation became a snarl and a growl. A distant whine and boom became the whistle of incoming rockets and the concussion of artillery. Nat was back in a half-flooded trench, staring at the crimson spreading across the coating of mud on his trousered leg.

God. . .oh God, save me. . . .

He jerked awake, a gasp on his lips. The coach car lay dim and quiet, most of its occupants still slumbering. Mr. Jensen snored softly, propped against the shaded window. Gently, so as not to disturb the older man, Nat eased out of his seat, dumping the blanket behind him, and slid out into the aisle. He needed a breath of air to clear the ghosts from his mind—but first, the necessary.

Over on the other side of the aisle, Gold's seat was empty but Frank slept, slumped against the window. In the seat behind him, Miss Shepherd leaned on her aunt's shoulder, both of them snugged under their blankets. Nat let his gaze linger as he made his way past them. Miss Shepherd's lashes draped the upper curve of her cheekbone, both shadowed by a wave of her hair, half fallen out of its knot. Full, soft-looking lips barely parted, just peeking over the edge of her blanket.

Oh so sweet. Just like when she'd charmed Mr. Jensen into conversation, she and her aunt, and remained unfailingly cheerful even in his grouchy moments. Nat couldn't help but be a little in love with her himself after all that.

He dragged his gaze away, forcing his feet to keep moving.

The men's room in the back of the coach was unoccupied, and he finished in short order, then stepped outside the doors. The small observation area at the side rail was likewise empty. Nat stepped up to the opening, letting the wind whip across his hands and face. The rising moon poured over a rugged, mountainous landscape, a valley with sparkling lights of a town spread out behind the train. Ahead the engine chugged and moaned as it climbed a hill, which must have been the source of the noise that invaded his dreams.

He gulped a deep breath, the wind tinged with coal smoke, and waited for his spirit to settle.

CHAPTER 6

Stella stirred from sleep but slowly, driven by a bodily need that became more urgent by the moment.

She knew she shouldn't have had that last cup of tea at dinner. But it was too enjoyable, being waited on, and the conversation too delightful, between the older Mr. Jensen, bantering with Aunt Lila, and the youngest Mr. Wise. Dinner coming to an end because other passengers still needed their turn was quite the disappointment.

But how to disentangle herself without waking Aunt Lila? She eased out from under her blanket and tucked it down around her aunt's side, then with a glance around to make sure no one was awake enough to witness such immodest antics, hiked her long skirt up around her knees and stepped over Aunt Lila's ample lap. The swaying of the car nearly pitched her onto the floor, but she gripped the back of the seat in front of her aunt and caught the side of the chair across the aisle—narrowly missing the shoulder of its sleeping occupant—and recovered. Then she tiptoed up the aisle to the ladies' room.

She lingered long enough to make an attempt at repinning her fallen hair, until a knock at the door demanded that courtesy triumph over looking put together. As she exited, she offered an apologetic smile to the rumpled-looking mother with the small boy in tow, and stepped aside to let them enter.

Away at the end of the car, Aunt Lila slumbered on. Climbing back into her seat would be a much more difficult undertaking. Did she really want to risk waking her aunt?

With a little sigh, she peered through the window of the closed doors on the near end of the car. Two figures stood silhouetted against the moonlight, standing too close to denote anything casual, and certainly not to invite interruption. Stella ignored the warmth washing through her at the very thought and trundled her way back down the aisle.

Still, standing beside her aunt, obviously lost in such perfect repose, Stella had not the heart to disturb her. She cast a glance at the closed door by the men's room at the rear of the car, then tiptoed down the narrow aisle to peer out through the glass.

A lone figure stood there. Her heart began to sink, until—was it? Yes, it was. The silhouette shifted, revealing arms extended over the rail, the hands busy in a way that had grown incongruously familiar over the past hours.

Her heart thudded. One hand went to her hair, trying to weave a couple of the loose pins back in, while the other rested on the door. Did she dare?

Another glance back at Aunt Lila, snug in her reclining chair, decided for her. She just could *not* discomfit the older woman just yet.

She pushed through the door, ignoring her hair in favor of

clutching her coat about her. Mr. Wise glanced over his shoulder, then visibly started and swung toward her. "Miss Shepherd! What finds you out here at this hour?"

Stella pulled the door closed then hesitated. She took in his one fist clenching and the penknife gripped in his other hand. A small bolt of alarm went through her. "Am I intruding?"

"I—oh, not at all."

He moved aside in the narrow space, as much as he could, and quickly pocketing whatever was in his hands, gestured her forward to the rail. Beyond, she glimpsed a forested hillside rushing past, bathed in moonlight, and without thought she sidled up the opening beside him. Above the hill, shadowed and mysterious, a moon just past full floated in a clear sky spangled with twinkling points of light.

"Ah," she sighed. "How lovely—so many stars!"

"Your namesakes, aren't they?" Mr. Wise said.

"Oh—yes." Stella grasped the rail with both hands and leaned out far enough for the wind to cool her cheeks. "Actually, I'm named for another great-aunt, Lila's sister Estelle, who passed away before I was born."

Mr. Wise made no reply this time. Stella peeked at him and found him half leaning on the rail, gazing out into the night.

"It's a fine name," he said at last.

"It's terribly old-fashioned," she said.

His mouth curved in a slow smile. "I'm no decent judge of that."

Should she—but the words were out before she could think. "Is it true, that you and your brothers are named—"

The question seemed just too ridiculous and died on her lips, but his grin widened and he met her gaze this time. His eyes glinted with the moonlight. "It is indeed true. My mother, God rest her soul, was fond of telling us how, after marrying our dad, she thought it would be amusing to name three sons after the gifts of the wise men. And so, here we are. Goldwin, Franklin, and Mervin. It amuses my brothers to go by Gold and Frank, but—well, I refused pretty early on to be called Mer, or Myrrh. By any spelling."

A giggle bubbled up at his words, and his chuckle answered it.

"And so I go by Nat, ruining the pattern a bit."

"And that's short for what? Nathaniel?"

"Close—it's just Nathan."

Still smiling, she peered up at the stars. "Mervin Nathan. I like it." Another laugh escaped her. "My next-younger brother goes by Frank, but it's short for Francis, after our great-uncle named Francis. My mama was visiting him when she met my papa."

His expression went strangely intent, as if he was studying her.

What was he thinking?

As the heat rushed into her cheeks again, she turned away, this time leaning just a little farther out. She did so want to peek at the length of the train, front and back. But her hair—

She reached up and simply secured the whole mass with one hand, then braced with the other and leaned, hesitantly, into the wind.

It was cold, fresh, smoky, but exhilarating, all at once. Barely able to hold her eyelids open when facing forward, she could only catch a glimpse of the moonlit expanse of train ahead, with smoke streaming back from the engine, before she had to turn to peek at the end of the train. It stretched on, longer than she expected for a passenger train.

Then she tipped her face to the moonlight and let a laugh escape her. A deep chuckle at her elbow told her that Mr. Wise shared the moment.

At last she pulled back, and steadying herself with a hip against the wall, set to fixing her hair in seriousness, or at least as properly as she could without a mirror. Across the small space they shared, Mr. Wise watched her with shining eyes and a small grin. "That was most unladylike of me, I'm sure," she said, still breathless from the wind.

He shook his head slowly. "I won't tell if you don't."

She laughed again and peered out into the moonlight. "So why are you awake at this hour, Mr. Wise?"

His smile grew thin, and settling himself more firmly against the opposite wall, he folded his arms and gazed out into the night as well.

"I'm sorry. I should not pry," she began, but he shook his head again.

"It was an honest question, Miss Shepherd. Would it come as a surprise to you that my dreams do not set easy with me after the war?"

She swallowed heavily at his suddenly grave tone, tucking in a last pin. There, not her best work, but the knot should hold for a little while. "Not a surprise at all. My Papa has shared—well, he shared that the front held some most terrible sights."

The corner of his mouth twitched, and he scuffed a shoe against the rough floor. "That's a polite way of putting it."

Stella frowned. What on earth could she offer this man, who so obviously carried hurts no earthly medicine could touch. "I am sorry that you have seen, and suffered, so much."

Mr. Wise's gaze returned to her, no trace of amusement in his expression this time. "I'm a lucky one—shot in the leg, but at least up and walking again. I shouldn't complain when others have lost so much more." He shook his head again. "Limbs—sight—or their very life and breath. But it's hard to come back to everyone just living their ordinary lives, when—when some of us will never be the same again, however whole we look on the outside, or not."

She cleared her throat. "Papa said something very similar when he first came home, months ago. I confess, although I knew his work was important, I did not think as much of it as I should have." She swallowed again. It must be the lack of sleep and the moonlight making her so sentimental. "I. . .thank you for your sacrifice, and that of your brothers."

His eyes were deep wells of emotion, and then he gave a single, grave nod. "Others have given more, as I said."

"But. . .your mama." Stella suppressed a wince at the words once more escaping her. Would her boldness know no end this night?

His head went down at that. "Yes," he said, finally, cutting his gaze out at the night.

The urgency to speak comfort still needled at her. "I hope at least that she was a woman of faith, and that you have the blessed hope of seeing her again."

His smile returned, sadly. "If anyone had faith, it was she. But oh, I'm not sure where I am these days."

An ache blossomed in her chest. "What do you mean?"

"I mean"—he ducked his head for a moment before his eyes met hers again—"well, that God feels very far away. Like I've seen too much, done too much, somehow. Ordinary church is fine for ordinary people but. . ."

Stella shifted from one foot to the other. *Lord, help me grasp just what it is he's trying to say—and give me words that might offer comfort and strength.*

"The thing is, Mr. Wise. . ." No. She had nothing to offer this man beyond prayers. No experience, no understanding, beyond the years of humble but wistful service in the home of a simple minister's family.

And that alone ought to be a shame to her. If she, a minister's daughter, could not find the words to reach across the divide to the spiritually needy. . .

"It's quite all right, Miss Shepherd. I should not have burdened you with such gloomy thoughts." And with that, Mr. Wise turned to lean out the opening himself, hands braced on the rail.

Stella's eyes burned. *Oh Lord. I am but one girl. You are God, and You alone know his heart. Will You not reach out and touch him, let him know You're here?*

Pinching her lips together—she must not cry, not here, right in front of a perfect stranger—she folded her arms and leaned against the wall, as he'd done only minutes ago.

Presently Mr. Wise stirred, glancing back at her with widened eyes. Apparently he'd expected her to make her escape. She could see the movement of his throat as he swallowed and then said, "And what of yourself, Miss Shepherd? Why are you out here?"

She gave a chuckle. "Because I had to use the ladies' room and then didn't have the heart to wake Aunt Lila by climbing back into my seat." She leaned a bit to peer out at the sky. Again. "And it is a beautiful night. I'd not have missed this."

He couldn't believe he hadn't scared her off. When he looked back and saw her still standing there, so obviously distressed and at a loss for words, yet stubbornly lingering, well—

Did she have any idea how lovely she was? And how completely vulnerable, if he'd happened to be the wrong sort of man?

Which he most emphatically was not, no matter where he felt he was with God—or where God might be with him. Mama had raised him far better than that, despite the weaknesses he'd fallen to while on the front.

Weaknesses that conversely made him not the sort of man to be standing out here enjoying a moonlit landscape with such a fresh, innocent young woman. He was anything but fit company for a church girl.

Beautiful night. . .beautiful girl.

He bit his lip hard to keep the words inside.

"Well," he said finally, when he could trust himself to speak, "I am glad to be sharing it with you."

And that itself was likely too much.

She offered a brief smile that was nearly his undoing. "So what of your other family, Mr. Wise? I confess I was not paying very close attention when your brother was chatting with my aunt at the start of our trip."

Some of the tightness around his throat eased. "Oh, I have a pair of younger sisters who divide their time between Dad and our cousins. All the cousins are girls." The grin he gave her was unforced. "They're the ones who call my brothers and me the 'Wise guys.' " He laughed. "They make us sound like we're a vaudeville troupe."

Miss Shepherd unexpectedly brightened. "Oh? Have you an interest in stage work?"

The awkwardness of a few minutes ago dissolved completely. "No. Not with all those eyes on me." Nat gave an exaggerated shudder and was gratified to elicit a peal of laughter from Miss Shepherd. "I suppose that's something you would enjoy, however?"

"Oh, not so much," she said, swiping a hand across her eyes. "Although. . ." Her gaze went distant as she gazed out over the rolling landscape. "I know I should be happy to just use my talent for the Lord, but sometimes. . .sometimes I dream of singing on stage, or even for radio."

He mimicked her stance. "It seems to me, Miss Shepherd, that if your singing brings joy to people, it wouldn't really matter how it's shared. Would it?"

She blinked. "I'd never thought of that. It just. . .well. . .my whole life has been church."

"Has it really?" And where were all these cheeky statements of his coming from? "Your father—he's a minister, right? And yet didn't he leave the church, so to speak, to join the war effort and try to bring comfort and help to men who perhaps would never dare walk into a house of worship?"

She looked at him for a moment, nibbling at her lower lip, before her chin came up sharply. "How is it, Mr. Wise, that you claim to feel so far away from the Lord, and yet your words are so—wise?"

They both dissolved into laughter at her pun. "I'm serious though," he said when he could speak again, "I suppose some might say it makes one, oh, more holy or spiritual somehow to use one's talent in church, and yet would that not cheapen your father's work in the war?"

She was smiling still, and nodding. "I see your point."

"Now, lest I be guilty of corrupting an innocent and encouraging her to run off to Hollywood, let me just say, there's certainly nothing wrong with singing in church either."

She laughed. "Of course not."

Their gazes held, and he went on, as quietly as he could over the rush of the train. "I am serious, Miss Shepherd. Innocence is a precious thing. Don't squander it lightly on the likes of Hollywood."

Her eyes flared, betraying surprise. "One might say the same of ministry, Mr. Wise. Especially in the case of those who are spiritually hardened or prideful. But if the Lord calls us to do it—it is spending ourselves, true—but can we consider it squandering?"

"Such sage words from your own lips as well."

He thought he could see a blush shading those pretty rounded cheeks, but she gave a small toss of her head and said archly, "Truth is truth, regardless of who speaks it."

"Touché, milady." He inclined the top half of his body in a tiny bow then settled back. "Your mention of pride though—doesn't that infect nearly everything? Those who think their talents are too good or too holy for the world at large, and—"

"And those who think somehow that their sin is too big for God to forgive?" she finished with a wry half smile. "That they've wandered too far for His grace to reach?"

His mouth opened, but no words came out.

Could it be true that what he thought proper humility in the face of a high and lofty God was, just as she suggested, merely another form of pride?

"Well," he said, laughing, "that was simply brilliant."

CHAPTER 7

S tella wasn't sure whether to feel pleased or dismayed. This wasn't meant to be a mere battle of wits and words, but an earnest appeal to the state of a man's soul.

She'd never wished so fervently that she could sit down and talk the whole thing through with Papa. He would know precisely what to say to this young soldier, wounded in both body and heart from his part in defending their homeland.

She thought of the newsreels over the past few years, of marching men in uniform, handling their rifles with ease, sporting jaunty grins and salutes when the camera drew closer. How easy to envision Mr. Wise and his brothers in that setting—and how amazing, if all Papa had told them was so, that all three had come home, alive and relatively unscathed.

"How bad was your leg wound?" Stella found herself asking.

Just that quick, a shadow fell over him again. He shrugged.

"Were either of your brothers wounded?"

"Gold caught a bullet in the arm, but it went clean through. Frank still carries a hunk of shrapnel, though you'd never know it." It seemed as though he would say more, but his mouth closed in a hard line.

Suddenly, he huffed, and in his face was only weariness. "I might as well tell you. Gold found work as a railway bull. A policeman or marshal, that is, on board our train, to guard it." He held up a silencing hand to Stella's exclamation of surprise and excitement. "It's only for this trip though, and neither Frank nor I qualify because, well. . .we're still convalescing. Frank only just returned a few months ago from a hospital in London."

Stella closed her open mouth. "I see."

"Do you? It's hard to find work right now, Miss Shepherd—powerful hard. And if an employer thought either of us unfit, well. . ."

"I do see."

His expression was slightly more alive now. "That's why Gold left the card game yesterday. Why you might have seen him missing from his seat, even now."

She felt her jaw falling again. "That's—that's absolutely swell!" Then she clapped a hand over her mouth at such slang, but Mr. Wise was laughing again.

"What, your proper aunt wouldn't appreciate your talking like that?"

She laughed as well. "No, she wouldn't. Nor my parents, I suspect. But still, that is tremendous. And"—she swiped a hand across her face, abashed to even admit it—"no wonder he seems, well, so fearsome."

"Fearsome? Gold?" He bent, laughing even harder this time. "Oh, that's rich! Wait till I tell him."

"Oh, please don't tell him! Please," Stella begged, suddenly mortified.

He chuckled, wiped his eyes, and peered at her for a moment. "No. . .actually. . .perhaps I won't after all."

"Thank you," Stella said fervently, then realized he was teasing her again and could only fall into helpless laughter. "Oh. . .you. Is this what it feels like to have an older brother?"

Another chuckle gusted from him. "Yes. Except. . ." He grew curiously sober, studying her again, then flashed another thin smile and said, "No, it's probably safest to think of it like that."

She smiled back, but hesitantly this time. "I would have liked an older brother, I think."

"Well then," he said lightly, "I'm happy to serve in that capacity."

They exchanged a grin, but a strange burning stirred inside Stella. Was it just the unexpected camaraderie? The knowledge that her feeling of safety with the brothers Wise was a well-founded one and not mere fancy?

Or something altogether different, where it suddenly occurred to her that a particular aspect of her interaction with Mervin Nathan Wise was particularly un-sibling-like?

It could not be. Not with her being a good girl, a Christian, and him being of uncertain spiritual moorings. Certainly any stray longings she felt must be only concern for his eternal soul.

That was it, surely. Just a wholesome concern for his well-being.

He was a liar, plain and simple. And he'd probably burn for it.

Because he could think of little worse at this moment than being relegated to a mere brother to this girl. Although he should be amazed and grateful that she didn't take one look at him and simply run.

No, somehow she actually seemed to enjoy his company, and that honestly baffled him.

"Are you warm enough?" he asked, watching her wrap her coat more firmly about herself.

"Yes, surprisingly. I expected it to be colder this time of year."

"Oh, that'll catch up with us the further north we go. But even so. . .shouldn't you go back inside and try to sleep?"

She moved enough to peek through the heavy glass and, after watching for a good half minute, drew back and shook her head. "Aunt Lila's still sleeping."

"I'm sure she'd rather be awakened and know you're safe than wake up and find you gone."

Miss Shepherd frowned at him. "Are you trying to be rid of me?"

"I. . . Not at all."

Her gaze remained searching. "What time is it, anyway?"

He pulled out his watch and consulted it by the moon's glare. "It's a little after midnight."

Was that all?

Her slow smile rivaled the moonlight in radiance. "Oh, we have hours then."

His heart stopped. Completely. Did she even know what she was doing?

He realized his grin must be absolutely ridiculous, but he couldn't seem to draw it in. "So. You enjoy singing?"

The trace of a flush touched her cheeks again. "I do. But I. . .I am terrified of singing in front of people. So I could never be a stage star."

"You—terrified?"

"Yes. Believe it or not. I can sing with a choir, no problem, but alone?" She shook her head.

"Why?"

"Who knows?" She shrugged. "Perhaps too much teasing when I was young. I don't really understand it. My stomach ties in awful knots when I even think about it, and my throat closes up so I can only squeak."

Now he was dying to hear her sing. "I could sing with you."

She gave a short giggle. "Oh no. Besides, I heard you and your brothers. You are amazing."

He grinned. "I cannot imagine that you are not."

Definitely blushing now. "Well, you won't get to find out, either way. Dancing, now. . ." She stepped away from the wall, glanced again inside both of the doors, then did a few steps of soft-shoe buck and wing that had him dropping his jaw.

"Where did you learn that?"

"What, you think I've never seen the outside of a church? We live in Charleston after all." She added several steps of something he thought he recognized as a brand-new dance that went by the name of the city, then stopped, laughing, reaching for her falling knot of hair. "Besides. Aunt Lila has a secret fondness for it."

"Simply shocking," he murmured.

He could not take his eyes off of her as she coiled and repinned the mass, her gaze bouncing between his and the glory of the moonlit night. "I'm not at all sure it'll stay," she said, her voice more breathless than it ought to be with just a few dance steps.

He felt his smile widening, and she grinned back. "Honestly though. My brother and I have fun trying to mimic the street performers we've seen. It isn't like we're allowed to frequent dance halls or anything like that."

"Of course not."

She sighed and swung back to lean lightly on the rail and gaze out over the hills. "It's so very lovely out there. I love the mountains. Where do you suppose we are at the moment?"

He sidled in next to her. There was just enough room for both of them, shoulders not quite touching. "Well, I've never traveled this way before, but from what I know of my geography, I'd say. . .we're somewhere between. . .Atlanta, Georgia, and St. Louis, Missouri."

Her laugh washed over him in a sweet wave. It really was too gratifying, the way she appreciated his sense of humor.

The train was at the moment sliding around a bend, and the hillside fell away to show the rails running along the upper bank of a river, tumbling and curling along in the moonlight below them. Miss Shepherd's exclamation was sharp enough to carry over the sound of the wind and the train itself. She shifted, and Nat stole a glance to see her once again leaning out into the open air, holding on to the mass of her hair, with a look of complete delight on her face.

"So—very—beautiful," she said.

"Yes. Yes, indeed."

But Nat was not speaking of the landscape, breathtaking as it was. He tore his gaze away from her and focused instead on the folded Appalachian ridges and peaks rising beyond the river.

The last thing he wanted to do was spook her or be guilty of anything inappropriate.

As if enjoying the moonlight alone with her was perfectly respectable.

She settled more firmly against the rail. "My mother and father have taken us to the mountains in upstate South Carolina—North Carolina as well—for holidays. This looks very like it."

"I have family up in Pennsylvania. Very like this as well, in places."

"Sounds lovely."

"It is." Nat blew out a hard breath. He wanted—no, needed—to busy his hands again. He reached into his pockets and fished out the penknife and the last block of wood. It was a great place to let the shavings fly. And perhaps Miss Shepherd would lose interest and go back inside.

"So what are you working on?"

He sighed again. Of course it would not do for him to go all shy on her about it—he'd pulled it out in front of her after all. Without a word, he reached into his coat pocket where he kept the most finished of the three and offered it to her.

She came upright, mouth rounding and, after a moment's hesitation, plucked the carving from his outstretched palm.

"It isn't so good, with the jostling of the train and all, but you get the general idea."

"Oh no, this is wonderful! I mean, I can see where your blade caught, but. . ." Her expression remained awestruck as she examined the piece.

He pulled the other out. "This one's roughed out, but not much detail yet. It's the kneeling wise man, which is a little harder."

She cradled both in her hands, side by side, then grinned up at him. "These are marvelous, Mr. Wise, truly!" She bit her lip, tucking her chin a moment. "It's probably silly to share, but I have my family's nativity in my satchel. My mama gave it to me to carry along, in case Aunt Lila and I don't make it back in time for Christmas. So I can feel a little closer to my family, that is."

"That's mighty sweet." Nat's fingers itched to snatch the pieces back even though she held them with the utmost care. "I'm sure your three wise men are very fine compared to these."

"Oh." She blinked at him, then the corner of her mouth lifted slightly. "That's the funny thing. Our set doesn't have wise men, or they were lost at some point. It's just Joseph, Mary, the Babe, and a shepherd. My great-grandfather carved them, way back, and painted them, so it isn't a very fancy nativity that way either. Not like the shiny bisque sets everyone seems to want these days."

Well, that was surprising. And the thought warmed Nat's heart, as well, that this girl could be able, because of her own humble origins, to appreciate the simple work of his hands.

Stella suddenly wanted to run back inside the car, grab her satchel, and drag it out on the platform to show Mr. Wise the nativity—but again, that would be silly. Why would he be interested in her family's sentimental hand-me-down, which wasn't even a complete set?

"It sounds swell, really," he said suddenly. "I'd love to see it—that is, when you don't have to wake up your aunt to get to it."

Speaking of Aunt Lila. . . Stella peered through the window again. Still slumbering on. Didn't her aunt have trouble sleeping on the best of nights? How was she so soundly out while on a train, and in coach seating at that? She should just go back inside to her own seat, wake Aunt Lila if necessary, and get it over with.

But not yet. Turning back toward the rail, she held the figurines up for closer scrutiny. Even in moonlight the wood grain was lovely and the proportions pleasing despite the crudeness of the carving. "Thank you so much for showing them to me," she said, offering them back to Mr. Wise. "I wish I could see them once you've finished."

His smile went wistful, a reminder that they'd all be parting once they reached St. Louis late tomorrow afternoon. "You're very welcome, and thank *you*."

He tucked them away, then wedging himself in the corner between the wall and rail, set to whittling again. Stella sighed, a wave of weariness stealing over her. She really should go back inside, but another peek confirmed Aunt Lila's unmoving state.

And when would she ever again have the chance to watch the wild mountains of Tennessee and Kentucky roll past by moonlight, in the company of a polite and affable young man?

She leaned her elbows on the rail and let her body sway with the rhythm of the train, while the wind teased her nose and cheeks and blew small tendrils of her hair about.

"So you have the guts to dance but not to sing?" came Mr. Wise's pleasant baritone above the rush of the train engine and rails. "I think you should sing."

She laughed but shook her head as heat washed through her, despite the chill of the night.

"Come on, I'll sing with you."

She peeked over and saw his grin.

"You heard my brothers break out singing when we were boarding yesterday, yes? And how everyone joined in? How hard could it be? Just pretend you're in the choir at home."

"You're relentless," she said. "I'd never have guessed that about you."

His chuckle warmed her again. "Come on."

She sighed noisily. "Fine. Pick something."

He aimed a rakish grin at her, took a moment to compose himself, then launched with, "We three kings of Orient are. . ."

She dissolved into laughter.

Mr. Wise motioned for her to join in and kept going. "Bearing gifts, we traverse afar. . ."

Whether it was the moonlight, or it being the middle of the night and she was half insensible with lack of sleep, or the fact that in the moment she felt like she'd known Mr. Wise forever, her throat loosened. As she closed her eyes, the words flowed and her voice soared along with his. "Field and fountain, moor and mountain, following yonder star. Oh-oh! Star of wonder, star of night. . ."

Mr. Wise surprised her—or perhaps it wasn't so surprising after all—by knowing, and staying strongly with her, through all five verses of the song that illustrated how each of the three wise men's gifts pointed in some way to the gift that Christ Himself was to the world.

They finished the last chorus and let the notes whisk away into the wind, then stood still, not daring to look at each other.

"You have a very lovely voice, Miss Shepherd," he said at last.

Stella ducked her head. "Thank you. Yours is also wonderful. But how can you sing a song like that and not believe?"

"I was raised in church as well," was all he would say.

She peeked over to see him leaning on his elbows on the rail, head bowed, heedless to the wind whipping his hair. At last he looked up and met her gaze, once again holding it as he'd done a few minutes ago and during dinner.

A pity they'd never have an opportunity to get to know one another better. He was someone she thought she'd like—very much.

Perhaps too much.

She dragged her gaze away. "Tell me more about your mama. She sounds like a marvelous woman, full of wit and good humor, to name the three of you the way she did."

Mr. Wise's low chuckle barely carried above the roar of the train. "She was that, for sure."

And so they continued for the next half hour and more, sharing stories, laughing far too much. Hushing each other then laughing again. Watching and reveling in the chug and sway as the train labored up one grade, slid over the summit, then gathered speed down the other side—only to repeat the process. Finally, Mr. Wise nudged her and assumed a stern look. "You need to go back inside. I don't want to get you in trouble."

She knew he was right. She glanced inside the coach, and her heart dropped to see Aunt Lila's spot empty and the woman nowhere in sight. "Oh drat! She's gone. I'll just go slip into my seat." Impulsively, she put a hand on his arm. "Thank you for—for the conversation! You should try to sleep again as well."

He smiled thinly, and though she so wanted to pry out of him just what he was thinking, she didn't dare linger any longer.

And sure enough, just as she slipped inside the door to the coach car, Aunt Lila emerged from the ladies' room.

Chapter 8

Well, everyone was back in their seats now. There would be no sneaking in. Nat could prowl the rest of the train, pretend to have been keeping a lookout for Gold, but neither of his brothers would buy that.

Nat strolled up the aisle of the coach as if nothing was out of the ordinary with him slinking back to his seat at two o'clock in the morning. While Stella avoided his gaze, he offered a smile to Mrs. Montgomery, who did not smile in return, and held the expression for both Gold and the bleary-eyed Frank. He doubted his middle brother would even remember in the morning. And then he bypassed them all for his seat next to Mr. Jensen, who snored on.

He could still feel their gazes boring holes in the back of his head.

"Were you outside with Mr. Wise?"

Did anything ever get past Aunt Lila? Her voice might be a whisper, but it held all the authority of Mama's and Papa's. Stella held her tongue because she could think of no good way to respond.

"Estelle Mary Shepherd. You answer me this instant."

"I went to the ladies' room, but you were sleeping so sweetly when I came back, I hadn't the heart to wake you to climb over. I know how difficult it is for you to fall back asleep once you've been awakened."

Aunt Lila's lips flattened, and her eyes seemed to shoot sparks. She inhaled deeply but then raised her eyebrows.

"He was already outside, standing at the rail. I just popped out for a moment to get some air."

"Young lady, I woke up three times and found you gone. It was not just for a moment."

So she was right—she should have listened to that feeling that told her to come back in—not to mention Mr. Wise's admonition.

She flicked a glance forward to where he was sitting.

Aunt Lila dropped her voice even further. "We do not know him, Estelle. We only just met him and his brothers yesterday morning—yesterday, for pity's sake—and while they seem like very nice young men—" She huffed, and when Stella still held her silence, she pressed, "Did he do anything untoward?"

"Not at all, Aunt Lila. I promise. He was the perfect gentleman." Perhaps too perfect, but she'd not say that. "In fact, he kept telling me to go back inside when I wanted to linger because the moonlit scenery was just so beautiful."

She bit her lip and moved her shade aside a smidge to peer outside. The train was still following the river, and all she could see on this side was a steep, tree-lined hillside rushing past. Aunt Lila made a sound of—was that disgust or something else? "I'm not so old that I don't recall what goes on under a moonlit sky, my girl. And your young Mr. Wise is winsome enough—"

Her aunt shut her mouth on whatever it was she wanted to say and shook her head.

"What is it?" Stella asked softly.

"Nothing for now. Just be as cordial as you like, but you are under no circumstances to allow yourself to be alone with a young man like that again. No matter how much I might push you to be a little more worldly."

"Yes, Aunt Lila."

The older woman gave a firm nod. "Now I suppose there shall be no more sleep for a while, after all that."

Feeling drenched in shame and disappointment, Stella covered herself with the blanket, turned toward the window, and leaned her cheek on her hand against the back of the seat. But when she closed her eyes, all she could see was a rugged landscape brilliantly lit by the moon and a billion stars, and hear the pleasant baritone of the young man bantering with and challenging her—and then raised in song with her.

In less than a day, they would part ways.

Oh how she wished that were not so.

"All off for Danville!"

Nat pried himself awake and looked around as the train squealed to a slow halt. Only the station lights illuminated the predawn outside—he checked his watch and found it right at four o'clock. The train was perfectly on time.

Beside him, Mr. Jensen sat up, rubbing his eyes. "Where are we?"

"Danville, sir."

As the man nodded and settled back again, Nat turned to look at Gold, also just stirring. Frank was out cold, and behind him Miss Shepherd curled in her seat against the window. Mrs. Montgomery's eyes were closed, but the crease between her brows betrayed her state of wakefulness as she shifted in her seat.

A pang gripped him at the thought of the trouble he'd caused. He hadn't even done anything—just slipped out for air—but he certainly should not have encouraged Miss Shepherd to stay there with him.

At least not for as long as he did.

A few people trickled off the train, but for the most part, this car seemed to contain folks who'd be traveling on toward Louisville and St. Louis. Slight movement and jostling bore witness to the reshuffling of cars, dividing the train between those headed straight north to Lexington and eventually Cincinnati, and those headed west. He'd nearly drifted off to sleep when the whistle sounded and the rising chug of the engine heralded their departure.

Another four hours and they'd be in Louisville. This was the stretch where Gold would need to keep closest watch, especially as they'd be stopping frequently again.

Speaking of Gold, his brother got up from his chair, thumped Nat's shoulder, then lumbered toward the back of the car. Nat watched as he bypassed the men's room and slipped outside, then got up and followed.

Gold was looking out over the rail when Nat pushed through the door and closed it behind him, but turned, his face like thunder. "Just how long were you out here with Miss Shepherd earlier?"

Nat slowly closed his sagging jaw. "I thought you brought me out here to share something about the job—"

"Just. Answer. The question."

Nat slid his hands into his pockets and straightened. "I don't know. Maybe an hour. But before you ask, nothing happened."

Gold glared for at least half a minute longer, jaw flexing, then swung back to look out at the edges of town sliding past them before turning to glare again. "Doggone it, Nat, it's one thing if she were one of those flighty, loose things that would throw herself at you, but she—she's too young and innocent and—and a minister's daughter besides."

Nat stepped up close, hands out of his pockets and in fists. "You think I don't know that? All of it?"

His brother's lips thinned.

"Even if I were worthy of her attention—*if*—I'd not treat her so lightly. I came out here because I couldn't sleep—you can't tell me your dreams are so easy either—and next thing I know, she's here as well, claiming she didn't want to waken her aunt by trying to climb back into her seat after a trip to the necessary."

Gold snorted and shook his head. "Can't really blame her there."

"No. And I tried to get her to leave at least a couple of times."

He huffed and leaned on the rail as well, where just a couple of hours before it had been Miss Shepherd.

Gold's shoulder bumped his. "You that gone on her already?"

Nat shook his head. "I don't even know her."

"We three kings of Orient are. . ."

It seemed foolish, but he could not get the sound of her rich contralto out of his thoughts.

His brother peered upward at the sky, darker now than before with the probable approach of rain. "Yeah, but sometimes the heart just knows."

And Nat's heart fairly throbbed with the weight of knowing he'd never see her again after tonight. "Doesn't matter. She's—well, she might as well be as high as the stars she's named for."

"Oh little Brother," Gold said with a groan, "you've definitely got it bad."

CHAPTER 9

When Stella woke, the sky had barely begun to lighten above hills that, while still rolling and thickly forested, were not quite as rugged as the ones they'd passed through hours ago.

A flutter went through her middle at the memory of just who she'd shared that sight with.

She glanced over to see his seat empty, but before she could respond to the alarm sending her butterflies into a new frenzy, Aunt Lila offered a slice of apple. "Good morning. Are you hungry?"

Stella rubbed a hand over her face and accepted the piece. "Yes. Thank you."

Her aunt dimpled as if the previous night had never happened, and cut another slice from the fruit in her hand. The simple action reminded her so sharply of Mr. Wise, and Aunt Lila's scolding, that Stella had to turn back to the window before biting into the apple. As the crisp flesh yielded to her teeth, the tart-sweet juice burst across her tongue.

"We may be able to have a proper breakfast after Louisville," Aunt Lila said, "but I'm not counting on it. The *Guide* said that last night's dining car detached from this route at Danville, so I'm not sure what will happen. They should be reattaching a dining car in Louisville, but I believe they won't be serving until luncheon."

Stella nodded because it was the obvious thing to do, but made no comment.

"If nothing else, perhaps there's a bakery near the station in Louisville where we could quickly purchase something."

"That would be good." Stella winced inwardly at her lack of tone.

Aunt Lila made a sound in her throat. "If you're still miffed about last night. . ."

"No," Stella said quickly. "Only still sleepy."

"Hmm, serves you right, I expect."

Stella glanced over to see Aunt Lila also looking away, so she had no idea whether the words were spoken in earnest or teasingly. With her aunt, it could be either.

Aunt Lila cut another slice and offered it to her. This one Stella nibbled, hardly tasting. "I suppose you never did anything in your youth that others considered a mistake. That was a risk but felt so wonderful in the moment."

Her aunt shifted slowly to look at her. Stella held herself still. Sooner or later she would have to learn to weather her aunt's disapproval.

"No, child. On the contrary, I have indeed done such things. Which is why I am so concerned for your sake."

Stella's eyelids stung, but she blinked and looked away again.

As the early morning wore on, the sky lightened with glimpses of amazing color at the edges of the horizon, and Mr. Wise returned to his seat, finger-combing his hair into relative submission and not looking her way. Stella hid a smile. She'd bet he'd stood outside for a while again. If she were not a young woman who had so recently been chided about propriety, she'd make her escape and go out as well.

And immediately she felt guilty for such a traitorous thought.

By the time they pulled into Louisville, at eight o'clock sharp, Stella felt drowsy enough to nap during the short stop, but Aunt Lila reached for her pocketbook and tugged at her sleeve. "Come. Let's go see if we can find breakfast."

Stella stifled a sigh and obediently climbed out of her seat.

"We'll be back," Aunt Lila confided in the older Wise brothers, also presumably preparing to go stretch their legs.

They smiled and gave her some cordial reply, but she didn't quite catch specifics, because in glancing aside to avoid eye contact with them, she happened to directly meet the gaze of the youngest brother. Mervin Nathan Wise.

Nat.

Not that they'd have the opportunity to become familiar enough for her to call him that.

The corner of his mouth lifted ruefully, and she couldn't help responding with a slight smile of her own, and then—before she could lose her nerve for it—brushed her fingertips across the shoulder of his coat as she moved past.

And then she and Aunt Lila scurried out into the chill morning, which Mr. Wise had been correct about. It seemed colder now than last night, even standing out at the rail with the wind rushing by. Aunt Lila stopped to inquire about a bake shop, then sped away across the station platform.

They located what Aunt Lila was looking for in short order, less than half a block from the train. She seemed quite pleased with that turn of events and bought no less than half a dozen sweet rolls, which were speedily slipped into a paper bag and handed over.

"Obviously they are used to serving passengers who have little time on stops," she commented to Stella as they hurried back.

Stella had to admit the fragrance of freshly baked sweet rolls had her stomach growling.

They were crossing the platform with still a few minutes to spare when Stella glanced over and saw the second-eldest Mr. Wise, the mustachioed brother, in conversation several paces away with a woman and a smallish boy. Of course she couldn't make any of it out at that distance, but he seemed so sober and intent, and the mother so apologetic, that Stella couldn't quite drag her gaze away before Mr. Wise pulled a wallet from his pocket and drew out a bill to offer the woman. Looking astonished, she shook her head, but he took her hand and pressed the money into her palm, closing her fingers about it.

Stella had to run to catch up with Aunt Lila.

Mr. Jensen's stop was actually the next one past Louisville, so Nat decided to sit tight until the crowd was past. Of course he couldn't resist looking up and over for Miss Shepherd, because true to her name—Stella—she drew his awareness as if she were the only point of light in a sea of darkness.

Her look of desolation wrung at his heart. Perhaps it was simply lack of sleep—or that her aunt had reamed her as thoroughly as Gold had him. And she was probably the kind to feel honest distress under a rebuke, however well-intentioned it was delivered, rather than becoming sullen.

But then she tried bravely to return his smile, and the way she'd reached out to touch his shoulder as she went past—

"That sure is a sweet girl," Mr. Jensen said, nodding toward her retreating form.

Nat froze. Had the older man witnessed the exchange?

"The niece ain't so bad either," Mr. Jensen added with a wink and chuckled at his own humor.

Nat gave a short laugh. "That's putting it mildly."

The older man peered at him. "If you like her, you should ask for her address. Write to her, take the time to get to know her better."

He lifted one shoulder. "She's so outta my league."

"Hmm. Maybe not as much as you think. And you never know until you try."

Huh, yeah, and after last night's shenanigans, her aunt would never let him close enough to even talk to her again.

"Maybe," he said.

"No maybe about it, young man. You should." Mr. Jensen sucked his cheek for a moment. "Don't wind up like me, old and lonely, because you were too shy or too proud to try."

Too proud. The words hit him in the chest like the report of artillery fire. It was the second time in just a few hours that he'd heard the term. Could it be pride, and not a good and right sense of reserve?

The train left the Louisville station a minute after schedule. Stella settled back, enjoying what was possibly the most delicious sweet roll she'd ever tasted. Taking in some sustenance might have done a bit to lighten her mood as well.

Even so, she glanced over the aisle before attending to her roll again. Mr. Nat Wise was busy with his carving. It would be fun to watch, now that she knew precisely what he was doing. She finished her roll, discreetly licked the glaze from her fingers, then wiped them as clean as she could on her handkerchief. Reaching down, she pulled her satchel into her lap.

She had the nativity pieces tucked into the very bottom, each of them rolled up in a stocking. Choosing one, she slipped it out of its cushion. The shepherd. She smiled, stroking the painted face of the figure. It really was the perfect picture of Papa, so willing to brave hardship for the sake of his flock, carrying their burdens and oftentimes his own children on his shoulders.

Her eyelids burned. How she would miss him and Mama these next few weeks, missed them already, in fact.

"Now there's something I wasn't expecting to see," Aunt Lila said softly.

When Stella glanced up, her aunt was looking at the nativity shepherd.

"Did you know that belonged to my older sister Estelle?" she went on.

"I did." Stella brought the figurine further out into the light. "Mama told me how Aunt Estelle sent it to her when she'd gone to stay with Uncle Francis that Christmas she met Papa."

Aunt Lila sniffed. "Yes, her daddy was quite the fool that year, and Estelle thought to offer a little comfort. So how do you happen to have it?"

Stella allowed herself a tiny giggle. "I have the whole set with me." The next piece she pulled out was Mary. "Mama thought they'd give me a connection to home while traveling with you."

Aunt Lila responded to Stella's hesitant smile with one of her own as she reached over to trace the folds of Mary's white mantle. "Jessy has always been so thoughtful."

"And—" Stella rushed on, not wanting to lose the moment. "See there, how Mr. Wise is always carving? Well, he's making a set of the three wise men."

Her aunt's smile deepened. "Hmm. Fancy that."

"He's very good at it too."

The older woman's blue eyes met hers, full of amusement.

"I'm not simply saying so, I promise."

"Oh, I believe you." But it was clear by her tone that Aunt Lila didn't, at all. Her gaze drifted toward Nat—*Mr. Wise*—and she sighed before turning back to Stella. "I never said I believe he's anything but a nice young man."

Stella sighed as well. "I know. It's just—"

How could she explain the contradiction of a man who claimed to feel far away from God but somehow knew all five verses of "We Three Kings" and saw through her fears to her heart?

CHAPTER 10

At the next stop, a little more than a quarter hour later, Nat got out of his seat and helped Mr. Jensen retrieve his suitcase from the top rack. The older man gave him a firm handshake, offered the same to Frank, Mrs. Montgomery, and Miss Shepherd, then taking his case, made his way up the aisle to the exit. Nat let out a breath and settled back in his seat.

Hearing Gold's voice close behind, he turned. His brother had stopped next to Mrs. Montgomery and was speaking to the older woman, who wore first a look of concern, then surprise, and at last nodded and prepared to leave her seat. Gold stepped up and clapped Nat on the shoulder, leaning down to murmur, "I happened to mention Mrs. Montgomery to Mr. Walker, and he's invited her back to his lounge car to talk business. Lucky break for both of them maybe."

Mrs. Montgomery herself hovered just behind Gold, catching Nat's gaze with her own suddenly severe one. "I presume you would not object to sitting and chatting with my niece for a little while? It appears I am called away, but I am not comfortable leaving her alone among strangers."

Heat swept through Nat. Her words were a barely veiled rebuke if he'd ever heard one. "It would be my honor, Mrs. Montgomery."

She nodded crisply then leveled the same look upon Gold. "You may escort me back, young man."

As she marched toward the rear of the car, Gold threw him a wink, then hustled after.

Miss Shepherd's wide sea green eyes met his. From the seat in front of her, Frank gave a cough and then noisily cleared his throat. Shoving down the urge to thump his older brother, Nat levered himself out of his seat. "Do *you* mind?" he asked, his gaze not leaving hers.

She gave a little laugh. "Not at all."

He settled in next to her, trying to ignore the crazy soft-shoe his heart was doing at the prospect of conversation they didn't have to steal time for.

With a grin, she pulled a bag from the floor into her lap, reached in a hand, and drew out a painted, carved figure no longer than her hand, of a robed, bearded man with eyes modestly downcast. "This is Joseph, and this—" A kneeling woman this time, clothed in blue with a white mantle over her head and shoulders. "This, of course, is Mary."

He gingerly took them from her, marveling at the detail, especially of their faces. "Your great-grandfather carved these, you said?"

"Yes." A dimple came and went, reminding him of her aunt.

She drew others out in quick succession, a shepherd with a lamb draped over his shoulders and a baby Jesus in the manger. The last, though ubiquitous, still tugged at him. He set Joseph and Mary between his knees and reached for the Babe. Simple, no different from the manger piece in any other nativity, and yet—

"It's almost too wonderful to believe, isn't it?" came Miss Shepherd's soft voice beside him. "The thought that God became a baby."

He blinked. It had been awhile since he'd considered it in such terms.

A God who made Himself vulnerable to human frailty, to the hurts and evil of this world.

"Is that the entire set?" he asked when he could speak.

"Yes." She leaned close, unintentionally he was sure, and fingered the edge of the manger. "Such a small, silly thing, but I'm happy my mama thought to send it along with me."

"No sillier than me trying to carve a set of wise men," he said gruffly, "simply because my brothers and I—"

His breath caught in his throat, his hands closing around the Holy Infant as hers withdrew.

"Not silly at all then," she murmured. "Especially where yours is concerned."

He snorted. "I don't know about that. I'm just fooling around here."

And a fool was precisely what he did not want to be anymore.

She stared at him, earnestness shining in her blue-green eyes. "Somehow I really don't believe that, Mr. Wise."

He forced a short laugh, but something in her gaze had gripped him, and he could not look away. "Miss Shepherd, I'm wondering, that is, might I have your address and write to you sometime? Just as friends, of course."

A slow smile curved her mouth and lifted the dimpled cheeks. "Or an older brother? I would like that."

She searched about in her satchel and found a sheet of notepaper and a pencil, then a book, presumably to use as a writing surface. "I'm not at all sure when I'll be home again, but it's possible Mama could forward a letter if we are gone too long." She finished and handed it to him.

"Charleston, is it?"

"Yes. We have a house, not too small but not too big either, west of the Ashley."

"The Ashley?"

Her cheeks turned rosy as she laughed. "The Ashley River. You aren't from Charleston, yourself?"

"No. My brothers and I came down from New Jersey a couple of months ago to try to find work, and—well, wound up looking westward."

Another curious look, and then another laugh. "The Wise men from far away in the East. 'Westward leading, still proceeding—'"

"Yeah, yeah, 'Guide us to Thy perfect light.'" Nat laughed as well. It really was too absurd.

"So, yes," Miss Shepherd went on, "the Ashley is one of two rivers that converge on Charleston—well, four, really. The Ashley and the Cooper Rivers form the peninsula that is Charleston proper, and then the Wando also converges to the north, and the Stono to the south. All those rivers—all those marshlands—that's why they call it the Lowcountry of South Carolina."

She stopped, looking abashed. "I'm sorry. Here I am, just rattling on."

"I'm enjoying it, Miss Shepherd."

She did flush at that and glanced out the window. "You are only being kind. No gentleman likes to listen to a lady's chattering."

He leaned back a little, frowning. "And what experience would you have with that?"

195

Not replying at first, she chewed her lip. "Everyone knows it. Aunt Lila says so, often, and she does have the experience. At least she wouldn't have gotten where she is in business without having some idea of how to comport herself among men, now would she? And even my Mama, who I know loves me, sometimes doesn't have the time or wherewithal to listen."

"Well, I can't speak for your mama—" Although if his own family was anything to judge by, if Miss Shepherd's younger brothers and sisters were all healthy and lively things, yes, her mama did indeed stay busy keeping up with them all. "But what has worked for your aunt in the business world may not be an accurate state of affairs in everyday life."

"Well, that may be so, but. . .still." She slanted him a glance. "You are kind, Mr. Wise, for saying so."

"You can call me Nat, you know," he found himself saying.

A tiny grin peeped through her gloom. "Then you should call me Stella."

He was as easy to converse with in daylight as he had been the night before, and Stella quite lost track of time as they continued to chat about everything from family to where they had grown up. Any embarrassment she might have had over presuming he was also from Charleston quickly vanished as he shared stories of small-town New Jersey, close enough to the city for a day of shopping when his mother wished it, but far enough out that the hustle and bustle did not touch them. But they had cold and snow, which Stella remembered from her childhood but almost never experienced on the coast of South Carolina.

In turn, she shared about visits to both the seaside and the mountains, of growing up in the shadow of an aunt who was vitally interested in her family's life but relatively important in her own right—as this trip had indeed borne out.

So it should have been no surprise when Nat's oldest brother suddenly appeared, looming over both of them, and announced to her, "Your aunt would like you to join her in Mr. Walker's business car."

"What? Me? Oh—"

And while Nat slid past him, out of the way, Stella fumbled over whether to bring her satchel or not. "Leave your baggage, Miss Shepherd," the eldest Mr. Wise—*Gold*, she reminded herself—said. "Frank and Nat will keep watch over it."

And so she found herself following him back, out of their coach and through the one behind it, through galley and dining cars, to an entryway where a smartly suited man stood as if on guard. "This is Mrs. Montgomery's niece, Miss Shepherd," Gold told the man.

The man nodded. "Very good, and thank you. Miss Shepherd, follow me, please."

She glanced up at Gold, and he gave her an encouraging smile. "It's all right. Mr. Walker is a good man."

They passed through another narrow hallway, this one with lovely wooden paneling covering the wall and closed doors on one side and burgundy velvet curtains above the windows on the other. The corridor opened out into the most beautifully appointed dining and lounge area she'd ever seen—far richer than she could have imagined finding on a railway car.

On the far side of the lounge area, among a small group of strangers, sat Aunt Lila, teacup in hand as if she'd known these folks for years and not a mere hour. "There you are, child," she sang out, and two men rose from their seats, an older one wearing round spectacles and a younger with a neatly trimmed mustache.

"Miss Shepherd, sir, as requested," said her escort, who bowed and whisked away into the hallway.

"Please, come and be welcome," the older man said, coming forward to usher her farther into the lounge. "I am so glad to make your aunt's acquaintance. Would you like some tea? Coffee, perhaps?"

Aunt Lila sat forward in her upholstered chair. "This is Mr. Walker, child. He owns shares in the railway, and we have the lucky happenstance of discussing some business together, but he's inviting us to have luncheon with him in a bit."

"Oh, that sounds lovely," Stella said, then suppressed a wince at how breathless she must sound.

As other introductions were made, she took a chair at the edge of the group and accepted a cup of coffee, already creamed and sweetened, making sure to thank the waiter.

The coffee was pleasing enough, although not any better than what they'd had in the dining car the day before, but given that it was the first she'd had today, Stella was grateful for it. She studied each of the people in the party in turn. Mr. Walker's family traveled with him, his wife a fashionable older woman, and their daughter, her younger mirror image, and then the young man, his son, who smiled at Stella, his gaze lingering as if she were indeed an object of interest. The women looked at her but said nothing.

Stella shifted her attention to the furnishings. The finish of the wood trim and paneling lent a warm glow to the interior of the car. The chairs and tables were beautiful as well as functional, and the velvet drapes completed the look of tasteful wealth.

She felt completely like the poor church mouse while the others chatted with ease.

A wave of homesickness overtook her, not just for Mama and Papa, but also for Nat and his brothers, who were the closest thing to friends she had on this trip.

Finishing her coffee, she cradled the cup in her lap, listening politely and sitting as properly upright as she knew how, until at last the waiter came in and announced that luncheon was ready, and would they be seated in the dining nook? Mr. Walker rose and indicated that they should all do the same, and Mrs. Walker led the way to the long, white-draped table.

While more coffee and tea were poured, Stella found herself seated beside the younger Mr. Walker, who bent another smile upon her, his brown eyes warm. "This is an unexpected pleasure. We do not often have company on these trips."

He offered the sugar bowl, and she took it with a word of thanks. "Do you often travel this route?"

"Oh, several times a year," he said lightly.

Stella compressed her lips as he handed her the cream next.

"And yourself?" he asked.

"This is my first time." She stirred in the cream and tasted her cup.

The waiter, accompanied by two others, brought in their first course—a delicious-smelling soup—and set it before them.

The consommé was as good as it looked, but Mr. Walker made a face. "Is there something wrong with your soup?" Stella asked.

"Oh, it's fine. I just prefer something with more substance."

She tried her best to keep her expression pleasant but could not help thinking of Nat and his enthusiasm for their meals the day before. "I'm sure there are many who would be grateful for such simple fare," she murmured.

Young Mr. Walker shot her a sharp-edged smile. "And what does your father do for a living, if your aunt is in business?"

She let her own smile widen at that. "He's a minister, Mr. Walker. A fine one, if I may say so of my own papa."

As she'd suspected, his expression flattened a little. "Please, call me Robert."

"Oh, I could not be so familiar with a young man I've only just met."

"Well, if the friendliness between your aunt and my father is any indication"—the young man nodded toward the animated discussion taking place between the two at the head of the table—"then unfamiliarity will not last for long."

She offered him her blandest smile and applied herself to the consommé.

It was the same through three more courses. Despite the excellence of the food, Robert Walker proved a steady if affable critic, and his mother and sister steadfastly ignored her after hearing she was a mere minister's daughter. Stella did not care. She'd already determined to make her excuses once the meal was over and make her way back to the coach car.

CHAPTER 11

He missed her, quite fiercely, even though he'd absolutely no right to.

Gold had given him a single shake of the head and unmistakable roll of the eyes on his pass through the coach on his way to prowl somewhere else. Lunch was past and then some, and still Stella and her aunt hadn't returned, but who knew how long they might linger. And with an invite to the private business car of one of the railway magnates, who could blame them?

Nat was nearly done roughing out the third figure. As he'd told Stella, he was looking forward to some quiet time so he could get the details just right—he'd barely enough time at stops for anything more than quick cuts—but he was cautiously pleased with the results so far. Although he'd shaken off a particular niggling thought, it kept coming back and back, until finally, after looking around to make sure Stella or Mrs. Montgomery weren't anywhere in sight to catch him doing so, he reached into Stella's satchel and pulled out one of the nativity figures so he could study its workmanship.

It was the shepherd that emerged in his grasp. Nat smiled a little at the irony.

Such fineness of detail, given the small size of the set. What sort of tools had Stella's great-grandfather had to work with? Certainly more than a simple pocketknife. Nat brushed the pad of his thumb across the texture of the lamb's white coat and the folds of the shepherd's tunic and cloak. Could he even hope to approximate the skill displayed here?

With a sigh, he nestled the shepherd back among its companions and gave attention to his own figurine. It seemed folly to even try, but having begun, he could hardly give up now.

At the next station, the train slid to a stop. Nat half watched, as he'd been doing so already, while a couple of passengers disembarked and a handful came on. In Gold's absence, Frank had moved to the aisle seat, presumably to discourage anyone from attempting to share the space, and Nat stayed put in the one he'd shared with Stella.

Among the other passengers, two men in expensive-looking suits and fedoras stepped inside, not removing their hats as they glanced about. Something in their manner set Nat's teeth on edge, but perhaps it was only the apparent lack of manners. He was still old-fashioned enough to believe that men should uncover their heads indoors.

Frank glanced back, caught his eye, and lifted a brow. Apparently the men's demeanor didn't sit well with him either.

Nat shoved down his gnawing restlessness and went back to carving.

The Walker women surprised Stella after lunch with an invitation to play cribbage. Aunt Lila showed no inclination to end their visit, so with a stifled sigh, Stella accepted and sat down with the other two ladies. The younger Mr. Walker hovered nearby, smoking a cigar but attempting conversation between plays.

Stella found it all exceedingly awkward and tedious, and kept having to swallow back a yawn. The rich meal had been delicious, but after a night with little sleep, all she wanted now was a nap. Fortunately, after a pair of games, Mrs. Walker begged off with her own need for a nap. The younger Mr. Walker tried to entice Stella into a game of checkers, but after a pleading glance at Aunt Lila, she forced a smile. "I'm afraid I'd be a poor partner if I continued any longer, after not sleeping so well myself last night."

"Ah, that's very much too bad," he said, tipping his head and squinting through a cloud of cigar smoke. Stella was at the moment having to stifle a cough as well as a yawn. "I was hoping we could persuade you and your aunt to stay and visit through dinner."

"Oh, I'm afraid we must return to our coach for at least a little while before we arrive in St. Louis," Aunt Lila chimed in.

Thank You, Lord! Stella could not hold back the impassioned expression of relief.

Rising, they shook hands all around. "You've given me much to consider," Aunt Lila said to Mr. Walker, "and I thank you very kindly for the lovely luncheon, but I'll need some time to consult my notes and think on the options before I give you any sort of answer."

He gave a half bow, and smiled warmly at both Stella and her aunt. "Of course, my dear lady. I look forward to hearing from you, whether in St. Louis or from Kansas City."

Aunt Lila beamed, but Stella could see that her usual cheer had worn a bit thin.

They made their way forward again, but not until the hallway of the galley car did Aunt Lila speak. "I declare, I could sleep for a week! So many sweets."

"But it was a delicious lunch."

"Delicious, but gracious, that man can talk."

Stella could not help but giggle.

As they reached the doorway between cars, Aunt Lila gave a sigh that was audible even over the noise of the train. "Wait a moment, child."

She stopped and turned. Her aunt's expression was sober but intent.

"Yes, dear Aunt?"

The dimple came and went. "You know I wish only the best for you."

Stella's skin prickled. What was Aunt Lila about? "O–of course," she said slowly.

"And you know, as well as your mama and papa have done, I've wanted better for you than life lived at the mercy of people's whims and preferences."

A frown gathered between Stella's brows. "Is that how you see what Papa does?"

"Well? Is it not?"

"It's—no. Ministry is much more than that. We live under God's own grace and mercy, not according to the will and pleasure of men."

"Oh child." Aunt Lila gave almost a full smile this time, but edged with pity.

Stella could feel herself flushing. "I realize how self-satisfied that must sound."

"Child, you are the picture of humility. And I am not surprised—your mother and father have always been nearly the perfect pair. It is just—I long for you not to have to struggle the way they did."

Was it Stella's imagination, or did her aunt's eyes glimmer a bit more than usual?

Aunt Lila cleared her throat and drew herself up a little. "I could not help but notice your disaffection for the young Mr. Walker. I would beg you not to be so dismissive of him. He has means to care for you that others may not."

The words tumbled over and over in Stella's mind. What was her aunt saying, truly?

"Others," she said slowly. "You mean such as Mr. Wise?"

Aunt Lila sighed again, heavily. "If you insist on bringing him up, then yes."

"If you noticed my disaffection for Mr. Walker," Stella said, "then you may also have noticed his family's marked dismissal of me once I mentioned that Papa's a minister."

"His mother and sister, perhaps, but Mr. Walker himself?"

"I'm sure that's nothing more than a passing fascination. What have I to offer a family such as theirs? That they'd be interested in?" she added.

Aunt Lila blew out a breath. "And what you feel for Mr. Wise is not merely a passing fascination as well?"

Stella's pulse stuttered. "I have no way of knowing that, no. But Auntie, I don't mean to be disrespectful, but your life has not been without trouble either. What with losing Uncle Amos and. . .and your sister. . .and—"

She faltered just short of mentioning Aunt Lila's lack of babies of her own. That would be just too hurtful.

Her aunt huffed again. "All I am saying is, do not be so quick to disregard someone based on his apparent material wealth and lack of interest in spiritual matters. The two are not always mutually exclusive, and you barely had time to get to know Mr. Walker."

And you should not be so quick to disregard someone based on his apparent lack of material wealth, she wanted to say but bit back the words. She could make only so many bold statements in one day. "Yes, Aunt Lila."

Turning, Stella made her way forward again through one crowded coach car and into the next, where the much-discussed Mr. Wise still sat, guarding their seats. He glanced up, a little startled, then smiled, his lips flattening when neither Stella nor Aunt Lila returned it with much warmth.

"Thank you so much for looking after our things," Aunt Lila said too cheerfully, and Stella wanted to cringe.

"It was a pleasure," Nat said with a dip of his head. When his brother Frank slid out into the aisle to let him in, he sat down next to the window directly in front of Stella's place.

She too settled in and caught him peeking around the seat for the briefest moment with a questioning quirk of one brow. A small shake of the head was the only response she dared give.

"How much farther to St. Louis?" she asked Aunt Lila, who checked her watch but kept her gaze averted.

"About four hours, perhaps less."

Stella set about making sure everything in her satchel was tucked back in, padding included, before pulling out her book. It lay in her lap, its title glittering in gold against the cover—*Riders of the Purple Sage,* quite a recent favorite among many and one Stella had read at least twice. But at present, she could summon no enthusiasm for the story within.

She found herself gazing at the unruly waves adorning the top of Nat's head in front of her. So Aunt Lila wanted her to consider a spoiled dandy such as Mr. Walker? Stella thought of his many complaints about the excellent meal. Somehow she could not see him ever consenting to endure standing with her in the cold, windy moonlight, content only with conversation, much less encouraging her to sing something as humble as a Christmas carol.

Lord, You know who is the true man of worth—and means—here. Or, if that even applies to either of them. Help me to trust You to show me who I should fix my attention on and to wait for the right time to do so.

As she ended the prayer, her fingers found the place where the crocheted lace bookmark peeped out from the pages. Opening the book, she tried to focus on the words and where she'd left off reading, but her mind still spun with the day's events. Perhaps a nap was in order after all.

She'd read the same paragraph three times over when the train jerked. The squealing of brakes announced an unplanned stop. As several passengers cried out, Stella glanced out the window. They were passing through what appeared to be the middle of a field—

"Stay in your seats!"

The command came from a well-dressed man standing at the front of the coach, brandishing a pistol. Stella's nerveless fingers closed her book and slid it down into her satchel while her heart thudded hard enough to make her head ache.

A second man, also suited and carrying a gun, stepped up behind the first. More cries and gasps echoed through the car.

With a jolt, the train came to a halt.

"Everyone just stay calm and hand over your valuables. Put 'em right here, in my hat. That's right, there you go—just like this gentleman and his good wife. Some swell folk, right there."

The muzzle of the pistol straying this way and that, he sauntered down the aisle in a grotesque parody of the collections Stella had witnessed so often. Her eyes burned. *Oh Lord, please help—and please, let no one be hurt!*

In front of her, Nat and his brother sat very still, barely glancing at each other. Aunt Lila was already grimly removing a diamond ring and her pearl necklace. Stella stayed quiet. She had nothing of value, not really. But would the robber believe her—

Frank exploded out of his seat. The first armed man swung toward him, and the gun went off, but Frank launched into him and knocked him onto the floor, scuffling for the weapon. The man still hovering by the door cursed but hesitated before dashing toward the fight. Frank came up, pistol in hand, and fired. The second man went down in a flurry of screams and small children wailing.

Nat too was out of his seat, and only then did Stella see, as Frank turned, the blood pouring down the front of the older Wise brother's shirt.

CHAPTER 12

It was just like war again. Shots, screams, and confusion. Only this time, his brother's was the face that had washed deathly white, whose gaze fastened blankly on Nat's, before he went down, heavily, in the coach aisle.

Nat half caught his brother, ignoring the stabbing ache in his own leg as he eased Frank's bulk to the floor. His brother's head was pillowed, incongruously, on the first fallen robber's leg, eyelids fluttering. Nat yanked back the lapels of Frank's coat, searching for the wound, then finding it, used the fabric bunched against the pulsing opening to stanch the bleeding. "Frank, stay with me, man. You're not allowed to die on me here."

The tumult in the coach was tremendous. Nat wanted just to put his own head down and cover his ears, but he forced himself to focus on Frank and his brother's labored breathing. "Come on, Brother. . ."

"Calm down! Everyone just be calm, please!"

Still the babies wailed and women sobbed. Nat glanced up to see Gold surveying the damage from the front, a revolver in hand as well.

"I'm with the police!" Gold called out. "Please, back to your seats and calm down." His gaze fastened on Nat's. "Is he—"

"Still alive. Not sure what else."

Suddenly, in the commotion, Stella was there at his elbow. "What can I do, Nat? How can I help?"

"I—" Nat swallowed.

God, help me. Help us. Yes, this is me asking, after all this time. . . .

A single thought dropped into his head—a memory. He looked up and met Stella's wide but determined eyes. "Sing."

"What?" Her whites showed now, her mouth rounding.

"Just sing, Stella. Something. Anything."

He watched her, saw the transformation, from shaking her head and shrinking at the thought, to acceptance. Squaring her shoulders. Rising to her feet, trembling, yet determination shining in her beautiful face. Drawing in a long, deep breath.

"Silent night, holy night. . ."

That rich, lovely contralto poured over him, swelled in strength and volume, filled all the cracks and crannies around them.

"All is calm, all is bright. . ."

Soothed. Settled. Voices lifted to join her as crying died to sniffles.

"Round yon virgin mother and Child. Holy Infant, so tender and mild. . ."

Gold was quietly at work now, recruiting help to bind the two fallen criminals. Frank's eyes opened, then closed again, but he was still breathing.

As the second verse began, with almost the entire car singing,

Nat's eyes closed as well, and he let the words wash over him. "Son of God, love's pure light. . ."

Thank You that You are with us in everything. In the heartache and the loss. In the mud of the trenches and all the blood. You are with us now, even if—even if Frank goes to be with You and Mama before I'm ready for it.

You are with us, and that truly is enough.

Epilogue

Kansas City, Missouri
December 23, 1919

Stella stirred the soup on the stove, and satisfied at last that it was ready, set the spoon aside and turned off the heat. Stepping into the dining area of their small rented house, she surveyed the table, set for four.

Who in the world was Aunt Lila bringing to supper two days before Christmas?

She'd been very secretive about it, saying something about the need to interview a new shipping manager for the Kansas City operations, but to have the meal ready at six o'clock. Stella peered at the timepiece over the mantel in the other room. Ten minutes after six now. Coffee was brewed, soup waiting, a roast still warming in the oven, the kitchen lamps flickering cheerfully. All lay ready, lacking only her aunt and unknown guests.

With a sigh, she untied her apron and hung it on its peg by the back door, then wandered into the sitting room where, in the light of several candles, the nativity stood in quiet dignity on a cloth-covered side table. The sight awoke a burn behind her eyelids, which no amount of blinking would banish.

The memory washed over her, as it had every day in the two weeks and more since it had happened, of standing in that crowded, noisy coach car and letting her throat open for the sake of offering comfort and peace to her fellow passengers. Of Aunt Lila, as Stella continued leading them in song, gently but firmly brushing past her to inquire after Frank's well-being and then taking charge of the situation, declaring that she herself would foot the bill for his care once they reached St. Louis.

Of watching the middle Wise brother and his laboring breaths, praying they would continue.

Of standing on the platform at the St. Louis station, feeling so lost as Gold and Nat prepared to escort Frank away to the hospital, while trying to explain the situation, along with Mr. Walker, to the police. Aunt Lila pulling both Gold and Nat aside, and the men saying their goodbyes to Stella as she fought tears. The press of Gold's hands around hers, thanking her for her help, though she felt she'd done so little. Nat grasping her shoulders, his eyes flinty as he gazed wordlessly into hers.

"Be well," she whispered, and he smiled a little.

"I'll write," he whispered back, and gave her shoulders a last squeeze. "You were absolutely wonderful. Don't stop singing."

And then he walked away, his stride marked, she noticed for the very first time, by a limp. And the tears did come, at that.

Aunt Lila's business in St. Louis had taken three days before they pressed on to Kansas City. Stella wanted to find out where Frank had been taken and visit him, but Aunt Lila's schedule proved too pressing, and she was unwilling to let Stella wander the city alone.

There had been no letter yet, but she knew that didn't mean anything. She couldn't really expect to hear from Nat until she and Aunt Lila were back home in Charleston, which would not be for at least another week or two. But she worried for Frank, though she tried to turn it to prayer, and she missed Nat.

She shouldn't miss him. She'd only spent a day and a night and another day with him. But she couldn't stop thinking about him.

A rattle sounded at the front door. Well, finally. Stella dashed the wetness from her eyes. Aunt Lila's gusty laugh preceded her into the house, and the resonant echo after of a man's voice wrung an ache from Stella's heart. She let a sigh escape before pasting on a smile and turning.

Her breath and heart stopped. Because right there, taking off hats and overcoats in the entryway, on the other side of Aunt Lila, were two of the brothers Wise. Gold and Nat.

They saw her and smiled, but it was only Nat she could focus on, that familiar wry grin, the rakish waves of hair now trimmed a little.

"Merry Christmas, Stella," Aunt Lila said, as saucy as could be.

"Oh—my—gracious!" was all she could get out.

Her aunt and Gold were both laughing, with Aunt Lila patting Nat's shoulder. "Go on then. I'll get supper out of the oven while you two take a few minutes to catch up. That is"—and she actually winked—"if that's what you wish."

"Soup is on the stove already," Stella said without thinking.

"Well, I expect I can ladle that as well."

Gold gave Nat a little shove before following Aunt Lila to the kitchen.

Stella stood, still frozen, as Nat came forward, chuckling quietly. "I'd ask if you were surprised, but. . ."

"Where is. . .Frank?"

The smile did not dim. "Still in the hospital over in St. Louis. It was a very near thing for a while, but he's mending."

"Oh—oh, I am so glad."

And then, somehow, Nat's arms were around her, and she sank gratefully into his embrace as if meant to be there, blubbering on his shoulder, but he seemed not to mind.

"You were so beautiful that last afternoon on the train." He stroked her hair with one hand while the other arm stayed fast around her. "It was like the angels themselves were singing, the way people quieted. And the way God's peace settled over my own heart, at last."

She drew away, wiping her eyes, able only to gape at him. The tender half smile came and went as he handed her his handkerchief.

"You really were like the star, you know, leading me back to Him. Just quietly shining, reflecting His goodness."

Stella sniffled. She had done that?

"And I hope you don't mind, but I talked with your aunt. She's offered Gold and me jobs, you know, and Frank too, once he's well enough."

"I didn't know, but that's wonderful."

Nat's lashes fell, and then he looked up again, all earnestness. "I asked her if she would approve of me seeing you again, that is, if you were willing."

Another wave threatened to overwhelm her. It was like standing on the beach at Folly Island while hurricane surf washed in. "Yes," she said, without hesitation. "Yes, oh yes, oh yes!" She laughed a little as the smile dawned again across his features, lighting his eyes like sunrise. "So which of you is the new shipping manager?"

The smile turned to a shy grin. "Me. Do you—do you mind?"

"I think it's brilliant," she said, dabbing her eyes with the hanky.

He chuckled. "Well, we'll see about that. In the meantime, I have another Christmas gift for you."

He reached into his pocket and drew out a paper-wrapped bundle. She accepted it with outstretched hands as the first breath of suspicion stole through her, and unwrapped it slowly.

One, two, three wise men, finished now. Two standing, one kneeling. All unvarnished and yet unpainted, but with amazing detail, so that she could see the jewels in their crowns and the looks of adoration on their faces.

"Oh Nat. They're perfectly wonderful!"

"So you like them?" Nat's gaze sparkled in the candlelight.

"Like them? I love them."

She looked from the figurines into his face, and then at the nativity on the table nearby. With deliberate movements, she set the wise men at the edge of the others, nudging them all a little to perfect the arrangement, before standing back. "There. They are home."

"Indeed they are," Nat said, but he wasn't looking at the nativity.

Her breath caught as he eased closer, one hand coming up to brush the side of her face, then his lips very gently testing hers.

"Merry Christmas, my star," he murmured, and kissed her again.

Transplanted to North Dakota after more than two decades in Charleston, South Carolina, **Shannon McNear** loves losing herself in local history. She's a military wife, mom of eight, mother-in-law of three, grammie of two, and a member of ACFW and RWA. Her first novella, *Defending Truth* in *A Pioneer Christmas Collection*, was a 2014 RITA finalist. When she's not sewing, researching, or leaking story from her fingertips, she enjoys being outdoors, basking in the beauty of the northern prairies. Connect with her at www.shannon-mcnear.com or on Facebook or Goodreads.

ON ANGEL WINGS

by Janine Rosche

DEDICATION

To those who served during the Second World War, both on the home front and abroad, especially the Angels of Bataan and Corregidor, 2nd Lt. George F. Mitchell Jr. of the 386th Division of the US Army Air Corps, and Corporal Robert W. Rosche Sr of the 309 Troop Carrier Group of the US Army Air Corps.

ACKNOWLEDGMENTS

Thanks to my fellow authors Susie, Shannon, and Deb for inspiring me and teaching me! Tamela, you are the best cheerleader I could ask for. Christina, Rachel, Janyre, and my brother, Bob, you helped make this story possible, so thank you. And finally, George, thanks for putting up with my Clark Gable crush all these years!

Suddenly there was with the angel a multitude of the heavenly host praising God, and saying, Glory to God in the highest, and on earth peace, good will toward men.

LUKE 2:13–14 KJV

CHAPTER 1

Hope Hill, Missouri
Thanksgiving Day, 1945

Ever since Elodie Wise was a little girl, she'd been told she carried a light inside her soul that even the darkest night could not snuff out. The only problem? When she wanted—or rather needed—to hide, she never could. That didn't keep her from trying, of course.

With hardly any sound, she crept backward, keeping her weight on her hands and heels until she'd settled into the blackest space she could find. Hugging her knees to her chest, she waited for the threat to fade away. Hinges squeaked, scaling up, then down, and a frigid breeze slithered through the darkness. It found her, coiling around her legs. While the chill snaked into the marrow of her bones, she remained still as the dead.

Something scurried nearby. Something big. Her heart drummed the rhythm of "Chattanooga Choo Choo" against her chest. Just as she'd done countless times before, she sang the words of Psalm 27 in her head, pairing the words to the beat.

*The Lord is my light
and my salvation;
who-oom shall I fear?
The Lord is the strength of my life.* . . .

And, like always, a nonsensical peace washed over her so completely that the hot breath against her neck hardly frightened her at all.

"I don't think she saw us." Benjamin. His whisper soothed away her remaining jitters. "We should be safe here."

"I'm not sure. She's relentless." Elodie rocked to the side, nudging her old friend.

On the other side of the cardboard box barricade, the door to the garage protested being opened again. Benjamin pulled Elodie against him, blanketing her back, shoulder, and arm with velvety warmth. A sharp contrast to the icy concrete below.

With a click, the single bulb attached to the ceiling flooded the space with light. "Elodie Lila Wise, you'll catch your death of cold out here." Her mother's voice carried over the maze of stacked boxes that held her family's memorabilia, old playthings, and Christmas decorations. "I'm getting the pies out, and I made all your favorites. Elodie?"

With a glance over her shoulder, she met Benjamin's mischievous gaze.

He raised a finger to his lips.

Elodie clapped her hand to her mouth, trapping her chuckle inside.

"Oh gracious. Ben, when you two are done playing hide-and-seek, bring Elodie inside, please."

"Yes, ma'am." The rich depth of his voice made one thing clear.

They were no longer kids hiding from chores. After the door shut, Benjamin circled Elodie's wrist with his thumb and middle finger. "Sweetheart," he said, in his best impression of her mother, "come inside and let me fatten you up. I've added extra lard to the chocolate pie. I shall spoon-feed it to you while your father smothers you with hugs." His voice cracked into laughter.

"It feels silly the way they baby me. But I can't say I blame them. I've only gained back half of what I lost over there."

"Give it time. It took, what? Three years to lose that weight? You'll get there. Even so, war heroes deserve some good pumpkin pie."

"Like you?"

"Oh yeah. I'm a real hero. All I did was babysit Mister America, Clyde Irving." The sarcasm was as thick as her mother's mashed potatoes. "I was a joke, and you know it."

"Benjamin Gabriel, you were not, and never could be a joke. You were the best soldier the army had. Why else would they assign you the job of keeping the most famous actor in Hollywood from getting killed?"

"Spare me, will you? It was nothing more than a parade of destruction through Europe. One that went past all the battles our real soldiers fought days before." Shame weighed on his brow.

Was there anything she could say to help him the way he'd always helped her? "You were a real soldier. I know you don't believe me, but other than MacArthur, I think you had the most important job of all. If something had happened to Clyde Irving, the whole country might have lost hope."

"Yeah, yeah."

She placed a hand on his face and offered him her best smile. "It kept us nurses going, I can tell you that much. The girls would fawn all over him. 'Clyde's going to set us free. Clyde's fighting the Nazis.

Clyde's marching on Tokyo.' And every time, I'd say, 'If he is, it's because of my Benjamin.'"

His eyes darted across the floor, then settled on her face. "You told them about me?"

"All the time." Her words unleashed a smile that lit up his face. "I'd tell them that you're the bravest man in the whole world—the brother I'd always wanted."

He blinked. His lips fell, then twisted into a smirk. "Why are you out here again? I mean, other than avoiding your mother's attempts to spit-shine your cheeks—which, by the way, are a little dirty." He pretended to spit on his thumb and reached for her face.

Intercepting him, she grabbed his forearm. He'd gotten so strong. And handsome. Of course, he'd always been that. She was the one who, as Mama said, had to grow into her beauty. By that time, she'd joined the Army Nurse Corps and took her first assignment at Manila's Sternberg Hospital in the Philippines six weeks before the attack on Pearl Harbor. Not long after, she and others were taken captive and sent to Santo Tomas, a university-turned-internment camp where beauty counted for nothing.

"I started remembering where I was this time last year. Just needed a few minutes." She wished she could blame the cold, dry air in the garage for the constricting of her throat. Her left hand quaked—something that might embarrass her around anyone but Benjamin. Straightening her fingers into rigid spokes, she turned her palm up.

Benjamin's hand slid across until it aligned with hers, his fingertips extending past hers slightly. After ten seconds or so, her trembling eased.

"Since Thanksgiving was a wash, I'd like to start thinking about Christmas. Perhaps I'll be better by then." She needed something to focus on other than the memories of war. Maybe then she could truly begin to live again. Accept the blessings God had placed right in front of her.

"Don't push yourself too hard, El." He wrapped his fingers around hers.

As a nurse, most of the hands she'd held were cold, frail, and waning of life. But Benjamin's hand was warm and strong. She hoped he didn't mind holding her hand a bit longer.

He didn't seem to. In fact, he held on tighter as they stood.

"Benjamin, will you help me find something? It's in one of these boxes labeled 'Christmas.' "

He was only a few inches taller than her. But what he lacked in height, he made up for in muscle, charisma, and a devout faith that had helped Elodie endure, even when half the world separated them. How he hadn't married already, she didn't understand. Any girl would love to have Benjamin gaze at her the way he did at Elodie now. Too bad she wasn't *any girl*. Not after what she'd been through.

Pressing his back against the wood, Benjamin held the door open for Elodie. With her arms cradling the wooden box, she had to turn sideways to fit through the frame. Her body brushed his, her hair wisping his nose. Every nerve in his body woke with a jolt. *This woman. . .*

"Now, Benjamin, I know you aren't making our little Sunshine carry that for you." Mr. Wise rushed to Elodie, but she shook her head.

Kneeling, she lowered the box to the carpet in the family room.

"I tried, sir, but she didn't trust me not to break it." Benjamin stayed close to Elodie. She breathed hard, the strain making her body waver slightly. He placed a hand under her elbow and guided her into a seated position, hoping her father hadn't seen. If her parents treated her any more like a porcelain doll, they'd hook her on a stand and place her on the highest shelf.

Mr. Wise had seen his share of combat during the Great War, and he and Mrs. Wise had fully supported Elodie's decision to join the Army Nurse Corps. But her being captured and held for three years had taken its toll on all of them.

"She says my mitts are too thick for handling this nativity set," Ben said.

"Did she bring up that broken angel again?" Mr. Wise reclaimed his spot in his leather chair. "At least it wasn't one of the heirloom figures or the wise men I carved for her mother. I think Stella bought that angel at Woolworth's for a dime the year Rhoda was born."

"Precisely. And it wasn't my fault Elodie has butterfingers. My throw was perfect. She was the one who dropped it."

Elodie slugged his arm. So much for that waning strength.

"Hey, bruiser, be nice." He deserved it though. She'd cried and cried when that ill-fated angel fell and broke in two. His penalty was seeing her front door shut in his face every day for two weeks. They'd only been ten the Christmas of 1931, but he'd vowed never to make her cry again.

She feigned a hateful glare. "Still, you knew that was my favorite piece, you big lug."

"That's why I figured you'd catch it."

Her mother appeared, wiping her hands on her worn checked apron. "The whipped cream is finished. Everyone to the table. Elodie, I got you a piece of chocolate pie and a piece of pumpkin pie, in case you're still hungry after one."

Mr. Wise met his wife in the doorway. He kissed her forehead and followed her lead into the kitchen.

Elodie met Benjamin's gaze. "That's my mother—sticking it to Japan and Germany, one dollop of whipped cream at a time."

At the table, Benjamin sat sandwiched between Elodie's two younger sisters. Although they shared their mother's golden hair and their father's light blue eyes, Charlie was Elodie's opposite in almost every way. He'd never once seen her wear a dress. And if anyone other than her family called her Charlotte, they'd be sure to get a fat lip. Ever since the war began, she'd been working for Heroes of Hope Hill, organizing support for the war effort on the home front.

The youngest of the Wise girls, on the other hand, idolized Elodie. Rhoda, the eighteen-year-old, dressed and acted just like her, with one glaring exception. Rhoda did not see Benjamin as a brother. Not one little bit.

Benjamin lifted Rhoda's hand off his knee and placed it on her own, shooting her a warning look in the process.

Elodie, sitting on his other side, smiled. Of course she found Rhoda's crush humorous. Last week she'd even encouraged him to take Rhoda out on a date. When he'd refused, she seemed puzzled. Yes, Elodie had been through a trauma in that internment camp, but had it made her utterly blind to his love for her? Driving his fork into the pumpkin pie, he prepared to eat his feelings, slathered with whipped cream.

"Benjamin, thank you for spending Thanksgiving with us," Mrs. Wise said.

"It's my pleasure, ma'am. Without you all, I'd be alone today, cooking for myself. And I'm not sure pumpkin pie comes in a can." He flashed them a grin of appreciation. After all, he loved them as much as he'd loved his own family. "My parents would thank you for taking me in."

"It can't be easy. Coming home to a world so different," Charlie said. She rested her elbows on the table, steepling her fingers. "It's all a mess. You know, I saw June Everhart at work the other day. Her kids asked if their daddy's going to be okay. He's struggling to cope with home life after returning from Europe."

"Charlie, please." Mrs. Wise's tone might have been enough to flatten the whipped cream if it wasn't already heavy with the heaps of sugar she'd added. She seemed to perform even the smallest task with her eldest daughter in mind.

Elodie poked at her pie but hadn't yet scooped a bite.

"Mama, we can't keep pretending all is fine around us. Of all people, Elodie knows that."

"That doesn't mean we should talk about it around the Thanksgiving table. Tomorrow we will discuss how our family can help, but not right now." She smoothed her hair behind her ear.

"How can we help people if no one is willing to talk about what everyone is facing? In our county, there are 132 empty seats at the table today. We have three people other than Elodie who are recovering from being prisoners of—"

"Charlie, we'll discuss this later," Mr. Wise said, a stern edge to his voice, which Benjamin knew from a childhood of playing in this home would only fuel the fire in Charlie's rebel soul.

As the argument over what constituted pleasant holiday table talk dragged on, Elodie straightened her hand. She flattened it on the table next to her plate. Her eyes met Benjamin's.

He put his fork down and, likewise, pressed his hand against the linen tablecloth, holding her gaze. He'd stay like this forever if she needed him to.

"I'd like to help." Elodie's voice was so low it burrowed beneath the plates and napkins.

No one heard her except him. Unacceptable.

Benjamin pounded his hand on the table.

The whole family stilled.

"Elodie has something to say."

She gave him a nod, then looked each person in the eye, one after the other. "Ever since returning home, I've been racking my brain to find some way to help others affected by the war—"

"You've done enough to help—"

"Mama, please. They didn't break me. I can do more." As she spoke, her hand relaxed, her fingers slowly curling. "Charlie, if I could raise money somehow for Heroes of Hope Hill, are there services you can provide to families like the Everharts?"

Charlie's eyes popped open. Her lips moved before any words came out. "Yes! We can provide counseling, loans, gifts, scholarships, if we have the money."

Elodie placed a bite of chocolate pie in her mouth and then dabbed her napkin where the two most perfect lips in the world came together. "I'll think of something." She pushed back her chair, stood, then kissed her mother's cheek. "Great pie, Mama." Elodie disappeared into the family room.

Mrs. Wise began to rise, but Mr. Wise's hand on her arm settled her back into the chair. He looked at Benjamin. "Stella, let's let Ben check on her."

"Yes, sir." Ben waved off Rhoda's hand, which, like an annoying mosquito, touched the nape of his neck. As he rounded the doorframe, he found Elodie unpacking the nativity set. Carefully, she unrolled each figurine from the newspaper and placed it in front of the wooden crèche. She flattened the newsprint and pointed to the headline of an article dated just after Christmas last year.

" 'Local Man Killed in Belgium,' " she read. " 'Mrs. Frank Dover received news that her husband, an infantryman, was killed earlier this month while defending the port of Antwerp. He is survived by his wife, his parents, Joyce and Elmer Dover of Park Street, and his two-year-old son, Frank Jr.' " Her fingernail marked an invisible line beneath the child's name. "Benjamin, if I can come up with an idea for a fundraiser to help the soldiers and their families, would you help me plan it?"

"You know I will." He unwrapped Joseph, handling the figure like a precious jewel. If he broke another piece, she'd never forgive him. Placing it beneath the roof of the crèche right next to Mary's kneeling form, he sang along to the song playing on the radio—"Chattanooga Choo Choo." Was she also thinking of the night they danced to that song?

"We could have a dance—a Christmas dance. We could invite the families but also people with deep pockets." Her words prattled faster with every detail about food, decorations, and possible locations. As she spoke, her spine lengthened. "With all the hoopla about the 'Battling Belles of Bataan,' maybe I could give a speech or show that star—"

"*That star?* You mean the Bronze Star?" He laughed at her near-constant humility.

"Yes, that one." Color tinged her cheeks. She was more alive than he'd seen her since she returned. "I could use my celebrity for good. Turn the darkness into light."

She leaned toward him in her excitement—almost close enough to kiss. Her nearness was entrancing.

"I wouldn't expect anything else from my girl." His thumb grazed her cheek. "I'm completely at your service, El. Anything you want, I'll get it for you. Just have to promise me one thing."

"What's that?"

"A dance," he said.

She smiled. "You got it."

His fingertips trailed down her jaw, settling on the side of her neck. Her skin was smooth as glass. Her eyes as soothing as the French sky when his feet were surrounded by bloodstained rubble. All those wasted years he'd spent during the war, protecting one man on a propaganda campaign, when he could have been doing more for his country, for his brothers-in-arms, for the interned people like Elodie. This was what kept him going. That one day he might dance with her again. And maybe kiss her the way he should have before the war.

"Benjamin." His name on her breath filled him with courage he'd lacked back in '41. He moved toward Elodie, and her eyes grew wide. "Do you think you could get Clyde Irving to make an appearance?"

CHAPTER 2

Y ou're a tough one to get ahold of, Clyde." Ben relaxed his grip on the telephone's handset. If his wartime pal hadn't answered this time, Ben was going to hop on the next bus to Los Angeles and track him down.

"If I weren't, everyone would get a piece of me. You know that." Clyde's movie star voice slid over the line smoother than hydraulic oil. However, Clyde Irving wasn't one to shy away from fans, cameras, or a good press opportunity. Over the years they'd spent together, Ben had seen the way Clyde offered pieces of himself to every passerby. "How are you, Benny? It's been too long. Have you reconsidered my offer to come out to Hollywood to be my assistant? There's a whole lot of pretty girls out here who'd love to meet an all-American kid like you."

Kid. Clyde was only five years older than Ben, although he acted younger than Rhoda. That didn't stop him from offering his wisdom.

And Clyde's favorite subject to lend advice about? Women.

"Nah. I'm calling about something else."

"Oh, that's right. You're back home with that pretty gal pal of yours. Goldilocks."

"Elodie."

"Goldilocks. Elodie. One and the same. Let me guess. You came back, dropped down on one knee, and now you've got the house, the wife, and the baby on the way."

"Not exactly." Ben hadn't hidden his adoration for Elodie from Clyde. They'd become friends of sorts, in the dark of night when the cameras shut off and they were just two soldiers in a foreign land dredged with the muck of war. And yeah, Ben had talked a big game about all that he planned to do when he saw Elodie again. It would involve just what Clyde had mentioned.

But the Elodie that Ben had parted from before the war had returned with a shadow lurking behind her. They all had. And the cottage with a front porch and a big oak tree needed to be put on hold. Not that she'd changed entirely. She was still Ben's childhood chum, but she needed to find her place again. Maybe this fundraiser would help.

"My manager wants me to settle down. Can you believe that? Clyde Irving settle down with just one woman? Foolishness. But he says it would be good for my image."

Just last week, Clyde had been spotted out with yet another young starlet. This one barely eighteen. The two were caught canoodling late into the night outside a Hollywood bar. While Middle America didn't love his gallivanting ways, they were still fascinated by his celebrity. And he'd bring in the big bucks for Elodie's cause.

"I have another idea for how you can rebuild your image," Ben said. "Elodie is hosting a fundraising ball on December 23. The money will go to helping veterans adjust to their lives at home as well as families whose soldiers won't come home at all. It's something she's passionate about and—"

"You're passionate about her."

Ben said nothing.

"You need me to make an appearance? Over Christmas?"

Clyde didn't have family. It was a topic they'd bonded over. But whereas Ben lost his father in '37 and his mother one year later, Clyde had been orphaned before he reached the age of ten. Another difference? Clyde liked to brag that he preferred to spend his holidays with a bottle of liquor. It'd be good for him to experience a Christmas in Hope Hill.

"It's a nice little place. Not the worst spot to celebrate Christ's birth."

Clyde scoffed. "Will I get to meet Elodie? The way you rattle on and on about the girl, I wonder if she exists at all. She might be one of those angels that book of yours speaks of."

"You mean the Bible?" Ben laughed. "You should pick one up. It won't burn your fingertips if you touch it."

"And read a list of all my sins? No, thank you," Clyde said. "I'll have to clear my schedule, but I can make that happen. We both know I owe you one."

Yes. Ben knew that all too well.

Judy Garland's voice spilled through the Chevrolet's radio. The toasty air kissed Elodie's face as she sat in the passenger seat next to Charlie. Through the windshield, the abandoned airplane hangar towered into the Missouri sky. Funny how the sight of an ugly steel building could summon sprinkles of joy. But there was a time not so long ago when Elodie, surrounded by concrete walls, shacks, the jungle, and fencing, wondered if she'd ever see anything like this again. Such a silly thought. She wouldn't share that with her sister. Now Ben? She could share that with Benjamin. He'd never think her silly.

She craned her neck to see if his old truck was in sight. Not yet. His shift as a mechanic on base ended only fifteen minutes ago. But soon she'd hear that old rumbling engine—a sound that, for some reason, was good for more than mere sprinkles of joy. Instead, she felt a blizzard of it whenever Benjamin was near. It swirled around her, lifting her hair off her neck and blanketing her with reminders of all the good that the war hadn't stolen.

"This song. . ." Charlie scooched across the bench seat, then latched onto the crook of Elodie's arm, hugging her close. "When I saw *Meet Me in St. Louis* last year in the theater, and she sang this song, I threw my box of popcorn on the ground and ran out of the theater."

Ooh. Must have been serious. Charlie loved her popcorn. Even more, Charlie, a big proponent of rationing, hated wasting food of any kind.

"All those promises she made about *next year*? I didn't believe one word of it. That loved ones would all be gathered 'round the tree together. That our troubles would vanish. With you still captured? My faith truly faltered."

"Aw, Charlie."

"Luckily, Ben stopped me from causing too big of a scene out there on the street. While I was trying to find a way to climb up to the marquee—I was going to tear down every letter from the movie title so no one else would see it—he talked sense into me."

Elodie stared hard at the hangar doors. "You went to the movie with Benjamin?"

Judy finished her song, and the jingle of a local shop's advertisement began. Charlie didn't answer. Ben had returned from duty last November, almost three months before Elodie's liberation. Why should she be so concerned, anyway?

"Did Mama tell you? Three boys from town are scheduled to arrive at the train station on the twenty-first, including George Weston."

"The same George that Rhoda has been writing to?"

"The very one. He'll be home for Christmas. And the ball."

"Charlie, what if the fundraiser was also a homecoming for George and the other men on the transport? The crowd will love to see them. And they may give more when they see the heroes their money will be helping."

Charlie grinned. "That's a fine idea. I'll have Rhoda write George about it and make sure he's on board. What about Clyde Irving? Will he make an appearance?"

"No word yet. Benjamin promised me he'd make it happen though."

"If he promised, then Clyde will be here. Ben's the reliable sort." Charlie sucked in a long, slow breath. A trick Elodie remembered Daddy had taught Charlie during childhood to force her to think through the words threatening to dart off her tongue. It didn't always work. "Hey, El. Do you plan to bring a date to the ball?"

"No. Why?"

"Have you thought much about dating, marriage, men in general?"

"Funny you should ask." Elodie brushed a stray hair off her forehead. She lifted her arm free of Charlie's hold, then worked to repin the tendrils at her crown. Difficult without a mirror, but if it looked a fright, only Charlie and Benjamin would see. And he didn't give a lick about what she looked like. "I always thought I'd be married by now. To a tall, strapping fella. With a kind face and a sophisticated style. Like Cary Grant or Jimmy Stewart."

"Clyde Irving?"

"Goodness. No. He's too handsome."

"Well, if you're opposed to handsome, I guess Ben is off the ballot."

Charlie found Benjamin attractive? Elodie rubbed a hand up the lapel of her coat then back down again. She'd expected Rhoda to go after Benjamin. Rhoda loved any boy who paid her mind. But Charlie wasn't to be swayed by an easy smile or smooth line. Any man she chose would have to be intelligent, funny, driven, and yes, handsome. That was Benjamin in a nutshell.

And Charlie was smart, witty, and full of life. Why wouldn't Benjamin fall for her in return? He'd be good for Charlie. He could encourage her passions while also tempering her fiery ways. So why did her chest ache at the thought?

"I'm not so sure I'd be a good girlfriend or wife to anyone right now," Elodie said. "There's still too much muddling my head. I can't imagine taking in a picture show or going to a fair. To pretend the world is fine? Every day we're learning more and more about the atrocities of the past few years. You understand, don't you?"

"Of course I do. But wouldn't you love for a brave soldier to get the help he needs so he could go to the fair and to picture shows without the memories of war haunting him?"

Elodie nodded.

"That's why our work is so important, Sis. We're bringing light one way or another."

The chug of an engine approached from the road. Benjamin's truck pulled up beside them. And when his eyes met Elodie's, his crooked smile beamed. She gave a small wave in reply. Elodie's joy, while still present, had calmed a bit from the heavy talk. Ben's eyes shifted to Charlie's, and he nodded. Charlie winked. *Winked.* At her Benjamin.

No. That wasn't right. Benjamin was a friend to her whole family. Elodie didn't get to claim him. Again, her joy dipped. Why though?

"I wonder who Benjamin will escort to the ball. Maybe he'll take a friend. That's allowed, you know." Charlie nudged Elodie—not as hard as she would have years ago. "Now, let's go see this place."

Inside the hangar, Ben could almost see the dance come to life as Elodie pointed out where the food and punch would be served and how the tables could be set up. He was glad for this project. Even moments ago, outside between their cars, darkness caped her eyes, just as it had so often since she'd returned home.

"We'll build the stage here, big enough for a full band." Elodie waved her arm toward the south end of the space, which currently held a stash of gasoline cans. She dipped her chin and spread her delicate hands out from her waist like she was smoothing sheets on a bed. "And this will be the dance floor."

An elbow dug into his ribs.

He pinned Charlie with a glare, but her eyes were full of challenge. The same elbow that had assaulted him now turned into a chicken wing that batted the back of his arm, nudging him forward. Ben refocused on Elodie.

She stood still, watching his exchange with her sister. Her

expression had sobered. Why?

"It's the perfect place for a dance floor. Let's give it a try." He moved forward, taking her hand and easing her toward him.

"Wouldn't you rather dance with Charlie? She's much better than me." Elodie spun on her heels and walked toward the space she'd designated as an auction display.

Over his shoulder, Ben glanced at Charlie.

She shrugged. "El, I promised I'd stop at the market for Mama. Ben will have to drive you home."

"I thought you had all these ideas to share."

"I do. I'll tell you later though. Mama wanted roast tonight, so I should get a move on. See you." Charlie scurried to the door before the confusion wrinkling Elodie's brow could fall to her lips.

Ben might have been miffed at Charlie's awkward exit if he wasn't so happy to have time with Elodie alone. Charlie was a fun kid sister–type, but after too much time with her, he was always ready for her metaphorical naptime. He joined Elodie but didn't try for the dance again. One rejection was enough for the day.

"I can build the stage if you want. Your father could help, I'm sure. I've got the hands for it, and the know-how." He held up his hands, only to notice how the oil from his job had stained his skin and lined his fingernails. Quickly, he dug them deep into his coat pockets.

Her gaze followed the movement then bounced back up to his eyes. "What about me? I can help. I know how to use a hammer. And as I recall, you only got through geometry with my help. And French class too."

"So you thought."

"What does that mean?"

"Did you ever consider that the reason I let you help me with my homework was so you'd lean in close to me?"

Elodie blinked several times before she responded. "Why would you do that?"

"Because when you concentrate hard on something, you whisper real soft. It's cute." Ben rocked on his heels. He should stop there, but he didn't want to. He ached to show her his true feelings. He stepped toward her, pausing at her side to speak into her ear. "And you smell nice too." He moved past her, checking the wall. A draft was coming in from somewhere. It would be hard enough to keep this place warm for the dance without rogue breezes finding their way in. Plus, this kept his flushed face out of sight. He wasn't used to such forward flirtation with her. Flirtation that dared take them beyond friendship. Or, in her perception, beyond brother and sister.

"Ben, do you. . . ?"

He turned to find her chewing her lip. That was no good. "Do I what?"

"Are you interested in Charlie?"

He nearly swallowed his tongue. Charlie? "Why on earth would you think that?"

Her blue eyes rounded beneath arched brows. "Because you two get along so well, and you share these moments. And last year you saw *Meet Me in St. Louis* with her."

Ben might've bored a hole in the ceiling if he concentrated on it any harder. How much to say? "I asked her to see the movie with me because I needed to be near a friend. I'd just gotten back from Europe, and I wasn't doing well. Not at all. Frankly, neither was she. I went with her because she was the closest person to you that I could find. And I needed to be near someone who was just as worried about you as I was."

"I heard you followed her out of the theater when she got upset."

"Yeah. She needed to calm down." He rubbed the back of his neck, still remembering how tight those muscles had been as he'd fretted over Elodie's safety for more than three years. "Elodie, I don't know if I ever told you this, but I missed you like crazy during the war."

"Oh Benjamin. I missed you too."

"I'm not interested in dating your sister." *I want to date you,* his heart begged his lips to say. But he needed to go slow with this.

She nodded but said no more. Perhaps he was mistaken, but relief appeared to wash over her. He'd never known her to be jealous of anything—not the neighbor girl's new bike or her friend winning the homecoming queen title. But he might have finally found something Elodie wanted only for herself. The possibility, slim as it was, brought a smile to his face.

"This dance is going to be a great success. The soldiers will get a fantastic welcome back. It will be a grand celebration for the whole town. And you'll raise a ton of money that will help these heroes and families." Ben urged himself not to pause too long. Otherwise Elodie would give him that same old lecture that he was a hero too. Not so. "Which brings me to the big news I wanted to share with you. I finally heard back from Clyde. He'll be here."

Elodie's brows shot higher than a cork on V-E Day. And the widest smile he'd seen in four years etched her face. Joy. Over Clyde. Once again, Ben's dream was overshadowed by his friend. When Elodie's bright blue eyes hazed and the first tears spilled over her lashes, she threw herself at him. His arms needed no message from his brain to know what to do next. She fit so perfectly against him that he figured God designed him for the specific purpose of embracing her. Growing up, he'd always wanted to be taller than his five-foot-ten frame, but he'd grown to like having only a few inches on Elodie. He liked that when they hugged, the slope of her slender neck aligned with the curve of his shoulder. It would make a kiss effortless if they ever got to that point.

"Thank you, Benjamin." Elodie's voice was small, and Ben wanted to take it and place it in his breast pocket to keep near his heart forever.

CHAPTER 3

How's the planning coming? You aren't overdoing it, are you? You look tired." The concern on her mother's face stretched wider than Manila Bay.

"Mama, I'm fine."

"If it gets to be too much—"

"I'll walk away. But it's all coming together swell. The community has been dropping off strings of Christmas lights, tables, and chairs. We've even had all the lumber for the stage donated. Benjamin and I will start building it tomorrow after we get off work."

"You let him build that. If you want, you can hold the nails."

"Oh Mama. . ."

Benjamin appeared at the back door, carrying two boxes. Elodie hurried to open the door for him. He passed by her, noting his thanks, then made his way to the family room. A few seconds later, he returned. "I think those were the ornaments and stockings. Just one more box. Are there more in the attic, Mrs. Wise?"

"No, dear. I think that's it."

"Okay, I'll be back in a jiffy." Benjamin flashed a grin at Elodie before disappearing out the back door that led to the garage.

"What a smile," her mother said.

"He's got a great one."

"I was talking about yours." Her mother dug her hands into the biscuit dough and began to combine the wet and dry ingredients. "Benjamin Gabriel will make a fine husband one day."

Elodie shook her head. At least her mother wasn't pushing her into marriage. Benjamin would have to deal with that himself. "Yes, he will. What a lucky girl she'll be. I'm going to look in the boxes for old time's sake."

"You do that, sweetheart."

In the family room, Elodie unfolded the flaps of the first box marked ORNAMENTS, finding its contents scarce. Where had all the colorful bulbs gone? Besides the heirloom nativity, they'd been among her mother's prized holiday decorations. Every year she'd added to the collection, even during the lean years before the war.

"Rhoda, where did all our ornaments go?" Her sister, who had been lying on her stomach and reading in front of the fireplace, didn't bother to look up.

"Mama pitched them."

"When?"

"After you left. No, after we joined the war, I think."

"Why on earth would she do that?"

"They were German glass, remember? She wouldn't let us hang those. No siree."

"What did you hang on the tree?"

Rhoda splayed her book flat on the ground, its front and back cover faceup. Then she rolled herself up to a seated position and sighed. "We didn't have one for that first year. In '42 there weren't men to chop them down, so the lots were empty. And we were too busy collecting materials for the war effort to do it ourselves. Not sure anyone was in much of a mood to celebrate Christmas anyway. Talk about crummy."

Elodie's thoughts trailed to her recent holidays behind fences topped with shards of glass. Even last Christmas Day, when the planes dropped flyers promising that liberation was near, it was hard to celebrate while the camp lost several to starvation every day. Thank the Lord that Rhoda didn't understand the full breadth of what others had endured. Still, Elodie forced herself to feel compassion for her little sister. "That must have been tough."

"We simply went to church and shared a meal. A small one with sausage disguised as turkey. Isn't that a hoot?"

"It sure is," Elodie said. Sacrifices were made on the home front as well. She mustn't forget that.

Benjamin rounded the corner with a large box propped on his shoulder. "I've got it."

"Thanks, Benny!" Rhoda popped up from the ground, then kissed him on his cheek. When she did, his eyes flickered to Elodie's, but she glanced away. Goodness. Her stomach twisted something awful. Like when she'd gone too long without food—a feeling she knew too well.

The box slid in front of her.

" 'Visca,' " she read off the side of the box. "What is this?"

Rhoda pulled on what appeared to be branches. "Our tree. It's not very big. A tabletop display is all."

Elodie hid her grin with a hand. Even before she had time to form words, the box got yanked away, leaving artificial needles

245

pinched between Rhoda's fingers.

Her mother heaved the box up into her arms. "This year we'll get a real tree. Like that last Christmas we were all together. They have some down at the lot. A fir, perhaps. There's no need to bring that hideous thing back out."

"Mama, I like it." Rhoda flattened her hands against the ground. Her brows pinched together above the bridge of her button nose.

"We'll have an old-fashioned Christmas or none at all." Mama's tone was resolute. Then she was gone along with Rhoda's tree.

Across from Elodie, Rhoda sat back and crossed her arms. Her lips pursed. She shot a brief glare in Elodie's direction before swiveling her whole body toward the window where flurries fell. It wasn't fair. At only eighteen, she was still forming childhood memories. And Elodie's presence was unspooling them all.

Benjamin rubbed his hands together. "Rhoda, what do you say we head down to the tree lot and pick out a tree so grand it will flatten my tires?"

She perked up. "Just me and you?"

"And Elodie. If she wants to go."

Rhoda groaned.

Elodie inched closer to her sister. "Rhoda, I bet that little tree looks pretty all lit up with lights." She placed a hand on her sister's forearm, but Rhoda shrugged it off.

"Go have fun with your boyfriend already." Before Elodie could lift her jaw off the floor, Rhoda had jumped up and skirted out of the room.

"What was that about?" she asked Benjamin.

Red splotches crept up his neck. "I have no idea." His voice cracked on the last syllable. He cleared his throat and held his hand out to her. "Come on. Let's go get that tree."

Benjamin finished loading in the back of his truck the tree Elodie had deemed perfect. Sap glued two of his fingers together. He separated them, but the stickiness remained.

Elodie eyed him. "Did you get a sliver?" She took his hand in hers, only to drop it. Her soft intake of breath sent his nerves into a tizzy. "Ew, sap."

He laughed, prompting her to lay a playful slap on his arm.

"You could've warned me." She studied her fingers, and then, with a smirk on her face, rubbed her hand down his coat, shoulder to ribs. Her touch was positively electric, like one caress on this tree could set it aglow, no lights required.

Lord, let her feel this too. Not that I deserve her. No one could. She's the closest thing to an angel I've ever seen.

Slowly, she withdrew her hand. Her crooked smile went flat as she raised her eyes to his.

"You practice your profession faithfully. Isn't that what that nursing pledge says? The one you recited at your graduation. You can't help but jump in, whether it's a sliver or something worse." He reached down into a pile of shoveled snow, grabbed a handful, then rubbed it between his palms. Once it had melted, he took Elodie's hand, and, not knowing the exact spot the sap had touched, methodically rubbed his thumb in circles over her palm. When she didn't recoil her hand, he continued, stroking his thumb down each of her fingers, knuckle to perfectly manicured nail. Her skin was so fair and unblemished compared to his knicked-up and stained hands. Embarrassment gnawed at him, and he released his hold on her.

"Thank you. I think you cleaned it off." Her voice was softer than usual, and she hadn't backed away.

"I should get you home."

"Or we could make a night of it." A touch of mischief danced across her face.

"Won't your mother worry?"

"Not if I'm with you," she said. "After all, the government trusted you to keep our country's most prized celebrity safe in a war. She knows there's no safer place for me than by your side." After she looped her arm around his, all other arguments fled.

A half hour later, they walked beneath colored bulbs that had been strung streetlight to streetlight. Main Street in Hope Hill was bustling on this Saturday night with shoppers eager to stuff presents beneath their trees Christmas morning. Lines of people waited outside the cinema to see *The Bells of St. Mary's*. Although he wouldn't mind taking in a flick and maybe placing his arm around her if she gave off the right signals, Elodie wanted to see the window displays. With the way she hugged his arm every time a chilly breeze passed between alleyways, that was just fine by him. And since it was cold, she remained quite close.

They paused a long while to take in a department store's window display. Children and their sleds rode a mechanical track down a glistening hill and around the back before appearing again at the top moments later. In the foreground, ice skaters skidded and twirled on a frozen pond. Benjamin, however, struggled to keep his focus off Elodie. How her face could still show such joy after the horrors she'd seen was a wonder. He could spend his whole life presenting her with simple pleasures if it meant seeing that gentle smile.

"I'd like to go sledding one day," she said. "It's been too long since I've gone."

"Next time it snows, I'll take you." The realization of what was to come struck him. Although Missouri was caught in a cold front, there was no more snow in the weather report. The likelihood of snow between now and the New Year was slim. It was high time he told her his news. Even if it might make her sad. Even if it would wreck her notion of having all her loved ones reunited in Hope Hill for the foreseeable future. He needed to tell her sometime.

"I got a call—"

"I used to hate snow—"

They spoke at the same time, then chuckled together.

Elodie tucked her arm around his and pulled him along the sidewalk toward the next storefront. "I was saying I used to hate snow. After college, I thought joining the Army Nurse Corps for a stint in the Philippines would be heavenly. And for six weeks, it was. Sun, sand, and sea. I had these wild notions of adventure and romance."

Ben's chin jerked her way. Here he'd been waiting for her to return to him after school, imagining a future for the two of them. No one was more shocked than he was to hear the announcement that she'd joined the military and accepted an assignment across the world. Yet she'd been so happy, he couldn't say a word. "When you shipped out, I was sure you'd meet someone. A doctor maybe. Or the rich owner of a sugar plantation. You'd have a tropical honeymoon then come back to Missouri a married woman."

Her cheeks lifted into a smile. "Me too. There was one man—a soldier from Fort Stotsenberg. He and I, along with another nurse and his friend, went picnicking on the beach one day. We had a grand time, splashing in the surf and relaxing beneath the palms. When the sun dipped low on the horizon, he kissed me."

The image slugged Ben hard in the belly so that the next breath seemed as far away as Bataan.

"Tuck was his name. From St. Louis. He was nice and polite although a bit dull. Not very interesting to talk to. Whenever there was a lull in the conversation, he would point out all the different birds around us—their species and unique characteristics. He'd mimic their calls even." Elodie's laugh was almost soothing enough to take away the ache. But then her smile fell. "As you might guess, it never went further than that one kiss. He asked me for a date, but I said no."

Her steps slowed in front of the next window. Inside, Santa Claus was placing presents beneath a Christmas tree. A model train circled the tree and passed by a toy gun. The lights on the tree glinted off the barrel of the rifle, draping it in red.

"The next time I saw him, he'd been hit with enough shrapnel to fill a gallon bucket—the result of one of the bombings on Corregidor. He didn't make it home to St. Louis." She blinked several times, forcing her tears to remain unshed.

"I'm sorry, Elodie." He placed his free hand over hers where it rested on his forearm. "Tuck seemed like a good guy."

"I didn't know him well, but he was nice enough. I only let him kiss me because—" Her lips closed, their heart shape reflecting in the glass.

Ben tucked her arm against his side. "You only let him kiss you because. . ."

She looked up at him and grinned. Either the red curtains surrounding the display cast a hue across her normally porcelain skin or she was blushing. "Because he looked like you."

CHAPTER 4

With a flick of Elodie's wrist, the hammer came down on the nail's head lightly, just enough to break through the wood's surface. After a full day of serving medicine at the base hospital, it felt good to do something with her hands that required muscle and force.

"That should do it." Benjamin stepped onto the stage, gingerly at first. When the plywood didn't give way, he jumped a few times. He moved a few feet to the left and jumped again. The wood creaked. "I think we need another nail right here." From a tin, he grabbed a carpentry nail and placed its point in line with the others.

Elodie kneeled beside him, hammer in hand.

"Hit it," he said.

"What if I get your fingers?"

"I trust you." His innocent grin beamed as he pinched the nail to hold it steady.

A couple of taps set the nail. He slid his hand back, giving her room to dig the nail deep into the stud.

Before he could get away, she grabbed his hand and pressed it tight to the stage. She held the hammer up and gave a teasing smirk. "Hang on, one more hit." She pretended to zero the head of the hammer on his thumb.

He laughed as he recoiled, taking her hand with him. "Oh, I don't think so!"

As she had so many times in the past few weeks, she reflected on how their hands fit together. This time, however, he pulled away, folding his hands tightly on his lap.

"Benjamin Gabriel, what are you doing?"

"My hands are stained with grease."

"And?"

"I'm embarrassed."

"Embarrassed about holding down a good job that you love? And one you excel at? Nonsense."

"I just doubt a woman would want to hold one of these calloused paws in her dainty hand."

"Well, I wouldn't want you with a woman who whittled down all your expertise for building and fixing things into a little grease anyway."

"Yeah, you're pretty good at building things yourself." He stood and perused the stage around them. Satisfied, he rested his hands on his hips and nodded. "Looks good to me. What do you think?"

"It should work." Elodie pushed herself off the stage floor then dusted off her aching knees. The accomplishment she felt outweighed the sore muscles she had from five nights of stage building. She also quite enjoyed the way Benjamin peered at her through the process of it. Impressed. Maybe proud. Not quite surprised though.

After all, they'd built a tree house together when they were thirteen. Of all people, Benjamin knew her capabilities.

Time with Benjamin was soothing to her weary soul. All the world had expectations of her—her town, her family, even herself. Some expected her to act like a heroine straight out of the movie *So Proudly We Hail*. But Claudette Colbert she was not. Others treated her with such fragility—a victim of war. Still others, like Rhoda, resented her for circumstances Elodie had no control over.

Not Benjamin. Yes, he still looked out for her, pausing the work when her body weakened and bearing most of the heavy lifting, but he didn't coddle her or keep her wrapped in quilts. And to him, she was still plain old Elodie Wise. Anything heroic was attributed to the nursing profession in general.

He hopped off the stage then turned and held out his arms. "We're a great team."

"We are, aren't we?" She bent forward, placing her arms around his neck.

He gripped her waist and lowered her to the floor. Then, together they looked over their handiwork. The stage would be big enough for a band, and Clyde Irving would look excellent standing at the center.

She still couldn't believe her luck. Clyde Irving would be cohosting Hope Hill's fundraiser with her, all thanks to Benjamin. "Come on. I have a celebratory treat for us." She tugged him over to one of the round tables they'd borrowed from the Episcopal church. They sat side by side in chairs dropped off by a group of high school teachers. Over the next two weeks, people all across town would deliver linens, decorations, dishes, and silverware, eager to help the returning soldiers in any possible way. From her purse, Elodie retrieved two bottles of Coca-Cola and a bottle opener. She popped the cap off one and offered it to him.

Benjamin's chuckle bounced off the high ceiling and the walls before settling deep within Elodie. "Don't mind if I do." He accepted the bottle but waited for her to remove her bottle cap. When she did, they clinked their soda pops together before taking a swig.

Elodie's eyes closed in surrender to the bubbly sweetness. Instantly, she was back on Leyte Island, just after liberation, tilting back the best Coca-Cola in the entire world. Even then, her thoughts had fallen on Benjamin. After all, it was his favorite drink, and they'd shared many. She had wondered for the ten-thousandth time if he was still alive. She shook off the memory.

He slid a coin across the tabletop. "Penny for your thoughts."

"You never talk about your time in Europe."

His shoulders bobbed in a shrug. "Not much to tell. I had an assignment, and I did it. Nothing more, nothing less."

"An important assignment."

"Babysitting detail." He gave his head a small shake.

"A necessary duty." She studied his face as he stared down at the bottle in his hands. His dark lashes shielded his green eyes. How often had she imagined his face on every dying soldier she came across? She still felt the guilt-tinged relief when the man was *another* woman's dearest friend. "You told me that you, Clyde, and the production team stayed behind the lines, following the last of our troops after the battle ended. Were you ever in real danger?"

Benjamin scratched at his collar before lifting his eyes to her. Still, he was silent.

"You can tell me."

"Once. The crew wanted to get footage of Clyde flying a bomber, so we went up with a skeleton crew on a B-24." He seemed to chew his next words. "We were hit with some flak that killed one of the engines and tore up the fuel line. We had to land in enemy territory.

Luckily, I was able to splice and reconnect the tubing. But some German soldiers came upon us. We exchanged gunfire, but in the end, we were able to get out of there."

"That's. . .that's amazing. Why didn't you ever tell me?"

"Clyde's studio made me sign a nondisclosure agreement. Some of that footage is supposedly in his movie."

"The one coming out soon? *Enemy Skies?*"

"That's the one."

Elodie swallowed hard. "Were you hurt?"

Benjamin tilted back the soda pop once more. If he thought she'd forget the question she asked, he had another thing coming.

She nudged his foot with hers, although she wanted to stomp his toes for keeping this from her since she'd been back. "Tell me."

He heaved a deep breath. Then, after setting the bottle on the table, he squared his body to face her. He unfastened the top button of his gray coveralls, revealing his white undershirt. With the fingers of his left hand, he yanked the collar of his shirt out wide. The trapezius muscle above his clavicle was mangled, the skin surgically tied back together.

Elodie lurched forward, hoisting herself to her feet and into a nurse's posture. With the gentlest touch she could muster, she inspected the site. Thank the Lord, this bullet seemed to have gone cleanly through. Still, something clutched at her throat.

"It happened while I was working on the engine." He stretched his neck to the side so she could get the full view.

"When?"

"September 28 last year. That was Clyde's last mission. The studio decided that was enough, and he was discharged while I recovered."

"Does my family know?"

"No one does. Nondisclosure agreement, remember?"

"Why did you tell me?"

His shoulders rose and fell on his heavy breath. "Because I'm tired of keeping secrets from you."

"Oh Benjamin." She could have lost him. Without thinking, her other hand cradled his neck. He turned to her. With only a few inches separating them, Elodie found something hidden in the depths of his eyes. Something she'd seen in glimpses before, but never like this. Never this strong. It called to her.

His hand reached toward her but paused midair. Waiting for permission, perhaps. To do what though?

Noises from outside challenged the thudding of her heart.

Elodie straightened, turning her attention to the door of the hangar.

Muffled laughter sounded on the opposite side of the door, followed by a familiar booming voice.

"Swell. This is just swell," Benjamin said as he rebuttoned his coveralls.

When the door wrenched open, Clyde Irving strutted through.

Clyde Irving was confident, charming, and sociable on his best days, arrogant, smarmy, and brutish on his worst. He had the reputation of wooing every woman he worked with. And once he set his sights on something, he got it. Right now, he gaped at Elodie.

"Clyde, I wasn't expecting you so soon." Benjamin fought the temptation to step between Clyde and Elodie to break the trance the actor had fallen into.

"Well, old pal, I decided to clear off my schedule a bit and experience Christmas in the heartland. I hope you don't mind." Clyde sported a grin as big as the Hollywoodland sign itself.

"The heartland would love to have you spend the holidays here." Elodie's cheeks had pinked, and she sounded breathless.

Benjamin rubbed his neck where just minutes ago Elodie had placed her hand. "Clyde Irving, this is Lieutenant Elodie Wise."

"Hello." Elodie offered a handshake.

True to his nature, Clyde took her hand, kissed it, and moved his chin in a slow circle, caressing her knuckles with his thin mustache. The same move Clyde used to bed women all over Europe. Ben couldn't feel queasier.

"Elodie, you are far more breathtaking than your picture."

A stronger wave of nausea roiled through Ben.

"My picture?"

Finally, Clyde shifted his gaze to Ben, letting a glimmer of mischief pass between them. "Well, your picture is all over. The youngest of the Battling Belles of Bataan? And the prettiest, if I do say so myself. Your reputation precedes you. You are quite the heroine, aren't you?"

"I didn't do anything that any other nurse wouldn't have done. In fact, of the nurses who were there with me, I probably did the least."

"El, don't sell yourself short." Ben wasn't sure Elodie heard him, considering the way she studied Clyde's face.

"Thank you for coming out to help us raise money for the veterans," she said.

"Believe me, it's my honor. Besides, I missed my old friend here and wanted to come back and see him."

"It's good to see you too, Clyde. How are things going in California?"

"Sadly, not as much fun as usual."

"I find that hard to believe. You're always up for a good time."

"Maybe I'm maturing with age."

"Oh, I doubt that."

"Elodie, this is the site of the ball, correct?"

"Yes. Benjamin and I built this stage."

"You did a great job. You've got some muscles, don't you? Remind me not to get on your bad side."

"Elodie wouldn't hurt a fly."

"Pretty, strong, *and* sweet? I'm in love." A sly smile appeared on Clyde's face. When he spoke to her, his head dipped forward, breaking the gentlemanly plane between him and Elodie.

To Ben's dismay, Elodie wore that same sleepy smile as the women along the battle route in Europe. And Ben had also seen where those nighttime trysts led. He wouldn't let Clyde break Elodie's heart. And he certainly wouldn't let him use her the way he often did other women.

"Where are you staying?"

"We found a motor lodge a few miles from here."

"You should stay with me, Clyde," Benjamin said without thinking.

Elodie snickered. "Where's he going to sleep? You only have one room and one bed."

"I'll sleep on the floor. It's no problem." Ben had done it before, and he could do it again. Although this time he feared something more dangerous than bombs falling on him.

"Clyde, my parents have an apartment over our garage. You are welcome to stay with us. They won't mind. It isn't the largest space, but it's better than a motor lodge."

"Sounds like we've figured it out, eh, Ben?" Clyde winked, and Ben felt his blood curdle.

Mr. and Mrs. Wise would love for that room to find use. They offered it to him when he returned from the front, but he hadn't wanted to inconvenience the family with his presence. Clyde didn't mind barging in at all.

"Gabriel. It's been a long time." The voice of Clyde's manager weaseled into Ben's ear from across the hangar.

Ben squeezed his eyes closed. Better and better. "Hello, Richard."

The man slithered in from the cold. He wore the same awful sports coat he'd worn during the campaign. Ben had never understood the motivation behind wearing that jacket while strutting past villagers who'd lost their homes, livelihood, and often, family members.

"We're glad you called." Richard pulled Ben's arm, forcing him to leave Clyde and Elodie to fawn all over each other. As if they wouldn't have plenty of time for that over the next two weeks. Once the couple was out of earshot, Richard spoke. "Clyde's gotten himself in some trouble in Hollywood recently. The long-legged variety. We need some good press. We drove past the theater on Main Street. I'm thinking we move the premiere of *Enemy Skies* to right here in Hope Hill."

"When?"

"December 22."

"The night before the fundraiser?"

"Yes. It'll bring in big stars and big money for Miss Wise's cause."

"Does *Lieutenant* Wise know?"

"I'm guessing Clyde's telling her as we speak."

Across the room, Elodie clapped a hand over her mouth. It would be a great thing to raise more money. The town would likely benefit from the press, and the businesses along Main Street would thrive. There wasn't a downside that Ben could see. Elodie caught his eye. When her hand lowered, he saw the biggest smile. No wonder Clyde was struck. She was as pretty as an orchid in spring. And with this fundraiser coming together, she was in bloom.

"I know I can count on you to keep things straight here. I'll need your help with Clyde. I can't have him getting in trouble again. We need wholesome. We need goodness. We need purity." Richard's gaze fell on Elodie. "Yes, this should work out just fine. I'll set everything up with the theater. You keep an eye on Clyde as much as possible."

Still on babysitting detail. Now in his hometown. Ben clenched his fists and counted to twenty in his head. When that didn't dispel the anger, he lifted his eyes to the rafters.

Lord, help me get through this.

Richard glanced back at the small crew that had traveled with them—three men Benjamin didn't recognize. "Time to start making plans, boys." He joined them closer to the door.

Elodie bounced over to Ben, the happiest he'd seen her since she'd returned home. "Did you hear? About the premiere?" Her eyes glistened with unshed tears.

"I did. That'll be great. With all those funds coming in, you'll be able to help those soldiers."

"I know. And how exciting for the town as well!" Elodie sobered, lowering her voice. "Clyde asked if I'd accompany him to the premiere."

"As his date?"

"Yes, but not in a romantic way. It's Clyde Irving after all."

"Exactly. It's Clyde Irving. Elodie, be careful."

"Oh please. I survived an internment camp. I think I can handle the wily ways of a Hollywood tomcat. I'm only going with him to bring more awareness to the needs of the soldiers."

"You're right. You can handle this. You already are. Everything is falling into place."

"You don't mind me stealing your girl for a night, do you, Benny boy?" Clyde lifted one side of his iconic mustache. Because of him, countless actors had copied the same style.

Not Benjamin. He'd stay clean shaven as a good soldier should.

"Elodie's her own person, and I support every decision she makes, especially if it will help a good cause."

"We'll make sure the charity is at the forefront because Lieutenant Elodie Wise said so. Gorgeous *and* sweet. No wonder Ben carried that picture of you during the war."

Ben's stomach dropped to his feet.

Elodie tilted her head. "Picture?" She pinned her focus on Ben.

"Ben carried a picture of you in his Bible over in Europe. If I asked him nicely, he would take it out and regale me with stories about the two of you."

Ben tried to swallow the putrid taste in his mouth. It did no good. As Clyde rambled on and on about what Hollywood royalty might attend the premiere and ball, Ben worked to keep his breaths steady. Elodie also remained quiet until Clyde asked her for directions to her home. He'd grab his luggage from the lodge and be over soon. She offered step-by-step directions and politely escorted them out while Ben collected their tools and shut off the lights.

Outside the hangar, she stood peering up at the crystal-clear sky dotted with stars. It was late, with no trace of twilight left on the horizon. With no trace of the moon either, the darkness shrouded any emotion on her face. Ben placed his toolbox in the bed of his truck and joined her.

"El, I hope you aren't angry with me."

"Why would I be angry? Although I am curious. Was my picture the only one you had with you?"

"Yes."

She nodded. "The soldiers I tended often had pictures with them of someone back home. Sometimes they'd tell me all about her. Or stare at the picture during frightening times. I never imagined I'd be anyone's someone."

He longed to tell her everything he felt. But to her, they'd always just been friends.

"Did it help? To think of me?"

He recalled how the photograph felt warm between his fingers on the cold nights. How her eyes swept peace over him on the frightening days. How her smiling lips whispered promises of a possible future when the war seemed endless. "It did."

"Benjamin, is there anything you'd like to tell me?" She turned to him, her eyes as wide as he'd ever seen.

This was it. His moment to come clean. But telling her too much might jeopardize everything. She must feel it also. She looked pale even in this starlight, and her jaw was set at an awkward angle.

"There is something I need to tell you." He took a steadying breath. "I'm getting redeployed after the first of the year. To Japan."

CHAPTER 5

All at once, the Missouri ground seemed to crumble and sink to the earth's center, taking Elodie's heart with it.

"Japan?"

"Yeah. MacArthur put out a call a few months back for replacements for his Eighth Army to occupy Japan. With Fairfax Field halting operations for the Air Transport Command, I knew I'd be out of a job. So I reenlisted and requested that assignment."

Elodie resisted the urge to take hold of his coat sleeves and cling to him. What would he make of that? "Why would you volunteer for that?"

Benjamin outstretched his hands, palms facing up. "I need to do something of value for our country."

"This all comes down to your inferiority complex? Freud and Adler would've had quite a time with you, Benjamin Gabriel." Elodie had seen the brutality of the war's Pacific Theater. The thought of Benjamin entering the land where those severe mentalities had originated did more than send shivers up her spine. It petrified her, and it took time for her voice to work once again. "How long have you known?"

"I found out the day before Thanksgiving."

"And you didn't tell me?"

"I was going to, but you said you were thankful for having everyone in your life together in one place. I didn't have the heart to ruin the holiday for you. And then there was all the excitement with the fundraiser. I figured I could help you pull this off, and maybe it would ease the jolt of my leaving."

"You think helping me raise money will make me feel better about the loss of the person I care most about in this world?" Elodie wiped away the tears.

She expected him to offer her a handkerchief or perhaps even brush the tears off her cheeks. Instead, Benjamin turned away, raking both of his hands through his dark hair.

"I guess you'll have to take that picture with you again."

"Not possible." When Benjamin faced her, the starlight passed over the twin canyons between his brows, leaving the darkness to fester. "It fell out of my Bible somewhere in France in the summer of '44."

Elodie made her best attempt at a smile. "I suppose I'll have to get you a new one to carry with you."

"I'd like that. But for now, we should get you back home. If your parents see Clyde Irving lurking around your house, they're likely to call the police. From what I gather, he doesn't need any more bad press."

"Nice house. Quaint." As he spoke, he wore a steady grin that Elodie couldn't read.

Her parents' house was surely a far cry from his California residence, but it was home.

"Thanks. Come on in, but be quiet. I need to tell my parents you'll be staying in the guest room, and they're likely asleep." Elodie led the way into the kitchen. "Stay here. I'll be right back."

At the top of the stairs, she rapped on her parents' door before opening it. It was dark in the room, but in the shadows, she saw two lumps. "Mama, Daddy?"

"What's wrong?" Mama asked, popping straight up in bed.

"Nothing, Mama. Clyde Irving came to town early. He's going to stay over the garage. Is that all right?"

"Clyde Irving, the movie star?" Her father roused more slowly.

"That's right."

"Where is he now?" Mama asked.

A scream broke through the dark, followed by a thump, a crash, then a manly groan.

"The kitchen," Elodie said as she darted out the bedroom door, then down the stairs.

Once she flipped on the light to the kitchen, she found Charlie, backed up against the sink with a book clutched to her chest. Clyde was on the floor, slumped against the refrigerator shelves with white liquid dripping off his signature hair and down over his mustache.

"What happened?" Elodie asked.

"He—he was rummaging through our refrigerator. I thought he was a burglar."

"Sweetheart, what burglar would steal a bottle of milk?" Daddy reached for a kitchen towel behind Charlie. He handed it to Clyde.

Clyde towel-dried his hair and face. "Actually, I was aiming for the ham. You didn't have to hit me with your book." He reached in the refrigerator, grabbed the paper-wrapped veal cutlets from the market, and pressed the package against the back of his head. "What is it? *War and Peace?*"

"*Gone with the Wind.*"

"Figures. I give up the Rhett Butler role to Gable, and this is my payback."

Mama sighed loudly. "Charlie, say your apology."

"No. Why is he in our kitchen?"

"He's our guest." Elodie extended her hand to Clyde. "Mr. Irving, I'm sorry."

He accepted her hand and stood, wavering a bit until he steadied himself against the counter. "Call me Clyde."

"*Clyde* shouldn't be in our kitchen at eleven p.m." Charlie inspected her book for damage.

"*You* can call me Mr. Irving."

"I'll call you a taxi and send you right back to Hollywood," Charlie mumbled before strutting out of the kitchen.

"Your sister is. . .sweet," Clyde said to Elodie. "Is she single?"

Twenty minutes later, after Elodie had helped Clyde settle into his lodgings, she slid into bed next to Charlie.

"Is Hollywood all settled?" Charlie asked.

"He is. Sorry for frightening you."

"I'm tough."

Elodie mashed her lips together. Silence followed, and she urged the sob caught in her throat not to disturb it. She'd handled worse news than this before. But she'd never had her sister there to lean on. "Char—" The name cracked in half, and the first tears burst forth.

"What's wrong?" Charlie asked, pushing a lock of hair off Elodie's cheek.

"Benjamin told me he's getting transferred."

"Oh, I see."

"Did you know?"

"I did. I'm glad he finally told you."

"Charlie, I'm so sad."

"Of course you are. You love him."

Elodie nearly laughed. "That's true. He's the brother I always wanted."

"No, he's the brother *I* always wanted. For you, it's different."

"What do you mean?" The chill in the room raised gooseflesh on Elodie's arms beneath her nightgown. She pulled Charlie's blanket up to her chin.

"I see the way you two look at each other. Like a walk down the aisle is the next logical step."

"You're silly. Not Benjamin and I."

"Have you ever imagined kissing him?"

"Charlie!" Elodie squealed into her sister's pillow. "You shouldn't say such things!"

"Have you?"

She'd imagined it just tonight when she'd seen where a bullet had tried to take his life. Elodie rolled onto her back and stared at the dark ceiling. "Maybe. He carried a picture of me during the war. Clyde told me. The men in my ward carried pictures of their sweethearts all the time. I knew what it meant to them. I never imagined Benjamin saw me like that until tonight."

"He loves you, El. It's clear to everyone but you. What you two have is already pretty special. Imagine what it could be."

"That's what I'm afraid of. What if I begin to see him in that way, and then he leaves in three weeks?" Tears burned Elodie's eyes once again. "What good is imagining what can never be?"

CHAPTER 6

Ben's focus burned straight through the windshield to the road ahead. Anything to keep from seeing in the rearview mirror the way Clyde poured his attention on Elodie, inching closer to her with every turn. It was enough to drive a man mad.

"So I said, 'I don't care if you are Frank Capra. I'm not dancing a jig with a poodle!' Everyone on set busted a gut," Clyde said.

"I bet they did." Elodie's voice, as always, held a polite lilt. She had to be as bored by Clyde's endless rambling as Ben was.

A laugh burst from the passenger seat—an exaggerated guffaw that rattled the seats more than the potholes did. "Tell us more about all the famous people you know, Hollywood. Maybe a bit more about Katharine Hepburn's dog. Or Gregory Peck's bathtub. It's all incredibly fascinating."

"Charlotte Jessalyn Wise," Elodie scolded.

"Yes, Mother?"

Ben pulled the car into a parking space. "We're here." And not a moment too soon. If Clyde wanted a night out on the town, he'd get it. And luckily, it wouldn't take long for him to experience all the nightlife Hope Hill offered. But then again, Ben wasn't in a rush to drop Elodie and Clyde off at her house to continue his flirtations late into the night. Maybe he should've driven them all the way into Kansas City. Topeka, even.

"The Barking Beagle?" Clyde asked.

Charlie twisted in her seat to face Clyde. "It may not have swanky enough clientele for the likes of you, Hollywood, but it has good food and even better music."

"You don't think much of me, do you, Charlie?"

"Oh Clyde. You think about yourself enough for both of us."

Ben bit his bottom lip to keep his snicker at bay. He opened his car door and stepped out into the crisp Missouri air. Not as cold as a week ago when he and Elodie had been on this same street buying her family's Christmas tree and taking in the window displays, but still frosty enough to nip at his nose.

He held the door for Elodie. Fortunately, Clyde had removed his mitts from her shoulder long enough for her to step out of the car.

"Thanks for driving, Benjamin."

"Happy to."

"And thanks for coming along. I don't want Clyde thinking this is a date."

Benjamin leaned in close. "Considering how he kept pawing at you, I don't think he got that telegram."

Inside the Barking Beagle, the light struggled to cut through the smoky haze. Still, it was bright enough for Ben to note how many liquor-filled glasses covered the tables. Clyde seemed to notice too, considering how he worked his lips. Ben had his work cut out for him tonight.

The foursome nabbed a table on the edge of the dance floor where a few couples swayed to "It's Been a Long, Long Time." Elodie watched them for several moments before dragging her gaze down across the table, then up to Ben's eyes. When he caught her glance, she turned away, touching her cheeks with her fingertips. Their pale polish contrasted sharply with the rouged color rising to her face.

They hadn't spoken about the photograph since Thursday night. The topic hung heavily between the two of them. At least it hadn't frightened her away. They'd worked all day in the hangar painting the stage, and she hadn't once looked at him like he was a creep. In fact, the day had been comprised of small glimpses, almost curious in nature. Like he was a puzzle piece she was trying to place.

"Looking to wet your whistle?" The waitress's final word faded as she recognized Clyde's mug.

"Certainly." Clyde sang the title line to the Andrews Sisters' "Rum and Coca-Cola."

"Give us a minute, will ya?" Benjamin waited for the waitress to stumble away before addressing Clyde. "How about we stay dry tonight, eh, Clyde?"

"Where's the fun in that?" Clyde winked at Elodie.

"Christmas in the heartland. Isn't that what you said you wanted? I think it's best we leave the alcohol for the other patrons."

Clyde rolled his eyes but settled for a Coca-Cola without the rum. He was drunk enough on the attention of the others in the place. At least half a dozen times someone asked him for an autograph or handshake. Clyde was keen to oblige.

Not everyone appreciated the fanfare though. Charlie had been bumped and bustled in each one of the encounters—something that appeared to amuse Clyde quite a bit.

"Do we have a backup plan for a celebrity host?" Elodie's whispering breath tickled Ben's neck marvelously. "Charlie might just kill Clyde before we get to the twenty-third."

"Well, if she does, she'll have to dress up as him."

"A little hair dye and a cut? That's doable. The mustache will be tougher." She bumped his shoulder with hers. The smile she offered may as well have seeped into his very soul. For the first time since Thursday, she held his gaze, until a hand reached in front of her.

"Let's dance." Clyde stood above Elodie—more than six feet of leading man interrupting their moment.

The band played the first few notes of Glenn Miller's "In the Mood."

"I'm not a great dancer," she said.

"I am." Clyde grabbed her hand and tugged her from the seat. On the dance floor, he took her in his arms and began rocking her back and forth, then swinging her to and fro.

The hollowing ache in Benjamin's chest conflicted with the happiness at seeing the joy on Elodie's face. Pure delight. Around them the crowd cheered. Clyde's smooth steps and eager expression only urged them on. A light flashed—a photographer's bulb from the far side of the bar.

Ben could only swig his soda pop. Meanwhile, Charlie was all smiles.

"What are you so happy about?" he asked.

"Have you any idea how much publicity this will bring to the ball? That's the reason why Clyde's here, isn't it? This is fantastic."

"For the soldiers, sure."

"And for us. Elodie needs this. She needs to see that our citizens will look after the soldiers if she doesn't. Only then will she be able to move on with her own dreams."

"Is one of her dreams to take up with a movie star?"

"Of course not. But would it be so bad if this opened her eyes to the love story she's meant to have?"

Ben scoffed. "You forget. I know Clyde. He always wins. He gets the glamour, the glory, and the girl. Every time."

Charlie patted his shoulder. "Not this time. Have a little faith."

The next morning, Ben awoke to see the local newspaper jutting beneath the door to his room. He rubbed the sleep from his eyes, threw off his covers, and sat up in bed. The first rays of sunlight sprayed through his window and honed in on the picture taking up space beneath the headline. Elodie smiled as her pin curls froze midmotion. In the arms of someone whose face was blocked by the door. Ben fell back onto his bed, covered his head with his pillow, and groaned.

Chapter 7

Elodie stared into the dress shop's fitting room mirror, tugging at the loose folds of fabric. There was a time she might have filled out this dress. But her three-year-long death march of starvation and disease had robbed her of her once-ample curves. At least she'd survived. Others hadn't been so fortunate.

Tremors in her fingers released the silky material. Would they ever stop? Might she ever look back at her time in the war and not quake with panic? Elodie stretched her hand taut and silently sang,

The Lord is my light
and my salvation;
who-oom shall I fear?
The Lord is the strength of my life. . . .

The verse was enough to ease the trembling. Once again she

took in her reflection. If there was a way to bring more focus on the Heroes ball without her name in lights, she'd surely do it. Perhaps she could keep her coat on the whole time. It would be cold on the red carpet as well as in the drafty old movie house. She'd just seen a picture of Rita Hayworth at her premiere. Covered by a fur coat, you couldn't see her dress at all.

No doubt all eyes would be on her. Especially after this morning's newspaper article. And that headline? "Clyde Irving Woos Bataan Belle"? Absurd. That morning at church, she'd had no luck getting the editor to consider a retraction. News was news, whether it was steeped in facts or not. And as Charlie told her as they fell asleep, this kind of publicity could only benefit Elodie's cause.

"El, are you decent?" Charlie called from behind the curtain.

"You could say that."

"Good. Ben's here. He says something bad has happened."

"What?"

"He wouldn't tell me, but he said it's about the dance."

Elodie pushed back the curtain and hurried out of the dressing room, still wearing the premiere dress. Sure enough, Ben stood near one of the dress forms, his face wrenched into a grimace. But when he saw her, his sorrowful expression faded away at once. As she neared, his lips shaped themselves to make words, but alas, no sound came.

She folded her hands again and again. "What's happened?"

He stepped nearer. "Elodie, you look. . .beautiful."

Holding her arms outstretched, she took a gander at herself. She felt naked with no hose or shoes on. But there was something about his compliment when she wasn't completely covered and done up that warmed her from the inside out. And the way he looked at her just now? It made her wonder if Charlie was right about his feelings.

She gathered a breath and lifted a curl off her face. "Thank you, Benjamin."

He nodded but stood in place.

"What's happened?" she repeated.

The question broke whatever trance he'd fallen into, and the frown returned. "There's a storm over the Pacific. The soldiers—the local guys we're honoring at the ball—are on a ship that's been detoured through calmer waters. They'll be landing on American soil a couple of days late. And rumor has it that soldiers are struggling to get out of port cities. Everyone's trying to get home for Christmas, and it's caused major traffic jams at airports and train stations. And with Christmas only nine days away, it's only going to get worse."

Elodie clenched her arms across her stomach, but they yielded no comfort. "That's why we're doing all this. If they aren't here, it will be for nothing." She squeezed her eyes closed.

A warm palm rested on the side of her neck. When her eyes opened, Ben was close enough for Elodie to see the tiny scar on his chin from when he'd fallen out of their tree house years ago. What strange comfort this familiarity was when everything between them seemed to be changing.

"It won't be for nothing, I assure you." He leaned in, cutting the space in half. "You've inspired all of us to get involved. And the money will be waiting for them when they get here, whether that's for Christmas or not."

The night's soft breeze sifted through her layers, and Elodie pulled her coat closed over her ward dress. Still, the walk home from her shift felt good, even as the day gave way to night. A streetlamp caught the last remaining leaves on the tree branches—the stubborn ones trying with all their might to survive until spring. Not unlike her own prayer in Santo Tomas. *Help me survive this day, Lord.* She hadn't the faith to trust Him for three years, but one day? That much faith she had.

From a medical standpoint, the past two days at the hospital had been uneventful. Dull, even. She liked dull. She'd learned her lesson from wanting more out of life. After all, that was what had brought her to the Philippines in the first place—the dream of an exciting adventure. She now understood the beauty of the mundane, although she did wish to do more for her patients than merely hand them a cup with medication in it.

But from a gossip standpoint, the past two days had been anything but uneventful. Whispers and side glances between her fellow nurses were enough to boil her blood. Truth be told, she had no interest in Clyde Irving. Perhaps she'd once been curious about him. What young female wouldn't be? But she'd seen enough these past five days to satisfy that niggling feeling. Clyde was egocentric and a showboat. There was absolutely zilch that was genuine or authentic. And apart from an appreciation to him for coming here, she felt nothing toward the man.

Elodie neared the entrance to her family's driveway. The warm glow reached through the windows into the night, drawing her home. Oh how she'd missed this place and the people in it. She checked her watch, tilting it so the face caught the light from the front porch—a quarter past six. Dinner would be ready soon.

Inside the family room window, she saw Clyde's profile. Her family had welcomed him in, personality flaws and all. They were kind like that.

Elodie heaved a deep breath. She didn't want to entertain Clyde tonight. There was someone else she wanted to spend the evening with instead. Someone whose residence she'd passed by four blocks back. Someone with a knack for always saying the right thing at the right time.

She reached for the front door handle, but before she could touch it, the door swung open.

Benjamin stood, blocking the frame. "There you are. Your mother was worried, so I was coming to look for you."

"I walked instead of taking the bus."

He stepped out of her way, then shut the door after her. He helped her with her purse and coat, hanging them on the rack. When Elodie shivered, his warm hands slid up her arms and down again. "Cold walk?"

"Yes, it was. But this helps." Had he always had such nice lips? Gracious. Now she was staring at his lips. She forced down a swallow. "What are you doing here?"

"I'm supposed to keep an eye on Clyde, remember?"

"What kind of trouble will he get into here?"

"With Rhoda and Charlie? Who knows?" He pressed his lips together for a brief moment. "Guess I also wanted to see you. I've only got a little more time to spend with you, so. . ."

"I'm glad you did."

"Elodie Lila Wise, is that you?" her mother asked from the direction of the kitchen.

"Yes, Mama. I'm sorry I didn't phone."

"Don't apologize to me. Apologize to my poor nerves."

Over a meal of meat loaf, mashed potatoes, and creamed spinach, Elodie's family listened to Clyde's tales about high jinks on movie sets. Equally entertaining were the various expressions Charlie employed while listening to them. Ben also enjoyed the show, tapping Elodie's knee beneath the table whenever an especially eccentric look appeared on her sister's face.

"What can you tell us about *Enemy Skies*? We're all looking forward to the premiere. Were there any funny stories filming?" Rhoda asked.

Clyde wiped his mouth with a napkin. "Most of the movie was filmed on a soundstage in Los Angeles, but as Ben here can attest, there were several scenes filmed in actual combat."

Ben shifted in his seat, keeping his head low.

"Filming that, as you can imagine, was a bit more somber," Clyde explained.

"That was very brave of you, Clyde, joining the war effort. I'm glad neither you nor Ben was hurt," her mother said.

Elodie stiffened.

"That isn't exactly true," Clyde said. "Combat was harder than I expected. You fought, didn't you, Mr. Wise?" Clyde sneezed, setting loose a dark lock of hair into his eyes. "I apologize. I—" Again, he sneezed.

"I hope you aren't getting sick ahead of your movie premiere," her father said.

"I'll be fine, Mr. Wise. Thank you for your concern."

Rhoda, sitting at Clyde's side, stared down at her plate with disgust. "Ew. Clyde sneezed on my dinner. Can I be done?"

Once the dishes had been collected, Benjamin began washing them. Elodie joined him, drying the plates and silverware with a dish towel. She'd suddenly become more aware of him, the way he moved about the kitchen. And how masculine his hands looked covered with soap bubbles. She found herself mesmerized by the way the muscles in his forearms worked as he scrubbed her mother's plates.

"Elodie, are you listening?"

How many times had her mother called her name? "Yes, Mama?"

Elodie turned, knowing full well her face was burning as red as the dish towel in her hand.

"Bob Hope's on the radio. He's recording from San Francisco. Rhoda's turning it on now. When you and Ben are finished, you should join us in the family room."

She nodded, then rested her hand on his bicep. "Do you need to head home yet?"

"I'm in no hurry."

"Good." Elodie took the last dish from him, drying it as he drained the sink. She opened the cabinet. The spot for the dish was too high for her reach.

"I'll get that." Benjamin took the dish, his fingers dragging against hers in the process. He stretched, bringing his body closer to hers, and stealing her breath in the process. After he'd placed the dish and closed the cabinet, he grabbed her hand. "Ready for some laughs?"

From her spot next to Ben on the couch, Elodie laughed so hard she had tears spouting from the corners of her eyes as Bob Hope and company acted out a scene. Even Rhoda chuckled a few times, although she didn't seem to like how close Elodie was to Ben. Not that they had a choice. With Clyde sitting on her right and Charlie at the far end, the sofa was cramped.

Skinnay Ennis sang a new song, "Let It Snow!" while Mrs. Wise handed glasses of eggnog to each person.

"This song is terrible. It will never catch on," Clyde said before unleashing yet another sneeze. His eggnog sloshed over the side of his glass, splattering on his trousers.

Elodie placed the back of her hand on Clyde's forehead. "You have a fever, Clyde. Do you have chills or aches at all?"

"A bit." Clyde handed the drink back to Mrs. Wise. "I think I'll turn in a bit early." Clyde stood. With a cordial bow, he excused himself through the back door.

When Elodie didn't move from her seat next to Ben, a new joy that had nothing to do with Bob Hope's humor flooded through him. After the radio show ended, Mrs. Wise yawned. "Time we head to bed. Rhoda, you too."

"Mama, I'm eighteen. I can stay up."

"Young lady. . ." Mr. Wise's final syllable rose in both pitch and warning, prompting the youngest daughter to stomp out of the room. "Charlie, please check on Mr. Irving. See if he needs anything."

"Why? He's a grown man."

"He's our guest," Mrs. Wise said.

"Why me? Elodie's the nurse in the family."

Mr. Wise lowered his stare on Charlie, who promptly rolled her eyes. "Right away. I'll be sure to fluff his pillow. . .right over the top of his smug face."

"Oh Charlotte." Mrs. Wise shook her head.

Charlie stuffed her arms into her sweater and went to the back door. With the door handle in her hand, she turned. "I'd take his temperature, but we already know he's full of hot air." She was out the door before her parents could respond.

Meanwhile, Elodie buried her face in Ben's shoulder, which did nothing to hide the laughter shaking her torso.

"These daughters of ours. Nat, I blame you," Mrs. Wise said to her husband. "At least we have Benjamin to keep things on the up and up. Don't stay up too late, you two."

"We won't. Goodnight," Ben said.

"Are they gone?" Elodie asked, peeking from Ben's shoulder.

"Yeah. It's just us."

"Good." She lifted her chin, then rested it on his shoulder. "Sometimes I like it better this way."

"Me too."

Over the radio, the lyrics of "I'll Be Home for Christmas" plucked at Ben's heart.

Elodie adjusted her head until her cheek rested against him. "We were allowed to listen to some American radio occasionally at the camp. Our captors couldn't give us enough food to nourish us, but they'd allow us to listen to music." Half a laugh followed her words past her lips. "When this song played, the whole camp went silent."

"It always made me think of you. Sure, I wanted to come home. But more than that, I wanted to be wherever you were." He chewed his lip, urged his breathing to remain steady. His hand sat awkwardly on his thigh, mere inches from hers. Close, but not together.

She sat up, inviting space between the two of them. Worry wrought her brow. "I'm ashamed to say I wanted you there with me too. Isn't that awfully selfish? That at one point, I wished you were one of the soldiers under my care, even knowing that would have meant starvation and disease? But at least then I could've had you in my keeping. I could've had a confidant. Someone who understood. So selfish."

"That doesn't make you selfish, El. It makes you human."

Her gaze fell to her trembling hands in her lap. She extended her fingers, keeping them taut. "My parents don't understand. Every night my mother checks on me as I sleep. She opens the door, then leaves the hall light on—a nightlight of sorts, thinking it will help. I know she means well, but it's strange. I'm more frightened in the light than in the total darkness."

"Because of the blackouts." Ben sighed. He held out his hand,

and she matched her fingers to his. "Light made you a target during the bombings on Bataan and Corregidor, didn't it? It was the same for us in Europe. Even the smallest light felt like a threat."

"Yes." Her soft voice weaved through his thoughts. Whatever she wanted, whatever she needed at this moment, he'd offer. If only he could read her mind.

The back door slammed. Charlie groaned. "That boorish, insolent, no-good, grandstanding crumb of a man." She never even looked their direction as she clomped through the room and up the stairs in the foyer.

Elodie's focus drifted back to Ben. She waited on something, though he wasn't sure what.

Sucking in a deep breath, he angled his body toward her, lifted his arm, and placed it on the back of the couch. "Come here."

She didn't hesitate to settle against his chest. He tucked her close to him. It took a few songs and a couple of commercials for their breaths to sync in a slow, steady rhythm. When she began to snore ever so slightly, he felt his heart surrender to her completely.

How was he supposed to leave for Japan now?

CHAPTER 8

Elodie knocked on the door to the guest room, the handles of the soup bowl nearing the point of scalding by the time Clyde opened the door. When he did, she burst past him and set the bowl on the bedside table.

Clyde cleared his throat. "Well, come on in, why don't you?"

She turned back to face him. He wore a white undershirt, untucked over a pair of trousers. His bare toes stuck out from beneath the hems. The man should be wearing socks on a day like today. "I brought you chicken soup. Mama wholeheartedly believes that will fix you right up. How are you feeling?"

"I think I'm through the worst of it. It no longer feels like an army is marching through my head." He grinned. Even sick, he hadn't lost his charm. Or his looks. With his hair falling over his forehead instead of slicked back with pomade, he looked like a younger, more innocent version of the Hollywood leading man he was recognized to be.

She pushed his hair back and felt above his brow. Nice and cool, though a bit clammy. "Feels like the fever broke. I believe you should be just fine to attend the premiere tomorrow night. The whole town is buzzing over the celebrities arriving. They've never seen such fancy cars."

"Glad to hear it. How are final preparations for the dance coming? Just about forty-eight hours to go, right? Or has my foggy brain got my days mixed up?"

"Close enough. Tomorrow my family and several others in the community are meeting at the hangar to put everything in place." Out of habit, Elodie straightened the bedsheets.

"Maybe I'll come by if I'm on the mend. Any news on the transport of soldiers?"

Elodie paused. Was Clyde Irving concerned about someone other than himself? The question both warmed and confused her. "They're still at a repatriation center in San Francisco. They were able to get seats on a bus though, and should arrive at the hangar during the ball. That's nice of you to ask about them."

Clyde scrubbed his hand across his unshaven jaw. "I hope you'll still be my date for the premiere."

"Date? Clyde, what the papers are saying about us being a couple. . . I don't want to fuel those rumors. But I'll attend the premiere as your guest."

Clyde cocked his head. "Is this because of Benny?"

Warmth gripped Elodie. "Perhaps. He's my dearest friend. And he's leaving soon." Her throat tightened with the admission. "I'd like to have him at my side as well, if you don't mind. I'll walk the red carpet with you, but I'd like to sit with him during the movie."

"I don't mind at all. I understand. I'm not sure I could've done what I did over there if I hadn't had him around like I did. He inspired courage in me that I'd never had before."

"Oh yeah?"

"Sometimes at night it got too quiet. Whenever I got to talking about the point of it all, he never told me to shut my trap. Instead, he encouraged me to keep gnawing on it. The truth is, sometimes the fame and glory don't feel like enough. Anyway, I've said too much."

Elodie rested her hand on his arm. "After you eat, if you're feeling up to it, we're going caroling in town."

"I'm still gathering my strength. And I'm not much for caroling."

"Okay. Charlie will stop by later to check on you, then."

Clyde's smooth grin fell in one swoop.

Ben shouldn't be expected to get anything done when Elodie was nearby. Even a task as simple as decorating the donated Christmas tree on the hangar's stage was more difficult when all his concentration was on her small movements.

"Whoever invented tinsel is surely laughing now at the mess they've created." He pulled a silver thread from its bundle and laid it across a branch.

"All right. Who replaced my Benjamin with Ebenezer Scrooge?" Elodie took a piece of tinsel and draped it over Ben's ear.

"Don't start, Wise."

She pursed her lips and held up another piece above his head. It caught in his hair, and an end fell between his eyes.

"That's it." He dropped the handful of tinsel. When she squealed and ran down the steps of the stage, he followed her, nearly clipping Mr. Wise as he nailed the curtain to the front of the stage Ben and

Elodie had built. "Sorry, Mr. Wise!"

Elodie hid behind Charlie, who was carrying a large stack of folded tablecloths.

"Don't use me as a shield," Charlie said, hurrying out of the way and leaving her sister exposed.

Benjamin pounced, but Elodie ducked out of his reach. He followed her to the vacant floor space near the back, where he grabbed her around the waist and spun her in a circle. Her laugh bounced off the steel walls. When he set her feet back on the ground, she turned into him, giggling against his neck most fantastically.

On Ben's right, something clattered on the concrete. There Rhoda stood above a dropped push broom, glaring at Elodie.

"It's not enough to steal all the attention. You have to steal Ben too?" Rhoda ran to the exit door while the rest of the volunteers watched the scene.

Elodie moved to follow her, but Ben caught her wrist.

"Let me talk to her first," he said.

Compassion swirled in her eyes. "Okay. Be gentle with her. Not that you'd ever need that reminder." A tiny slice of tinsel had threaded itself into the curl in front of her ear.

Benjamin carefully removed it before grinning and excusing himself. He grabbed his coat from the stack by the door and stepped into the deceptive December sun. It may look warm, but that ice-blue sky wasn't playing games. He glanced around. "Where'd you go, Rhoda?"

From the far side of the lot, a metal barrel drummed and rocked a bit. Behind it, a bobby-socked and saddle-shoed foot slid out of view. Ben jogged toward it.

Rhoda had her hands crossed over her stomach. Already she was shivering. Twin trails of tears streaked her face.

Ben spread his coat wide and placed it over her.

"Thank you."

"You got it." He took a seat on the gravel and allowed the chittering of a field critter to fill the silence for thirty seconds while he thought of what to say. "I bet it hasn't been easy for you."

Rhoda stared straight ahead, her chin trembling slightly. She sniffed then pulled her legs up to her chest, using the coat as a blanket.

"I remember how close you and Elodie were before she left for Manila. It was hard having her leave, wasn't it? I know I felt like that. Getting left behind never feels good."

When her face crumpled, Ben put his arm around her shoulder. Rhoda sniffled. "I was so mad. I wanted something bad to happen to her. Then when it did. . ."

"You blamed yourself? Rhoda, that's not why she was taken prisoner."

"Then why was she?"

Ben fumbled for a word, any word at all. But how many times had he asked God the same question?

Rhoda heaved a breath. "Once she was taken to that camp, Elodie was all anyone cared about. We didn't celebrate anything. Not birthdays or holidays. Only anniversaries for Elodie's enlistment, deployment, and capture. Those Mama treated like funerals. And everything was about sacrifice for the war effort. Everyone said it was my duty, but I never signed up for that." Rhoda wiped her nose on his coat—a move that might have made him laugh in other circumstances. "And then she came home, but still it was all about her. Finally, we get a Christmas without war, but here we are, giving more of our time to Elodie and her dreams. Why don't I get to have the goals and the dreams and the romance?"

"You do get to have that, Rhoda. After tomorrow, it will be different. You'll see. And George Weston will be coming home, right?"

"What does that have to do with anything?"

"I've seen those letters from him sitting on the table. And the outgoing ones with the heart over the *i* in Wise." He squeezed her tight.

"Ben!" Her face flamed bright pink.

"I'm just saying you have a lot of great things coming your way. And you may not see it now, but you're fortunate to have your sisters."

"Even Charlie?"

"Even Charlie. Come on. Let's head back in and get warm."

As they walked back toward the hangar, Rhoda kept tight to Ben's side. "Hey, Ben, if Elodie chooses Clyde, do I get you?"

He chuckled. "Oh Rhoda. . ." He held the door open for her, then stepped inside, perusing the scene until he spied Elodie.

She was up on a ladder finishing the tree trimming. Clyde stood off to the side with his hand on the small of her back. When Elodie saw him, she turned a bit, and Clyde's hand moved to her hip.

Ben worked to loosen his clenched fists as he approached the two of them.

"Is Rhoda okay?" Elodie asked.

"She will be. The place looks almost ready. Everyone is packing up, I see."

"This is the final touch." Elodie held up a star tree topper. "Star or angel?"

Clyde removed his hand from Elodie and held up a knit angel.

"Angel. Always," Ben said.

"I had a feeling you'd say that," Clyde said. He lifted the topper to Elodie.

She placed the angel on top of the tree. "Perfect. We're all ready for tomorrow."

Clyde lifted Elodie down from the ladder. "Excellent. It's nearly time for your red carpet debut, Lieutenant Wise."

CHAPTER 9

Over the span of a few hours, her small town had been transformed into Tinseltown. The movie house had been scrubbed and painted. The burned-out bulbs surrounding the marquee had been replaced, and Clyde Irving's name, along with the film's title, *Enemy Skies*, shone brightly above the red carpet.

Inside the car, Elodie adjusted her gloves where they bunched on her wrists.

"You look ravishing, my dear," Clyde said.

"I'm not sure why I must walk the red carpet. Are you sure this will help bring attention to the needs of our soldiers?"

"Trust me. It'll do wonders for the charity." He took her hand. "Let's go shine."

As Elodie followed Clyde out of the car, flashbulbs, reporters, and a film camera bombarded them. A blond woman she recognized as a famous actress—what was her name again?—pushed her way in between Elodie and Clyde.

"Hi, doll. Patricia Ridgeway, I'm sure you know. Listen, hon, I'm interested in playing you in an upcoming film."

"Patricia, please. This isn't the time," Clyde warned. He tugged Elodie past the woman.

There was too much noise. Too many flashes. People crowded her, and she lost Clyde's hand. The scene spun, and she was back on Corregidor, dodging debris and explosions. It was challenging to find breath amid the chaos. If only there were someone she could help. Then maybe she'd find her way through.

Past the faces, some familiar, others not, she caught sight of Benjamin. All it took was one glance, and soon he was right at her side, shielding her from the bulk of the intruders. Still, breath eluded her.

"Lieutenant Wise?" Through the commotion, a motherly voice broke through. It belonged to a short woman who might have once had a friendly face before war riddled the world. Her brow hung heavy over weathered eyes that wore sorrow like a cloak.

Elodie was drawn to her. "I'm Lieutenant Wise."

"I'm sorry to bother you, especially on a night like this. My name is Florence Uchermann. My son served in Manila before the war began. Sadly, we received word that he was killed early in '42."

A hand to her chest did nothing to soothe the pain Elodie felt pierce her heart over the woman's loss. So many had died, yet the loss of even one life still shattered. "I'm so sorry."

"We know nothing else. I was hoping you might have run into him. His name was Tom."

Benjamin whispered in Elodie's ear. "You don't have to help her."

"It's okay." Elodie searched her trembling hands like they might hold an answer for this woman. She'd seen thousands upon thousands of soldiers during her tour of duty. Tom. Tom Uchermann. Her breath rushed out, carrying one name with it. "Tuck."

"Yes, Tuck was his nickname at Fort Stotsenberg. Did you know him?"

"A little. He and I picnicked together on Thanksgiving Day of '41." Elodie felt a smile stretch her lips even as tears filled her eyes. "I liked him."

Tuck's mother smiled as well. "He was a good boy. Everyone liked him. Can you tell me anything else?"

Benjamin took Elodie's hand, steadying it as she pondered what she might say to a mourning mother.

"I didn't see him again until he was brought into the ward we'd set up in the jungle that January. He'd been gravely injured, but he wasn't in pain. He'd received morphine, but he was still lucid. I held his hand, and he spoke of fishing the Mississippi with his father and your dancing lessons beneath a weeping willow."

His mother's chin quivered. Elodie released Benjamin's hand and took both of Florence's in hers. "I'll never forget his last words. He smiled up at the palm fronds above him and said, 'I sure would like to dance again.' And he was gone."

Mrs. Uchermann closed her eyes, and tears fell, creating tiny starbursts on the red carpet down below their interlocked hands. The noise surrounding them had hushed at some point. Every person stilled, listening to their conversation. Every person except Benjamin, who tugged a handkerchief from his pocket and held it out to the woman. She accepted it, but when she noticed Benjamin, perhaps for the first time, she froze.

"You look very much like my Tom." She studied his face, placing a hand on his cheek and turning his head. Benjamin obliged, and when new tears came, he covered her hand with his.

Elodie sniffled. "This is Benjamin Gabriel, my closest friend. He fought alongside Clyde Irving in France."

Mrs. Uchermann nodded. She dabbed the handkerchief against each eye, then offered it back to Ben.

"Keep it, in case the tears keep coming," he said.

"Thank you. Both of you. You've brought much peace to an old mother's heart."

"Will you stay for the movie?" Elodie asked.

"No, I've had enough war. I think I'll return home and finally lay Tom down to rest."

Elodie and Benjamin watched her slip through the crowd. Once she'd disappeared, Elodie's lungs opened and she could breathe again. She shared a glance with Benjamin, but it was short-lived as Clyde stepped between them.

Clyde took Elodie's hand. "Time to head inside. My movie's about to start."

Enemy Skies was precisely the kind of film audiences needed one year ago. A final push to support the troops to finish the race and bring home the victory. But now the battle scenes and trauma felt gratuitous. Then again, Ben wasn't a filmmaker.

Clyde's role was as a soldier named Edmond, who falls for Marguerite, a French nurse who is betrothed to a Nazi officer. The crowd oohed and aahed at all the right moments, even if it was fantastically unrealistic.

Elodie sat between Ben and Clyde in the front row. She seemed unimpressed by Clyde's performance. Whenever the battle scene did bend toward reality, she leaned Ben's way, not Clyde's.

Most of the scenes were filmed on a stage, but a good deal of footage from their time in Europe had been added. Every familiar scene gave Ben a jolt. He could still smell the concrete dust, feel the smoldering heat from the dashed fires, and see the tear-streaked faces of the people offscreen.

One particular scene gutted Ben. In it Edmond laments the horrors of war in the rubble of a French church. In actuality, it had been Ben who'd let loose his prayers of abandon in that church. Some of the lines Clyde's character spoke were too close to Ben's heart, stolen from his most vulnerable moments. He'd only pulled himself back together when something in the rubble reminded him of Elodie.

He shifted in his seat.

"Are you doing all right?" Elodie whispered.

One look at her soft eyes and one whiff of her flowery perfume steadied him. She turned her hand palm up on the armrest, stretching her delicate fingers to their full length. He slid his hand over hers, fingertip to fingertip.

"I am now," he said, interlocking their fingers.

As the film headed toward its climax, antiaircraft flak hit the engine of the bomber Edmond flew in. Sure enough, the plane went down behind enemy lines. While the rest of the soldiers provided defensive gunfire and the real mechanic in the crew hid in fear, Edmond fashioned a new fuel line. As he worked, enemy fire sprayed the plane and hit Edmond in the shoulder. He fell back, surrendering to despair. He withdrew a small black-and-white picture of the film's heroine from his breast pocket—an image that looked remarkably like the one of Elodie that Benjamin had lost. The sight of his dame was enough to spur him on so he could finish repairing the bomber.

Benjamin gritted his teeth. It was no wonder the studio made him sign a nondisclosure agreement about the events of the war.

They'd been using him to get material for a film. Ben leaned forward in his seat to see Clyde's face cast with light from the screen. The man stared straight ahead, too low to see the rubbish spanning wall to wall in front of them. His gaze flitted to Ben's then fell even lower to where he wrung his hands in his lap.

The ignition of the bomber's engine drew Ben's focus back to the film. When the pilot slumped in his seat, succumbing to his bullet wounds, Clyde's character took the helm. Amid enemy fire, he taxied the plane down a makeshift runway and lifted his crew out of danger and into freedom. The cheers from the audience cut straight through Ben.

To think he'd once called Clyde his friend. Nausea wrenched his stomach. His hand felt slick where he held Elodie's. She was no longer watching the movie. One hundred percent of her attention fell on Ben.

He was ruining this for her. The screen's light faded as Edmond pondered the reality of war. Ben used the cover of darkness as he sought the exit door to the right of the screen. On the other side, the hall was barely lit, perfect for sinking into his shadowed thoughts. He heard voices. No, this wasn't quite private enough. A velvet curtain blocked a doorway on his left. Ben ducked inside, where a few steps led up onto the stage. From behind the screen, Ben watched Edmond reunite with Marguerite. Clyde got the girl again.

A hand touched Ben's arm. He jerked back.

Elodie, in her delicate satin dress, looked elegant and classy. "I'm right here, Benjamin. Talk to me."

A few yards away, the film played on the back side of the screen. The soldiers were welcomed home with a grand parade. Edmond stood in the center with Marguerite at his side as he addressed the crowd, thanking them for their support on the home front.

"That was your story. You were the one who took the bullet, fixed the fuel line, and saved that flight crew. Did you fly the plane too?"

"No. When Mickey, our pilot, got shot, the copilot took over, but I took over his duties. It was a team effort to get home." All except Clyde, who'd hidden in the plane the entire time. They'd never have been in that mess if it weren't for him. Fortunately, they'd all escaped with their lives and a command to remain tight-lipped—for the sake of morale, they were told.

It was all clear now. Clyde Irving's fledgling career was riding on his wartime heroics.

"When I got the order to keep him alive, I knew my strengths would go to waste. I didn't think I was providing him and the film-makers with material. That scene in the church, those were my cries, my prayers. We'd just come upon a ghastly sight, and I'd sought the Lord's presence in the church. I opened my Bible to Psalms, where I kept your picture. You were gone. I searched my bag, but it was nowhere to be found. Just that day we'd received news about the worsening conditions of Santo Tomas. It was too much. And Clyde—my friend—used that."

The film's final scene culminated in a musical crescendo. The credits began with the first image displaying Clyde Irving's name. The writing was mirror-imaged, but it was easy to decipher: "*Based on the true heroic acts of Captain Clyde Irving.*" The audience cheered for each of the big names. There was no mention of Mickey or the others who'd risked their lives so the filmmakers could get their footage. Certainly no mention of Ben.

And after all the conversations he and Clyde had shared. It had been Clyde who'd helped him find the bronze angel in the rubble of the church—a part of a wall sconce that had been broken in pieces by the bomb blast. It was that small, palm-sized angel that Ben had carried around for the remaining few months of his time in Europe. The one he held whenever he longed to remember Elodie's kind heart, good soul, and loving ways—all the good he'd enlisted to protect.

"And then he came here to woo you, knowing good and well how I feel about you."

The golden hue of the credits set Elodie's face aglow as she inched closer. "How do you feel about me?"

How many times had he held back his feelings because of timing, school, war, or most recently, her health? But more than that, she'd never seemed ready to hear it. Things had changed this past month though. And the hunger in her eyes was nearly enough to make his knees buckle.

As if to urge him on, she hesitantly slid her gloved hand over his scarred shoulder to his neck. The gentle touch roused enough courage to finally unlock the caged words he'd so long wanted to say.

"I love you, El."

She stilled a long moment, but then, a coy smile arose. "Why haven't you said anything to me before?"

"Because I never imagined you might feel the same."

Her hand on his neck guided him toward her. The fingers of her other hand pinched the lapel of his suit jacket, tugging him closer until no space remained. Her breath teased him. "And what if I do?"

"Then, I'd say we have a lot to figure out," he whispered.

The moment her lips brushed his, the loudest orchestra in the world couldn't have drowned out the pounding in his chest. He slid his hands around her waist, taking in the silky feel of her. She melted into his embrace, tilting her head back to welcome the full breadth of his kiss.

He slipped his hand beneath the curls on her neck. It didn't seem real, sharing this intimate moment with her. After imagining it countless times, her mouth was warmer, her lips smoother, and her hair softer. There weren't enough prayers in his heart to show his thankfulness.

CHAPTER 10

Elodie held her hands over Ben's eyes as they walked into the hangar. She knew him. He'd sneak a peek if she just told him to close his eyes. He got too excited around surprises.

"This had better be worth me nearly breaking my neck," he said.

"It's worth it."

"I hope it involves a kiss."

"Only if you're good." Elodie bit at the grin taking over her face. What kind of dream had she stumbled into, where Benjamin Gabriel desired to kiss her? She took in a deep breath. "Almost there. And stop." She didn't drop her hands quite yet. He was warm despite the frigid prairie air they'd just escaped. And he smelled like cinnamon. Like home. After all, he'd spent the morning baking cinnamon-swirl bread with her mother for tonight's dance. She stood behind him, resting her cheek on his shoulder. Still unbelievable. This was Benjamin, her friend. And now, much more.

She had no idea how he might react when he saw her surprise. Hopefully, he'd appreciate it, but as she could attest, not all wartime reminders were welcome. "Three, two, one." She dropped her hands and stepped to the side to gauge his response.

When Benjamin saw the B-24J Liberator, he inhaled sharply. "Is this. . . ? It is. The *Elmira Jane*. I was wondering why you wanted to leave a big empty spot on the floor."

"I had it flown in for the occasion. I hope you don't mind."

"I think it's great." Like he had done a dozen or so times since they'd first kissed last night, Benjamin took her in his arms and held her tight against him.

She allowed herself to soak in his tenderness and warmth. Her Benjamin. After a few moments, she skimmed her lips over his earlobe. "Will you show it to me?"

"Absolutely." He led her to the side of the plane, where he explained the origin of the name and all about the crew assigned to it.

But as he spoke, Elodie could only focus on the bullet holes dotting the fuselage. Ben caught her concern, stopping his story about an Oklahoman named Rip, who was a gunner. He kissed her forehead. "It's okay. We all survived."

Barely. He found a ladder and opened up the panel concealing the engine they'd lost. This engine had since been entirely replaced, but Benjamin explained the mechanics of the trauma inflicted by the antiaircraft flak. Flying with only three engines was difficult but not impossible for a B-24. But the flak also severed the main fuel lines leading to one of the remaining engines. Benjamin described how he finagled a temporary fix to get them back up in the air. According to him, the *Elmira Jane* flew five more missions in late 1944 and early 1945. None of those missions were as problematic as the one with Clyde and Benjamin though.

An hour later, the two sat in the back of the plane, enjoying their newfound closeness. She dragged her fingertip along his jawline, hinge to chin. His lips, full and soft, contrasted quite nicely to the slight scratch of his skin. Each time he smiled, it only enticed her to kiss him again. Would she ever tire of it? Unlikely. She'd kiss him forever and a day.

If only things were different.

"Eight days. That's all the time we have left together."

Benjamin said nothing. He merely dipped his chin.

"Are you sure you have to leave? Japan is so far away."

"You know how the army works. Still, it's going to be a tough goodbye." He squeezed her tighter to himself.

"Let's not think about it, okay? We have a big night. Can you believe we're pulling this off?"

"I knew you could do it. When you put your mind to something, whether it's nursing soldiers back to health or throwing a spectacular fundraiser to help those soldiers and their families, you do it. I couldn't be more proud of you. I know your family and this community feel the same way. We are so fortunate to know you, Lieutenant Elodie Wise."

When tears blurred her vision, she buried her face against his collar. She'd always loved him as her friend. But that love had transcended to new heights in the last few weeks.

"I know you'll be busy with your hosting duties tonight, and I'll be busy making sure everything runs smoothly behind the scenes, but remember, you promised me a dance."

She looked up. "I wouldn't miss the chance." She welcomed his next string of kisses until he mumbled something against her neck.

"What did you say?" she asked.

His eyes lifted to hers, and his thumb caressed her cheek. "*Mon ange.*"

Her thoughts flitted back to her high school French class when he'd asked her to translate those two words. *Mon ange*—"my angel."

CHAPTER 11

"B en, Mrs. Handel brought all kinds of delicacies from her bakery. Where should she set them?" Mrs. Wise positively beamed as she received a platter of croissants and scones from his landlady.

"Those look delicious, Mrs. Handel. Thank you for the donation. All the food will be set on that table back there by the bomber." Ben motioned to the long table they'd borrowed from the local art gallery. Food had started piling up, thanks to the generosity of the townspeople. From the looks of it, folks had saved up their rations for a celebration such as this. Everything had come together perfectly. Soon guests would start arriving and the festivities would begin. Last he heard, the three men Elodie had hoped to honor tonight had boarded a bus in San Francisco and were en route to Hope Hill. If all went well, they'd arrived at the hangar around nine o'clock.

Ben had a great feeling about all the good that would come from this event. Yet he was most excited to see his girl and finally continue that dance from more than four years ago. His thoughts drifted to the way it felt to hold Elodie in his arms.

"Ben?" A most unwelcome voice clamored over his memory of her kisses.

Clyde Irving sported a much more elegant suit than Benjamin's. His hair had been expertly slicked back, and his mustache was trimmed and oiled. All in all, he looked slimier than Ben had ever seen him. Close behind him, Richard followed.

Ben tried for a greeting but found none to suffice.

"Looking sharp, brother," Clyde said, dusting Ben's shoulder.

Brother. What a term. He knocked Clyde's hand away.

The smarmy smile disappeared from Clyde's face. "I wanted to speak with you before everything gets started. About the movie."

Ben didn't try to hide his disgust. It was undoubtedly written all over his face. When Clyde saw it, he retreated a step. "I hope you enjoyed it and it didn't bring back too many terrible memories."

The scoff burst from Ben's throat before he could trap it. "Oh, it brought back memories. But I remember things a bit differently than you. 'Based on the true heroic acts of Clyde Irving,' isn't that what it said? This was never about serving the country, was it? It was all about image. You were foolhardy before the war, but rather than letting the horrors of what we witnessed change you for the better, you held tight to your reckless behavior."

Clyde bristled under the barrage.

"You know, when I was first assigned to be your guardian, I was angry. What sense did it make to take a good mechanic and sock him with babysitting duties when he could have been making a real difference in the fight? But in time, I got to know you. I considered you a friend, and I would've been honored to risk my life to save yours. So this is a bit of a sucker punch for me. I was a pawn, wasn't I?"

"No. Ben, I don't have a lot of close friends. You're one of the few—"

"Is Elodie part of your plan too? She is, isn't she? It was you and your team that leaked those stories about the two of you being a couple. You don't care about her or Heroes of Hope Hill. You only care about cleaning up your image so you can sell more movie tickets."

"Ben—"

All the heat building within Ben seemed to center beneath his ever-tightening collar. He pinned Clyde with a glare. What possible excuse would the man give now?

"I need to get ready for my hosting duties. Excuse me." Clyde walked toward the stage where the swing band was warming up with their instruments.

The anger within Ben threatened to consume him. He focused his sights on the angel topping the Christmas tree at the center of the stage. He'd told Elodie to take her time getting ready. He'd handled all the prep work. But he needed to see her right about now.

A brisk draft tickled his cheek, and he turned toward the door. Elodie seemed to glide in on the wintry breeze. Her father welcomed her, helping her slide out of her coat.

Everything else in the hangar faded out of focus. All he could see was her in that candy apple red dress. It wrapped her waist in folds of fabric then splayed out in a full skirt that showed off her lengthy gams. Urging his eyes back to the prettiest of all faces, he couldn't remember what it had been like not to long to kiss her. Her glossy lips formed a heart of a smile in his direction. Probably due to the way he was gawking at her beauty. He wanted to welcome her, but he didn't remember how to walk.

Instead, she came to him, sauntering the whole way, as if to tease him even more. "Aren't you handsome all dressed up."

"And you. . .you are too heavenly for this world."

She curtsied. "Why, thank you." She kissed his cheek, then laughed. "I think I've staked my claim on you with lipstick." She rubbed at his cheek with her thumb. "Is everything ready?"

"Yes, we are. Are you nervous?"

"No. All I have to do is tell people about the good this charity does. Nothing I add will be more powerful than that. And afterward, you'll be the one walking me to my door and kissing me good night. If everything falls apart, at least I'll have that."

The hangar thudded with the beat as the band played "Chattanooga Choo Choo." The familiar lyrics tickled Elodie's funny bone, especially when she met Benjamin's gaze through the crowd. Joy threatened to burst forth from her in a Lindy Hop, but she settled for tapping the toe of her sling-back against the floor until she finished her conversation.

"As I was saying, we'd love to bring on a medical professional such as yourself to help with the veterans at our clinic," Dr. Carol Phelps said. As a board member for Heroes of Hope Hill and a notable name in the area of psychology, she was someone Elodie had long admired. "We're funding research into the treatment of flak happiness. You know, shell shock."

Elodie's heart swelled. "What important work. Your early research on the effects of trauma on the brain has helped many people. I've seen how flashbacks following stressful events, especially battle, can be debilitating. I'd be honored to play a part. Where is your clinic?"

"We'd like to open one right here in Hope Hill. With the proximity to Kansas City, we can serve many returning soldiers." The doctor patted Elodie's hand. "Let's stay in touch. Great work tonight. No matter how much money is raised, you've brought much-needed awareness to our cause."

As Dr. Phelps breezed through the crowd, gentle hands settled on Elodie's shoulders.

"Is it time for our dance yet?" Benjamin cooed in her ear.

She leaned back against his chest. The gossip hounds in town might get enough fodder for a week, but Elodie didn't care. With their time together ticking down, she wouldn't miss a moment of affection over the fear of what others might say was appropriate. Elodie guessed he felt similarly considering how he pecked her cheek.

A dozen yards away, Richard spat words at Clyde and poked a finger into his chest. Clyde shook his lowered head but didn't look up at the man. Elodie had managed to avoid Clyde all night. After what she had seen in the film and learned from Benjamin, she no longer admired the man behind the handsome face. She was thankful for the crowd he'd attracted to the dance, but she'd be just as happy to bid him farewell.

"What do you think? Trouble in paradise?" she asked.

"Knowing Clyde, I'm sure there's something in the works. Let's not let him ruin our dance." Benjamin stepped around her. He took her left hand in his and circled his arm around her waist.

Over Benjamin's shoulder, she caught Clyde's eye. He skulked over to the two of them. "Elodie, I need to speak to you."

Before Elodie could voice her refusal, Benjamin turned sharply to Clyde. "Do you mind? I want one dance with her."

"It's important. It might change some things."

Benjamin stiffened. He clenched his fists, and Elodie tensed. Benjamin Gabriel wasn't one to make a scene, but Clyde's antics might have pushed him too far. Fortunately, her father appeared in the nick of time. He glanced curiously between the two men, then at Elodie.

"Sweetheart, there's a telegram—from George." He held out the paper. "It isn't good."

She snatched it, then thought better of the action. "Sorry. Thank you, Daddy." As quick as she could, she skimmed the words, pressing a hand to her heart as if to keep it from thudding to the floor. She placed the telegram in Benjamin's hand.

With Clyde peering over his shoulder, he read the bad news silently to himself.

"I guess I should make an announcement."

"Good idea." Her father blew out a breath. "I'll find Mrs. Weston."

"And I'll see to Rhoda," Benjamin said.

Clyde grabbed Elodie's arm. "When you're done, come find me outside. Out the back door."

"All right." As Elodie took to the stage, Benjamin moved between the dancing couples to where Rhoda was sipping punch.

As the song concluded, the band leader stepped back from the microphone and waved his hand to welcome Elodie to it.

She mouthed a thank-you, then positioned herself to speak to the more than three hundred attendees. "I'd like to thank all of you for this united effort to raise support for Heroes of Hope Hill. Clyde and I are both honored to thank our soldiers and welcome them home. However, we've just received a telegram from our local son, George Weston. He, Willis Cathy, and Eugene Rosenthal were able to board a bus in San Francisco. But this morning the bus broke down on the Colorado and Wyoming state line. Unfortunately, they won't be able to make it home tonight."

A lament rippled through the crowd. Locals and celebrities alike covered their mouths. When Rhoda's shoulders rolled forward, Benjamin held her, then nodded at Elodie. What a great man he was. For the thousandth time, she begrudged his transfer. If only there were something to be done. Some reason for him to stay here that would still allow him to use his talents for good. *Please, Lord.*

"May we all pray that they make it home for Christmas Day. When they do, your generous donations will be here waiting for them." She left the stage to the band and hurried down the steps.

Clyde was nowhere to be found. Must already be out back waiting for her with whatever gobbledygook he had to say. Chatter and a new song filled the hangar as Elodie made her way toward the back door.

Her mother appeared, her face beaming when she found Elodie. "Dear, you need to come with me. There's someone you must talk to." With hands on Elodie's shoulders, she gently steered Elodie back into the gathering of people.

"Sorry, Mama, I'm supposed to meet with Clyde. He says it's important."

"I don't believe anything he says could be more important than this. Trust me."

CHAPTER 12

Once Ben had convinced Rhoda that the sky hadn't fallen, that George would indeed be home soon, he left her to rejoin her girlfriends. If anyone knew the pain of having a love miles away, it was Ben. The back door of the hangar where Elodie was meeting with Clyde was only one hundred feet from where he stood, and Ben couldn't wait to get to her side. How much farther was Japan than that? It had been hard enough during the war, but now that he knew how good it felt to kiss her, hold her, and tell her he loved her?

The tension in his shoulders pulled his scar tissue taut, and he scratched at it. If only he'd trusted God with his future, his worth, his identity, he wouldn't have looked for one more way to prove himself and volunteered for this next assignment a world away.

He headed toward the door, bypassing the *Elmira Jane* and the guests examining the bullet holes in the side. When he opened the hangar's back door, a welcome gust rushed into the space. The heaters hadn't been necessary after all the folks had begun dancing.

Outside the night offered a peaceful contrast to the soaring noise of the dance. While he'd expected to hear Clyde's camera-ready voice spinning some tale for Elodie, the only sounds were the whooshing grasses of a moonlight-tinged field. Where had the two of them gone?

Thud.

It sounded like something had bumped against the hangar's wall, but there was nothing out here. He crept to the corner and peeked around.

The tall form of a man stood against the hangar's steel side, where even the moonlight couldn't reach. He was facing away from Benjamin and dredged in shadow, but his broad shoulders and slick, dark hair erased all mystery. Clyde.

Ben's fists clenched. Finally, he could tell the guy just what he thought about his stunts over the past two and a half years. He opened his mouth to call out his former friend's name but paused when a woman's hand curled around Clyde's upper arm. More than the December air, the sound of kisses sent a chill into the marrow of Ben's bones.

Clyde shuffled his feet.

Thud, thud.

A golden blond curl fell over Clyde's shoulder as he and Elodie giggled together. Nausea arrested Ben's stomach, and when the two resumed their kissing, Ben backed away, nearly tripping on a rock.

Elodie was merely confused. In just a few weeks, Ben had pushed her from friendship to, well, what was it? They hadn't defined it yet. What point was there in going steady or courting when Ben was leaving in a little over a week? It had been an emotional night following a hard few years. And Clyde Irving was Clyde Irving after all.

He shouldn't blame her.

He could forgive a few stolen kisses, couldn't he? They would talk about it and figure out what their future might hold.

Still, anger raced through his veins, and he cursed it. If he had one of Elodie's syringes, he'd bleed himself dry if it meant being rid of any malice toward her.

A lanky man with thinning auburn hair turned toward Elodie and her mother, greeting them with a smile. "Lieutenant Wise. Woman of the hour."

"Elodie, this is Colonel J. P. Chesterton. Your father and I have known him for a long time," her mother said.

He held out his hand. Though a bit more aged, the skin was stained with the same grease that marked Benjamin's calloused palms. "Sorry about that. These mechanic mitts always give me away before I can introduce myself." He recoiled his hand, but Elodie grasped it, shaking it firmly.

"A colonel with grease on his hands?" Elodie raised a brow. Normally, she wouldn't speak to a superior with such informality, but it was a night of goodwill and celebration, and Colonel Chesterton had a gracious way about him.

"I work for the War Department, specifically in the area of aircraft procurement. I was up at Fairfax Field earlier today checking the quality of the remaining C-47s before they head to Topeka. Can't let the young ones have all the fun, can I?"

Elodie grinned.

Her mother pressed her hands together in front of her waist. "While he won't tell me specifically what special projects they have going—"

"It's confidential. You understand," Colonel Chesterton explained.

Her mother continued. "He said he's heard about how skilled Benjamin is."

Elodie nodded. "Oh yes. Benjamin's a genius when it comes to engines. Cars, trains, and aircraft, especially."

"As you know, threats still abound in the world, and we're always looking to create the strongest aircraft for our boys. We're looking at some contracts with outside companies to develop new aviation technology, and I'd love to have Benjamin's knowledge and experience."

Hope flitted inside Elodie. "I'm sorry to tell you, sir, that Benjamin is one of the replacement troops being sent to occupy Japan just after the first of the year."

"Well, that won't do. If he doesn't mind staying closer to home, I believe his skills would be put to better use here in the US. I can move some chess pieces on my end to make that happen. Is there anything you could do to convince him to stick around Missouri?"

The warmth of a hundred Filipino summers flooded Elodie. Her happily ever after was so close, she could kiss it. "I'm sure I could think of something."

Elodie's mother tilted her head as if to say, *I told you so.*

Perhaps her hovering ways weren't so terrible after all.

"Now, ladies and gentlemen, the band has a special Christmas treat for us," Clyde said from the stage. Whatever had been bothering him, he must've forgotten about it, for he was sure beaming now. "And if you don't mind, I'd like to welcome to the stage, my cohost, Lieutenant Elodie Wise, for a dance."

Elodie shook her head, but the crowd's applause urged her forward. She climbed the stage with hesitation. He was not the man she wished to dance with tonight. Especially not now. She longed to find Benjamin and tell him about Colonel Chesterton's job offer.

She scanned the audience—no Benjamin. As the band began to play "Have Yourself a Merry Little Christmas," she accepted Clyde's hand, though she reserved her smile.

"Why so glum? This is going well."

"I'm not glum. Tonight *is* going well. But it would be better if the soldiers were home. And if the right people were getting the glory."

His brow wrinkled. "I saw you go after Ben during the final part of the movie last night. He was pretty upset, wasn't he?"

"Yes. He's an honorable man with the heart of a hero. It's a shame he wasn't able to prove that to the world." What was on his lips? They were tinged pink.

"Yes. A shame to be sure." He clamped his lips together. "You really like him, don't you?"

"Yes, Clyde. I love him."

"Excuse me, folks." Richard's voice in the microphone brought the band's music to a dissonant halt. "I hate to interrupt this great music, but while we have our two hosts up here together, this appears to be the best time to make an exciting announcement. If you think these two lovebirds look good together on stage, just you wait."

"Do you know anything about this?" Elodie whispered.

Clyde leaned in. "This is what I was trying to warn you about."

Richard motioned to two of his crew members. They pulled strings connected to something Elodie hadn't seen earlier. A stage-wide roll of paper had been tacked to the wall behind the Christmas tree. When the roll released, it displayed a poster with both Clyde and Elodie's pictures. In big block letters, it read THE IRVING-WISE TOUR. Below that, in smaller print, it promised visits to A TOWN NEAR YOU.

Elodie dropped her hands to her sides.

"That's right. These lovebirds are hitting the rails on a fifteen-city

314

tour to raise money for our brave soldiers returning to the home front. The first stop is on December 27 in Birmingham."

Lovebirds? No. This was all wrong. The walls of the hangar swayed like the trees in the jungle. Elodie needed to settle her breathing, or she wouldn't be able to think.

"Elodie?" Clyde was too close. He looked pale, but perhaps that was her vision succumbing to the headache.

"I never agreed to this, Clyde."

"Elodie, I'll make this right. I promise."

"Now back to the music," the bandleader said. "How about some 'Jingle Bells'?"

Elodie backed away from Clyde and nearly stumbled down the steps of the stage. Benjamin. He needed to know this was not her doing. But where had he gone? Above everyone's heads, she saw the exit door swing closed. She pushed her way through the dancing couples.

Patricia Ridgeway tugged Elodie's hand. "Congratulations on the tour. Like I was saying last night, I hope to play you in a movie." She twirled a barrel curl around her finger. "I've already got the hair for it."

"I'm sorry, but I must go." Elodie withdrew her hand, but by the time she pushed her way through the door and out into the crammed parking lot, all she saw was taillights.

CHAPTER 13

Ben sat outside the Wises' dark home in his truck. In his hands, he held a box big enough to hold his heart, but not all the emotions he felt for Elodie. The thin wrapping had torn at the corners from too much handling and fretting. He'd already held on to it too long. He may as well give it to her. And maybe that way he could let her go.

Where had he gotten things so wrong? Why had she allowed Clyde to kiss her? And why had she agreed to go on this tour without telling him? His brain hurt trying to process it all. That was the problem. He loved her too much to see things as they were.

He dropped the small box onto the stack of presents he'd brought for the members of the Wise family. Beneath Elodie's, he saw Rhoda's name on the tag. What was Elodie's philosophy when she felt troubled or scared? Look for someone to help. That he could do. But it would take time and space, which was exactly what he needed right now.

Elodie stepped into her home as the clock struck midnight. Was this how Cinderella felt in that old story by the Brothers Grimm? Her time of festivities was over. Now she must return to her ordinary life, but in this version, it was she who was searching for her prince. No golden slipper in sight.

Only a dim light filtered down the hall—from the Christmas tree most likely. Still, her home lacked its usual warmth, and she kept her coat on to fight off the chill pressing against her bones. She made her way into the family room.

Her mother sat in her rocking chair with a cup of tea in her hand. "Any luck?"

Elodie slumped on the couch. "I can't find him anywhere. No one in town has seen him since the dance."

"Give him time, sweetheart. The two of you have made it through far worse things than this."

Elodie swallowed against the lump in her throat that might never dissolve. "We didn't even get our dance."

"Have faith. Hope is never lost when you have faith." Her mother sipped her tea. "I can't tell you how often I reminded myself of that very thing while you were gone. And here you are—still my courageous girl, helping others at every opportunity."

"You and Daddy taught me well. I never agreed to this publicity tour. If Benjamin thought I did, it would break his heart. He'll think I chose to spend his last week with Clyde rather than him. No wonder he left."

"Wherever he went, he stopped by here first."

Elodie angled to face her mother. "How do you know that?"

"Look under the tree."

Elodie kneeled at the foot of the fir she and Benjamin had purchased at the tree lot. Her heart panged at the sweet memory of strolling down Main Street with him, making sledding plans that would never come to pass.

A stack of gifts rested on top of the tree skirt. A joint present for her parents, one for Charlie, one for Rhoda, and finally a small one for her. All from Benjamin. On hers, beneath his name, it said OPEN IMMEDIATELY.

"I'll let you be alone. Would you like a lamp on?"

"No. I prefer the dark. Thank you."

Elodie waited for her mother to leave the room, then untied the ribbon, letting it fall to her lap. She slipped her nail beneath the seam, loosening the tape. Once the paper had been removed, all that remained was a simple white box. She lifted the lid carefully. Inside, on a pillow of tissue paper, a bronze cherub greeted her. She lifted it out and held it, taking in the intricate curves of its wings. A small slip of paper stuck to the inside of the box. She unfolded it and read his words to her.

Mon ange,

There was a time in France when everything I understood about the world was turned upside down and covered in rubble. What good could exist in a world so overcome with evil? It was the question that led to my wrestling with God in that church. That was when I found this angel. I believe it had once been part of a sconce. When I saw it, I thought of you and the others in this world that seek to do good in the hardest of circumstances. I carried this with me in my pack for the remainder of my time. In the absence of your picture, this is what I held to think of you. I thought you might like to add it to your nativity set to replace the one I broke years ago.

Love to you always,
Benjamin

A tear dropped onto the note. Elodie wiped her cheeks on the sleeve of her coat. She stood, carrying the angel and the note to the mantel where the crèche sat. Inside, the Holy Family was flanked by the three wise men and the shepherd. Elodie carefully placed the angel behind the manger to watch over the infant Jesus.

She backed away and pressed the note to her chest. *Oh Benjamin, where are you?*

CHAPTER 14

The day before Christmas crawled by. Elodie drove to Benjamin's home several times, but he still hadn't returned. Mama made supper, but Elodie couldn't find the appetite to eat. Neither could Clyde, it seemed. She didn't like having him across the table from her, but Daddy forbade her from sending him packing when they'd promised him a place to stay for the holiday.

Elodie stared hard at the man who wouldn't meet her eye until Charlie kicked her shin. "Ouch! What was that for?"

Charlie said nothing, just scooped a bite of pickled herring into her mouth. Nasty stuff.

At Elodie's side, Benjamin's seat remained empty. They'd all hoped he'd be back by now. After dinner, while the family settled in to listen to carols on the radio, Elodie excused herself to bed. She stared at the ceiling, praying for Benjamin wherever he might be.

As a girl, she'd listened for St. Nicholas's sleigh bells on Christmas

Eve, but now she listened for any sign that her love had returned to her. Around eleven, a scuffle sounded from the side yard beneath Elodie's bedroom window. She bolted upright, listening. A muffled man's voice rose from below.

Elodie threw on her robe and hurried out of her room, padding past Mama and Daddy's door and down the stairs. She left the house through the back door. If it was Benjamin, she didn't want her family waking up to witness their reunion.

A few light snowflakes drifted lazily past her nose. All was calm this Christmas Eve. No more scuffling.

"Benjamin?" she whispered into the night.

There was movement by the garage. Someone was hiding in the shadows.

Elodie took a few steps forward.

A man coughed.

"It's me." Charlie wore the dark quilt from the family room over her shoulders like a cape.

"Charlie. What on earth are you doing out here in the cold this late? Are you alone?"

"Yes," she stammered.

There was more noise from the shadows. Clyde Irving leapt into the yard, brushing the top of his hair.

Elodie squinted. "Clyde?"

"I thought a bat landed on me." After realizing he was safe from the invisible creature, he fixed his eyes on Elodie. The same sheepish expression slid over his face as her sister.

"What are you two. . . ? Oh!"

Upon closer inspection, Clyde had lipstick smeared over his mouth. Elodie didn't know if she should laugh at them or scold them.

"Um, I should head to bed. Good night, Hollywood," Charlie said.

"Good night, Charlie."

Charlie pressed past Elodie, raising a brow and challenging her to say something in the process. But Elodie kept her mouth closed. Charlie wasn't one to take a reprimand lightly, especially after a long day. Elodie let the door shut behind her before looking back to Clyde.

"Sorry to interrupt," Elodie said. "I thought you might have been—"

"Ben?"

"Yes. Clearly, I was mistaken." Without a good night, she spun on her slippered heels and went inside the kitchen.

Clyde, however, followed. "Elodie, wait. We need to talk."

"I don't want—"

"Please? I need to apologize, and that isn't something I have a good deal of experience with."

Elodie groaned softly. She grabbed the bottle of milk from the fridge and a saucepan. Perhaps some warm milk would help her sleep. For once, she wanted Clyde to share one of his dull stories about life in Hollywood. That would put her out like a light.

"I had nothing to do with the tour. I've already told Richard you aren't going."

Elodie lit the burner and stared hard at the milk, willing it to warm quickly. She grabbed a wooden spoon and swirled it around the pot.

"I fired him. I'll be looking for new management in January."

Elodie stopped stirring.

"I don't like the direction my career has taken over the last few years under his guidance. I knew he was the one fueling the headlines about you and me. I didn't stop him though. I'd gotten myself in trouble in California, and I thought being tied to you might help my reputation recover. Last night when I was waiting for you so I could warn you about the tour announcement, your sister followed me out of the hangar. She gave me a grand lecture on learning to speak for myself."

Elodie swiveled to face him. Those ridiculous lips were stained pink like last night—proof Charlie had given him a lesson on more than merely being spineless.

"I shouldn't have used you like that. Or Ben. The events in *Enemy Skies* were based on his heroic acts. Not mine. He took the bullet, fixed the plane. In reality, I was the reason we were behind enemy lines in the first place. When the camera was filming me in the cockpit, I steered us in the opposite direction than the pilot instructed. It was my fault we were hit by flak. I almost took Ben's life, and he responded by saving mine. He's the hero."

"I appreciate you saying that. Now, if Benjamin ever returns, will you say it to him?"

"Yes."

"And will you come clean to the papers about it?"

"Absolutely. No more lying." He scratched his cheek. "But there's more." He reached into his breast pocket. He took out a small rectangular paper, looked at it for a long moment, and then with a sigh, he slid it across the counter.

The black-and-white photograph featured Elodie smiling and looking off at an angle. Her parents had arranged it for her college graduation. The edges of the picture had frayed. Part of it had faded, and there was a crease across her arm.

She picked it up, holding it gingerly, as if too firm a grip might harm the wide-eyed, naive girl in the shot. "My photograph?"

"This was the one Ben carried in his Bible."

On her right, the milk bubbled up and over the side of the saucepan. She grabbed a towel, pulled the pan off the burner, and then switched off the flame. The burnt smell wafted past her nose, and she felt ill. "The one he lost?"

"Yeah. But he didn't lose it. I took it one night when he was sleeping."

Elodie pinched the collar of her robe together at her neck. A throb drummed her temple. "Why would you do such a thing?"

"I was jealous. I was jealous of the way he thought of you. I had no one in my past, present, or future to give me peace. I wanted you for myself. Even if it was just your picture and the childish stories he'd told."

"Why would you rob him of that?"

"Why have I done anything? I've been a selfish fool, and I'm sorry." Clyde fought to clear his throat. "He does love you, you know. It's clearer to me than the sky over the Pacific Ocean."

CHAPTER 15

With the light streaming past the curtains, Elodie rolled to her side and bumped into a warm body in her bed.

Rhoda's wild hair fell across her face. For a moment, she looked like the fourteen-year-old Elodie had once left behind in favor of excitement and adventure. When had she slipped beneath Elodie's covers? No matter. Elodie's heart swelled seeing her baby sister do something other than pout or roll her eyes in her presence. She almost didn't want to wake her.

But she could smell bacon. Mama's Christmas morning breakfast was worth a few extra sneers from Rhoda. Elodie brushed her sister's hair off her face. On the pillowcase, beneath Rhoda's eye, a faint stain was circled in salty white. "Rhoda," she breathed.

When Rhoda awakened, she seemed as confused as Elodie over her bedfellow. Then, after a moment, tears came.

"Oh Rhoda. What's wrong?"

"I've just missed you."

"Oh honey." Elodie nestled Rhoda close. "I've missed you too."

"And I'm sorry I've been such a brat. I was mad that you left me. And then even when you came home, you weren't here. Not really. Your mind was still over there in the Pacific. I needed my big sister."

"I know. I'm sorry." Elodie stroked Rhoda's face gently. "At least you had Charlie."

Rhoda snorted, which sent Elodie into a fit of giggles. *Just wait until Rhoda finds out about Charlie and Clyde.*

"Still no word from Ben?"

Elodie rubbed the sleep from her eyes. "No. Have you heard from George?"

"No. Bing Crosby just keeps dashing my hopes with that 'I'll Be Home for Christmas' song."

"We'll keep praying. Merry Christmas, Rhoda."

"Merry Christmas, Sis."

A heavy knock from downstairs made them both tense up. They held eye contact and their breath.

"Rhoda! Someone's here to see you," Mama called.

Rhoda's eyes rounded, and she pulled her lower lip into her mouth.

"Go on," Elodie said.

Rhoda hopped out of Elodie's bed, nearly catching her foot on the sheets. She grabbed Elodie's robe and swung it over her.

"Hey, that's my—"

And Rhoda was gone.

Elodie smiled and swung her legs off the side of her bed. She dressed quickly, craving that bacon. She might eat the whole platter now that she had her appetite back. She brushed her teeth and ran a comb through her hair, but the makeup could wait until church.

She headed down the stairs. A glance into the den showed that yes, indeed, George Weston had made it home—or at least into Rhoda's arms—for Christmas. Elodie gave George a small wave, then proceeded into the family room, allowing them their privacy. She'd known Rhoda's crush on Benjamin wasn't something to fret over.

She gathered a deep breath. If only the promise of Christmas morning presents could soothe the ache she felt in—

"Benjamin!"

He was there. Sure as Christmas morning, he was there, with one elbow leaning on the mantel by the nativity set. When he laid eyes on her, he straightened up, and his apology was written all over his face. Although she wanted more than anything to run directly to his arms, she needed understanding first.

"Where did you go?"

"Wyoming."

Elodie gasped. "You brought George home!"

"After the dance, I needed some time to think. When I was dropping off your gifts, my thoughts were really muddled, so I did what you taught me. I looked for someone I could help. I was able to fix the bus's engine so the rest of the soldiers could continue on to their families. But I made George ride with me. Wasn't taking a chance on him not making it back to Rhoda."

"Why didn't you tell me?"

"I wasn't sure I'd be able to find them. The last thing I wanted to do was get Rhoda's hopes up, so I didn't leave a note. And once I got there, I tried to call, but lines were jammed with soldiers trying to get in touch with their families."

"And you love surprises," she said, rounding the rocking chair.

Ben lowered his gaze. "Not all surprises. I didn't like stumbling on you and Clyde kissing."

Elodie nearly swallowed her tongue. "I beg your pardon?"

"At the dance, when you and Clyde went out behind the hangar."

Oh! "Benjamin, that wasn't me kissing Clyde."

"Then who was it?"

Clyde strode into the family room, stopping on a dime when he spotted Benjamin. "Oh, hello, Ben."

"Clyde, give us a few minutes?"

Realization dawned on Clyde's face. "Absolutely. But first, Elodie, have you seen Charlie?"

"I don't think she's up yet," Elodie said. "I'll tell her you're waiting for her."

Clyde remained still.

"In the kitchen." Elodie nodded for him to leave.

Clyde winked. "Right. In the kitchen."

Once Clyde had left, Ben rubbed his hands down his face. "I'm a fool."

"Maybe a bit. But you're my fool." She lifted her lips into a smile and broached the space that separated them, hopefully for the last time. "I said no to the tour."

When she neared, he squared his shoulders to face her, leaning ever so slightly. Longing swirled in his eyes. "Elodie. . ."

She sprang forward into his arms, forcing him to grab the mantel to steady himself. Unable to hold back, she pressed her lips against his, releasing all the frustration of the past thirty-six hours into him. He was strong enough to bear it. They—Elodie and Benjamin—were strong enough to bear it. Like Mother said, they'd been through worse.

Her kiss softened, welcoming his tender caresses that poured over her lips like waves on the sand. The warmth inside her flamed hotter than the fire in the hearth. She pulled away slightly, and he touched his forehead to hers.

A grimace bent his features. "I can't bear to part from you after this," he whispered.

"Funny you mention that. Do you know who Colonel J. P. Chesterton is?"

"Yeah, sure."

"He's got some top-secret project he wants you to work on with him. Rumor has it, our guys are trying to produce a jet bomber to rival the Luftwaffe's. He said he could get your assignment changed *if* you had a reason to stay close."

His smile shone light straight into her darkness. It was a great smile.

"And if for some reason they don't approve the move, I can flaunt my angel wings—that's what they're calling us now—the Angels of Bataan and Corregidor."

"That's what I heard. How did the fundraiser end up?"

"Outstanding. We more than tripled our goal, and we don't even have the final tally yet. We'll be able to help so many soldiers and families, Benjamin. And look at this." Elodie lifted her hand out to the side for him to see the way her fingers only quivered the slightest bit. "I don't know that I'll ever completely forget my past. Maybe I'm not supposed to, but with the Lord, my family, and you by my side, I'm no longer afraid of my future. In fact, I've been offered a job at the clinic to research how to best help those who have endured traumatic events like war."

He smiled as he took her hand in his. "Where?"

She felt heat rise to her cheeks. "Right here."

"The more I see what you're capable of, the more I'm convinced that you truly are an angel." He nodded to the nativity set. "Speaking of, do you like your gift?"

"I love it. It's the perfect addition to my family's set. I look forward to passing it on to my children and my grandchildren one day."

"And will you tell them the story of how you got it?"

"The story of how their grandfather salvaged it from the rubble during his time in the Second World War?" She twisted her lips into a playful smirk as his eyes lit up. "I won't spare a single detail."

He studied her face, pushing a curl behind her ear and letting his hand trail down the nape of her neck. "I'm not sure our grandchildren will want to know about the many kisses involved."

"Perhaps we'll keep that to ourselves."

On the way to the kitchen, they passed the window where more snowflakes flitted around.

"Too bad the snow isn't sticking," she said. "You owe me a sledding date."

Benjamin stopped and pulled her tight against him, one arm around her waist and one holding her hand against his heart. "And you owe me a dance."

"Well, you can dance with me whatever the weather for the rest of our lives. And one day, the time we've spent apart will be a mere breath compared to the years we've shared. I love you, Benjamin Gabriel."

"And I love you, mon ange."

Janine Rosche lives in northwestern Ohio with her husband, four children, and two sweet dogs. She is a certified family life educator and teaches college courses in human development, love and marriage, psychology, and family relations. She infuses this experience into her contemporary romance novels by creating relatable characters and relevant conflict. Her website is www.janinerosche. com. Janine is represented by Tamela Hancock Murray of the Steve Laube Agency.

MAKING ROOM AT THE INN

by Deborah Raney

DEDICATION

For our three newest grandbabies: Ivy Corinne, Beckett Ryan, and Baby Smith-to-be. What joy you bring to our hearts! May you always make room in *your* hearts for the Reason.

ACKNOWLEDGMENTS

There aren't enough pages to thank everyone who has poured into every book I write, but I offer deep appreciation to my agent, Steve Laube; my editors, Rebecca Germany and Ellen Tarver; my precious writing critique partner, Tamera Alexander; my early readers, dear friend Terry Stucky and my sister Vicky Miller; and my precious family, most especially the love of my life, Ken Raney. Special thanks to Susanne, Shannon, and Janine for their charming stories that gave my characters families and a history before I even got to know them!

Finally, and most importantly, I owe my life, my all, to Jesus, the Reason for the season.

Joseph also went up from Galilee, out of the city of Nazareth, into Judea, to the city of David, which is called Bethlehem, because he was of the house and lineage of David, to be registered with Mary, his betrothed wife, who was with child. So it was, that while they were there, the days were completed for her to be delivered. And she brought forth her first-born Son, and wrapped Him in swaddling cloths, and laid Him in a manger, because there was no room for them in the inn.

LUKE 2:4–7 NKJV

CHAPTER 1

Benjie Gabriel shifted in the uncomfortable auditorium seat and coiled the loose wire on her spiral notebook around one finger. Would this professor *ever* shut up? She'd be late for her interview if she didn't get out of here in about five minutes. And the guy seemed nowhere near ready to wind down, droning on and on about supply-side economics.

She'd taken a seat near the front of the auditorium, but now she'd have to climb all the way to the back while everyone watched, no doubt envying that she was escaping early. She waited five full minutes before quietly gathering her backpack and water bottle and starting the long ascent to the balcony-level doors.

She didn't make eye contact with the other students, but she could feel their eyes on her just the same. Being a twenty-six-year-old college student was awkward. It wasn't as if she was a slacker who hadn't done anything with her life until now. She had a certificate from a respectable culinary school. Never mind she'd worked two jobs for four years after high school to save enough for only two years of culinary training in Chicago. It irked her more than a little that she'd had to pay thousands of dollars for a certificate saying she had a marketable skill when the truth was, thanks to her dad, she'd already possessed her talent for cooking the day she entered her first classroom at the culinary school. And so far, that certificate had landed her exactly zero chef's jobs. Not that she hadn't learned anything at all in those two years, but surely there were better ways to spend the money it had taken her so long to save.

She jogged across campus to her car, working to stay beneath the canopy of trees as much as possible to avoid the warm October sun, but she was a damp, hot mess by the time she got behind the wheel. She blasted the AC, hoping to cool down before she got to the inn. Even though she knew where Keye's Inn was, she plugged the address into her phone. It had been years since she'd actually been there, and she didn't have time to get lost on one of the dead-end streets down by the river.

She'd come back to Cape Girardeau to satisfy her mother's request and earn a business degree at the university. Mom hadn't been willing to foot the bill for culinary school, but apparently a "real" degree was different. Benjie felt a little guilty that even though she was working on that degree, her goal hadn't changed whatsoever. Despite being a smaller town, Cape boasted dozens of restaurants, and Benjie held out hope that she'd find a job she could love here in Missouri—hopefully long before she graduated. Would Mom be so eager to help with tuition if she knew that?

The job she was interviewing for in ten minutes was her dream job—the one she'd envisioned herself doing since she was a little girl twirling in a fancy dress during Christmas tea at Keye's Inn. Despite the fact that it was eighty-five degrees with the trees in full leaf instead of the snow-covered streets and leafless branches from her memory, she sighed, her thoughts floating back to that winter day at Keye's Inn when she was six. It was the one memory of Mimi that she treasured above all others.

Mimi, her paternal great-grandmother, had brought her again when she was twelve, and that day was magical too, but by then she'd been more concerned about missing out on what her friends were doing than spending time with Mimi. She wished she could go back in time and lecture her twelve-year-old self. Or give her the swift kick her bratty self deserved.

At the top of a hill coming down Broadway, she caught a glimpse of the mighty Mississippi through the open floodgates. Her turnoff was just ahead, and she slowed the car, trying to read street signs that were mostly hidden behind overgrown branches and shrubs.

Turning north, she smiled as Keye's Inn came into view, its two chimneys popping up through the trees like periscopes. Adrenaline kicked in as she pulled into the brick circle drive of the stately 1920s home. But even as her heart beat faster, she steeled herself for disappointment. She'd heard "no" too many times to think this might be different.

The plane of the pine felt smooth beneath his hand, and Trevor Keye switched to a finer grain of sandpaper, moving the block over the surface of the bench with practiced strokes. Almost there. Sure, he could have saved time using an electric sander, but to him, that would have felt like cheating.

He would treat the white pine with a simple oil finish, no varnish, and the bench would sit at the foot of a bed in one of the guest rooms at the inn. His dad would deem the piece too humble for the award-winningest bed and breakfast in Cape Girardeau County, but then, there wasn't much he and his dad agreed on these days. And besides, the inn was his now. For better or worse.

Trevor pushed harder on the block and inhaled the pungent scent of sawdust, forcing the troubling thought aside. He glanced at the clock over the workbench. He had an interview in five minutes. And if this one didn't gain him a cook, he'd be slaving over a hot frying pan the rest of the week instead of over this fine piece of wood.

He slipped off his carpenter's apron and went to wash up. A quick glance in the dusty mirror over the shop sink told him it would take more than a little soap and water to look presentable, but there was no time to do anything about that. He scrubbed his hands, splashed water on his face, and ran his fingers through hair that hadn't been cut in two months.

He locked up the shop and walked across the gravel drive to the inn's kitchen entrance. The front doorbell was ringing when he stepped inside.

He hurried past a sink overflowing with this morning's breakfast dishes. He didn't have guests checking in until after five, so the inn was quiet, but if this applicant was serious, they'd want to see the kitchen before they said yes to the job, and its current state did not speak well of the inn.

Trevor wasn't even sure if it was a man or a woman he'd be talking to. The name was Benjie something-or-other. The only image that popped up every time he saw the name on the application was that runaway dog from the movies when he was a kid. Chuckling to himself, he made a mental note not to mention *that* Benji during the interview.

The doorbell rang again, and he flipped on lights as he hurried through the dim hallway and opened the door to a person undeniably of the feminine persuasion.

She looked up at him, the breeze playing havoc with a tumble of wild auburn curls. "Hi." She smiled timidly. "I'm Benjie Gabriel. I have an interview with Mr. Keye."

"Come on in. We'll go back to my office." He held the door for her then closed it behind her and started down the hall. It wasn't really his office. It was Mom's, still decorated, like the rest of the inn, in the Victorian-era style she loved. The room still held most of her things too, including an ancient desktop computer that could still connect to the internet if he held his tongue just right. He'd booted it up this morning so he could print out Benjie Gabriel's application and have it in front of him.

"So, *you're* Mr. Keye?"

He glanced over his shoulder at her. Who did she think he was, the doorman? "Yes. I'm Trevor Keye." He entered the tiny room that was used only on rare occasions. If anyone saw his real office out in the woodshop, they'd likely report him to the sanitation department.

He scooped the cat off the chair in front of the desk and deposited him on the floor. "Have a seat. You're not allergic, I hope."

"Excuse me?"

"To cats." He went behind his desk and pulled out his chair.

"Oh. No, I like cats just fine." As if to prove it, she stooped and scratched Pumpkin under the chin, speaking in that baby-talk voice women always used with animals. "What a pretty kitty you are!"

He waited for her to sit down, then reviewed her application on the computer screen before looking up at her. "So you studied at Kendall?"

"Yes. I earned my certificate from there. I can show you, if you'd like. . . ." She reached for the small purse she'd placed on the floor beside her.

"That won't be necessary. I believe you." Although maybe he shouldn't, given her eagerness to produce the certificate. He glanced over her application again, even though he pretty much had it memorized. He'd only had two other serious inquiries about the opening. Given that the first guy had been fired from his last three jobs, he wasn't even an option. The second one came highly recommended but couldn't start until mid-November. There was no way he could do this on his own for another week, let alone a month. The young woman sitting in front of him didn't look like she could heft a twenty-pound sack of flour if her life depended on it. But he didn't have the luxury of being picky. He tapped the papers in front of him. "You've never worked as a chef?"

"No, sir, not officially. But I've been cooking since I was a kid, and—"

"Um. . . This isn't exactly a peanut-butter-and-jelly establishment."

She started, as if she'd been stung.

He hadn't meant the comment to come off as gruffly as it had, but "cooking since I was a kid" was not at all the kind of reference he hoped for. Too much was riding on him keeping up the inn's award-winning reputation.

She blinked and seemed to recover. He couldn't help but notice that she had beautiful eyes. Not quite brown, not quite green, but something in between. Maybe what they called hazel? They reminded him of the topaz tiles in the inn's fireplace surround.

"Actually"—she cleared her throat—"you'd be surprised how popular peanut butter and jelly has become in the food industry. It's actually quite healthy if served on whole-grain bread and with all-fruit jam or apple butter or a—"

340

"Hey, hey. . .I was only teasing. But I rather doubt my guests will be expecting peanut butter and jelly as breakfast fare."

"You'd be surprised what a delicious breakfast a peanut butter and bacon sandwich on homemade sweet potato bread makes."

Not on his watch, it didn't. "I'd be surprised, all right."

She narrowed her eyes at him. "Would I be using your recipes? If I got the job, I mean."

"Is that what you'd prefer?" This woman might be a loose cannon. He dare not encourage her.

"Actually, I prefer being creative." Her smile turned impish.

"We can discuss that later perhaps. But we'd need something tried and true. Our guests can't be guinea pigs."

"No, of course not. I wouldn't serve anything until it had been properly tested."

"It might be best if you start with our tried-and-true, award-winning recipes. Then we can discuss adding something a little more. . .creative to the menu."

She looked hopeful. "I don't mean to be too forward, but do you know when you'll have made a decision?"

"Oh, the job is yours if you want it." Hadn't he made that clear? Maybe not. "I'm getting desperate, and right now you're my only option."

She laughed, an airy, musical giggle that made her auburn curls dance around her cheeks. "Wow, then I'm honored."

Hearing more than a trace of sarcasm in her tone, he let himself smile. "That didn't come out so well, did it?"

"No, it did not. But I'm desperate too, so I guess we're even."

Touché. He laughed, then quickly sobered. "You do understand the position of chef is only temporary? My regular chef has twins on the way, and she's been put on bed rest."

"Yes, I read that in the classifieds—that it was temporary, I mean. When will she return to work?"

"The babies are due in early February, but her doctor said she'll probably go into labor as early as mid-January. With another six weeks for maternity leave, probably through February, but it could be a bit longer. Will that work? We'll know more after the babies are here."

She sighed. "I'll make it work. To be honest, I'm looking for full-time work."

"Oh, this *is* full-time. You'll start at six each morning and be finished by twelve thirty. Sometimes sooner. But it's six days a week. Sundays off, but you cook for Sunday on Saturday, since we book guests all weekend. It was all in the ad." She said she'd read the ad.

"Yes, I understand that. What I mean is, I wasn't looking for temporary work. I'm hoping for a career. As a chef."

He nodded slowly. "I see. My misunderstanding." If he wasn't careful, he was going to scare her off by his sheer rudeness. And he needed her. He shuffled the pages of her application. "It says here that you could start immediately? You're not currently employed?"

She laughed nervously. "I'm a full-time student. Here at the college. But I've scheduled all my classes for the afternoons," she added quickly, "so I'm free the hours you're talking about."

"I see." Not ideal. But beggars couldn't be choosers. "Well, I'm looking for a self-starter. I work from home, so I'm here most of the time, but I'm usually in my shop out back, so I can't be running in and out to supervise."

"I understand. I consider myself very independent. A self-starter, like you requested."

Ah, so she had read the ad. "Well then, when could you start?"

"Right now, if you need me." She glanced around the room as if looking for a clock. "I guess it's after hours, but I can be here first thing in the morning."

"Then you're hired." He gave her his best smile and came around the desk to shake her hand. "I assume you'll want to see the kitchen?"

Her expression said it had never crossed her mind. That didn't bode well.

But she brightened. "I'd love to. I came here for tea with my great-grandmother when I was a little girl, but of course that didn't include a tour of the kitchen."

"Well, let's take a quick run-through before you leave. I'll be here in the morning to get you started, but you might feel better knowing exactly what you're getting into."

If it were physically possible to kick oneself, he would have taken full advantage. He'd never claimed to have personnel skills. Or, for that matter, any of the skills necessary to run a bed and breakfast. But his mother had taught him how to be polite. And kind. And he was failing miserably at both. He squared his shoulders and determined that for the next twenty minutes he would be the nicest man Benjie Gabriel had ever met. Because he needed her to say yes to this job.

CHAPTER 2

Mentally pinching herself, Benjie followed Mr. Keye from his office and down a different hallway than the one they'd entered by. Either he was really tall or the ceilings were low in this hallway. The wood floors creaked gloriously beneath their feet, and Benjie was glad his back was to her so she could gawk at the architecture—the transom windows over each doorway, the elaborate ceiling cornices. She would live here in a heartbeat. Well, minus the profusion of tchotchkes and doilies she'd encountered in the living room off the entry. She was not fond of dusting.

Still, this house was incredible. Maybe the squeaky floors would muffle the pounding of her heart. She had a job at Keye's Inn! It seemed too incredible to be true. She reminded herself that the position was only temporary. Not even six months. Still, she would relish every single day and pray that by some miracle the job might turn into full-time.

The large orange tabby cat had followed them from the office and now slipped silently past her to wind a figure eight between Mr. Keye's feet.

"Oh no you don't, buddy." He picked up the cat and carried it in a football hold. "He's not allowed in the kitchen."

"I'll remember that. What's his name?"

"Pumpkin. I didn't name him."

"Oh, but it fits." She laughed, even as she wondered why he felt the need to give a disclaimer.

They came to a set of french doors that overlooked a flagstone patio lush with flowerpots and a trio of vintage ice cream parlor tables that sat beneath the shade of black-and-white-striped market umbrellas. Mr. Keye stopped and opened one of the doors, depositing the cat outside. Pumpkin hopped onto a cushioned settee and curled up in a patch of dappled sunlight. Benjie was jealous.

Her new boss turned to her, running a hand over the shadow of a beard at his jawline. "This is where you'll enter. Parking is around back. You'll see my Jeep out there. You can park beside it. This door will be open during the day, but I'll get you keys in case it's locked when you arrive. And by the way, the cat usually hangs out in the woodshop or in my basement apartment, but if he's at the door when you arrive in the morning, don't let him talk you into coming inside, persuasive as he can be."

She smiled, trying to imagine how a cat would persuade her of anything. But she nodded, taking note of every detail, wishing she could start work this very minute.

"The kitchen is around the corner here." He motioned for her to precede him. "It's small, but I think you'll find it adequate for your purposes."

A lingering fragrance of cinnamon and vanilla met her even

before they reached the kitchen. And then she turned and stepped through the wide doorway and stopped. She had to work to stifle a gasp, for she was standing in the kitchen of her dreams. The *absolute* kitchen of her wildest dreams!

An ornate chandelier hung over a table and chairs tucked cozily into one end of the room. The walls rose at least ten feet to pressed tin ceilings, and the back wall of the nook was bricked from top to bottom. An old hutch leaned against the brick. Painted her favorite robin's-egg blue, the hutch held an exquisite mismatch of old dishes. No doubt the same cups and saucers she and Mimi had taken tea from that long ago Christmas. Oh how she wished they'd taken a photo that day!

She turned to her right and could no longer hold back her amazement. The narrow galley kitchen boasted stone floors, glass-front cabinets, and a beefy gas range with a pot-filler faucet at the back. The range looked new, but the faucet, like nearly everything else in the kitchen, looked original to the house. She pointed. "Does that work?"

"I think you'll find everything in working order. At least as of this morning when I made breakfast."

"Oh, so you're a chef too?" Now she felt intimidated.

"No. Oh no." He held up a hand, palm out. "I can scramble eggs and shove a slice of bread in the toaster, but I'm no chef. I've just had no choice with Megan out of commission."

She nodded. "This kitchen is beautiful. Truly gorgeous."

"Megan complains it's too small, but then she's a little wider now than when she first started working here."

"The downside of being a good cook, I guess. I just hope I don't gain thirty pounds working here." His look of confusion made her realize what he'd actually meant. "Ohh. . . You mean because of her pregnancy?"

"Yes." His eyes held amusement, but he kept a straight face. "The pantry is back here. I think it's stocked to get us through the weekend, but you'll want to start a grocery list around your own plans. I think you'll find Megan left excellent notes on the laptop"—he pointed back to the round table in the nook—"and that's where you'll find all the recipes as well. But if you're like my mom and prefer a recipe card, those are all in the recipe box over there."

She nodded, feeling the weight of responsibility grow heavier. She was starting tomorrow, cooking in a kitchen where she didn't have a clue where things were kept or what guests were accustomed to. Not only that, but she would apparently be making his mom's recipes. What had she been thinking? "Um. . . What are you expecting me to cook for breakfast tomorrow? And how many will be here? And what time do you usually serve breakfast?"

He held up that "stop-sign" hand again. "Whoa, whoa. . . One at a time. Our guests pay a premium because of our breakfasts. Believe me, they haven't been getting their money's worth the last few days while I've been cooking." He rolled his eyes. "Megan usually serves an egg dish with meat, a fruit cup, and a coffee cake or scones or something else good and carb-y. That way there's something for everyone."

"Do you have a gluten-free or keto menu?"

He shook his head—rather adamantly, she thought. "If guests request it, you can substitute extra fruit or nuts for the bread or cake. But I'm not running a health-food store. We win awards because we serve *real* food, and I've yet to taste a gluten-free bread that would win anything other than an all-expense-paid trip to the dumpster."

"Wow." She couldn't help it. She laughed. "But tell me how you *really* feel, Mr. Keye."

"Sorry. Pet peeve. And you can call me Trevor. Please. Mr. Keye is my father."

"I wondered. That's why I was surprised when you answered the door. I was expecting someone much older and—" She waved a hand. "Never mind."

"And what should I call you? Is Benjie short for Benjamina?"

She cast him a wry smile. "Please, no. Benjie is my given name. It's a combination of my great-grandparents' names—Benjamin and Elodie. Dad thought it was cute. Most people just think I'm named after that dog from the movies."

He laughed out loud. "I know the one. And that thought did cross my mind. Sorry."

"Well, FYI, his name—the dog's—is spelled *B-e-n-j-i*. There's an *e* on the end of my Benjie."

"Noted." He looked like he was about to choke on laughter. Whatever.

She changed the subject. "So, you manage the inn now?"

"I own the inn now."

"Oh. I'm sorry. But it was your family that started it, right? Same Keyes?"

"Yes. I bought it from my parents."

"They're retired?" It struck her too late that his parents may not be living, though she hadn't found any mention of their. . .demise when she explored the inn's website yesterday. But then, there was no mention of Trevor Keye either. Apparently the website had been updated about as recently as the rest of the house. Which was still lovely but a little frillier than she remembered. At least it still matched the photos online.

But Trevor looked young. Not much older than she was. Of course, she was only twenty-six and she had only one living parent.

Oh Dad. . . She swallowed back the memories that threatened. "I'm sorry if I'm asking too many questions. It's just that I think I remember your mother from when I was young and came here with my great-grandmother. Your mom was so pretty and cheerful and welcoming."

That comment earned her a smile. It was one worth earning. "She still is. Pretty and cheerful. She moved to Nashville two years ago." His smile faded.

"Your inn has had a fond place in my heart ever since Mimi first brought me here. Even though I haven't had a chance to come back since I was a little girl."

"Oh? You're not from Cape?"

"No, I grew up in Kansas City. I'm not sure how Mimi—my great-grandmother—knew about this place, but we made a special trip here for tea when I was six and again when I turned twelve. I don't know why I remember it so well, but it was kind of. . .magical."

He nodded. "Yeah, we get that a lot."

"Especially at Christmas. Both times Mimi brought me, you were all decorated for the holidays. It was just lovely!"

"Which reminds me. . ." He brushed an invisible crumb from the granite countertop into his hand and deposited it in the deep farmhouse sink. "We're always extra busy during the holidays. . . probably starting early next month. Part of your job will be to help with decorations around the inn and with baking some seasonal items for the teas. We serve afternoon tea three days a week in December for various groups. We can talk later about the other tasks, namely, some flower arranging, decorating, and of course, the kitchen cleanup."

She opened her mouth to protest, but now that she thought about it, those things had been mentioned in the ad she'd seen online. She'd been so focused on the "chef" part of the job description, she'd blown off the rest. But she needed this job, and it was the only thing she'd interviewed for that worked with her class schedule at the college. At least it got her a foot in the door and something to put on her résumé when the perfect job came up. Although, when she thought about it, she couldn't think of anything more perfect than cooking in this inn that had such a special place in her memories.

"I trust you're okay with the extra duties? The hours wouldn't change from what was in the ad, and Megan was able to do everything without putting in any overtime." His voice broke through her reverie.

Did she have a choice? "I'll do my best. Cooking is really my gifting. I'm not much of a decorator, but if you can show me what to do. . ." If he could see her apartment right now, he would not be talking to her about decorating.

"We try to do something a little different each year. Keeps it fresh for people who come back. So you do whatever you think looks good. Time at the inn has become a tradition for a lot of people. Of course, we only have five guest rooms, so we fill up fast. I've had every night in December booked since the first of the year."

She lifted an eyebrow. "Well, that's great job security, I guess."

"Yes, and speaking of which, I have work in the shop calling me." He turned and started back down the hallway.

"The shop?" She trailed behind him, hurrying to keep up. "Is there a gift shop here at the inn?"

He laughed but kept walking, not turning to look at her. "No. By shop I meant woodshop. I build furniture—benches and such—and make cutting boards and utensils and. . .I do a little carving." He almost sounded embarrassed at the admission.

"Ah, so you're an artist. That's really cool. So is that a full-time job? What kind of things do you carve?"

"Oh, not full-time. Running the inn is the full-time job. The woodworking is more of a hobby. The inn's office is out in the shop too, though not where you interviewed, but where I keep the books and handle reservations and such. When I'm not mowing and keeping up with the gardening and watering."

"The patio is gorgeous."

"Thanks." They came to the french doors again, and he stopped, pointing outside toward a quaint-looking shed that was mostly hidden behind a tangle of evergreen trees and overgrown shrubs. "That's where you'll find me most of the day. But don't worry, I'll be available tomorrow to help you get started. We have a pretty light schedule this weekend. Three couples checking in tonight. They'll all be here two nights, and one couple for Saturday night only, so you'll need to vary the menu so we don't repeat. You'll find the menus on Megan's laptop."

"What time does breakfast need to be ready in the morning?"

"I'll have to check. I'm not sure my guests have let me know yet. We always say any time after seven, so you'll have at least an hour to prep."

"Oh. Okay. And do you serve buffet style, or do I need to plate breakfast?"

"Buffet. Unless someone requests it brought up to their room. Megan likes to serve on the patio when the weather is nice, but if not, you saw the dining room as you came in. You'll set the buffet up there. You'll need to be in chef's whites anytime you're with guests. I trust you have your own uniforms?"

She nodded.

"If you prefer, we can launder them here."

"No. Thanks, but I'll do my own." She had one good set of whites that had broken the bank when she was in school. She wasn't about to trust them to the inn's laundry. But she'd have to buy another set with her first paycheck.

"Megan left a couple of coats here." He regarded her for a moment, seeming to literally size her up. "But you'd be swimming in her coats. Of course, you'll put your hair up. I don't require a toque, but if you want to wear one, that's great. Megan did, and our guests always seem impressed when the chef wears the white hat. Oh, and I almost forgot. The teas I mentioned run from November through Christmas. These are afternoon teas for community members by reservation only. You'll be baking ahead for those daily starting the first week in November. There's a deep freeze in the pantry where we stockpile finished pastries for the teas. Not everything can be made ahead, but we do what we can."

"You said afternoon? But I have classes in the afternoon. All semester."

"Oh no. I didn't mean you'd have to be here to *serve* tea. I hire temp help to serve. Your job is just to bake the goodies."

No wonder he was so desperate to replace Megan. "What a time to lose your chef, huh?"

He rolled his eyes. "Tell me about it. And if you have any spare time on days we're not fully booked, you can use that to work on the seasonal decorations."

This was getting more complicated by the minute. She had not hired on to be a decorator! And she didn't own a toque. But she'd get one. And wear it proudly. Just probably not by tomorrow.

For now she would simply be thrilled that she was finally a chef—a *real* chef. At Keye's Inn.

CHAPTER 3

By the time Benjie parked beside Mr. Keye's Jeep the following morning, she was sweating like meringue on a humid day. She was operating on about two hours of sleep since, while ironing her chef's whites last night, she'd thought of a dozen questions she should have asked her boss. Important questions like where was she supposed to change into her uniform? Which serving pieces should she use, and where were they stored? What if she couldn't get the gas stove to light? They'd had all kinds of trouble with the gas lines in one of the brand-new ranges in the culinary school's kitchens, and one guy had almost blown up the place trying to light a stubborn back burner.

She'd finally convinced herself that she was being ridiculous worrying about questions that likely had easy answers. And things seemed a skosh brighter now with the sun just starting to peek over the Mississippi in a blaze of sherbet pinks and oranges. Mr. Keye had said he'd be here to get her started, but there were no lights on at the back of the house where she was to enter.

"Breathe, Benj, breathe. It's going to be fine," she whispered, eyeing her reflection in the rearview mirror. She'd tied up her hair in a regulation topknot, but someone forgot to inform her unruly curls about said regulations. The toque she'd ordered off of Amazon last night was due to arrive Monday. She'd have to make do with the can of hairspray in her tote until then.

She opened her car door, gathered the hanger with her crisply pressed uniform, and her bag, which weighed approximately 372 pounds since she'd thrown in every possible item she might need before her shift ended at one o'clock this afternoon. Locking the car behind her, she hiked the bag up on her shoulder and walked across the patio to the french doors. Taking a deep breath, she reached for the handle. *Locked.*

He'd said he'd get her keys, but. . . She looked around, wondering if she should go to the front and ring the bell. But she didn't want to wake the guests. That would not be a good way to start her first day at the inn. She knocked quietly on the glass, hoping to rouse her boss. But hadn't he said he lived in the basement? Doubtful he'd hear her knocking from all the way down there. And the shop windows were dark. She waited three minutes—still no answer.

She left her bag by the door and hooked the hanger with her uniform over the edge of a hanging petunia. Picking her way around the side of the house on grass still wet with dew, she climbed the wide stairway to the inn's front door. Maybe it would be unlocked.

Nope. Fort Knox.

She retraced her steps to the back entrance and tried again. No luck. She checked her watch. It was almost ten minutes after six. Let the record show that she had been here at six o'clock sharp. And time was wasting!

She knocked one more time, a bit louder this time, but when there was no answer, she went to sit at one of the ice cream tables on the patio where she could see the doors. The striped market umbrellas had been rolled down for the night. After waiting five minutes, she decided to put all the umbrellas up. Mr. Keye had said Megan liked to serve breakfast on the patio. The sun would be up by the time she served—assuming she ever got in!—so she may as well do what she could out here. If someone didn't hurry up and let her in, the guests would be dining on cold cereal!

Once the umbrellas were up, she checked the doors once more, then headed across the gravel driveway to see if perhaps her boss was in his woodshop. She mentally corrected herself: *Trevor.* That would take some getting used to. It felt too familiar to use his first name, even though he couldn't be much older than she was. Maybe early thirties?

The light beneath the canopy on the small stoop was on, but she couldn't remember if it had been on when she arrived. She climbed the two steps and knocked. Loud, desperation setting in.

No answer. Seeing a window to her left, she walked along the flower bed that ran across the front of the shed and peeked in the window, cupping her hands around her eyes. . .and came face-to-face with Trevor Keye!

Eyes wide, he stared back, headphones on, wood tool in hand. Benjie jumped back and staggered to catch her footing. But couldn't. She landed on her backside in the soft grass edging the flower bed.

"What on earth. . . ?" Muttering, Trevor swiped off his headphones and pushed away from his workbench, pulling his carpenter's apron over his head as he ran to the front door. The window peeker was dusting off the seat of her jeans. "What are you doing?"

She huffed. "I couldn't get in." Benjie Gabriel's curls had escaped from the bun on top of her head and formed a wild halo around her flushed face. She took a step backward and pointed over her shoulder, looking sheepish. "I tried the side doors like you said, and they were locked, so I went around front, but I didn't want to ring the bell and wake your guests. So I thought maybe you were out here."

"You might have knocked—"

"I did knock!" Fire lit her eyes, turning them more topaz than green.

"If you'll let me finish." He spoke slowly, trying—and failing—to hide his amusement. "I was going to say, you might have knocked, but I had my music turned up. . .headphones. . .so I didn't hear you."

"Oh." She looked appropriately cowed, but only for a moment. "I'm sorry. But it's twenty after six. If I'm supposed to serve breakfast at seven, I— Well, that's just not going to happen." She swallowed hard, and for a minute he was afraid she might cry.

Pumpkin sauntered out of the shop door he'd left ajar and made a beeline for Benjie. He had a feeling she wasn't in the mood for a feline bath right now, so he intercepted the cat and deposited him back in the shop.

"I'll help you with breakfast. Just. . .calm down." He'd lock up later. Right now he needed to keep his new chef from having a stroke. Fishing the house keys from his pocket, he started toward the patio. He heard her traipsing behind him on the gravel, huffing—whether because she was out of breath or furious with him, he wasn't sure.

As they approached the house, he hid a smile, seeing her chef's uniform dancing in the breeze hanging from a bedraggled pot of pink petunias. He made a mental note to start pruning the spent flowers and putting away pots for the winter. As if he needed one more thing to do.

He hefted the large tote bag that sat by the door, groaning involuntarily under its weight. "Good grief, did you bring your own brick oven? What have you got in here?"

She giggled, and some of her steam seemed to dissipate. "I wasn't sure what I'd need. I brought my favorite pots and knives. I should have brought something to pick locks with."

Zing. Chuckling, he unlocked the door and motioned for her to go in. He set her tote on the kitchen table and indicated the arched opening ahead of her. "There's a powder room around the corner. You can change there and keep your things in the walk-in closet beside the sink. Meanwhile, I'll go scramble some eggs."

She rummaged in the tote and pulled out a smaller bag. "I'll be right back."

True to her word, five minutes later, she appeared beside him looking sharp in baggy houndstooth drawstring pants and a slim white coat. Her hair had been tamed back into its bun—much to his chagrin. He checked the thought too late.

She must have noticed, for she patted her hair as if checking for loose strands. "I don't have a toque yet, but I will by next week."

"No problem. Your hair isn't going anywhere." With a wink, he scooted over to make room for her at the stove. "I hope you don't mind using our pots and pans this morning. I already have the scramble started. Friday is Farmer's Scramble and English scones with clotted cream."

She stared at him. "I seem to recall that clotted cream takes twenty-four hours to make."

"Ah, we do it the old-fashioned way." He opened the fridge and produced a glass jar labeled Devon Cream. "Special order. Amazon.

And please treat this like the gold it is. You'd have to ask Megan, but I think this is twelve bucks a jar or something like that."

"Ouch. I'll make it next time. It'll save you a small fortune."

He didn't trust that her recipe would meet the standards of the good stuff he ordered—which Megan thought was superior—but now wasn't the time to burst Benjie's bubble. They had guests to feed. He noticed that rather than using the laptop, she was consulting his mother's recipe that he'd stuck to the range hood with a magnet.

"I see you're a recipe card kind of chef." He pointed to the stained recipe for Farmer's Scramble. "I've got the sausage already browned. Can you prep the vegetables, and I'll grate cheese?"

She glanced at the clock. "Don't we need to get the scones in the oven first?"

"You get a small reprieve this morning. Megan left scones in the freezer. We'll heat those up to serve since we're getting a late start. And by the way, I'm sorry about this morning. I completely lost track of time."

She shrugged. "It's okay. I'm just glad you're walking me through things this morning."

He went to the fridge for the cheese and veggies for the scramble. He rolled a red pepper and a green one onto the cutting board beside the deep sink, along with an onion and the last of the tomatoes from the vine behind his shop.

She ran a hand over the surface of the cutting board, a simple utilitarian version he'd made from scraps several years ago. "This is too pretty to cut on."

"Thanks, but that's what a cutting board is for: cutting." The piece did have a unique striped pattern, and Megan had kept it nicely oiled, but it didn't have the flair of his recent work.

"You made this?"

He shrugged. "It was a practice piece."

"It's gorgeous." She selected a knife from the block on the counter and set to work. With his back to her, he couldn't watch her work, but under the guise of supervision, he snuck glances now and then, impressed with her skill. And more than a little disconcerted by her presence in his kitchen.

Benjie finished chopping the peppers and cleaned the knife, then searched for a tomato knife in the wood block on the counter. When she was finished, she slid the diced vegetables off the cutting board into the large sauté pan where Mr. Keye had butter melting over a low flame. A delicious aroma wafted through the kitchen. She moved the pan back and forth over the flame, tossing the vegetables while she studied the recipe on the stove's hood.

After a few minutes, he looked over her shoulder. "Ready for the eggs?"

"I believe so." She stepped to one side, and he poured the eggs into the pan then sprinkled the browned sausage on top. She gently moved the mixture around in the sauté pan until the eggs were set, then lowered the fire under the pan. She turned to find her sous chef—or was she his?—at the kitchen table with his laptop.

"Mr. Keye, did you season the eggs?"

He looked up. "I did. Though you might want to taste them. And please. . ." He cleared his throat. "It's Trevor. I'm too young for that Mr. Keye business."

She replied with a nod and turned back to the stove, sprinkling the grated cheese on top. She lifted a handful of the cheese closer to her nose. "This smells like cheddar. Mild cheddar." Nothing more boring.

"Is that a problem?"

"It's just that the recipe calls for Dubliner."

"Oh? I just grabbed what Megan had in the fridge. I've made it this way before. Nobody complained."

She grinned up at him. "Just don't tell anyone I made the scramble. It would be a whole different dish with the Dubliner. A delicious dish. I don't want to get a bad reputation my first day on the job."

"Well, *excuse* me. I didn't know cheddar was such a lowly cheese." He wasn't smiling.

"Cheddar has its place. But Dubliner would be the star of this scramble. I'm just saying. . ." She risked catching his gaze.

He didn't quite roll his eyes, but close. He pushed the laptop away and rose to join her. "I'll get the scones in the warming oven, and then I'll walk you through the coffee routine."

Routine? How hard could it be to make coffee? Biting her bottom lip, she curbed a sigh. Grateful as she was for his help with breakfast, Benjie wished she had the kitchen to herself on this first day of work. And she especially wished she could have wowed him with her own recipes—or at the very least, used the right ingredients in Megan's recipes. She prayed today's guests were from far, far away and only passing through. She would never forgive Trevor if word got around town that the new Keye's Inn chef served a bland scramble and frozen scones with clotted cream out of a jar!

She checked her thoughts. Definitely a first world problem. And the truth was, if she hadn't been so nervous after getting such a late start, she would have been singing her heart out over the circumstances that had placed her in this kitchen of her dreams.

As it was, she would just be thankful if they got breakfast to the patio—or wherever her boss wanted to serve—on time and without any mishaps. She was still slightly annoyed that his negligence had barely given her time to change into her whites, let alone find her way around the kitchen. But tomorrow was a new day. And she—only 240 days after graduating from culinary school—was finally a chef!

CHAPTER 4

Trevor locked the side door behind him and headed across the dark yard. Once past the patio, the gravel crunched beneath his feet and Pumpkin meowed behind him, trying to catch up. Early morning was his favorite time of day, mostly because it allowed him uninterrupted time to work in the shop. The bench was finished, and now he needed to get some new cutting boards glued and ready to oil before the art fair a week from today. For some reason, those things had been his top-selling item the last few fairs. He'd sold out at the last one and had even filled a couple of special orders.

But first he set a timer on his phone. He didn't dare get lost in his work again and risk the ire of his new chef. He really did feel bad about locking her out on her first day of work yesterday and made a mental note to get her a key before she left today. He hoped his apology had smoothed things over with her.

Today would be a rather easy day breakfast-wise. Most people wanted to sleep in on Saturdays, and the majority usually opted for breakfast in their rooms, so all she'd have to do before scrambling eggs was bake a coffee cake, fry some bacon, and toss together a berry compote.

He'd happily show her where everything was for the morning's menu, but he wasn't going to coddle her. Or listen to her insults if he dared to use a lowly cheddar. He chuckled to himself. He wasn't sure why the woman brought out his snarky side, but she did. Cute as she was with those big topaz eyes and that unruly hair, she had a bit of a bite to her bark. He hadn't decided yet if he liked that about her.

Almost an hour had passed when his phone signaled it was time to go unlock the doors for Benjie. But he'd made good progress gluing wood strips for the next batch of cutting boards. He cleaned off his work surface with a damp rag, wiped the excess glue from the assembled boards, and washed his hands in the utility sink near the door. The boards would have to wait until tomorrow to get planed and trimmed. Then he could sand and oil them the next day.

He'd been surprised by how much Benjie's compliment about the cutting board in the kitchen pleased him. He'd found himself trying to think of a way for her to "accidentally" see one of his nicer, handled boards. Now those were works of art, if he did say so himself.

He'd heard compliments like hers from countless others. Why then did they fade away, all but drowned out by his father's well-aimed criticism?

He dried his hands and locked up the shop, then headed to the house. Her car was already parked beside his Jeep, and she was sitting on the settee by the door. The three umbrellas were up, swaying in the morning breeze. Good. She was a self-starter.

When she spotted him, he raised a hand in greeting. "Morning."

"Good morning."

He checked his phone. "I have five fifty-seven."

That impish grin lit her face. "That's right. Just giving myself a little cushion."

"Again, I'm sorry about yesterday."

"All is forgiven. You're on time today."

"And so are you apparently." He let himself smile. "Come on in, and I'll show you where everything is."

Trevor led the way to the kitchen, and Benjie followed, inhaling the aroma of fresh-brewed coffee.

"Oh, I went ahead and made coffee." He flipped on the kitchen lights, and she mentally pinched herself. Yep. Still her dream kitchen.

"You didn't have to do that."

"Yes, I did." He tossed her a sheepish look. "I wanted a cup myself."

"Oh, well then. . . Thank you."

"But I need to show you how to use the espresso machine in case anyone orders a latte this morning. Unless you were a barista in a past life?" He looked so hopeful.

"No, afraid not." She frowned. She'd expected making a pot of coffee to be part of her duties, but it hadn't crossed her mind that she'd also have to figure out how to serve up an almond honey flat white on command. That was a whole different school, and that had not been in the job description. But she wouldn't let on. "I'm a fast learner."

"Let's go, then."

The espresso machine was on a cart in a corner of the dining room, and the knobs and dials on it made the process look about as easy as learning to fly an airplane. Without actually using coffee, he talked her through making a shot. But that was the problem. She'd told him she was a fast learner, but she was a hands-on learner. She actually had to perform a task before she figured it out. But she didn't have time for that this morning, so she pretended she understood his instructions and hurried back to the kitchen to start on the coffee cake.

She heard the back door close, and the house was cloaked in silence. Good. She could work much better without him looking over her shoulder. She'd taken a quick inventory of the cupboard and pantry yesterday but decided that while she was baking, the easiest thing would be to leave all the cupboard doors open so she could see where things were. She didn't have time to wash her hands every time she needed to locate an ingredient.

As she tried to decipher the traditional buttermilk coffee cake recipe through the smudges on the yellowed card, she plotted how she could convince her boss to let her use some of her own recipes.

She'd earned an impressive number of As in culinary school with her original recipes. Her adviser, who'd taught two of her classes, told her she had a talent for taking an ordinary dish and adding a fresh twist to it. She had her dad to thank for that, and oh how she wished he could have heard those golden words. They played often in her mind, especially while she was sending out her résumé—such as it was—all over the state, trying to land a job that paid enough to—

A loud bang sounded behind her, causing her to nearly drop the carton of buttermilk into the mixing bowl.

"Ouch!" Trevor stepped from behind an open cupboard door, holding his right hand over one eye. One by one, he slammed the open doors closed. "What in blazes?"

"Oh!" Benjie covered her mouth with her hands. "I am so sorry!

I thought it would be easier to find things if I—"

"It's fine," he huffed. "I should have watched where I was going."

Her thoughts exactly, but she wouldn't say that, of course.

He pulled his hand away from his eye and blinked.

"Oh! You're bleeding!" She sucked in a breath and ripped a length of paper toweling from the dispenser on the counter.

He touched his eye again. Seeing blood on his hand, he gave a low growl but took the paper towel from her, wadded it up, and pressed it to his eyebrow.

"Let me see." She had to stand on tiptoe to get a look at the wound. He closed his eyes and let her inspect it. It wasn't too deep, but he definitely took a hit. She couldn't help but notice that his dark eyelashes were longer than hers. And his hair, peppered with sawdust, smelled woodsy and delicious. She took a measured breath before managing, "It doesn't look like it needs stitches, and it's under your eyebrow, so any scar will be hidden."

He opened one eye and cast her a look that said a scar was the last thing he worried about. He took a step backward. "I need to get a bandage. But I came in to tell you that the couple in the Garnet Room needs to check out by eight, so they're requesting breakfast in their room at seven sharp."

He dabbed at his brow again and hurried from the kitchen.

Great. She went to the sink and thoroughly washed her hands. There was probably some complicated protocol for dealing with a bleeding incident, but she had thirty-five minutes to get breakfast plated and a tray up to the Garnet Room. The coffee cake would barely be out of the oven by then. And that was if she ever managed to get it in the oven!

With panic rising, she systematically opened the cupboard doors Trevor had just closed, looking for a serving tray. She finally gave up and cleared off a tray that held condiments on the kitchen table. It would have to do for now. But since she didn't have classes today, she could stay after her shift ended and try to learn her way around this kitchen. Maybe even organize things a bit more to her liking.

By some miracle, she managed to get breakfast finished and a tray ready for the departing couple. She didn't even know for sure where the Garnet Room was, but she'd find it. There were only five rooms in the inn, counting the upstairs suite.

She checked her reflection in the bottom of a large stainless frying pan hanging from a pot rack over the sink. The distorted image didn't hide the fact that her hair had escaped the bun and was out of control, as always, but she didn't have time to do anything about that.

She made sure all the burners were off, covered the tray with a clean tea towel, and headed into the front foyer where she'd entered for her interview. Gripping the tray, she started up the stairs, anticipation rising at a chance to see the rest of this inn. She'd caught glimpses of the inn when she interviewed, and again yesterday, but this was her first chance to go upstairs where the guest rooms were. The gorgeous oak floors in the long hallway featured a runner in shades of red and gold that led past four doorways to a bay window with space for a settee and chair and a collection of healthy houseplants. If she had her directions straight, the window overlooked the courtyard below. Once she delivered this breakfast tray, she'd go take a peek and get her bearings.

Each of the doors bore a signpost with the room's name. Garnet was the first door on the left. Next door was Emerald, and across the hall were Opal and Topaz. She'd have to ask Trevor how the rooms got their names.

Balancing one edge of the tray on her shoulder, she knocked quietly on the door. "Breakfast is served."

She heard stirring in the room beyond and waited until a sleepy-eyed man in pajamas answered. "Can you just set it outside the door, please?"

"Of course. Be careful," she whispered. "This coffee is extremely hot."

"Okay. Thanks." He disappeared, closing the door behind him, but not before Benjie got a peek at the room beyond—and a hint of the source of the room's name perhaps? She cringed. Not that she didn't love a pop of red here and there, but sleeping in that room would feel like being trapped inside a silk-padded box of Valentine chocolates. Everything in sight was red. Even the sunlight that canted through the room's tall windows had a red glow.

Benjie carefully lowered the tray to the floor, then hurried to the end of the hallway, careful not to make any noise. Peering down through the wavy glass in the bay window, she saw the tops of the umbrellas through the leafy branches. Such a pretty view, with many of the summer flowerpots still in bloom and the leaves tinged with the beginnings of fall color. If she lived here, she would have her coffee and quiet time with the Lord right here every morning. But not until she'd redecorated the Garnet Room.

By eleven o'clock, all the guests had checked out and the kitchen was halfway to sparkling. Except for Trevor's mishap with the cupboard door, the morning had gone surprisingly well, and Benjie was feeling rather proud of herself. Thankfully, no one had requested a latte—and she'd made sure not to offer one. She did have to call Trevor out of the shop to help a guest find the right kind of artificial sweetener for his coffee, but other than that, she'd managed everything just fine and without his help.

She spent the next hour and a half familiarizing herself with the kitchen and making notes of things she needed to add to the grocery list, a list that she'd discovered only a few minutes ago was her responsibility.

She should have known though. This wasn't like cooking for a big restaurant where suppliers delivered ingredients on a regular schedule. She needed a few items for Monday morning, so she'd leave her apartment early and do the shopping before work. She rather enjoyed being up before the sun, and she'd seen a couple of glorious sunrises on the river from the top of the hill, driving down Broadway each morning.

She changed out of her whites and redid her bun. But with half an hour still left on her shift, she decided to retrace her steps upstairs and finish checking out the lay of the land up there. And to discover whether the other rooms lived up to their jewel-toned names. Tiptoeing up the stairs felt a bit like trespassing, but she did need to know her way around the inn if delivering room service was going to be one of her duties.

She peeked into the Garnet Room and confirmed the room was even redder than she'd suspected, right down to the tile in the en suite bath. *Ugh.* On down the hall, the door to the Emerald Room stood open. She peered through the door before walking in. Yep. Green. Although this room seemed to be more recently—and tastefully— decorated. Emerald green was only an accent color, and the curtains were a lovely, modern floral print that let some light into the large room. The bed had been stripped and the duvet folded at the end of the mattress. For the first time, she wondered about the staff that cleaned bathrooms, did laundry, and made up the beds. She hadn't seen anyone come or go, but then, they probably wouldn't arrive until her shift was over, since check-in time wasn't until three.

The bathroom door was partially open and a light was on. She stepped in and took in the beautiful room with its old-fashioned soaking tub and creamy marble tile. There were two pocket doors at one end of the large room. One was slid open a few inches, but she didn't feel right about exploring beyond the doors without permission. She located the double light switch and flipped both switches off on her way out, closing the door behind her.

"Hey!"

She jumped back, stifling a scream.

"Could I have a little light, please?" Trevor's voice came from somewhere in the room she'd just vacated.

"I'm sorry! Where are you?" Cautiously, she opened the bathroom door and flipped the light back on.

"Thank you." One of the pocket doors slid open, and Trevor appeared, his arms loaded with sheets. "Do you need something?"

"I'm sorry. I was. . .I was trying—" She stammered, her face warming as she noticed the laundry room behind him. "I was just trying to familiarize myself with the inn."

"Well, this is the laundry. How about you familiarize yourself with these sheets and help me make that bed in there?" He brushed past her, shaking out a pillowcase, leaving the fresh scent of clean cotton in his wake.

"Is your housekeeping staff on leave too?" She definitely hadn't signed on for laundry duty, but she followed him nevertheless.

"Housekeeping staff?" He gave a dry laugh. "You're looking at him."

"What? You do all that yourself?" She could hardly believe he was still standing.

"All that and sometimes play chef too."

"Why don't you hire someone?" She took a contour sheet from

him and shook it out over the king-size bed.

He laid the other linens on an overstuffed chair and went to the opposite corner of the mattress. "I prefer to make a profit."

"Oh. I guess there is that." She laughed, suddenly feeling a little guilty for how well she was being paid.

"Been doing it since I was twelve. My parents both believed in child labor."

She laughed. "I wish more parents did."

"Well, I did earn a nice allowance for helping out at the inn, but it wasn't optional."

"I'm sure that's served you well." She looked pointedly at the small bandage spanning his right eyebrow. "Is your eye okay?"

He reached up and touched the bandage as if he'd forgotten it was there. He gave her a wry smile. "I think I'll live."

"I'm sorry."

"Sorry that I'll live?" His eyes held mischief.

"No, no. Sorry it happened. I shouldn't have—"

He waved away her apology. "No need to be sorry that *I'm* a klutz."

Relieved, she tucked her corner of the fitted sheet around the thick mattress. They worked together to make up the bed with Benjie following his lead. When they were finished, he lined up half a dozen throw pillows along the headboard like so many soldiers. The decorative items on the nightstand looked like a toddler had played with them, and it was all she could do not to group the pillows neatly and tidy up the top of the nightstand. But she resisted. It was his inn after all.

When they were finished, he met her gaze. "Thank you. That took about a quarter of the time with you helping."

She threw him a smirk. "Yeah, well, I think I'll be more careful about where and when I explore from now on."

His laughter was free and genuine. "I promise I won't take advantage. But thank you."

"I'm going to get groceries before I come Monday, so I might try to get here a little early so I can put them away."

"Let me get you a key."

"That'd be great. Thanks."

"Just promise me you'll turn it in when Megan comes back. I don't like to have too many of those floating around out there."

"Of course." She was happy he trusted her with a key. "Do you have any other sheets ready? I'll be happy to help for a while. I don't have class on Saturdays."

"If you're sure you don't mind. It'd be great to get in the shop earlier today."

"What are you working on?"

"Cutting boards. There's a big pumpkin festival up in Washington next weekend. I've got a booth there."

"Washington State? Or DC?"

He laughed. "Washington, M-O. It's a little town west of St. Louis. On the Missouri River."

"What do you do about the inn when you're at festivals?" She felt a little panicked at the thought of being on her own here at the inn. There was still so much she didn't know.

"Oh, I just have my stuff in someone else's booth on commission. I don't go to the festivals myself. That would be a dismal existence."

"Oh heavens, yes. Much better to be here cleaning toilets and making beds instead of eating corn dogs and getting a little sun."

He grabbed a throw pillow and, without warning, lobbed it at her.

Surprised, she threw it back. This was a side of him she hadn't seen. And she liked it. "Now where are those other sheets? I don't want to be here all day."

CHAPTER 5

Putting the throw pillow back in place, Trevor shot Benjie a self-satisfied look and headed to the laundry room for another set of sheets. "Follow me."

"Oh wow! Look at this!" Her voice came from behind him and he turned, laughing. "Megan had the same reaction the first time she saw the laundry room. Apparently it's every woman's dream to have two washers and two dryers. What would you even do with two of each? Well, unless you have a family of six you failed to mention."

He was kidding, but now that the words were out, he realized it was actually possible that she had a family. Of course, he couldn't ask such questions in the interview, and she hadn't volunteered that information one way or the other. He watched her, waiting for her reply, unsettled that he felt so much riding on how she answered.

"No, but I can see how Megan would want a setup like this with twins on the way. And it makes perfect sense for the inn. I guess I've only thought about the logistics of running a B&B where the second *B*—breakfast—is concerned."

He let out the breath he'd been holding. "Understandable." He pulled the still-warm linens from the second dryer and piled them in her outstretched arms. Opening the door to the side hall, he motioned her to follow.

"Ooh, a secret passageway."

He laughed. "Not all that secret, and for future reference, we do keep both entrances to the laundry locked when guests are here. Too many supplies went missing when we left them unlocked."

"Really? How sad! What is wrong with people?" She frowned.

"If I had to guess, I'd say it has something to do with them being human."

She clucked her tongue. "Still. That's just wrong."

"I couldn't agree more." He appreciated how indignant she was on his account. "The key I give you will lock the laundry doors too."

"Good to know. Not that I plan on ever being in the laundry room again." She winked.

He liked this playful side of her, even as he was disappointed to hear she didn't intend to help him make up beds in the future. It really did make a world of difference, and he wished he'd added it to her job description.

"So I guess it's futile to ask you to help me clean bathrooms too? Oh, and also, for future reference, cleaning supplies are in the cupboard over the washing machines."

"Most definitely futile! Don't even give me that information." Her eyes flashed. "Besides, it wouldn't be very sanitary having these hands that prepare the food also in the toilets, now would it?"

"Well, I hate to disappoint, but. . ." He held up his own hands.

"Eww." But her expression said she was teasing.

He grinned. He hadn't enjoyed making up rooms this much since—well, ever. He quickly turned away, pushing the thought from his mind. The last thing in the world he needed was to get tangled up with an employee. "I shouldn't keep you," he said over his shoulder. "I'm sure you have better things to do with your Saturday."

He led the way to the Opal Room and started to work on the bed. They worked together in silence until the bed was finished.

"What about towels?"

"They're in the other washer. I'll take care of them later."

"I haven't seen the other rooms. Would you mind if I take a peek before I go?"

"Of course. I know sometimes you just need a break from the kitchen, so feel free to wander around. As long as it doesn't interfere with guests' privacy—or mine—you're welcome to any of the public areas of the house. The basement is my territory, just so you know."

"Oh, of course. And thank you. I'm curious which came first, the rooms' names or their color schemes?"

He cocked his head, thinking. "You know, I don't think I've ever heard. I've always assumed Mom just kept the names they had when they bought the place. And decorated them accordingly. But I could be wrong. I'll have to ask her."

"So your parents redecorated when they bought the inn?"

He nodded. "They bought the house in the late 1980s when I was two." He could almost see her doing the math. He wondered if she considered thirty-two "old." Lately it sometimes felt old to him.

"Oh how wonderful it must have been to grow up here!"

He shrugged. "I suppose I took it for granted. It's all I ever knew. Although, once Mom opened the bed and breakfast, she completely redecorated."

"So it was just a private home when they bought it?"

"Oh no, it'd been an inn since the early seventies. We lived here for about four years before Mom reopened it as an inn, but that was her goal from the day they bought it."

"Your mom ran it by herself? Not with your dad?"

He turned away again and straightened an already perfectly straight bedspread. "My father was. . .*is* an attorney. That paid the bills. The B&B was Mom's dream. And a bit of a money pit, according to my father." His laughter rang false in his own ears. How many nights had he lain awake in bed listening to his parents argue in the next room? Listening to his father berate Mom for every penny she put into the inn?

"Aren't all old houses money pits? But how cool that you've taken it over now. I bet that thrills them."

"Mom's happy about it," he admitted. "Dad—let's just say he has different ideas about how it should be run." Or if it should be running at all. And why was he spilling his guts to this woman?

"I get that." She nodded knowingly. "My mom thinks a career as a chef is a bad idea. I think she still holds out hope I'll find a. . . *reasonable* career."

"Reasonable? Like what?"

"Oh, just about anything besides cheffing. Secretary. Nurse. Garbage collector. . ."

He laughed. "What does she have against cheffing?"

"Mostly the kind of hours I'd have to work. And that it would tie me down. . .especially once I have kids, I think is her concern."

He started to ask how many kids she wanted but caught himself. Instead, he said, "I'm sure our parents only want what's best for us. It just doesn't feel that way sometimes." He gave the room a once-over and moved toward the door. This conversation was getting entirely too personal. "I should let you go."

The look she gave him made him think she could read his mind. But she remained silent. And he was grateful. He didn't like thinking about everything that had happened with his dad, let alone telling a virtual stranger the details. Even though Benjie Gabriel did seem like someone who might be sympathetic.

Now though, she took his hint. "Okay. If you don't have anything else for me, I'll just go down and get my things."

"Of course. You're well past your hours anyway. You can leave early some day next week to make up for the time."

"Don't worry about it. And thanks for the tour."

"Sure. Oh, and the other rooms are open if you want to take a peek. Everyone has checked out." He pointed across the hall. "See you Monday."

"Oh. You said you'd get me a key? In case I come early with groceries. . ."

"Right. Let me—" He'd started to say he'd go down with her, but he just wanted to let her go home. He'd kept her too long. And she'd stirred up too many emotions best left dormant.

He fished in his pocket and unclipped the master key from his keychain. He'd replace it before he went out to the woodshop tonight. He handed it to her. "This opens the front door and the back french doors where you come in. Best to use those rather than the front. Also, like I said, it'll open both laundry room doors." He didn't tell her it would also open his woodshop. She had no reason to be out there.

"Thank you. I'll see you Monday."

He gave a nod and forced a smile. "Thanks for your help."

"No problem." But her teasing tone was gone. And he knew he was to blame.

When Benjie got home, an Amazon box waited in front of the door to her apartment. A little spark of excitement shot through her. She hadn't expected to get the chef's toque until after work Monday, but opening the box before she even let herself in, she saw it was indeed her toque.

She was thrilled Trevor had suggested she wear one. A lot of her classmates in Chicago eschewed it in favor of ponytails or scarves, but she'd earned the right to wear it and saw it as a symbol of her accomplishment. Besides, she rather liked the way she looked in the white hat, probably because it tamed her insufferable curls.

She closed up the box and tucked it under one arm before unlocking her door. Now that she worked in such a charming house, this tiny, sparsely furnished studio apartment depressed her even more than it had when she first moved in three months ago. She'd purposely not done any decorating to the shoebox studio, not even bothering to unpack most of the boxes she'd moved from Chicago. She didn't want this studio to feel like home.

She put the Amazon box on the kitchen counter and opened the fridge in search of something that could stand in for supper. While she hoped Cape Girardeau would eventually be her home, she didn't want to settle in anywhere until she could afford something better—and bigger—than this place.

Her gaze landed on a stack of mail and a care package her mom had sent a few days ago. Guilt nipped at her as she realized she hadn't even let Mom know it had arrived. She needed to call and thank her, let her know how the job was going. They'd had a brief text conversation after she was offered the chef's position, but Mom had made it clear she wasn't too happy about Benjie wasting her time on a temp job, and Benjie didn't want to get into another argument, which they surely would if she called.

She hadn't realized, until Dad was gone, how much he'd played the role of mediator between her and her mother. And now that he was gone, it sometimes felt like she'd lost both of her parents.

Benjie sighed and pulled a soggy bag of salad from the fridge. Would she ever be able to speak of her mother with the same affection Trevor obviously felt for his mom? Of course, he might be wondering the same about her relationship with Dad. At least from their conversation this afternoon, she'd picked up that tension was pretty thick between Trevor and his father. It seemed they each had one parent they adored and one they struggled to get along with. She wanted to ask him about it, but it seemed that every time they talked about anything too personal, he got antsy and retreated from the conversation.

If she didn't want to risk losing her dream job, she'd better take a hint and keep it business only. Trouble was, Trevor Keye was exactly what she was looking for in a friend. And she was lonely for a friend.

CHAPTER 6

Benjie took a breath, tightened her hands on the shopping cart, and made a dash through the rain across the parking lot, dodging puddles as she searched for her car in the crowded parking lot. Since when was five thirty on a Monday morning rush hour at Walmart?

Thank goodness she'd left plenty of time to unload groceries at the inn, because it would take her twice as long to put everything away since she'd have to dry things off before placing them in the cupboard.

By the time she returned the cart to its stall and drove to the inn, she looked like a wet poodle. Thankfully, she'd practiced with the toque over the weekend and discovered the hat did a decent job of covering her unmanageable mop of hair.

She let herself in the back door, put away the food that needed refrigeration, and went to change. When she emerged from the powder room, she felt a little self-conscious about the toque. She'd chosen a conservative one with a flat band and a low, pleated crown. Still, she wished she'd started out wearing a hat her first day so it didn't feel so. . .pretentious now.

She finished putting away groceries then checked the clock and set to work on breakfast. Monday's menu called for a hash brown casserole, the usual side of bacon, and gingersnap muffins. She was itching to try some of her own recipes, but she was learning some delicious new ones too. As Trevor had said, the inn had won awards for its food.

Her third day in the kitchen proved far less intimidating than the first two. Or maybe it was only because Trevor wasn't there watching her every move. The lights were on in his shop when she'd parked by his Jeep half an hour ago. He must still be working on finishing the cutting boards for the craft fair he'd mentioned.

She didn't know how much he charged for his boards, but she planned to talk to him about buying one if they weren't too expensive. She had Mimi's old cutting board that Great-great Grandpa Nat had made. She'd never known Mimi's father, of course, but she almost felt as if she did from the stories Mimi had told of her parents' grand love story. Benjie had always thought she'd like to name a daughter after Great-great Grandma Stella if she had a girl. Of course, Papa and Mimi had a pretty romantic beginning themselves.

Benjie had always dared to hope for one great love for life—the kind of love her parents and grandparents going generations back had all experienced. But with each birthday, that dream dimmed a bit. She could be content with a career she loved and a place like Keye's Inn to spend her days. Still, she didn't want to grow old alone. She wanted a family someday. And a man who would be her friend and confidant.

As she slid a pan of muffins into the oven, a thought popped into her mind. Did Trevor Keye have a girlfriend? She closed the oven, blaming it for the heat rising to her face. Maybe he'd been married before, although as shy as he sometimes seemed with her, she doubted it.

The squeak of the french doors in back drew her attention, followed by whispers in the hallway. She set the timer and wiped her hands before going to greet guests. "Good morning! You're up early."

"Just took a little stroll around the block." A middle-aged man turned to greet her.

"You didn't get wet?"

"Aw, nothin' that won't dry out in a day or two."

She laughed at his attempt at a joke.

His wife seemed to notice Benjie's toque for the first time, and her eyes widened. "You must be the chef Mr. Keye was talking about!"

"Yes, I'm Benjie. I'd offer a hand, but mine are a bit sticky right now." In truth, she just didn't want to have to wash her hands again. She wondered exactly what Trevor had said about her but couldn't think of a way to ask that wouldn't sound like she was fishing for a compliment. "Breakfast will be ready at seven. We'll serve buffet style in the dining room, but it looks like the rain has let up. So if you'd like to take your food to the patio, we'll get the cushions dried off for you."

"Oh, don't bother on our account. We'll take ours up to our room later, if that's okay."

"Of course. Or I can bring up a tray if you'd like."

"You don't need to do that. We'll carry it up when we get back. We're going to take a longer walk down to the river first."

"Enjoy! Breakfast should be ready when you get back." She gave them her best smile and retreated to the kitchen, feeling a bit like a fraud. She'd acted as if she practically owned the place and knew all the ins and outs. But at the same time, she loved interacting with the guests and playing hostess. It was the very thing that had drawn her to the idea of being a chef for an inn. Being cooped up in a kitchen without access to the people she was cooking for would have taken the joy out of her job. Running an inn would be the best of all worlds.

If she owned Keye's Inn, she would hire out the cleaning and laundry and do the cooking and hostessing herself. And give the Garnet Room a major overhaul! She smiled at the thought. But of course, she didn't own the inn. She was only here for a few months. She needed to remember that.

Benjie could hardly believe the week was almost over. A week ago today, she'd come to her first day of work feeling green and unsure of herself. And already she felt comfortable in her role here and lucky beyond words that she'd managed to land this job. She adjusted her thought: no, not lucky. Blessed. This job was a gift. Even if it was only for a few months, she had no doubt it was an answer to her prayers, pure and simple.

She loved coming to work. She awakened each morning before sunrise with a sense of excitement and then was sorry when her shift ended and she had to change clothes and hurry back for her one o'clock class. In fact, this job was the only thing that helped her bear the ridiculously boring business and econ courses she was taking for no good reason she could see.

As the professor droned on and on, her mind would wander to what new recipes she might cook up for the guests at Keye's Inn. Maybe she could put together a cookbook for the holidays that would benefit the inn. A little "pay it forward" gesture to show her appreciation for how the inn had inspired her as a girl. And still inspired her now. They could offer it on the website and even have a book table for visitors during the upcoming holiday teas. What would Trevor think of that idea, she wondered?

You're only temporary, Gabriel. It wasn't her place to be ramrodding ideas through. And for all she knew, they already had a cookbook.

They'd had a light guest load for breakfast this morning, and Benjie had the kitchen cleaned up before nine o'clock, but as she had each morning this week, she changed out of her whites and headed upstairs to help Trevor with the beds.

She'd teased him last Saturday that she would make herself scarce where laundry and beds were concerned, but since she had the time in her schedule, and seeing how much more quickly things went for him when they worked together, she would have felt selfish not helping.

And though Trevor looked surprised when she'd appeared in the laundry room doorway on Monday, he hadn't protested. If anyone had told her that she'd spend the last half hour of her workday helping him make up beds and that it would become her favorite thirty minutes of her new "chef's" job, she would have called them crazy. But it was true.

At the top of the stairs, he greeted her with a smile—and a pile of clean linens that he transferred into her arms. "Emerald Room. I'll be right there. Need to move a load into the dryer first."

When he joined her a few minutes later, they worked in silence until he straightened and sighed, rubbing the small of his back.

"Are you hurting?"

"Not now, but I will be next week when I lose my laundry assistant."

"Lose?"

"Remember, I told you November is when we start baking for the teas. Much as I hate to lose your help up here, I don't want to risk not having the freezers stocked. And also, we need to start thinking about getting the holiday decorations up."

She didn't reply, sad that these mornings with him would soon come to an end.

"I should probably be worried that our calendar is so light this month, but I'm thankful for extra time in the woodshop."

"Oh, that's right. You've got the pumpkin festival this weekend. Did you make your quota?"

"Not yet, but I will. Just barely. The gal picks up the order for her booth tonight."

"I'd like to see your work sometime." She hoped it wasn't too broad a hint.

If it was, he didn't seem to mind. "If you have a few minutes, I'll show you what I'm working on."

"Oh yes. I'd love to see."

"Let me turn off some lights and close up the rooms. I'll meet you out by the shop."

By the time Trevor got downstairs, Benjie was already waiting outside the shop. He unlocked the door, feeling suddenly nervous about her seeing his work. He hadn't decided yet whether to show her his carving. That was more personal. And he didn't trust his own talent where the carvings were concerned. He thought it was good, but he'd met too many self-assured artists who didn't have a clue how bad they really were. He didn't want to be one of them.

He knew his woodworking was up to par—the furniture and the

cutting boards and utensils. Patrons raved about his work on display at craft fairs. And the items sold well. That, after all, was the true test of excellence. At least according to his father.

He mentally rolled his eyes then just as quickly shot up a silent *Sorry, Lord*. He'd been working on a better attitude where his father was concerned. Not very successfully, unfortunately. And not for Dad's sake as much as for his mom's. How Mom had forgiven the man, Trevor didn't know. She was a better Christian than he'd ever be.

"Come on in." He flipped on the fluorescent lights and waited for them to quit flickering.

She inhaled deeply. "I love that smell. Sawdust?"

He nodded, gratified that she appreciated it. "Unless you like the smell of turpentine and linseed oil, I'd guess it's maple wood you're smelling. That's the last thing I sawed in here." Best smell on earth as far as he was concerned.

"Different woods have different smells?"

"You've smelled a cedar chest before, right?"

"Oh yeah. I guess that makes sense. I just never really thought about it."

He led the way to the workbench where a lineup of cutting boards in various stages of finish waited. Most were finished except for being oiled.

"You made all these?" Her voice held admiration.

"Unless some elves snuck in during the night and added a few. Which would be fine with me."

She smiled. "I wouldn't hold my breath."

He glanced up at the window over the workbench and couldn't resist giving her a hard time. He pointed. "If you need a frame of reference, that's the window you were peeping in."

She hid her face in her hands, but she was laughing. "I'm not going to live that down, am I?"

"Probably not for a while anyway. I mean, it's not every day we get window peepers here."

She gave a little growl and drew back her arm like she might sock him but then seemed to think better of it.

"You weren't going to punch your boss, were you?" He was having entirely too much fun teasing her.

"It did cross my mind." She wrapped her arms around her middle. "But I need my job."

"And I need a chef, so you're safe. Here, come this way." He walked to the far end of the workbench. "These are the finished ones."

Benjie followed then gasped. "These are gorgeous! I want one! Can I buy one of these from you? Seriously. . ."

He frowned, even as his chest puffed out a little at her compliment. "I barely have enough to fill the display for the pumpkin festival, but tell you what, if any of them come back from there, you can take your pick."

Her face fell. "What are the chances of that?"

He shrugged and gave what he hoped was a humble smile. "I usually sell out. But when I start the next batch, I'll save one out for you. Will that work?"

"I guess." Still frowning, Benjie ran her hand over one of the striped ones that was a favorite of his. "Just so you know, I'm going to pray that this one right here doesn't sell."

He laughed. Then, surprising himself, he picked up the board and handed it to her. "It's yours."

"What?"

"I don't think I've ever had anyone pray over one of my cutting boards before."

"I bet you have and you just don't know it."

That made him laugh harder. And feel it was worth every one of the fifty-five dollars he would have made from that board after the booth took their commission.

"Are you sure?" But even as she said the words, she hugged the board to her chest as if to say he'd have to fight her for it if he changed his mind. "How much do I owe you?"

"No. It's yours. Call it a bonus."

"You can't do that."

"Um, I believe I just did. I know you'll appreciate it more than most. As a chef, I mean."

"Thank you, Trevor. So much."

"I'm glad you like it. You have good taste. That one turned out especially nice, if I do say so myself. And it's probably not the end of the world if there's an empty spot in the display case."

"So what kinds of wood are in this? Is there anything I need to know about taking care of it?"

He answered a dozen questions, then took her to the back room to show her the benches he was working on. "Now don't go praying over these," he warned with a grin. "They're for the inn."

She giggled. "I promise. But they're beautiful too. Not as gorgeous as my cutting board though."

He was pleased to find someone who seemed genuinely interested in this little hobby of his. So pleased, he couldn't seem to shut up, despite the warning bells going off in his head. He prattled on and on about his love of woodworking, then finally sighed. "Honestly, if I could, I'd shut down the inn in a heartbeat and spend all my waking hours out here." He looked up at the clock over his desk in the corner. "Uh oh, don't you have class today?"

She trailed his line of vision to the clock. "Yikes! I'd better go!

I need to run back in and get my purse. But thank you for the tour, Trevor. I'm so impressed. And my cutting board!"

He shrugged, feeling embarrassed for wearing his passion for this hobby on his sleeve the way he had. He grappled for a way to change the subject and let the poor girl escape. "We'll probably start decorating tomorrow, if that's okay with you."

"Sure. Do I need to bring ratty clothes?"

He opened the door for her and walked with her across the drive toward the inn. "The attic—where everything is stored—does get pretty dusty, but I'll try to pull everything out while you clean up after breakfast."

"Please tell me we're not doing Christmas decorations yet. It drives me nuts when people start putting up Christmas before Halloween and Thanksgiving even happen!" She met his bemused gaze and winced. "Uh-oh. We're decorating for Christmas, aren't we?"

He laughed. "No. My Mom always felt the same way. But she hates Halloween, so she always went heavy with an autumn theme. Said that made it easy to move right into Thanksgiving."

Benjie nodded. "Makes sense."

"Although Mom would have a cow if she knew I didn't even have the fall stuff up yet."

"I promise not to tattle on you."

He laughed. "Okay, then. That's what we'll go for. An autumn look. Or I should say, that's what we've got to work with in the attic. But you're free to do whatever you think looks good. I could probably even find a little wiggle room in the budget if you want to shop for something to freshen up the decorations we've always used."

She shrugged as they approached the back door. "Let me see what you have first."

They both looked up at the sound of rustling leaves overhead.

"The leaves are sure cooperating with you on the autumn theme." As if to prove her point, she tromped through a pile that had collected on the patio near the doorway.

"I'd rake, but it would be futile."

"Oh no, I like the way they look."

"I like your attitude." He smiled. The autumn colors, even faded as they were now at the end of October, never got old to him. "But I'll at least blow them off of the furniture before guests arrive. It looks like it might be nice enough to use the patio this evening."

"Lucky guests."

He wished it would be her sitting on his patio this evening. Startled by the thought, almost afraid he'd spoken it aloud, he nodded toward the door, hinting that she needed to get her stuff and leave. "I hope I didn't make you late for class."

She checked her phone. "It wasn't your fault. And I won't be too late."

But it was his fault. And he needed to Cut. It. Out.

CHAPTER 7

Benjie frowned and studied Megan's recipe one more time. For the first time, breakfast had bombed, and she couldn't figure out why. The cream-cheese-filled french toast had looked fine. So good, in fact, that it had disappeared from the platter almost immediately. So there wasn't even any left for her to taste, but she knew within five minutes of serving that something was wrong with the main dish. None of the guests had complained, but she didn't miss them pushing it around in the puddles of syrup on their plates before coming back for seconds of scrambled eggs and hash browns. In fact, there were no leftovers at all this morning. Well, except for the french toast.

Embarrassed, she determined not to blow it next time that dish came up on the menu. She hadn't noticed if Trevor went through the buffet this morning. He didn't always. And part of her wanted to ask if he'd noticed the french toast tasting off. But if today had been one of those days he grabbed a granola bar, she'd just as soon not bring up her culinary failure. Maybe she'd call Megan and introduce herself, ask the *real* chef if she had any idea what could have gone wrong.

Or maybe this was a good time to hit Trevor up about introducing some of her own recipes to the menu. She'd created several in culinary school that were every bit as good as the inn's own recipes. And a couple that she thought were superior. Of course, she'd be careful how she approached the topic, since she suspected most of the recipes had originated with Trevor's mother.

She hadn't learned what the deal was with his parents, but it was obvious he was very fond of his mother. His father—not so much, it seemed.

Just then he poked his head into the eating nook. "I'm ready whenever you are."

She almost felt like she'd been caught gossiping about him behind his back. "Just finishing up. I'll be right there."

She closed the laptop and made a mental note to revisit the french toast problem next week. She'd changed into street clothes earlier and put her hair in a ponytail, since it refused to stay in a bun once she corralled her stupid curls in a toque. Especially since her hair had been damp from the shower when she put on the white hat this morning.

She followed the racket to the front parlor. "What on earth are you doing in here?"

He looked up from where he knelt on the floor, a mound of Christmas light strings tangled in front of him. "It's the annual untangle-the-lights wrestling match."

"Who's winning?"

"Not me."

She slipped off her tennis shoes and knelt beside him. "Let me see what you've got going there."

She worked for fifteen minutes and produced ten strands of lights, seven of which worked.

"Will that be enough for what you have in mind?"

"Me?" She stared at him. "Was I supposed to come up with a grand plan? I thought you were going to walk me through this. I told you decorating isn't exactly my gift."

"I'll walk you through it if you need me to, but I'd rather see something completely new and different. If I just tell you where to put stuff, it'll look like it always does. Decorating was always Mom's gig. You think it isn't *your* gift? It isn't even in my wheelhouse."

"What'd you do last year?"

He shot her a hangdog look. "I called my mommy."

"And she came running all the way from Nashville?"

"Actually, I went and picked her up."

She laughed. "Seriously?"

"Well, she was due for a visit anyway." He grinned then a shadow clouded his expression. "I realized then that she's just not up to helping out at the inn anymore. She's still in her own apartment, but I'm not sure how much longer that will be an option."

"I'm sorry. It's got to be hard watching that happen."

"I didn't come along until she was close to forty. I think that kind of did her in."

Benjie couldn't tell if he was joking or if he really thought that. "Is your father. . .not in the picture?"

"Not for Mom, he isn't." He busied himself with the plug of one of the strings of lights in the "does not work" pile.

She sensed he didn't want to go there, but her curiosity won over propriety. "They're divorced?"

Another nod. "Four years ago. He. . .had an affair."

"Oh. Ouch. I'm so sorry."

"Yeah. You and me both. He and his. . .the other woman. . .live in Florida."

"Do you see him often?"

His jaw tensed. "As little as possible. Unfortunately, he bought out my mom, and then I bought the inn from him. Or I should say I'm buying the inn from him. Hence, the reason I see him at all."

"I'm really sorry. That must be hard. Your mom hasn't remarried?"

"No. And she won't. She still loves my dad. I don't see how. What he did to her. . ." A muscle in his jaw twitched.

Benjie scrambled to think of a way to change the subject.

He changed it for her, gesturing to the far wall of the parlor. "Those boxes over there are full of different decorations." He rose and panned the room, turning a one-eighty on one heel. "To be honest, I'd love to get some of the junk out of these two front rooms. It's just a lot of dusting, and it's not my style. Not that I know what my style is, but it's not this. I wouldn't mind dialing it down a notch or two. If I'm going to be the one putting up decorations in the future—or hiring someone to do it, I'd like to keep it as simple as possible. I mean, we still want it to look festive for all the holidays, but after all, the inn is already pretty tricked out."

"I've always thought less was more. And you're right. The inn has its own beauty. You could put up a few greens and some twinkle lights, and they would enhance what's already here. And draw attention to the home's features instead of the decorations themselves. Not to mention if you keep it simple, switching from fall to Thanksgiving to Christmas—and even to Valentine's Day—would be a breeze."

"Okay then. I like the way you're thinking. Sounds like we're on the same page."

"Do you want me just to clear all the flat spaces off, and we can dust and then go from there putting things back?" She had to admit she'd been itching to pare down these rooms. She wasn't Marie Kondo or anything, and she didn't know that much about decorating. But she knew she wasn't a maximalist, and Trevor's mom clearly was.

"Hey, go for it." He rose and stacked some of the empty boxes together.

"You're sure your mom won't be offended if we put some stuff in storage?"

"I'll be honest. I'm not sure my mom will make another trip back here. Her health just isn't that good." His shoulders drooped with the words.

"I'm so sorry, Trevor." Benjie felt his sorrow deeper than he likely suspected. It was how she'd felt that first Christmas home after Dad's first heart attack, knowing then that she wouldn't have him in her life much longer. That he probably wouldn't live to walk her down the aisle. He'd died the day before Valentine's Day. And it still seemed unreal. Still broke her heart.

"Thank you." He shrugged. "It is what it is. Now why don't I get you some boxes so you can start clearing things out of here."

She let that close the subject, but sadness lingered in the room like a palpable presence. She cleared all the knickknacks from the mantel, side tables, and the narrow desk in the entrance hall, placing things she thought she might use again in one pile and packing away anything that felt too "busy" or dated. She left all the books on the built-in bookcases, and after dusting the dark mahogany woodwork and furniture, she stepped back to appraise the space. Despite the sunbeams that streamed through the narrow spaces between the forest green draperies, the room had a gloomy appearance. Lights and greenery would help, but she wanted to use something lighter to brighten the rooms.

An idea formed, and when Trevor returned with boxes, she ran it by him. "What would you think about taking these heavy draperies down and just leaving the sheers underneath? This room doesn't really need the privacy and—" Too late, she realized her suggestion might seem critical of his mother's decorating taste.

But Trevor shrugged. "Why not? We can always put them back up if it doesn't look right without them." He went to the nearest window and inspected the curtain rod. "Let me run and get a ladder."

He was back in a few minutes and climbed the ladder to release the curtains from their clips then handed them down to her in a billow of dust that made them both sneeze. But half an hour later the heavy draperies had been shaken out and folded into boxes, and the room looked bright and cheery—and twice as big.

Trevor went to the entryway and studied the transformation, hands on hips. "I don't know why we didn't do that years ago."

Pleased that he approved, Benjie closed up the boxes and stacked them on top of one another.

Trevor lifted them and started for the stairway. "I'm going to take these up to the attic. If you want to come and see what else is up there that might work for the season, feel free."

She jumped up. "Oh, I'd love to see the attic! I've always wondered what's up there."

"It's nothing very exciting, I can assure you. But come on up."

The attic proved to be a veritable treasure trove. "Are you kidding me?" Benjie stared into the dim space with her jaw agape. "Trevor! Your idea of 'nothing very exciting' is seriously flawed. Just look at this stuff!"

"I don't even know where half of this stuff came from. Mom loved to dig around in the antique shops downtown. But I'm guessing a lot of this came with the house. I was never allowed to play up here when I was a kid."

Benjie crossed the dusty floor to a stack of crates that had an old radio on top. She blew off the dust and lifted the radio up to inspect it. "This would be a fabulous conversation piece for the parlor."

"Well, bring it down, then. See what else you want." He brushed his hands together. "If you don't mind, I'll just leave you here to 'shop' for whatever else you think might work. Just stack things here by the steps, and I'll carry them down."

She panned the dim attic. "It doesn't look like anything is labeled. You don't mind if I open boxes?"

"Have at it." He went to a small window at the opposite end of the attic and moved a stack of boxes blocking the sunlight. "Is that better? Get a little light on the subject?"

"Much better. Okay, I'll be down in a few minutes."

"Have fun."

He had no idea! She felt she'd been given a blank check to her favorite kitchen store.

CHAPTER 8

Benjie scarcely knew where to start. The attic was like a messy thrift shop—no, antique shop—with dusty items piled on top of boxes stacked on top of furniture nestled among rolled-up rugs. A glorious jumble of treasures waiting to be discovered.

Everything hovered under a veil of fine dust, but despite the dim light from two bare bulbs that hung from the ceiling, she could almost see the patina of age shining through the grime on boxes and bottles and even books. She emptied an attractive wicker basket and collected a few promising items in it, then opened the top cardboard box in a stack of several. It contained scrapbooks, certificates, old grade cards—not Trevor's—and other random ephemera. Nothing that really struck her as holiday decor. She moved on to the next box and found old spools of ribbon, crocheted doilies, and run-of-the-mill flower shop vases.

Moving several large boxes out of her way, she unearthed several vintage valises, the kind with interesting latches and straps. Stacked, these would make a great plant stand and were just the muted colors she had in mind—moss green, a lovely antique brown, and a smaller case in a pale mustard yellow. Lifting them one by one, she judged them to be empty but opened each one to be sure.

A musty, yet not unpleasant, odor wafted from the first two. The green case felt a bit heavier and lopsided. Setting it on the floor and kneeling in front of it, she undid the straps and latches. Empty. And musty. She started to close it again then noticed a bulge in one of the gathered pockets in the silk lining. Slipping her hand inside, she retrieved a carved wooden figure.

She moved to the window where it was brighter and inspected the piece. It was a man in an ancient robe, lifting a lantern in one hand. At his waist was tied a piece of twine with a tiny brass key dangling from the "belt."

She turned the figure over in her hands. The paint was faded and scuffed in places, but the wooden character had a certain charm to him and felt almost. . .*familiar* in her hands. The piece was about seven inches tall and expertly carved with a fancy design bordering the robe, and detailed facial features, including a rather scruffy beard. She smiled. Maybe that was why it looked familiar. It reminded her of the "designer stubble" Trevor always sported, what her dad had called "five o'clock shadow."

The figure seemed like it might belong to a set. A nativity, maybe? Although the character didn't look like the traditional shepherd, and surely wasn't as regally dressed as a wise man.

She held it up again, fingering the brass key. "Oh duh. Of course! It's the innkeeper." Her own voice startled her in the quiet of the attic space. She'd ask Trevor if he knew the history of the little man, but it definitely went into her basket. It would be cute sitting among greenery on a shelf—and perfectly fitting for an inn.

A memory came, and she realized why. The worn painted wood finish on the figure reminded her of the nativity set Papa and Mimi always put out for Christmas at their house in Kansas City.

Their set hadn't included an innkeeper, but when she thought about it, unlike the wise men, the innkeeper would have been present the very night of Jesus' birth. She liked the idea of it and wondered why more crèches didn't include that character. She tucked the wooden figure into the basket where she was collecting items to use downstairs.

She heard footsteps below and turned to see Trevor coming up the attic steps. "Have anything for me to carry down yet?"

"You can take these valises if you would. And this basket, but I may want it back to haul more things." She lifted the carved innkeeper from the basket. "You don't know anything about this, do you?"

He took it from her and inspected it. "Nice. It looks a little bit like the pieces from a nativity set my mom had, but I've never seen this guy before." He looked past her to a pile of boxes. "That nativity is up here somewhere, but I couldn't tell you which box it's in if my life depended on it."

"Well, lucky for you, it doesn't. I thought it might be part of a nativity set too. He's an innkeeper, I think. See his key?"

He gave her an amused look. "Oh, I get it. Innkeeper? Keye? No wonder he ended up here. But seriously, I've never seen him before."

"He even kind of looks like you. That scruffy beard and all." She held the carving up beside Trevor's face as if comparing.

He stroked his chin, looking self-conscious, and Benjie wished she hadn't said that part. She tapped the green valise, trying to diffuse the uncomfortable moment. "I found him in the lining of this case."

He took the bait. "Oh, those cases came from an estate sale. The nativity probably did too. This guy must have gotten separated and hitched a ride."

"Did you get the valises at the same sale as the nativity?"

He shrugged. "I don't think so. For a while there, Mom was going to sales every week. Then she. . .um. . .didn't want to get nominated for one of those hoarders shows, you know?"

She laughed. "I love it. There's some cool stuff up here."

"Plus, my dad didn't like the clutter." His countenance darkened as if a memory disturbed him. But then he brightened and cocked his head, studying her. "You look like you're kind of getting into this decorating thing."

"Maybe a little." Her cheeks warmed, but she wagged a finger at him. "I'm still a chef first though. Don't you forget it."

"Duly noted." He gave a mock salute and piled the overflowing basket atop the stack of valises, hefting them all in one load. "Have fun!" he called over his shoulder as he disappeared down the stairwell.

She laughed, thankful for the easy way they'd come to have with each other in the not even two weeks she'd been working for him. She'd quit feeling nervous about coming to the inn and had begun to enjoy each day, even if it was with just a trace of sadness, since this job would come to an end for her in a few short months. Because the truth was, she loved this place, loved her job. Maybe it was crazy to consider that she wouldn't want to keep climbing the career ladder, but she sincerely thought she could be happy being a chef here at Keye's Inn for the rest of her career. Even if it meant helping Trevor make up the beds each day. Maybe *especially* if it meant helping him make up the beds each day.

She stretched and panned the room, looking to see what other treasures she might find to use downstairs. She'd told Trevor she didn't have a gift for decorating, but already ideas were swimming in her mind. Something about clearing everything away from the shelves and mantel in the parlor had opened new vistas, and now her imagination took over.

She tackled another stack and discovered two identical boxes full of red and green decorations. She set them aside so she'd know where they were when it was time to decorate the inn for Christmas.

She opened a third box stuffed with crinkled brown paper. Whatever it held must be fragile. She removed the paper section by section and discovered that one clump cradled a heavy metal object. She tore away the paper to reveal a bronze angel. She gasped. Mimi had owned an angel exactly like this! She'd often told Benjie the story of how Papa had rescued that angel.

Wondering where Mimi's angel was now, Benjie added the one she'd found to a small pile she was collecting to take downstairs—that was, if Trevor ever brought the basket back up.

The angel was a beautiful piece and would look nice in the parlor year-round. It was pretty cool that she'd found an angel like Mimi's here at the place that held her fondest memories of the woman.

Trevor appeared on the narrow stairway again with the empty basket. "Anything else?"

"Just those few things there. But look at this." She told him about finding the angel that was so like her great-grandmother's. "Mimi told me that Papa, my great-grandpa, found her angel in the rubble of a bombed-out church in France during World War II. He called Mimi *mon ange*—it means 'my angel' in French—and he carried it in his pack the rest of his tour and brought it back to her. You don't know anything about where yours came from, do you?"

"I don't. I'm sorry. I'm guessing it was in a box of things Mom bought at some estate sale or garage sale. But I couldn't be sure. If you'd like to have it, you're welcome to it."

"Oh, I couldn't." But oh how she wanted to say yes.

He seemed to read her thoughts. "Take it. Please. It doesn't mean anything to me, and it sounds like it would bring nice memories for you."

"If you're sure. Thank you. I love it." This was the second gift he'd given her in as many days. She'd have to be careful what she admired from now on.

"You're welcome." He loaded the basket with the items Benjie had piled at the top of the steps. "You said your great-grandpa found the angel in France? What are the chances that one just like it would show up in Cape Girardeau, Missouri?"

"I know. It doesn't really seem like a mass marketed piece, does it? But I'm glad it did end up here. Especially since the inn was such a special place for Mimi and me."

"Pretty cool," he said. "Have you come across the nativity yet? I'm curious if that innkeeper you found maybe goes with part of that set."

"Part of it?"

"I think the set my mom had included pieces from a couple of different nativities. But this looks hand-carved to me, like the rest of them."

"Well, I don't know anything about woodcarving, but the innkeeper does have a certain flair to it."

"I don't know how it would have gotten into the valise, but I suppose Mom could have bought them at the same place." He shrugged. "I don't remember. A lot of stuff came into this house from her shopping trips."

"I haven't found the nativity set yet, but the last few boxes I looked in held Christmas stuff, so I think I'm getting warm."

"Okay. Well, I'm going to take these on down."

She nodded, distracted by what she was finding as she pulled more crinkled brown paper from the box where the angel had been. "I think I found it—" She turned to tell Trevor, but he was already downstairs.

She lifted a trio of carved wooden figures from the box. Wise men. One kneeling. They were carved out of a light-colored wood, rubbed smooth by the years, none of them painted as the innkeeper had been. She turned the pieces one way then another and shook her head in disbelief. These too looked almost identical to the ones from Papa and Mimi's set. How strange. Maybe her mind was playing tricks on her and looking at these pieces made her remember the ones from her childhood differently. She scrambled to remember when she'd last seen them. They'd moved her great-grandparents into a nursing home two years before Papa passed away. Mimi had lived only a few months after that. But that was at least five years ago. Maybe six now.

She hurried to unpack the rest of the box, and as she did so, her breath caught and her mind whirled. She withdrew a shepherd from the box—a shepherd with a sweet lamb slung around his neck like a scarf. Unlike the wise men, this piece was painted, though most of the color was chipped and worn thin. But she wasn't imagining things. She knew this shepherd!

She dug in the box again and pulled out Mary and Joseph and the manger with baby Jesus nestled inside. Her jaw dropped. She knew these too. And knew that it was too much of a coincidence that someone else had collected the exact same mismatched pieces as Papa and Mimi had. No, this wasn't a set just like theirs. It *was* theirs. The exact nativity she'd played with as a little girl. She lifted the shepherd and inspected his face. There it was. A tiny nick out of his nose. And Mary's robe bore a smear of orange crayon. One she'd probably put there herself when she was a toddler. This was without a doubt the set she'd played with as a child.

How could that be?

As a little girl, she had played with Mary and Joseph, the baby in the manger, the shepherd with a lamb on his shoulders, and the three carved wise men bearing gifts. She and her cousins had played with them for hours on end at Papa and Mimi's house. The bronze angel too. The angel she'd sent downstairs with Trevor had to have belonged to her great-grandparents as well.

But how in the world had they ended up here, 350 miles away?

CHAPTER 9

Trevor headed back up the stairs with the empty basket. Benjie hadn't made much headway putting up decorations in the parlor and entryway, but she seemed so happy rummaging through the attic that he hated to be a spoilsport. "How's it going up here?"

She had her back to him but turned at the sound of his voice. "Um. . .good. You're going to think I'm crazy, but. . .I found the nativity."

"What's so crazy about that?"

"It's. . .my grandparents' nativity. Great-grandparents, actually."

He gave her a blank look. "The angel, you mean?"

"No, Trevor. The whole thing! Mary, Joseph, baby Jesus, the shepherd, the wise men—all of them." Her voice picked up speed as she rattled off the nativity characters. "They all belonged to Papa and Mimi. My dad's grandparents."

He narrowed his eyes. "You mean the set is just like theirs?"

"No, I mean it *was* theirs! Look." She struggled to her feet and carried an armful of carved figures over to him. She tapped a manicured finger on the shepherd's nose. "See this nick?" She set the shepherd down and thrust Mary at him. "See that crayon smudge on her hem? I probably put that there myself."

"Seriously? This very set? I don't understand. Your great-grandparents didn't live in Cape, did they?" Maybe he'd just assumed her whole family was from the Kansas City area, but he didn't remember her saying anything. Surely she would have. "You don't know what happened to their set?"

"I do now. It ended up here." She almost sounded like she was accusing him of having something to do with that. "Do you know where your mom got it?"

"I don't. Sorry. I assume an estate sale. I can ask her, but honestly, Benjie, I'll be surprised if she even remembers it. We never used it. In fact, Mom was going to sell it in some church rummage sale, but I asked her to keep it because I liked the carving. They're really well done. I thought I might be able to learn something from studying the—" He stopped. He hadn't shown Benjie his carvings, and he really didn't want to answer questions about that right now. "I'll ask my mom next time I talk to her."

"Oh, would you please? I'm so curious. And a little upset, if you want to know the truth."

"Upset?"

"I feel bad that Papa and Mimi's things ended up in a rummage sale. Mimi would be so sad if she knew that. I should have paid more attention, but I think it was handed down for a few generations. I know my dad played with it when he was little. I always kind of thought my kids would too. And then. . ." She shook her head as if she hadn't meant to reveal so much. Or maybe she was just sad.

"Well, you can certainly have it now. Like I said, it doesn't have any sentimental value to my family. I only liked it because of the carver's skills." What was he thinking, giving her all these gifts. It went against everything he'd lectured himself about after their far-too-cozy conversations of late. He was surprised she didn't think he was trying to woo her. But was he? He brushed away the uncomfortable thought. "You don't know who did the carving, do you? On the nativity pieces?"

She shook her head. "I don't. This is when I wish I'd asked my dad more about our family history."

"Well, it's not too late to ask now."

"That's just it." She pressed her lips together and her chin quivered. "It is too late. Dad had a heart attack two years ago last July. He'd survived a bad one the winter before. But this time. . . He was out working in the backyard and. . .Mom found him there on the ground when she got home from work."

"Benjie, I'm so sorry. I didn't know."

"No, of course not. How could you?" She gave him a smile he knew was meant to forgive him for his gaffe.

But he felt awful. "Would your mom know, do you think? How the nativity might have gotten here?"

She shook her head. "I doubt it. Mom inherited a fancy crèche from my grandmother and grandfather Tyson. That's the one that was always set up in our house at Christmastime. But it was breakable— and valuable—so I wasn't allowed to touch it. That's why I loved this one so much. Because we got to play with it."

"I'm serious though. Please take this. You have far more right to it than anyone in our family."

"Thank you, Trevor. . .really. But I don't have anywhere to put it. I'm in a tiny studio apartment. I doubt I'll even put up a Christmas tree."

"Well, if you change your mind. . ."

"You keep it. Study the carving or whatever it is you do with carvings. And maybe. . . Would you care if we set it up on the hearth in the parlor? Not until closer to Christmas, of course. But that was where it always lived at Papa and Mimi's house—on the hearth in front of their big wood-burning fireplace."

He shrugged. "I don't see why not. It's the reason for the season after all. It's really not too early to set it out now, if you'd like."

"We'll see. And we can add the scruffy-bearded innkeeper to the set. I think he'll fit in nicely." The grin she cast his way gave him great relief.

"Sounds like a plan. And"—he turned and pretended to leave—"I guess I'll go shave. I can take a hint."

She laughed and tugged on his shirtsleeve. "Hey, I'm just teasing you. You look good in a beard."

He stroked his rough cheeks. "I don't know about that, but thanks." Right about now, he was thankful for a few whiskers, scruffy though they were, that hopefully hid the flush creeping up his neck and heating his cheeks.

Benjie brewed tea in the tiny microwave and poured it over ice in a tall glass, which she carried out to the narrow patio behind her apartment. She slipped her phone from her jeans pocket and plopped into the lone chair. It was chilly in the shade of the apartment building, and she scooted her chair out farther to catch the last of the day's sun.

A couple and their dog were chasing a Frisbee on the weed-strewn lawn of the common space, and half a dozen noisy children played tag at the playground at the far end. She dialed her mom, taking a deep breath to gather her patience, which lately seemed in short supply whenever she and Mom talked.

"Benjie? Is that you?"

She laughed. "No, Mom, it's a stranger calling from my phone." Why did her mother do that? Benjie knew good and well that a huge photo of her popped up on Mom's phone as soon as it rang, because she'd set up Mom's phone herself.

Her mother gave a short laugh. "Well, you just never know. How are you?"

"I'm good. Work's going great. I love it."

"And what about school? Classes are going well?"

"They're okay."

Mom was quiet a moment too long. "You don't sound like they're okay."

"No, they're fine. I'm not flunking out or anything, if that's what you're worried about."

"I'm not worried about anything. I'm just asking."

Benjie took a sip of her iced tea and let it cool her throat before she replied. "School is fine. I just like work better."

"Well, nothing wrong with that, I guess. Are you doing okay for money?"

"Mom! I don't only call when I need money."

"Did I ever say that? No, I did not."

"Sorry. And no, I'm fine for money. And I appreciate you paying my rent last month. Pretty sneaky, but you didn't need to do that."

"I didn't need to, but I was happy to. I thought it might help out until you got your first paycheck."

"Well, thank you. And I get paid next Friday, so I'm fine." She did appreciate it. What she didn't like was the way her mother used money to affirm—or censure—her choices. She took another sip of tea. "Listen, Mom, I wanted to ask you something."

"Oh? What's that?"

"Remember Papa and Mimi's nativity set? The one they always set up on the hearth?"

"I think I remember it. A wooden one, right? Why?"

"I found it today." She waited for her mother's reaction.

"Found it? You mean one like it?"

"No. I found their exact nativity. At the inn." She told her mother all about how she'd found the set in Trevor's attic. "When I saw that orange crayon mark, there was no doubt in my mind that it was Papa and Mimi's nativity."

"You remember orange crayon?"

"I did when I saw it. How in the world do you think that got all the way to Cape Girardeau?"

"I have no idea. Your aunt Kathy handled the estate sale. She swooped in and took what she wanted well before we moved Dad's parents into the home."

Benjie remembered Dad grousing about it, but Dad had never been one to hold a grudge.

"Your dad wasn't really interested in any of that junk," Mom said. "Although I wouldn't have minded having some of Mimi's jewelry."

Benjie was surprised to hear that. Mom wasn't the least bit sentimental. Everything was about practicality. She'd even gotten rid of her and Dad's wedding dishes a few years ago. Until Benjie had moved into her own apartment, she hadn't realized that Mom's minimalism meant there was nothing to pass down. Not from Papa and Mimi and not from Dad.

She swallowed back a wave of bitterness. "Trevor—my boss—gave me the angel. The one Papa brought back from France for Mimi. Would. . .would you like to have it, Mom?"

"Angel? Hmm. . .I don't really remember an angel."

"It was always with the nativity, but it was bronze. Not carved wood like the rest of the set."

"No, I don't have any use for that. Don't you want it?"

She let out a breath, more relieved than she realized that Mom didn't want the treasure. "Yes, I'm thrilled to have it."

"Well, good."

"I wish we could solve the mystery."

"It is kind of strange. You said the lady bought it at an estate sale?"

"Yes. Trevor's mom. But how did it get to Cape from Kansas City? That's what I don't understand."

"No telling. If those wise men could talk, huh?"

"I wish they could. I'm so curious!"

She chatted with her mom for another few minutes and hung up feeling grateful that they'd been civil—actually, more than civil—to each other. Of course, it helped that she was doing something now that Mom saw as productive—working toward her bachelor's. If she ever dropped out of school, she'd be back to the silent treatment from her mom. Not that she intended to drop out, tempting as it was.

Only this afternoon, she'd gotten a stark reminder of why she was in school. Why she couldn't drop out. And it stung all over again, remembering. She'd asked Trevor if she could reorganize a few of the cupboards and the spice cabinet. Now that she'd cooked in the kitchen for a while, she realized there were more efficient ways to arrange utensils and ingredients for the way she cooked.

Trevor hadn't hesitated for a moment, had readily agreed. But he also asked her to please put up sticky notes where things originally belonged so she could put everything back in place for Megan. It hurt, but it was a wakeup call. This might be her dream job, but it was only temporary. Just until his *real* chef came back.

CHAPTER 10

Benjie put her bag in the powder room closet, quickly changed into her whites, and tucked her hair under the toque. She marveled a little at how comfortable and confident she felt in her job already. Today began the fifth full week since she'd started working at the inn, and since her one o'clock class had been canceled, she'd agreed to stay late to help Trevor put up the Christmas trees.

As had become her habit once she was in uniform each morning, she walked quietly through the downstairs rooms of the inn, checking for dishes guests had left out the night before, and tidying up the public rooms. It had become her favorite time of the morning, especially now that it held memories of the day she and Trevor had put up the decorations for Thanksgiving. They'd laughed so hard together that night as their efforts to hang lights and greenery became a comedy of errors.

Despite Pumpkin pulling down twinkle lights as fast as they

could hang them—and then a real pumpkin rolling off its perch atop a pile of Indian corn and gourds before smashing into a hundred slimy pieces—they'd finally finished. And it looked really lovely, if Benjie did say so herself.

Something had changed between her and Trevor that night. They'd gone from being merely boss and employee to being friends. Now Trevor seemed to find excuses to spend time in the kitchen helping her with meal prep and cleanup. And since it was time to start making pastries for the Christmas teas, he helped with that too.

He'd given up protesting when she came up at the end of each shift and helped him make up the beds, and time flew much, much faster than she wanted it to.

He still spent most of his time in his woodshop, which was where he was this morning. She'd seen the lights burning in the shop windows when she parked beside his Jeep at six o'clock. For some reason, it comforted her to know he was there, making beautiful furniture and objects of art. She thought it had something to do with seeing how happy the work made him. More than once he'd told her that he wished he had more time to spend out there. His reluctance to follow through on that desire seemed to have less to do with an actual lack of time and more to do with his father's strong objections.

She had yet to meet the senior Mr. Keye, but she hated that there seemed to be such animosity between father and son. She'd tried several times to talk to Trevor about it, but he always clammed up or changed the subject. Of course, she probably did the same when it came to the subject of her mother. No one wanted to admit that they had trouble getting along with the one who gave them life. But she had to admit, the whole thing had made her more aware of her own role in the friction between Mom and her, and she was actively working on nurturing a better relationship with her mother. And things did seem better when she talked to Mom on the phone, but her efforts would be put to the real test when she went home for Thanksgiving next week.

Home. Kansas City hadn't felt like home since Dad's death. Even her apartment wasn't home. The inn was what felt like home to her now. At the thought, that constant ache—the one that gauged how quickly time was passing and how soon Megan would be back to take her rightful place as chef—pressed harder against Benjie's chest, even as she tried to ignore it.

Back in the kitchen, she mixed scones and patted out the dough. She checked the fridge to be sure the two jars of clotted cream she'd made before leaving work on Friday were still there. She'd slid them behind the condiments to hide them from Trevor, lest she not have enough to serve with today's scones. Apparently the man had a major thing for clotted cream.

She smiled to herself, remembering his reaction to the first batch of her homemade clotted cream she'd served guests two weeks ago. One taste and he'd instructed her to cancel the order for "that second-rate stuff in the jars" and teasingly ordered her to keep a supply at the ready at all times.

"You'll have to teach Megan how to make it," he'd said, licking a bit of the buttery confection off his fingers.

"I'm sure she knows how. It's one of the things they teach you in culinary school."

"Well, be sure she does before you leave. Please. I'll never be satisfied with the old stuff again."

"Before you leave. . ." She didn't like it when Trevor brought up Megan. She hadn't even met the woman she was filling in for—who sounded plenty likable—but hearing the *real* chef's name only served to remind Benjie that her days here were numbered. And

if she were honest, it bothered her more than a little that Trevor seemed so indifferent to that fact.

Pulling a skillet from the pot rack over the sink, Benjie reviewed the steps for the mushroom spinach frittata she was trying this morning. It was a new recipe she'd experimented with at home but had never served guests. She was grateful Trevor was giving her a little leeway but also aware that one flop and she'd be back to the tried-and-true recipes.

She drizzled olive oil into the pan, swirling it to coat the bottom. When it was hot, she slid in the mushrooms she'd sliced earlier. While they sautéed, she piled fresh spinach on top. Then, while waiting for it to wilt, she cracked a dozen eggs and whisked them with a half cup of heavy cream. The beauty of a frittata was that it could be served at any temperature. It was delicious warm or at room temperature, but some people actually preferred it chilled. So unlike the breakfast casseroles on the menu most mornings, no matter what time guests came down to breakfast, this dish would be the right temperature to serve.

She grated a bit of soft fontina cheese over the eggs. *Mmm. . .* If she had to live on one food the rest of her life, it would be cheese.

"Good morning." Trevor appeared in the doorway, sniffing the air appreciatively. "Something smells delicious."

"I'm making that frittata I told you about."

"Okay. Well, it sure smells good."

"Have you had coffee?"

He shook his head. "Not yet. I'll make it though. You're busy."

"If you have time, that'd be great. Thanks. Did you have a good weekend?"

He grunted. "The usual. Cleaned the house, worked in the shop a bit. Church yesterday. Nothing to write home about. You?"

"Same." Except she hadn't gone to church. It was just too hard going by herself. "Have you carried down the Christmas decorations yet?"

"Not yet, but it's on my to-do list."

They'd found a pleasant rhythm together that filled her workdays with joy and laughter. And sadly, made her dread going to class each day even more. She was making good grades, and as much as she hated to admit it, she was learning some things that might prove helpful, if not in her work life, at least to her personal finances. But mostly those dreary classes made her realize that the job she had right now was the job she ultimately wanted. And she didn't need quantitative analysis or microeconomic theory for that. No, what she needed was a micro miracle.

Trevor stood beneath the archway between the foyer and the parlor and appraised their work. He felt Benjie's eyes on him, no doubt holding her breath, hoping he approved of her ideas. He had merely been the muscle behind everything they'd accomplished this afternoon, the gopher at her beck and call. She was the creative brains behind this impressive display.

Benjie had ordered him around as if she were the boss and he the employee. And he'd loved every minute. When they'd taken the draperies down last month, she had also gotten rid of every last doily in the parlor. Same with the stockpile of teacups and saucers, figurines, and silk floral arrangements that had been fixtures in the built-in bookcases and on the mantel for as long as he could remember.

He said good riddance to all the frilly things, even though, for Mom's sake, he packed them all away in a box in the attic, just in case. But what a revelation not to have to dust around those annoying breakables.

In their place, Benjie had artfully arranged rows of old books beside stately vases or single teapots and the old radio she'd admired in the attic. In fact, she'd used many of the pieces his mom had collected from estate sales and garage sales over the years. But with all the other clutter gone, each item had a chance to shine.

Benjie's smile said she was quite pleased with herself, but he made her suffer for a long minute before returning that smile. "It's a masterpiece. Seriously, Benjie, these rooms have never looked better."

She clapped and cheered. "It's a little plain for Christmas, but it'll look better once we get the rest of the ornaments on the trees. And light some candles and fire up the Christmas carols."

"All true. But it looks fantastic just like it is. And if I didn't think guests would complain, I'd say leave it this way." He liked the trees a little bare, with only white lights and snowflakes and a few pine cones tucked in here and there. He thought Mom would approve too, but he probably wouldn't mention the changes to her. She'd had enough upheaval in her life, thanks to his father.

"Do you think they'll complain?" Her pretty brow creased. "I don't want anyone to be disappointed they're not getting the frilly, over-the-top Christmas experience they remember."

"Would you be disappointed if you came for tea and it looked like this?"

She thought for a minute, panning the room. "No, I wouldn't. I think the magic of this house is in the architecture and the. . .soul of the house. Does that sound weird? It just has a good feel."

"Not weird at all. And I think you're exactly right. I think the way you've decorated, a little sparsely and with more natural materials, actually highlights the architecture." He slanted a suspicious look at her. "Are you sure you're not a decorator?"

She laughed. "One hundred percent positive. But I'd be lying if I said this wasn't fun. It really was. And satisfying."

He brushed his hands together as if finishing a job. "Then I say we call it done. If we sense for a minute that anyone is disappointed, we can gussy it up a little. But personally, I think this is perfection, right here."

She moved to the hearth where the nativity was the star of the show. She turned the shepherd a few degrees and repositioned one of the wise men, then stood back to inspect her work, frowning.

"I'm serious about you taking that when you go. It's rightfully yours, and it should stay in your family."

"I'm not sure I'd feel right about that, Trevor. I—"

"Not another word. I want you to have it. But thanks for letting it stay here till after Christmas. Except for this guy—" He picked up the innkeeper Benjie had discovered in the attic, then placed him back where she'd positioned him to one side of the scene. "I'd like to hang on to him, if you don't mind."

"Of course. He belongs here. He wasn't part of the set I remember anyway."

"Well, he sure seems like a good fit." He hadn't let himself think about what it would be like here once Benjie was gone. Megan would do the fine job she always did. But she would hurry home after work each day—as she should—to be with her twins and her husband. He'd be back to making beds by himself. And unlike Benjie, Megan didn't like anyone in the kitchen when she was cooking. Megan didn't sing while she cooked. And she didn't toss snarky barbs his way to make him laugh.

"Thank you, Trevor. I really can't thank you enough." Benjie's voice brought him back to his senses.

"You're welcome. Now you'd better run. Don't you have class at four?"

She checked her phone. "I do. I need to go. But if you change your mind about the rest of the ornaments, I'll make time tomorrow to hang them."

"Oh, that reminds me. Hang on a sec." He went down the hall and ducked into the office he never used. He returned a minute later and handed her the check he'd written this morning.

"What's this?" She looked up at him, confusion clouding her expression.

"Just a little bonus. For all the extra help you've been giving me with decorations and the pastries for the tea and—"

"Trevor! You didn't need to do that. Those were all in the job description."

"And helping make up the beds."

She laughed. "Okay, now that might warrant a bonus. But seriously"—her tone turned sober—"you've already given me so much. The cutting board, the nativity, this job I love—" Her voice broke.

He studied her, surprised at her emotion. "Are you okay?"

She gave a shaky laugh. "Sorry. Didn't mean to get all sentimental there. But I do love this job. I. . .I'm going to miss it."

"Well, I'll miss you too." *Take it easy, Keye. Don't show any cards you can't play, man.* "I mean"—he feigned a grin—"just think how long it'll take me to make up the beds without you."

She gave him a playful elbow in the side, and they were back to normal. No, that wasn't right. Benjie Gabriel had rocked his world in ways he wasn't ready to acknowledge, even to himself. But he knew one thing: Nothing would ever be *normal* again.

CHAPTER 11

Trevor flipped the page on the lumber yard calendar past November to a brand-new month. December. The beginning of the Christmas season in earnest. He never felt quite ready for it.

He went to his workbench and settled into the chair he favored. He untied the tool roll he kept his knives in, along with the chunk of balsa wood he was working on. He'd snuck the innkeeper Benjie had found in the attic and the shepherd from her great grandparents' nativity set out here so he could study their craftsmanship and hopefully find some inspiration for this next project.

He felt certain the two figures had been carved by different people. They may not have ever been part of the same nativity, but the "scruffy" innkeeper certainly looked comfortable nestled on the hearth along with Benjie's nativity.

Over Thanksgiving, he asked his mother if she remembered where she'd picked up the nativity. She didn't remember the set at all, but she solved at least part of the mystery after he told her about Benjie finding the set in the attic and recognizing that it had belonged to her great-grandparents in Kansas City. Apparently Mom and a group of friends had gone antiquing in Kansas City a few years ago. "We only did that once though," she told him. "We discovered we were such good friends and had so much in common that we were fighting over the same antiques. We decided our friendship was more important." She'd leaned in then, chuckling. "Now don't you dare tell Miriam, but I did sneak back to some of those stores a few months later—by myself."

Trevor smiled, remembering. Mom seemed older and frailer each time he visited, but they'd had a good time together, and he thought her health seemed a little better than it had on previous visits.

He picked up the balsa wood and turned it slowly in his hands. He'd considered making a second shepherd to add to Benjie's set, but after doing some research online, he learned that most of the nativity sets that included an innkeeper also had an innkeeper's wife. That would finish out her set nicely. Though he was pretty sure the Bible never mentioned an innkeeper's name, let alone the actual innkeeper, some of the manufacturers did give the couple names, like Fontanini's *Thaddeus* and *Elizabeth*. Another maker had labeled them *Benjamin* and *Leah*. The thought made him smile, since he'd taken to calling his creation Benjamina. Not that he'd ever tell anyone—especially a certain someone—that.

Benjamina was giving him problems too. Unlike the other figures he'd carved, he'd started working on this one from the bottom up, partly because he was trying a new technique on the hem of the robe. It was intricate work, and if he messed up, he didn't want to have spent hours on the face only to ruin the whole piece with his experiment. Of course, that could backfire on him the other way, and he could carve an elaborately feminine robe only to have the face turn out looking like a strong-jawed sailor. There was a learning curve to this art.

But the main reason he'd started carving at the bottom was because he didn't yet have a clear image in his head of the character's features. Often the wood itself informed how his figures turned out and helped him picture what their features should look like. But so far this hunk of wood wasn't telling him anything.

At least not anything he was ready to listen to.

The morning's guests had all checked out, breakfast dishes were in the dishwasher, and Benjie stirred a custard on the range. It would be the filling for the cream puff shells she'd made yesterday, and it was tricky getting it to thicken without curdling, but so far, so good. The inn's first Christmas tea was this afternoon, and she didn't have time to start over if she messed up this custard.

She could tell Trevor was nervous about hosting the tea. This was his first year to do the teas without his mom's help, and yesterday he'd let slip that last year Megan had stayed to help too, with setup and instructing the college girls they'd hired to help serve. So he was truly flying solo this year.

Right now he was in the dining room scooting furniture around and setting up round four-tops wherever they would fit.

Something crashed in the living room, and she dropped her wooden spoon and jumped back, heart racing.

But Trevor hollered, "Don't worry, nothing broke."

She laughed and hollered back, "Not my house." *But oh that it was!*

A minute later he stuck his head around the kitchen door. "Can you help me for two minutes? Just two, I promise."

She looked pointedly at the saucepan in front of her. "As long as you don't mind scorched custard in your Christmas tea cream puffs."

"Never mind. It can wait." He came and leaned against the counter next to the stove. Crossing his arms, he watched her stir.

She tossed him what she hoped was a sympathetic smile. "Listen, I would have gladly skipped classes today to help out, but this econ test is half our grade and I'm barely hanging on to a low B in there right now."

He shook his head. "I'm not asking you to skip."

"I know. I'm just saying I'd rather be here if I had a choice."

"Yeah, well I'd gladly skip this entire month of teas if I didn't already have 150 people signed up. Well, that and if it wasn't such a moneymaker."

She lifted the spoon, checking her custard. "This needs to cook maybe another seven or eight minutes, but once I get it in the ice bath, I can help."

"No rush. Take your time."

She'd been able to make most of the pastries ahead of time, a recipe or two each day, and she'd taken enough out of the freezer to thaw this morning for serving today's twenty-five guests. The cream puffs and some mini tarts were the only things that wouldn't freeze well. "I have everything on platters except the cream puffs, so once the tables are set, all you really need to do is just put everything out on the buffet. It's not rocket science, Keye. You've got this."

He rolled his eyes at her. "Easy for you to say as you trot off to campus. Mom always made it all look so effortless."

"Hey, you never told me how your trip went. I'm jealous you got to spend Thanksgiving in Nashville while I was in Kansas City where it was ten degrees colder than here. What's up with that?"

"It was nice. Nashville and my time with Mom. How about you?

Well, except for the weather?"

"Also good. My mom and I didn't get into one argument the whole weekend. I'm rather proud, if I do say so myself."

"You usually do? Get in arguments? Why?"

She told him then, things she'd never told another soul. About her resentment that it was her beloved dad who died, while Mom, whom she'd always had a tenuous relationship with, lived. "I know that isn't fair to Mom. And I know I was horrible to take that out on her when she was grieving Dad and needed me most. But I'm happy to report that I managed to be nice to her the entire time I was home for Thanksgiving."

Trevor shook his head. "I'll be honest, I have a hard time picturing you being mean to anyone. Snarky maybe. But mean? No."

"Hey!" She laughed, glad for the levity that softened this hard admission. "That's just it though. Mom doesn't do snark. She doesn't get it. Now Dad got it."

"Well, of course. That's probably where you got your, um. . .*gift* for it."

"I will take that as a supreme compliment."

"As I intended it." He tipped an imaginary cap to her.

"It's not only my snark I got from Dad. I don't think I realized till he was gone how much he had to do with me wanting to be a chef. We cooked together when I was a kid, and I was always inventing new dishes for him to test. He did most of the cooking at our house, since he got off work before my mom. He was a great cook too." The memory made her ache for Dad. His teasing smile, his encouraging words, his strong arms. It still seemed impossible that he was gone. Every time she went home, she expected him to greet her at the door like he always had, a twinkle in his gray eyes and a big bear hug that made her feel like everything would be okay now that she was home.

She looked up at Trevor, aware she'd drifted away in her thoughts. "I love my mom. I don't want you to think I don't. But home just isn't the same without Dad."

"No." He shook his head. "It probably never will be. And that says a lot about the kind of man your dad must have been. One of the good guys."

It meant more than he could possibly know to have him say it. But she could only nod and whisper, "The best. The very best." Tears threatened, and she stopped stirring and turned away from him, busying herself with wiping the counter where she'd mixed the custard.

When she'd collected herself, she resumed stirring and changed the subject. "But enough about me. What did you and your mom do?"

"We cooked together, actually. Not turkey, but we did a pork tenderloin on the grill that turned out pretty amazing. And Mom made all my favorite desserts. Fed me till I about popped. We watched the parade on TV and had some good talks too. And *I* was nice the entire time as well."

"Yes, but you get along with your mom, so I still get more brownie points."

"Oh, that's where you're wrong. Well, half wrong. I get along with Mom as long as I talk nice about my dad."

She rested her spoon on the side of the pan and regarded him for a moment. "That's not easy for you, is it? Talking nice about your dad."

He picked up the recipe card for her custard and worried the edge of it. "No. It's not easy."

"Because he cheated on your mom?"

He nodded. "Yes. And I know it doesn't say much for my Christianity, but it rankles me that she can forgive him so easily."

"That would be hard to do," she admitted.

"But it's more than that. By doing what he did, my father undermined any confidence I ever had in myself. I know that sounds self-centered as all get-out, but it's the truth."

She frowned, not wanting to say the wrong thing. "I don't understand."

He put the recipe card back on the counter. "Never mind. I don't need to burden you with my issues."

"Maybe you don't need to. But what if I want you to? I. . .I care about you, Trevor. And I'm here to listen if you need a listening ear."

"I appreciate that, Benj. I really do."

She loved that he'd shortened her name, calling her by the nickname Dad had given her. "So talk to me."

"I don't think this is a conversation I'm ready to have. Not with you."

She swallowed hard. That hurt. Deeply. She turned back to the range, stirring harder than the custard warranted. "Okay."

She half expected him to walk away. But he stayed. His breathing was punctuated by little huffs that made her think he was considering saying something but couldn't decide. She chose to stir in silence. Trevor didn't seem like a man who'd be persuaded by begging and pleading.

The pudding bubbled and thickened, and still he was silent.

She turned off the flame and took the pan off the stove. She turned to the sink behind her and set the pan down in the ice bath she had waiting. She felt his presence behind her.

"Benj. . .The reason I don't want to have this conversation with you is because it's *about* you."

"Me?" Her voice came out in a squeak, and she turned to face him, leaning against the sink across from him.

"I like you, Benjie, as a friend, but. . .more than that. This might surprise you, but it's crossed my mind to ask you out. If you didn't work for me, I might. Except. . .I wouldn't."

She tilted her head and studied him. "Now you're not even making sense."

"I wouldn't ask you out because that wouldn't be fair to you."

"How about you let me be the judge of that. And what do you mean, not fair?" Her breaths came quickly, and she'd never been so aware of his closeness. The way he looked into her very soul.

"My parents loved each other, Benjie. I know they did. Mom believes they did. But somewhere along the way, something happened to my dad. . .something that let him throw away everything they had together. Including this inn, if I hadn't stepped in to buy it so Mom wouldn't lose the only thing she had left that she cared about."

"Oh Trevor. I didn't know. I'm so sorry." She'd always thought he'd bought the inn because it was in the family, because he had a passion for it. Now she wondered if he merely felt saddled with it. But if that was true, he hid it well. She said as much.

"I don't hate it. And it's home after all. But honestly, if money were no object and Mom wasn't part of the equation, I'd probably sell it and open my own woodworking shop."

She smiled softly. "Now that's something you don't hide so well. You come alive when you're working in that shop. But I still don't understand what this all has to do with me."

"Because, what if. . ." He held up a hand and looked at her with a vulnerable grin. "Just work with me here. Let's say I asked you out on a date and you said yes, and we. . .I don't know. . .hit it off? Like big-time?"

"You mean like hit it out of the park?"

"Out of the park and busted a stadium light."

She wasn't sure if she adored where this was going or was terrified by it. "Would that be so horrible, Trevor?" she whispered.

"It would be if it ultimately turned out like my parents."

"Trevor. You can't think that far ahead. And there's no way you could know if it might turn out that way."

"Exactly. You can't know. But what if these things are genetic or generational or whatever. I don't think my dad set out, the day he proposed to Mom, to cheat on her years later. So what if I ended up doing the same thing to you—I mean, to a woman I loved?"

She didn't dare think of the implications of his slip-up right now. "Trevor, you can't think that way. Have you ever cheated on a girlfriend?"

"No. Of course not."

"Well, see?"

"That's because I've never had a girlfriend long enough to find out."

"What do you mean?"

"Every time I feel like things are getting too serious, all I can think about is what if I do to this woman what my dad did to Mom? I can't let that happen." He gave a little laugh. "Just for the record, it's not like I have a string of forty-three women I've almost fallen in love with. But there've been a couple."

"Then go find them! Well, one of them. Tell them you made a huge mistake." *What is wrong with me?* The last thing she wanted him to do was to go track down an old girlfriend! "Trevor, the very fact that you're so worried about this is probably the best proof possible that you won't do what your dad did."

"Brittany is married, and I don't know where Jill is. I think she moved to California after college."

Brittany and Jill? Good riddance.

"But that's not the point, Benj. I don't even think about them anymore. Except that they helped me know that. . .I hold back."

"Then stop it. Stop doing that! I'm here to tell you, you are not a man who would do that—what your father did. I would bet my life on it."

"Would you bet a date on it?" He rubbed a hand over his face. "I didn't mean to say that out loud."

"Well, you did." She couldn't help the smile that came. "Um, do you have a company policy about dating the help?"

"I haven't checked the policy manual lately, but if we do"—a slow grin bloomed on his face—"I know the guy who makes the policy. I could probably talk him into changing it."

She gave a single bob of her chin. "Then, yes, I would bet a date on it."

CHAPTER 12

Reaching in to flip on the light and holding the door open for Pumpkin, Trevor entered the woodshop with a greater sense of purpose than he'd felt in months. He really should be gluing the next batch of cutting boards, but tonight he felt like carving.

He went to the stool and methodically untied his tool roll. The hunk of wood was waiting at the center of the leather pouch, and he placed it in the palm of his left hand and started in where he'd left off. An intricate border was taking shape on the hem of the robe. But tonight he was going to attempt to find the heart and soul of this character.

He glanced over at the wooden innkeeper that stood sentinel on a shelf beside him. He chuckled to think that Benjie hadn't discovered yet that the innkeeper had gone missing. He'd put the shepherd back in place with the nativity before the tea this afternoon, but he needed the innkeeper beside him for inspiration.

"*He kind of looks like you,*" she'd said.

He whittled a thin strip from the top of the balsa piece. And then another. The tea had gone surprisingly well. Thankfully, he'd been able to get a couple of the servers from last year and they'd done a fantastic job. He could hardly wait to tell Benjie about it when she came in tomorrow.

"*I would bet a date on it,*" she'd said.

With Pumpkin purring at his feet and the feel of the wood in his palm, he settled into the thing he loved most about carving. The gentle rhythm of knife against wood as he scraped away each bit that didn't belong, leaving only what was the very essence of the character he was creating.

Chip, chip, chip. . . Scrape, scrape. . .

He had a feeling he'd make some real progress tonight.

He had to. Because Friday night he had a date with the sweetest girl in Missouri.

In the dusky twilight, Benjie looked over at Trevor from her perch in the passenger seat of his Jeep, appreciating her view. He'd picked her up at her apartment, and now they were on the road, headed to a parade of lights festival in nearby Sikeston. Her spirits were high, even if she still had trouble wrapping her mind around the way this had all come about.

He looked over and caught her smiling. "What?"

She shook her head, unable to wipe away the smile. "I think I'm still a little in shock that I'm on a date with my boss, that's all."

"So you can imagine how I'm feeling." He gave a wry smile before turning his eyes back to the highway.

"Did you ever find that policy manual?"

"Yep." He wriggled his eyebrows comically. "It said, 'Go for it!' in great big capital letters."

She laughed. "Well, there you have it."

As they got closer to downtown, they drove along streets lined with people bundled up against the cold night, waiting for the parade to start. They finally found a place to park on a side street in the crowded town. "Hope you don't mind a little walk," he said as they climbed out of the Jeep. "I didn't realize this was such a big deal."

"I don't mind. I could use the exercise." *And all the more time to spend with you.*

Heading to the historic downtown area, they walked by the floats and marching bands and merchants' cars that were lining up on a side street.

"We might've had to park a mile away," she told him, "but we've got a ringside view of the parade." They stopped to admire a few of the parade entries, and Trevor ran into someone he knew and briefly introduced Benjie as "my friend."

The temperature dropped as the sun disappeared, and their breaths formed clouds that mingled in front of them. She sniffed appreciatively as the enticing aromas from the food trucks wafted toward them. "I think I smell fajitas. Now I'm starving."

"Me too. Let's go!" The sidewalks grew more congested with festival-goers, and Trevor took her gloved hand in his. They found a spot on the corner, mid–parade route, and stood there taking in the Christmasy window displays and laughing at a group of small children, apparently oblivious to the cold, making up a game that involved hopping off and on the curb.

Benjie hadn't realized how much she was really dreading the holidays. Another Christmas without Dad, another trip home where nothing would be the same. But as the night wore on, as she and

Trevor laughed and joked and cheered on the floats and marching bands that paraded by, she suddenly began to find glimpses of the Christmas spirit she'd been resisting.

After the tree-lighting ceremony, the crowd dispersed and she and Trevor stopped at a couple of food trucks for fajitas and then funnel cakes. They stuffed themselves, talking with their mouths full, and still not getting everything said that there was to say. Not ready for the night to be over, they walked until they found a little cafe on Main Street. Trevor ordered apple pie a la mode, Benjie ordered lemon meringue, and after that, reluctant for the night to end, they both ordered hot chocolate. They finally left when the servers started putting chairs on top of tables and mopping around them.

All the way back to her place, they groaned and laughed about how stuffed they were. And then they sat in his Jeep in front of her apartment and talked and laughed some more.

It was after midnight when he finally said goodnight and walked her to the door. As much as she wanted him to kiss her—and she sensed he wanted to—she was strangely glad he didn't. Glad they still had a first kiss to look forward to. And hopefully so much more.

Benjie came to work as usual Monday before sunrise. But the day was anything but usual. She couldn't stop smiling. By the time her shift ended, her face actually hurt from smiling. She thought her time with Trevor might possibly have been the best weekend of her entire life. And the hyperbole of her thoughts made her smile some more.

Trevor had opened up to her while they drank hot chocolate after the parade. His father had belittled so many of his decisions, especially the one to save the inn for his mom's sake. His dad saw

Trevor's woodworking and carving as a waste of time. *"You can have it built cheaper than you can make it yourself. It's like a woman knitting. Waste of time."*

Benjie wanted to smack the man, who seemed blind to his own guilt. She pointed out that Trevor's carving had proved to be anything but a waste of his time. Only partly kidding, she said, "Besides the extra money you bring in from the craft fairs and the furniture you've made for the inn, look how much you've saved on counseling."

He laughed and agreed that the woodworking was a bit like therapy for him. Especially the carving. Still, she could see that his father's words and attitude cut deep, and she prayed that God would help him heal from those wounds.

When they'd come back after the parade of lights, Trevor invited her to go to church with him—the Saturday night service, since he had guests at the inn for breakfast Sunday morning.

How comforting to have someone to sit with, to stand and sing Christmas carols beside. And then, while they sat side by side listening to the sermon, something wonderful had happened.

Sighing, Benjie rolled out biscuits and let herself relive the memory. The pastor had preached from Exodus 35 about how the Lord had chosen a man, Bezalel, from the tribe of Judah—Jesus's line. The Lord had filled Bezalel with the Spirit of God, "with wisdom, with understanding, with knowledge and with all kinds of skills—to make artistic designs for work in gold, silver and bronze, to cut and set stones, to work in wood and to engage in all kinds of artistic crafts."

Benjie quietly tapped those words—"to work in wood"—in the Bible on Trevor's lap, wondering if he'd noticed too.

He threw her a sideways smile, then underlined the words in his Bible.

On the drive back to the inn, Benjie had nudged him. "See, it's in the Bible! Woodworking is a noble artistic skill."

"That did catch my eye."

"And not just the artistic skill, but it was connected to wisdom and understanding and knowledge. I see all those traits in you, Trevor. Don't let anyone ever tell you otherwise."

Smiling at the way God had already begun to answer her prayers for Trevor, she slid the pan of biscuits into the oven, realizing her cheeks were wet with the memory. Then she was smiling again as other memories of their weekend played through her mind. She was still smiling when it came time to serve breakfast.

An elderly guest took one look at her and clucked her tongue. "Well, aren't you the cheery one at seven a.m. Did you win the lottery or something?"

Benjie laughed and said, "Not exactly. You have to play to win." But she did feel like a winner.

She'd worried that it might be awkward coming to work this morning when their date had so obviously shifted their relationship.

But Trevor must have felt the same apprehension, because he'd met her at her car in the predawn darkness and walked her to the house. "I just wanted to tell you that I had a great time this weekend."

"Me too. It was a good bet."

That earned her a knowing smile. They'd talked more while he helped her empty the dishwasher and get breakfast started. And they were still talking when he finally said he'd get out of her hair and go get some work done in the woodshop.

They'd discovered so much about each other in those hours together. Benjie felt she would never tire of hearing his voice, and that they'd never run out of things to talk about. Her rational mind knew that every couple falling in love probably felt this way. But there was a little part of her that believed they were different, that for them it was actually true. Silly as it was, the thought made her smile some more.

Trevor was smiling too when he came in from the shop around noon to start making up beds. But it wasn't Benjie he was smiling about. "I just got a call from Jason, Megan's husband. As of ten o'clock this morning, they have two bouncing baby boys!"

Her breath caught. "She had her babies? But isn't it too early?"

He nodded. "About seven weeks early, but they both weighed over four pounds, and according to Dad, they're doing great. Jason sounded pretty hyped."

"Aw, that's really great." She had to work to pump enthusiasm into her voice. Why did she feel so deflated?

"Yeah, I told Jason I'd go up to the hospital and visit right after lunch, so"—he winked—"lucky you, you get out of making beds today."

"Don't you need help setting up for the tea?" Tomorrow was another of the Christmas teas. "Or I can come in early tomorrow if you want me to."

"You don't need to, Benj. They went so well last week, I'm not nearly as nervous about it now."

"Okay. Well, I guess I'll see you tomorrow, then."

"See you then." He put a hand briefly on her shoulder. "Have fun in class." It felt like a dismissal.

She watched him retreat, then gathered her things from the powder room and hurried to her car. Unshed tears made her eyes ache and her head throb. How could things have gone from the elation of this morning to this dull ache in mere hours?

She felt foolish for being jealous of two tiny babies. And their mother. That was the real issue. Trevor seemed so happy that the babies were here. And now he'd get his *real* chef back.

She pinched the bridge of her nose. She was being ridiculous. She'd always known that when the babies came, her countdown would begin. Hadn't Trevor been clear with her that first day when she interviewed? Megan planned on taking a six-week maternity leave, and then she'd be back. *Six weeks.*

Benjie took a shuddered breath. She'd already been here for seven weeks, and every one of them had blown by like a hurricane. Now today was the beginning of the end.

CHAPTER 13

Trevor heard tires on the gravel and watched out the window as Benjie parked beside his Jeep. As he had yesterday morning, he went to meet her at the car and walk her into the house. If they were going to be "an item," he would have to be the one to set the tone of their relationship at work. But at least it was only six weeks, give or take, before Megan would be back and he wouldn't have to feel so torn about the fact that he was dating his chef. In love with his chef. Maybe it was too soon to say that, but he'd never felt about anyone the way he felt about Benjie Gabriel.

"Good morning," he said as she climbed from her car. His heart lifted, just seeing her face, that halo of curls, untamed and still damp from the shower, the way he preferred it.

"Good morning." Her smile dimmed too soon, and she turned to retrieve her bags from the passenger seat.

He pulled out his phone and scrolled to the photos he'd taken at the hospital last night. "Look at this." He thrust the phone in front of her.

She looked at the photo of Megan holding both of the babies, and her smile brightened again.

"I even got to hold one of them," he bragged.

"Aw. Did you get a picture?"

He shrugged. "I didn't think about it."

"They're awfully cute. They don't even look like preemies."

"If you saw them in person. . . They're pretty tiny." He shrugged. "Not that I have anything to compare them to. Maybe all newborns are."

"So, Megan is feeling good?"

"She looked great. Could hardly tell she'd just been through fourteen hours of labor."

Her "Wow" was oddly guarded, and she hurried across the gravel ahead of him.

"Is everything okay, Benj?"

"Yes. Why?" She kept walking, not meeting his gaze.

"Because you seem. . . You don't seem like yourself." He stopped at the back door but didn't open it. Stood there, blocking her way. "Listen, I know it's a little awkward to be working together now that we're. . ." He let his voice trail off. He wasn't sure what they were. What she thought they were. "But now that the babies are here, it'll only be six weeks, and then I won't be your boss anymore. I can just be your. . .friend."

Her shoulders slumped and she turned to face him. Tears welled in her eyes. "You don't get it, do you?"

"Get what?" A blanket of dread fell over him. "What's wrong, Benj?"

"In six weeks I'll lose the best job I've ever had. The only thing

I ever wanted to do in my life. I feel like. . . I feel like I'm already in mourning," she wailed. "I can't even let myself think about not getting to come here. . .like this, and—"

"What? You can still come here. And I hope we'll still be able to see each other."

"That's not the same!"

"Benjie. . . You knew this was only temporary. Until Megan had the babies. You knew that." He put an arm around her, but she shrugged him off and fumbled in her bag until she produced her keys.

"It's unlocked." He tried not to smirk.

"Oh." She turned the handle and swept through the door, heading straight for the powder room.

A few minutes later, he heard pots clanging and silverware rattling in the drawers. He decided it might be best to make himself scarce. He'd talk to her after the guests checked out this morning.

With a heavy sigh, he walked across to the woodshop to clear his head.

Benjie scrubbed the frying pan with a vengeance, blowing a puff of air upward to ward off a curl that had escaped her toque. For a full week now, she and Trevor had tiptoed around each other at the inn. Spoken politely to each other as they worked together. Yet somehow politeness had never felt so offensive.

She rinsed the pan, dried it, then set it on a burner for a few seconds before hanging it on the pot rack. She'd made up her mind that it would end today. This ridiculous politeness between them. She would have it out with him. Lay it all on the line, and if he fired her on the spot, well then it would be over. But she couldn't live this way.

Tears threatened as she sent up a prayer that God would give her the right words to say. But almost instantly she knew that her "confrontation" needed to begin with an apology. And probably end with one too. With maybe another one in the middle. Trevor had done nothing wrong. Nothing at all. She was the one who'd let her dreams and expectations get out of hand. Trevor had only offered her what he had to give: a temporary job. It wasn't his fault that she'd fallen in love with the job—and then with him. It wasn't his fault that Megan's babies were here and that she would soon be back at the job. The job that had been hers first.

She heard him come in the back door and quickly wiped her tears and slipped out the hairpins that secured her toque. She pulled her apron over her head and stood in the kitchen, waiting.

"Oh, hi. All finished?" That dreadful politeness.

"Could we talk, Trevor?"

He stopped in his tracks. "Sure."

She looked past him, wondering if there were still guests about, though she hadn't seen anyone since breakfast.

As if reading her mind, he pulled out a chair for her at the kitchen table. "Everyone's gone for the day. Can we sit here?"

"Of course." She took the chair he held, and before he'd even sat himself, she blurted, "I'm so sorry, Trevor. You've done nothing to deserve my stupid attitude. I just. . . I love this inn, and I can't imagine being happy anywhere else. But it's more than that. I'm so afraid you won't feel the same about me once I leave. I love who I am when I'm here. But crazy college business major Benjie, she's. . .kind of a crank." She attempted a smile.

"Benjie, I will feel exactly the same about you when this job ends. How can you think I won't? When I said 'temporary' the other night, I didn't mean us. That's not what you thought, is it?"

"No." She gave him a sidewise glance. "I'm not that stupid. But will you even have time for me once—"

"Of course I will. We'll make time."

"You say that, but. . ." The tears threatened again. "I'm so sorry, Trevor. It's just that I think I love you, and I don't want to lose you."

He stared at her, as if her confession had just registered. But then he rested his elbows on the table and put his head in his hands. When he looked up a minute later, it scared her that she couldn't read his expression.

After a minute, he scraped back his chair. "Come with me."

"What?"

He didn't reply but walked purposefully toward the back doors.

She hurried to follow him, curiosity rising. She trailed him silently to the woodshop, and by the time she caught up, he had the door unlocked.

"Come here." He beckoned her across the shop and led the way to a worktable at the back. "I have a little Christmas gift for you."

"Trevor. . . Oh, I. . .I feel bad. I don't have anything for you."

"Well, you might, actually."

"What do you mean?" She looked up and noticed the innkeeper she'd found in the valise sitting on a shelf beside the worktable.

"Open my gift and you'll see." He pulled a wad of red tissue paper from the drawer and handed it to her.

The tissue paper wasn't taped or secured like a gift, just wadded around something solid in the middle. The humble wrapping made her feel a little better about her lack of a gift for him. She looked for the edge of the paper and carefully unwrapped the object. It was a carved figure made of soft, pale wood. A woman wearing a robe with an intricately designed hem and carrying a basket with a loaf of bread. The figure was a bit shorter than the innkeeper figure, but the robe had been painted the same shade of green, then sanded and scuffed to match the aged look of the innkeeper. They were obviously made to be a pair. She held out the gift and set it on her open palm to get the full effect. "Trevor, this is beautiful! You made this? For me?"

He didn't reply.

She turned the piece in her hand and laughed, noticing the corkscrew curls that poked out from under the figure's kerchief. She looked up at Trevor with a smirk. "Poor girl has crazy hair like me."

"Poor girl *is* you, silly." He took the figure from her hand, but his gaze stayed intent on her. "The innkeeper you found needed a wife. So I carved him one." He set the "wife" on the shelf beside the innkeeper then took her hand.

"They're perfect together!" Her mind was reeling.

He squeezed her hand. "Benjie, I know we've had exactly two dates with each other and this might feel a little. . .premature, but hear me out. Over these past weeks, I've had the distinct advantage that a guy doesn't get with just any date. I've had you in my house six days a week since that first day you knocked on my door. I walk into my kitchen, and there you are." He squeezed her hand tighter, his words came faster. "I come in from the shop to talk to my guests, and there they are, laughing and happy because you're serving them with your gift of hospitality. I open my fridge, and there's my clotted cream that has spoiled me for any other."

She laughed. "You and your clotted cream!" But she didn't want to stop the flow of his sweet words.

"Let me finish before I lose my courage." He ran a finger down the bridge of her nose. "When I think about a time when you won't be here every day, banging around in my kitchen, making my guests feel like kings and queens. . .and yes, helping me make up the beds. . .I can hardly handle it, Benj."

"Really?"

"Really."

She narrowed her eyes. "This isn't just about help with the beds? Or clotted cream?"

"No, Benjie. It's about you. It's about the fact that I want you here. This place wouldn't be home anymore without you here. So. . . Here's what's happened. Jason called me today and asked me how upset I'd be if Megan stayed home with the twins."

Her heart leapt to her throat. "He did?"

"Seems she's decided she doesn't want to miss a single moment with those babies, and apparently Jason loves her enough to make her dreams of being a stay-at-home mom come true. So, come February, I'm short one chef, and I'm wondering how you'd feel. . .if we made yours a permanent position."

She looked at him, hoping the twinkle in his eye meant what she thought it meant. "Listen buddy, if you know what's good for you, you'd better tell me quick that you're offering me something more than just a full-time, non-temporary chef's job."

"Would you consider a lifetime, non-temporary job? And I don't mean chef. Well, not *only* chef anyway."

She would have tried to come up with a signature snarky reply if the hope in his eyes hadn't been so pathetic. "This sounds pretty serious," she whispered. "Like. . .shatter the stadium lights serious."

He laughed. "This makes that look like nothing." His smile faded, and he took her hand. "I love you, Benjie. I want you in my house every day for the rest of my life. You're already in my heart. . .so deep. I want you by my side, as my wife. I've been searching my heart, but more importantly, I've been searching the heart of God." A crooked smile tipped his lips. "Carving affords a man some good thinking time. And I promise you, in God's sight, and only with His help, that if you will be mine, I will be faithful and true to you until my dying breath."

"Oh Trevor. . .I—"

He put a finger gently to her lips. "Hear me out before you answer. Please. I didn't intend to ask you so soon." He looked around the dusty shop and smiled. "And I sure didn't intend to ask you out here in this. . .lowly stable. But Benj, I didn't want you to think for a minute that I could ever be happy without you."

She couldn't speak, her heart was so full.

He studied her, obviously concerned about her silence. "Do you need some time? To think about it?"

"I do." She bowed her head, then quickly looked up. "Okay, I've thought about it. Yes. Oh yes, Trevor."

He laughed, but his eyes glistened as he took her face in his hands, brushed his thumbs over her lips with utter tenderness. He bent to kiss her. Softly at first, then claiming her lips with more urgency, his fingers weaving through her hair.

She wrapped her arms around him, loving even the five-o'clock whiskers that scratched her cheek. Being in his arms, their first kiss—it was everything she'd dreamed of, everything she'd hoped for, prayed for. She pulled away to look at him, placing her palm on the side of his face, memorizing its planes. Then, looking heavenward, she whispered, loud enough for Trevor to hear, to know that he was the real gift He'd given her. "Thank You, Lord. Thank You."

After a second kiss and a third, he reached around her for the carving. "I'm not quite finished with this, but I thought I'd have more time."

"Not finished?" She took it from him and turned it in her hand, inspected it from every angle. "It's perfect, Trevor. Please. Don't change a thing!"

He tapped the hand of the innkeeper's wife, her left hand that held the basket. "I thought I'd add a ring to this finger."

Benjie looked up at him, flushed with pleasure at his words.

He set the carving back on the table and took her left hand in his. "Thought I'd add one to this finger too." He lifted her hand and kissed the spot where a ring would go.

"That would be the best Christmas present I could possibly imagine."

Deborah Raney's first novel, *A Vow to Cherish*, inspired the World Wide Pictures film of the same title and launched Deb's writing career. Twenty-five years, thirty-five books, and numerous awards later, she's still creating stories that touch hearts and lives. Her novels have won RWA's RITA Award, the ACFW Carol Award, the National Readers Choice Award, and the HOLT Medallion. She is also a three-time Christy Award finalist. Deb is a recent transplant to Missouri, having moved with her husband, Ken Raney, from their native Kansas to be closer to kids and grandkids. They love road trips, Thursday garage sale dates, and breakfast on the screened porch overlooking their wooded backyard. Connect with Deb at www.deborahraney.com.